Evil of the Age

Evil of the Age

A Thriller

Allan Levine

Skyhorse Publishing

Skyhorse Publishing books may be purchased in bulk at special discounts for sales promotion, corporate gifts, fund-raising, or educational purposes. Special editions can also be created to specifications. For details, contact the Special Sales Department, Skyhorse Publishing, 307 West 36th Street, 11th Floor, New York, NY 10018 or info@ skyhorsepublishing.com.

Skyhorse® and Skyhorse Publishing® are registered trademarks of Skyhorse Publishing, Inc.®, a Delaware corporation.

Visit our website at www.skyhorsepublishing.com.

10 9 8 7 6 5 4 3 2 1

Library of Congress Cataloging-in-Publication Data is available on file.

Cover design by Brian Peterson

Print ISBN: 978-1-5107-2648-2
Ebook ISBN: 978–1-63158–027-7

Printed in the United States of America

For Angie, with love
Thirty-two years and still smiling

CONTENTS

"He maketh his sun to rise on the evil and on the good, and sendeth rain on the just and on the unjust" (St. Matthew 5:45). What is the evil that St. Matthew speaks of? Does he mean the serpent in the Garden of Eden and the inhabitants of Sodom and Gomorrah? Does any mortal truly know? Only God can judge man and therefore the hazy line between light and darkness is for him, and him alone to determine.

Charles St. Clair, "Evil of the Age," Fox's Weekly, Vol. LXX, New York, Monday, September 4, 1871

New York City
Courtesy of the University of Texas Libraries,
The University of Texas at Austin.

PROLOGUE

—————✦❖✦—————

Fox's Weekly
Vol. LXX, New York, Monday, August 14, 1871
"New York Street Scenes: Number 12"
A monthly series by Charles St. Clair

ANY VISITOR TO NEW YORK this hot summer will surely notice the contrasts that now characterize the city's various neighborhoods. It may be only a few miles from Fifth Avenue to Five Points, but who could imagine, unless you witnessed it with your own eyes, that such a short distance offered so completely opposite scenes of streets and people? The last census revealed that New York and the surrounding area will soon boast a population of more than two million people. And yet, how many of our citizens live in abject poverty and misery?

The grand mansions on Fifth Avenue, department stores on Broadway and Sixth Avenue, exquisite horse-drawn carriages seen on Sunday afternoons in Central Park, and the daily crowd of superbly attired gentlemen and ladies at Delmonico's and other fine dining establishments are testimony that many New Yorkers enjoy everything modern life has to offer. For these select men and women there are festive balls, literary clubs, and enchanting theatre to attend.

But should our visitor take a ride on a congested omnibus east or west of Fifth Avenue and south of Houston Street, provided of course that he can tolerate the foul odors of these public transportation wagons, he would discover an entirely different environment where crime, prostitution, and drunkenness are rampant. Whether it is in Five Points, Hell's Kitchen, or

Kleindeutschland (east of the Bowery and north of Division Street) there are Irish and German b'hoys to contend with. They are never to be trusted. Most are thieves, robbers, and pimps who will slit their own mothers' throats if they thought they could get away with it.

If not confronted by the criminal element, then our visitor is more than likely to be accosted by beggars. Most readers will agree that it is seemingly impossible to go anywhere in New York lately without being pestered by veterans of the last war. If truth be told, they are a pathetic bunch. Many of them have lost an arm or leg, others are blind or deformed. As a group they are seemingly without hope.

They served their country protecting the Union and fighting the Confederacy. Once the battle had been won, the government instructed them to return to their former lives as clerks, blacksmiths, dockworkers, laborers, and bar keeps. Many were able to do so. But for thousands more who were wounded on the battlefields of Shiloh, Vicksburg, and Gettysburg their options were limited. Most drink too much whiskey and are forced to beg on the streets in order to survive. They sell used shoelaces or stand begging with organ grinders. They are in railway stations, at ferry houses, and by the waterfront . . .

~

Lucy Maloney was late. Her appointment had been arranged for two o'clock in the afternoon. Why had she not listened to George and permitted him to hail her a hansom cab? As one of a dozen or so doormen employed by the Fifth Avenue Hotel, where she resided, George made it a habit to keep his eye on the street traffic. For a Negro, she had decided, he was unusually astute. He sparkled in his blue uniform with its distinctive tails hanging down below his waist, gold string tassels on his shoulders, and a smart-looking hat with a black patent peak.

"You heading downtown, Miss Lucy?" he had asked her. "I think a cab would definitely be quicker. I hear there was an accident at the corner of Broadway and Ninth. Some foolish boy on a wagon ran right into a carriage. At least two horses went down. It may be hours until they clear it away."

"That's fine, George, I think I'll walk," she had told him.

"In this heat, you'll likely faint again, Miss Lucy. Be sure to use your parasol."

"Of course, George. I can always count on you."

She began walking down Broadway, then turned and waved to him one last time. George was correct about something else too— She had not been feeling well of late.

Each morning for the past two weeks, she had awakened nauseated and her stomach uncomfortably queasy. She had instructed the hotel maid to leave a bucket beside her bed and had regularly made use of it. What was the point of dining out if her dinner was only to end up at the bottom of a bucket? Then, only two days ago, she had collapsed in the reception area of the hotel. Such a fuss. George and Mr. Buckland, the hotel's manager, had helped her into to her suite. It was merely the heat, she had told them. The summer weather was unusually hot, the mercury and humidity high.

But even as she spoke the words, she knew it was a lie. Mildred Potter, one of her closest and dearest friends, who knew nearly all of her secrets, had insisted that she see her physician.

"It could be the consumption, heaven forbid," Mildred had warned her.

She reassured Mildred that she was not going to perish. That it was another ailment, not life threatening, but serious nonetheless. She was unwell, as Mildred and the other ladies she had tea and cakes with each afternoon would have so delicately put it. Her time of the month had come and gone and there had been no blood flowing. She was experienced enough to know what had to be done, and immediately before quickening occurred.

Once there was quickening, once she could feel movement in her belly, finding a solution to this problem would be much more difficult—not impossible, but definitely more dangerous. She had told no one about her predicament, not even the father of her unborn child. It would have caused so much confusion and pain. She had stupidly allowed herself to become involved in a situation that she could not control. And after she had worked so diligently to make a decent life for herself. She blushed at the thought of her foolishness.

There were no available cabs in sight. A Broadway omnibus was approaching and she decided to climb on board—as distasteful as she found public transportation. She walked straight ahead, delicately lifting up her canary yellow organdy dress so that it would not come into contact with the dust and dirt on the floor. She deliberately did not look at any of the other passengers and attempted not to inhale the foul air. Still, she felt nauseated and dizzy, as she had at the hotel. She found a seat near the middle of the bus, drew her shawl around her shoulders, and tried to make herself as inconspicuous as possible.

As the bus lurched forward, Lucy began to perspire and her hands started to shake. She breathed deeply and tried to calm herself. But she was frightened—there was no denying it. Who knew what terrors awaited her? She had heard stories of girls who had visited midwives and abortionists and who had bled to death or died in tremendous pain from ingesting poisonous concoctions. According to newspaper and magazine accounts she had seen, these women had taken a variety of strange herbal medicines including, ergot, savin, and black hellebore.

Only last month, Lucy had read about the case of Maria Alder, an unmarried woman found dead in a boarding house in Philadelphia. The police had discovered that the poor woman had visited a quack named Benson, who had operated on her. Yet there had been medical complications, bleeding and infection, and he had cruelly left her to die an agonizing death. Lucy had plans for the future and much to live for. She was not about to meet such an unsavory end.

She tried to put these horrific thoughts out of her head. Over and over again she told herself that within a few hours her problems would be resolved. There was no other way. But it was to no avail—she could not stop shaking and felt sick to her stomach.

As the two great horses slowly dragged the bus down Broadway, she clasped her hands tightly together. At that moment, she felt more alone than she ever had in her entire life.

A few feet away, the dark eyes of another passenger locked on to her. He pulled his hat low, and contemplated his next move.

Chapter One

A Trunk at Hudson Depot

*P*addy Tritt pulled tight on the leather reins. So hard that Queenie, his chestnut nag, lurched forward before she completely stopped. "God damn horse," he muttered. "What's wrong with you today? I'll bet it's that racket. Can't say I blame you, girl." There was no mistaking his thick Irish accent.

Like most of his friends and acquaintances who also resided in the dilapidated slums of Five Points or Hell's Kitchen—quarrymen, street laborers, sewer and ditch diggers, and dock workers—Paddy was dressed in a white shirt streaked in dirt, brown pants held up by thin suspenders, and old, dusty, black boots. On his head was—apart from Queenie and his wagon—his most prized possession, a black plug hat.

Paddy found a secluded alleyway close to the corner of Eighth Avenue and Twenty-Second Street to leave his rig. He gave his hungry horse some feed, and could not help but take a moment to admire his wagon. It wasn't much to look at, he knew—no more than a large open wooden box sitting on top of four spoke wheels, one of which was badly in need of repair. Nonetheless, there was his name, *P. Tritt* printed on the side in large black block letters. What a beautiful sight that was, he thought.

He chuckled to himself as he recalled, yet again, how two years ago, he had had a rare streak of luck at the faro table. The money he won was enough to buy himself a cart and horse. Since then, he had sufficient work to keep a roof over his head and some food on his table each day. He was a truckman with a fairly good reputation. Patting the side of his hat, he had to laugh out loud. What would Jimmy think of him now?

Jimmy Doyle.

Hardly a day went by when Paddy did not think about him. Jimmy, as every rogue south of Canal Street still acknowledged, was one of the meanest cusses to ever lead a gang in Five Points. Back in the forties, Doyle's Plug Uglies ruled the Points like a band of medieval outlaws—and Jimmy was their undisputed prince. They protected their home territory with the cunning and ruthlessness of a pack of wild dogs, yet regularly exploited, stole from, and even murdered their own people if *law and order*—as Jimmy defined it—in the Points required it.

The stylish high hat Paddy wore so proudly was a gift from Doyle. When Paddy was about six years old, Jimmy had found him wandering the streets and had taken him in. In those days, every Irishman was called *a damned Paddy* so that's what Jimmy named him. He even taught Paddy how to read and write. When Jimmy was murdered in a gang brawl in 1851, Paddy was on his own again at fifteen.

Paddy Tritt—he took the last name Tritt because he liked the sound of it—always took pride that he was a survivor. And he had seen it all—cholera, Nativists, who lived by the code 'Life, Liberty, and the Pursuit of Irishmen,' Know-Nothings, gang wars between the Bowery Boys and the Dead Rabbits...Paddy had fought on the side of the Bowery Boys...the Draft Riots of '63 when he had watched a Negro beaten, lynched, and finally burned on Clarke Street, and more saloon fights than he cared to remember. He had cheated death a thousand times.

Paddy was running his long grimy fingers through Queenie's mane, when the horse was startled by the sound of gunfire. He steadied the nag and slowly made his way through the mud and manure to investigate the disturbance for himself. He had only taken a few steps when more gun shots echoed through the air. Ahead, he heard angry shouting and terrified screams. His good sense told him he should turn around and flee.

Only last evening, however, he had assured his friends over a bottle of whiskey at Pete Ruley's saloon that he would gladly join them to jeer the Orangemen who dared to flaunt their Protestant flags in a parade through Irish Catholic neighborhoods. And Paddy Tritt never broke a promise.

He turned the corner onto Eighth Avenue and was nearly run over by a burley omnibus driver, who had left his rig and hackney a few feet away with the dumbfounded passengers still inside.

Behind the terrified driver was a group of shrieking women.

"Run for your life," one of them yelled.

There was blood streaming down her face. She desperately tried to grab hold of his arm. At that moment, a heavy-set soldier, wide-eyed, with a thin moustache, marched up behind her. Two more soldiers accompanied him. Before Paddy could react, the first solider thrust his bayoneted rifle into the woman's back and swiftly retracted it.

"Irish scum," he muttered under his breath. "You don't belong in this country."

The woman stared into Paddy's eyes, a look of horror mixed with enormous sadness on her face. Blood spewed from her mouth as she slumped forward. Paddy dropped her and turned. One of the other soldiers aimed his rifle directly at Paddy's head. He cocked his trigger, yet as he did so the woman's friends rushed him. They grabbed at his hair and tore at his eyes with their fingers.

Paddy frantically searched for something he could defend himself with, a piece of wood or a metal bar from a wagon. But there was nothing on the street he could use. His instincts of self-preservation were strong. Although no one could ever accuse of him being a coward, he realized that if he helped these women he would surely die.

So he ran. In seconds all around him were more people fleeing from the soldiers and police firing indiscriminately into the Catholic masses, which had gathered along Eighth Avenue to protest the Orange parade.

"Paddy, over here." The familiar deep voice came from behind another abandoned omnibus.

"Is that you, Big Frank?" he asked peering around the large passenger wagon.

"Get down you fool or you'll get us both killed."

Frank Connolly was at least ten years older than Paddy. He was not a particularly large man, other than around his midriff, and Paddy wasn't certain why he was nicknamed Big Frank. Perhaps it was because his most distinguishing feature was two thick mutton-chop red side-whiskers that drooped onto his collar. Paddy immediately noticed that Connolly's right arm was limp and that he was in pain.

"Frank, what happened? You look as white as a ghost," said Paddy in a whisper.

"You got any chaw?"

Paddy reached into his jacket pocket and broke off a small piece from a stringy plug of chewing tobacco he had been saving.

Connolly took it with his left hand and pushed into his mouth between his teeth and gums. "Much obliged. My arm feels better already."

"Is it broke?"

"Don't know." Connolly spit a yellowish brown spew on to the road near Paddy's boot. "I got here at about noon with Little Philly and Punk Tyler. About thirty minutes later, those damn Orangemen arrived with their banners and flags. There must've been a hundred of them. And behind them were soldiers cheering them on. As soon as they started singing the bloody Star Spangled Banner, the men and even some women beside us started throwing bricks and stones at them. And then all hell broke loose." He paused to spit again. "The soldiers began firing at us. I don't know what happened to Philly or Punk. I got clubbed on my arm with a bloody rifle butt. Lucky for me I had a bottle in my hand. Smashed it right over the arsehole's head. Then I decided to take cover over here."

"Damn it. Didn't Fowler say there'd be no soldiers or police? That we'd be safe. That's why the women came out."

"I guess even the Boss can be wrong or maybe…"

"Maybe what?" asked Paddy.

"Maybe Fowler lied to us."

Paddy shook his head. "Why'd he do a thing like that? Mr. Fowler's a great man, the greatest there ever was. He's always taken care of us. Why would he ever lie?"

Frank Connolly laughed. "Paddy, you're just a stupid Irish truckman. Now, help me up."

～

The streets were quieter by the time Paddy found his way back to Queenie and his cart. He had taken Connolly to a nearby saloon. There was a barkeep named Shaw. He said he would have one of his boys fetch a madam he knew who could mend Connolly's arm.

Before he left his friend, Paddy gulped down a glass of whiskey and then another.

"You can take the bottle with you if you want," Shaw offered with all the sincerity the barkeep could muster.

"Probably not a bad idea," said Paddy, his hand shaking. "But I better keep my wits about me today."

Paddy had seen many people killed before—stabbed in bar fights, beaten to death in gang brawls, even shot at point-blank range over a stupid argument in a card game. Yet, the image of the dead woman stabbed by the soldier was stuck in his head.

～

Queenie was exactly where he left her. Paddy was climbing aboard his wagon, when he heard a rustling sound on the other side of the horse. He clenched his fists.

"Who goes there? Show yourself," he commanded.

A young boy, maybe thirteen or fourteen years of age, dressed in raggedy pants and a torn filthy blue shirt, stepped from behind Queenie.

"Get away from my nag," ordered Paddy. "What you doing here, kid?" he said more firmly.

"Hiding. Hiding from the soldiers and police," said the boy looking downward.

"You hurt?"

The boy shook his head. "I came to throw a bottle at those bloody Orangemen. I hate'm all."

"Yeah, me too."

"You the truckman, Paddy Tritt, aren't you?"

Paddy gestured to the sign with his name on the side of the wagon. "Don't you read, lad?"

The boy didn't answer him. "Speak up, kid," said Paddy, his voice rising. "What the hell are you really doing here? You got shit for brains? You'll feel my knuckles in a moment."

"Name is Corkie," the boy interjected, more bravely. "I was hiding, mister. Honest. But I also got a job for you. I was told you're reliable."

Paddy stepped down from the wagon. "You got a job for me? Is that right?" He sized the boy up and down. "You got five dollars? Because I don't work for free, if that's what you're after."

The boy reached into his pants pocket. He held a crisp five-dollar bill in his greasy fingers. He handed it to Paddy, who grabbed it.

"Where do you get that kind of money, kid? You steal it? I don't want no trouble from the cops. Not after today."

"I didn't steal it and there's another five for you when the job's done."

Paddy stared hard at the boy. Ten dollars was about as much as he could make in a very good month of business. "What do I have to do?"

Corkie climbed up on to the wagon. "I have to show you. Let's go."

Paddy shrugged and climbed up beside the boy. "Where to, sir?" he asked with a sly smile.

Corkie chuckled. "Turn around and head down toward the corner of Broadway and Broome. You know where that is?"

"Shit, kid, you think I'm a dumb Croppie? I've been to places in this city you'll never see. You come with me down by the docks, I'll introduce you to a few of my friends," said Paddy laughing. "How old are you, boy?"

"Fourteen," mumbled Corkie.

"You ever tasted sweet cunny before? Ever had your hands on a pair of teets?" His grin widened. "I'd bet not. Once this job is finished, maybe I'll take you to see this gal I know. Her name's Bridget. She's got big eyes and long dark hair." Paddy whistled. "She can cure any ailment I know of."

Paddy reached under his seat and pulled out a small box. "Here. Hold on to these for a moment," he said handing the reins to Corkie. "Don't pull too hard, Queenie knows where she's going."

"I've led a wagon before, mister."

"I'm sure you have, but you got to keep your eyes opened down Broadway. There's liable to be some damn fool trying to cross the avenue when he shouldn't. Or there's cripples and stray dogs to watch out for." He opened the box and took out two thin cigars. He lit his own and grabbed the reins back from Corkie. "Have one of these. About the best you can buy for a nickel."

Corkie took the cigar, lit it and inhaled sharply. Immediately he started coughing uncontrollably. Paddy roared with laughter as he urged Queenie on toward their destination.

❧

Corkie instructed Paddy to park his wagon in an alley off Broome Street, next to a two-story red-brick building—Anthony's Carriage Supplies.

The building was squeezed between the neighborhood's infamous tenements, where Paddy knew thousands of immigrants—most of whom were Irish like him—lived in the most crowded and fetid of conditions. He had seen the despair with his own eyes when he had recently visited Joseph Walker's home. Walker was a pleasant enough fellow, who assisted truckmen loading and unloading freight at the St. John's Square Station.

About three weeks ago, after an unusually busy day, Paddy had driven Walker home and could not refuse an invitation to join him for a drink. Walker and his family of six lived in a run-down tenement on Prince Street. They had one room and a small alcove where Walker's wife, Frances, sewed dresses. With so many people in such a tiny space, it was impossibly crowded and even more so in the summer heat. The stench from the excessive garbage and manure in the streets below wafted throughout the building making Paddy even more uncomfortable. He drank his glass of whiskey quickly that day, fearful of contracting the consumption that the tenements were famous for spreading.

"You know what I'm supposed to haul?" Paddy asked Corkie. But he wasn't heard.

Out and about on Broome Street there was a lot of commotion from the small army of men making their away along the cobblestone road with their pushcarts filled with food, fruit, cloth and metal utensils. Even noisier were the newsies—young boys hawking newspapers—as well as an assortment of girls selling flowers. Paddy glanced at one pretty lass with a green dress. He figured she could not have been more than fourteen years old and like the rest of them likely worked at a nearby brothel for such well-known madams as Red Light Lizzie and Hester Jane Haskins.

"What am I supposed to haul?" he repeated, shouting.

This time Corkie heard him. He nodded, but remained silent, and instead beckoned Paddy to follow him. Corkie threw down what remained of his cigar and stomped into the mud. Muttering, Paddy stepped down, lightly patted Queenie on her nose, and trailed after the boy into the alley. There were pieces of broken glass and furniture scattered about. Suddenly, Corkie stopped at a dilapidated wooden shed. He pointed to a black medium-sized trunk with a rope tied around it.

"Yeah, I see it. Now what?"

"Here's what I'm supposed to tell you," the boy whispered. "You're to deliver this trunk to the Hudson River Railroad Depot by three o'clock," the boy continued, louder. He pulled a card from his pocket and handed it to Paddy.

"What the hell is this?" He glanced at the card. It was a ticket for the eight o'clock train to Chicago. "What am I to do with this?"

"Show it to the baggage master. Deliver the trunk. Tell him the passenger, an old lady, will be by at about seven-thirty. Then, leave the check he gives you with a beggar who'll be near the main door to the depot."

"With the beggar?" asked Paddy. "That's what I'm to do?"

"That's right. His name's Flint. He's an old soldier, bald with a silvery moustache and bushy side-whiskers. You'll see him, but don't shit yourself. Just hand it to him and he'll give you the rest what's owed to you."

"Sounds kind of peculiar to me."

"Trust me, old man, Flint'll give you another five when the job's done."

Paddy stared at the boy for a moment. He had to admit the kid had as much pluck as he had when he was that age. "I've delivered just about everything in this city," said Paddy. "Chairs, tables, even a piano from Steinways to a fancy house on Fifth. But this is the strangest job I've ever had. You know what's in the trunk, boy?"

"No, mister, I don't know and I don't want to know. I'm being paid to talk to you and then keep my mouth closed." At that, the boy turned and ran back toward Broome Street.

"Hold on," yelled Paddy. "I could use some help lifting this damn thing."

He kicked the trunk and tried picking it up. "Not too heavy," he mumbled. "What I do for cash."

He wiped his hands clean, grabbed hold of the trunk, and lifted it up off the ground. It was, in fact, heavier than he thought and had an unpleasant odor. As he loaded it on to his wagon, he thought nothing more about it. He climbed up on the driver's seat, took hold of the reins, and got Queenie moving again.

~

An hour later Paddy was parked outside the Hudson River Railroad Depot on Thirtieth Street and Ninth Avenue. He was greeted by the usual hubbub of travelers, street vendors, cartmen, truckmen, and carriages. Paddy did exactly what Corkie had told him to. He unloaded the trunk and delivered it to the baggage master inside the station house. He handed him the ticket to Chicago and explained that the owner of the trunk, an elderly lady, would be by at 7:30 in the evening to retrieve it. The baggage master handed him a check, as was routine.

"There's a strong smell coming from that trunk," said the baggage master, a short and stout fellow with a white moustache and a full General Grant style beard. "You know what's in it, rotten food or something of that sort?"

"I was paid to deliver the trunk, that's what I'm doing."

"All right, off with you."

Paddy exited the station, bit off a piece of tobacco and scanned the street for this beggar named Flint. He spotted him by a line of carriages and wagons down the street.

"You Flint?" asked Paddy, as he approached him. For a beggar, Paddy thought he looked rather neat and clean. Like other veterans of the Civil War who took to begging on the streets, he wore a dusty blue uniform. Yet his moustache and side-whiskers were trimmed and he appeared to have all of his limbs. He wore a grey Confederate kepi that was pulled down over his eyes.

"You have the baggage check?" Flint grunted. His voice was deep and gruff.

Paddy handed him the piece of paper. "Now the rest of my money."

"Don't spend it on whiskey. Irish scum. You're ruining this city." He threw a five-dollar bill at Paddy's face.

"You're a shit-sack, anyone ever tell you that?" Paddy picked the money off the ground.

With a deft movement that caught Paddy by surprise, Flint pulled out a knife from his overcoat pocket. It had a black handle and its razor-sharp blade glistened in the sun. He grabbed Paddy by the collar and poked the knife hard against the bottom of the truckman's chin.

"I'd advise to you mind what you say, otherwise they'll be one less Irishman to kick around. Now get the hell out of my sight."

Paddy drew back and without another word walked back towards his wagon.

≈

Flint placed the knife back under his coat along with the rail check. As soon as Paddy was out of sight, he headed north toward the corner of Thirty-Fourth Street and Eighth Avenue. A driver and a private stage with pearl handles on the doors, pulled by two fine black horses, were waiting for him. He climbed in and immediately the driver snapped the reins. The horses turned east on Thirty-Fourth heading toward Fifth Avenue.

≈

It was about five o'clock when the baggage master's curiosity finally got the better of him. The stench from the trunk had become unbearable. Other passengers were clearly uncomfortable and more than one of his porters wondered if they should allow the trunk on the eight o'clock train.

"Lift it down and put it on the ground," the baggage master commanded two of his men. He examined the trunk for a moment, cut the rope with a knife, and opened it. The strong smell almost overwhelmed him.

"So what do you see?" asked one of the baggage men.

"A red quilt."

"That it?"

The baggage master reached for the quilt and opened it up.

He covered his mouth. "For the love of Jesus."

"What is it? Let me see."

Both baggage men moved forward and gingerly peered over the top of the open trunk. "God damn," said one of them.

Inside was the naked body of a woman. Her knees were pulled up to her chest and her feet were twisted. It was as if she had been folded in half. Her long blonde hair swept around the bottom part of her face. But her eyes were wide open. This poor girl died in a terrible fright, the baggage master thought. He noticed, too, that there were no bruises on the body. He peeked a little more closely and abruptly stepped back when he saw the splotches of dry blood at the bottom of the trunk.

"Go fetch the police," the baggage master ordered one of his men. "And hurry."

Chapter Two

———◆———

At Fox's Weekly

Charles St. Clair would have conceded that he did not look his best. He thought that if he wore his finest black suit, white shirt, and tapered vest, along with his summer white derby, no one would notice. He was fooling himself. His right eye was plainly black and blue and his face more than a bit banged up. He was thirty-five-years old, lean and trim, but he looked a little older on this day.

"Mr. St. Clair, my word, what happened to you?" asked Molly, as she rose from her chair.

Molly Lee warmly greeted each and every writer and client who stepped into the offices of *Fox's Weekly*. She was twenty-seven, never married, and had been working at the magazine for more than three years.

"I had a bit of an accident, I'm afraid," replied St. Clair. "I could tell you that I fell down the stairs at my flat."

She smiled. "I suppose you could," she said softly. Molly was not a beautiful or striking woman, yet she did possess a quiet attractive quality that St. Clair found impossible to ignore. She sounded as gentle as she always did, like a mother hen tending her chicks.

He trusted her discretion. He also knew that Molly would never pry into his private affairs nor was she prone to gossip—a noble characteristic in New York City, where in St. Clair's experience, everyone talked behind his neighbor's back if given the opportunity. At the same time, he could not stand there and lie to her.

"I'm afraid my poor luck at the poker table last night got me into a difficult predicament," he said without hesitating. "You don't have to tell me how foolish this looks." St. Clair's face reddened ever so slightly.

"You know I'd never do that, Mr. St. Clair. But you should take better care of yourself. There are people around here who care about your welfare."

St. Clair smiled. "Your concern is much appreciated. Truly. And I shall make every effort to be more careful in the future."

"Wonderful," said Molly. "You've always been a man of your word, Mr. St. Clair. Now why don't you see Mr. Fox and I shall prepare you a cup of tea."

"An excellent idea, Molly. And thank you."

"For what?"

"Your kindness and good sense. It's a rare attribute, in my view."

She smiled warmly at him.

In fact, St. Clair greatly appreciated the fact that Molly did not launch into a preachy Sunday school lecture about the evils of gambling. He knew all too well that he had shown poor judgment in this matter. And the consequences had been an altercation the previous evening with Captain Jack Martin, the meanest and most vicious thug in Hell's Kitchen.

His dilemma now, and it was a ticklish situation indeed, was to find the money and get Martin out of his life. Perhaps his luck at the poker table would change—it couldn't get much worse.

Until about a month ago, faro had been his game of choice. It was the most popular way to gamble in the city. St. Clair generally preferred a high-class gaming establishment on Park Row, where amidst exquisite paintings and rosewood furniture he could enjoy himself with fine food, whiskey, cigars, the company of some of the most beautiful women in the city, and the excitement of the game.

Yet St. Clair had had a terrible run of bad luck—he was simply unable to pick the winning cards no matter what he did. And so, after due consideration, he had opted for poker, a game that was becoming more fashionable. He reasoned that if he sat in on a game at Martin's saloon, his luck would have to change. He always had been able to take care of himself, although he often carried a pistol with him when he ventured into one of New York's many squalid neighborhoods.

Still, in retrospect, he realized that in his imprudent desperation to succeed, he had overestimated his abilities. His inexperience at poker proved costly. He had lost $1,500 in the past two days, betting far too much on cards he believed he could win with. Holding three jacks, he thought he had a winning hand and had foolishly borrowed money from Martin to increase his bet. Everyone around the table stayed in the game during this round, even those players he later discovered—curiously enough—were holding lousy cards. The pot was worth a few thousand dollars by the time the betting stopped. He was sure it was all his. Yet he was beaten by one of Martin's cronies, who was holding three kings. His losses mounted.

Worse, he was short of cash and could not meet his debt obligations to Martin. For the moment had no idea where he would find the $1,500. His bank account was depleted and his $150 monthly salary fell far short. He had forty-eight hours or so to arrive at a solution. If he did not pay by six o'clock the following evening, he'd owe Martin an additional $200 and $100 every day after that. Martin and his hoodlums had also warned him that next time, the beating he got last night would seem like a gentle pat on the back.

St. Clair's desk was near the front of the spacious office, next to the desk belonging to one of his colleagues, Edward Sutton. A tall and handsome man in his late twenties, Sutton was busy working and barely acknowledged St. Clair's arrival. Smoke from the cigar he was puffing lingered overhead.

St. Clair would never have interrupted him—it was the custom of the office not to bother a colleague while he wrote unless absolutely necessary—and was thankful that he did not have to explain why he looked the way he did.

As Molly arrived with a cup of hot tea, he filled his pipe with tobacco. It was an aromatic Dutch blend that he had picked up from a tobacconist on Bleeker Street, a block from his flat. He found a wooden match amidst the pile of papers on his desk, struck it hard against the bottom of his boot, and lit his pipe. After a few deep puffs, he felt slightly more at ease. Then he sipped his tea—even in the summer heat, Tom Fox, the magazine's proprietor and chief editor, insisted that the wood in the office stove be burning and the water in the iron kettle be warm.

"A hot cup of tea feeds the brain," Fox always said. "Makes a man work harder." Ever since he had arrived from the *New York Times* a few years ago, St. Clair had appreciated Fox's good sense.

"St. Clair, where've you been? I need the next installment?" It was Tom Fox. He was standing at the door to his private office on the far side of the room, chomping on a cigar, the first of several he'd consume during the day. "Get in here," he barked.

At fifty-five-years of age, Fox was a large man. He was tall, about six feet and four inches, heavyset, with a belly that made his vest jut out. The hair he had left on his head was white, as was his moustache and beard.

St. Clair began walking slowly among the desks and furniture.

"You look terrible, St. Clair, rough evening?" asked Fox with a yawn.

"I'd be lying if I didn't say I'd been better. And what about you? It doesn't look like you got much sleep either, my friend."

Fox chuckled so hard that his belly jiggled. "A glass of Bushmills is the cure for both our troubles." Fox may have promoted tea drinking, but he generally preferred a glass of Irish whiskey to quench his thirst.

St. Clair waved his hand. "None for me right now, Tom, but thanks."

Fox's inner sanctum was separated from the main area of the *Weekly*'s newsroom by a thin wood wall and a door that was rarely closed. A sea of paper and files greeted a visitor entering his private quarters. The clutter on his desk was legendary, with documents dating back twenty years rumored to be among them. On three walls from the floor to the ceiling were shelves of books—many of which he and his late brother John had published in the early 1860s when they began the company-journals, magazines, and an ever-growing stack of newspapers.

Fox was not only a clever publisher—his success in establishing *Fox's Weekly* in the summer of 1862 as a magazine of general interest was testimony to that, St. Clair always argued with anyone who suggested otherwise—he was also a voracious reader and always on the lookout for the next Dickens. At the moment, as St. Clair had been told repeatedly, he had his eye on the journalist and humorist Samuel Clemens.

"Wittiest writer I've read in years," Fox had maintained. "If his next novel, a tale about a boy in the American backwoods, is half as good as *The Innocents Abroad*, I'll be very pleased."

St. Clair had been reminded time and again that two years ago an excerpt in *Fox's Weekly* of Clemens's first novel—under his pen name Mark Twain—had sold out within two days.

Directly behind Fox's desk was a large window overlooking Park Row and the streets beyond. From this vantage point, four stores high, it was possible to see the headquarters of the *Weekly*'s various competitors, the *Tribune, Times,* and *Evening Post*. It was said that printers' ink ran through the streets below.

"How's the next piece coming along?" asked Fox, adopting a more serious tone. "I've got three messages from Fowler already today. He wants to meet with you. I'd say he's as scared as a jackrabbit right now. Stewart's already working on the next illustration. So how much longer?"

"I need to hear from my snitch. Anything arrived for me this morning?" asked St. Clair.

"Not as far as I know. Remind me again how you continue to acquire such information." Fox's eyebrows tightened. "And why I've risked the wrath of city hall and the magazine's reputation on this?"

"I wait," said St. Clair with a sly grin, ignoring Fox's rather pathetic effort to feign anger. "Don't worry, Tom, he'll deliver something soon. He always does."

"You still won't tell me his name. I run this goddamned journal, in case you've forgotten."

"I gave him my word that I wouldn't reveal his name to anyone. You'll have to trust me," said St. Clair, patting Fox on the shoulder.

"I want something for this week's issue, Charlie. We have to drive those bastards out of city hall. You understand?" said Fox.

"You know I do."

A slight smirk crossed Fox's mouth. "By the way, Fowler sent me a personal message, too, this morning. It seems he didn't appreciate your latest 'Street Scenes' column. He said those references to crime don't put the city in the best light. Have you ever heard anything so ridiculous? Talk about the kettle calling the pot black."

St. Clair had listened to Fox's rant about Boss Victor Fowler many times. How Fowler, Tammany's Grand Sachem and president of the Board of Supervisors, had organized, in his opinion, the most corrupt municipal regime ever launched on New York. The 'Fowler Ring' is how Fox described it—a hard band in which there is gold all round and without end." The name stuck.

About six months ago, a person of some importance in the civic administration and close to Fowler had contacted St. Clair. He wanted to talk. After that initial meeting, the first package soon arrived. It contained facts and figures about the huge contracts the city had awarded to the New York Printing Company. It did not take St. Clair too long to determine that the Printing Company's majority owner was none other than Victor Fowler. There were invoices for city hall stationery that at the most should have cost $1,200. Except the bill the city paid was for $7,500. Each week thereafter, St. Clair received new and potentially incriminating information.

Patronage was seemingly doled out at a rate that shocked both St. Clair and Fox. The graft was scandalous—or, at least, that was how St. Clair described it. There was some exaggeration and embellishment to be sure—it was the way a journalist worked after all. And, perhaps, in a court of law St. Clair might not have been able to prove every allegation he leveled at Fowler. Yet according to the records he had examined, thousands of dollars had flowed to Fowler's friends for work that was never completed. One construction company doing road and sewer work charged the city ten times what the labor should have cost.

St. Clair had put it this way in the inaugural story:

The Ring and the Boss command an army composed of elements as dangerous as those which make up the crew of a pirate ship. The instant the slightest sign of weakness is shown, each man aspires to be commander, and is willing to sink the ship and all on board rather to forego his own ambitious schemes.

As the articles continued to flow, St. Clair identified the key members of the Ring, giving each a suitable nickname. There was Governor "Dandy" Archibald Krupp—Fowler's man at the State Assembly in Albany, Mayor Thomas "The Prince" Emery—who in St. Clair's opinion was "an opportunist of the worst variety."

Mayor Emery dresses in the finest clothes—his suits are imported from Paris. He smokes the most expensive Egyptian cigars, drinks only the best Scotch whiskey, and is known to dine regularly at Delmonico's.

There was also, "Slimy" Bob James—the cunning and sly City Comptroller, and Isaac "The Wizard" Harrison—the City Chamberlain.

Harrison is possibly the most treacherous of the "Ring Rascals," a man never to be trusted.

What made the stories even more sensational were Peter Stewart's fantastic and highly amusing cartoons. In the *Weekly*'s last issue, he lampooned Fowler as King Louis XIV, fat and pompous with a tilted crown on his head and gold coins bulging in his pockets. Beside him stood his Royal entourage—Krupp, Emery, Harrison and James—dressed as consorts and jesters. St. Clair had heard through his confidant that Fowler was so livid when he saw it that he punched a hole in his office wall.

In the last month, St. Clair had documented how the annual budget of the office of the Street Commissioner, which now answered to Fowler, had increased from $650,000 in 1864 to more than $3 million—except no one at city hall was certain where all of this money went.

New York has more manure inspectors than any city in America, yet as any citizen can attest, there is manure everywhere you look.

Then, in last week's article, St. Clair had chronicled, "A Day in Judge Silas Smith's Courtroom."

Judge Silas Smith likes to wear a large white hat while he deliberates in his courtroom. He usually keeps his legs up on his desk and has a bottle of whiskey nearby in case his throat becomes dry—which it does from time to time during a session.

The first defendant brought before him on this particular day was one Christopher McGunn, a well-known rogue from Hell's Kitchen. On this occasion, McGunn was charged with robbing a druggist's shop on Hudson Street owned by a Mr. Manuel Morrison. The city lawyer prosecuting the case, Jack Duncan, called five witnesses. All of them testified that they had been in the store at the time of the offence, that they had seen McGunn enter the shop, threaten Mr. Morrison with a pistol, and then depart the store with a handful of money from his cash box.

During much of the witnesses' testimonies, Judge Smith whittled on a pine stick, as he is apt to do.

McGunn's lawyer, Samson Simons, offered no defense other than the word of McGunn himself, who claimed to have been at the Black Tavern on Water Street at the time of the robbery. No witnesses from the Black Tavern were called to testify as to this alibi.

Judge Smith retired to his chambers for about fifteen minutes, before delivering his verdict. Upon returning to the courtroom, the judge stated that, "there is not sufficient evidence against Mr. McGunn and I have no choice but to acquit him." At that the courtroom erupted in shouts of "Shame, Shame."

The next case involved Miss Flo Taylor, a woman known to manage a brothel on Wooster Street. She was charged with assaulting one of her young girls, a thirteen-year-old child named Suzie. The only witness to this alleged crime was the girl herself. In a matter of some ten minutes, Judge Smith also dismissed this case for lack of evidence.

Judge Smith is known to be an associate of Mr. Victor Fowler. In the possession of this reporter is a cancelled bank note from Miss Taylor to Mr. Victor Fowler for $3,000.

"Charlie, you know the rule around here," said Fox.

St. Clair smiled. "I'm only as good to you and the magazine as my next article."

"Exactly," Fox said, glaring at St. Clair. "So you have until tomorrow afternoon to come up with something new. Otherwise…otherwise, you'll hear some screaming in your left ear."

St. Clair nodded, again ignoring his boss' efforts to be tough.

"Go see what Fowler wants," continued Fox more calmly. "Maybe that'll lead to something. But watch your back. It's like going into the lion's den."

"Agreed, but you know I can handle myself…at least most of the time. Besides, Fowler wouldn't dare try anything. We've got him on the run."

"Maybe," said Fox, rubbing his beard. "But don't underestimate him, Charlie. The man is dangerous. Your articles have stung him, but you know as well as I do that the Ring is stronger than ever."

～

"That is so," conceded St. Clair. "You know Fowler is an opponent who I'd never dismiss, despite any claims to the contrary."

"Good. Now, do you want to tell me about that black eye?" asked Fox.

"It's nothing to worry about." St. Clair peered downward.

"Nothing? My arse. My finest writer walks in this morning looking like he just stumbled off the battlefield at Gettysburg, and he says that nothing is wrong. If you're in trouble, Charlie, I can help. How much do you owe this time?"

St. Clair shook his head. "I appreciate the offer, Tom. But I think I need to solve this problem on my own."

He was hardly convincing and he knew it. A few months back, Fox had loaned him a couple of hundred dollars to pay off another gambling loss and he wasn't about to ask him again. Foolish pride, dear Caroline used to warn him, would be his undoing. How right she had been.

"Have it your way, Charlie. But you know where to find me."

"I do and thanks for respecting my wishes in this matter." St. Clair stood up.

Fox paused to strike a match and light another cigar. "There's only one more thing we need to discuss. I want your opinion on another feature I'm planning." He stood up, poked his head out of his office entrance and called out in Molly's direction. "Get Sutton in here and please show in Miss Cardaso."

Within moments, Molly and Edward had appeared followed by a striking woman. St. Clair immediately jumped from his chair. She was perhaps twenty-seven or twenty-eight-years old, he guessed. She wore a bonnet of white ribbons from which hung a sheer veil. He could plainly see her olive skin and raven black hair that loosely dangled in ringlets on to her shoulders and down the back of her powder blue dress. Her nose was long and slender, her cheekbones high, her lips full and red. Through the veil, he could detect that her eyes were large and a deep hazel. Even with the numerous petticoats she wore beneath her frilly dress, St. Clair noticed her exquisite and shapely figure. She had a certain Mediterranean charm about her.

"Thank you, Molly," said Fox. "Charles, Ed, let me introduce you both to Miss Ruth Cardaso."

St. Clair nodded. "Miss, please take my chair. I'm Charles St. Clair, this is Edward Sutton."

"Why thank you, Mr. St. Clair. Mr. Fox has told me all about you."

"Is that so?"

"That's right, Charlie," said Fox. "I've explained how things work around here and Miss Cardaso was especially interested in your articles on the Ring."

"You're interested in civic politics, Miss?" asked St. Clair.

"Does that surprise you, Mr. St. Clair?" replied Miss Cardaso, pursing her lips.

St. Clair smiled. "My experience is that most women prefer less complicated matters." Even as the words tumbled out of his mouth, he wasn't sure what the hell he was saying. He did know, however, that he couldn't take his eyes off of her.

"Such as?" asked Miss Cardaso, her voice slightly sharper.

"Yes, Charlie," added Sutton, "please continue. This is fascinating."

"All I meant was that it has been my experience that ladies find the intrigues of city hall rather droll," he said as his face flushed and tiny beads of sweat formed on his forehead and palms.

Miss Cardaso smiled and nodded. "You feel, Mr. St. Clair, that I would find conversation about fashion and children more to my liking?"

"Perhaps. That...that has been my experience, as I said," St. Clair added, wringing his hands.

"I'm afraid that for such an accomplished journalist, your experience in matters about women has been limited," she said, arching her eyebrows.

"Touché," declared Sutton.

"If you're finished, Charlie," said Fox, "I will uncomplicate things for you."

St. Clair remained silent and offered Miss Cardaso the chair beside Fox's desk. He and Sutton stood to the side close to a bookcase. She lifted her veil and gently folded it on top of her bonnet. St. Clair could not take his eyes off of her. Her skin looked as smooth as silk. She was even lovelier than he had first thought.

"If I may, this is a rather delicate matter," began Fox, sounding as officious as he could. "As you both know, there have been several stories in the *Times* recently about the plight of women who have been victims of vile medical malpractice. Physicians and midwives advertise services for women with female problems. They're often at their most vulnerable and these quacks, for that is what they are, are quick to take advantage of the situation. They offer cures for pregnancy, pills, and other remedies, most of which have no effect or, in some cases, can be deadly. You recall reading about the case of the women found dead in Philadelphia."

"In a boarding house, I believe," said Sutton. "It was a bloody mess—"

"Exactly," Fox cut him off. "I can list another dozen or so cases like that in New York. Women nearly bleeding to death or left at the mercy of a butcher like Madame Philippe. The woman has made millions of dollars dispensing her French Pills and performing dangerous surgery. She lives like Queen Victoria in that mansion on Fifth Avenue. Blood money, that's what she has. I've also heard . . . and please pardon this, Miss Cardaso . . . that she even makes a profit selling the dead corpses."

"To whom?" asked Sutton. "Who would want such a horrific thing as that?"

"Does it matter?" blurted St. Clair. "It's an abomination of the worst kind. The woman should be hanged from the nearest lamp post."

"That wasn't always your opinion," said Sutton.

St. Clair glared at him, but did not respond. He would have conceded that Sutton was correct—his views on abortion had been more liberal in the past. But that was hardly the point. And, frankly, he didn't care. All he knew for certain was that now his blood boiled any time this issue was raised.

"Ed, be quiet," said Fox. "No God-fearing man can ignore this, which brings me to the point of this gathering. Miss Cardaso has come here all the way from San Francisco highly recommended by a friend for her numerous acting talents. She arrived nearly a week ago and has been enjoying the city's sights until now, but is anxious to get to work. I've hired her to accompany Sutton on visits to every midwife and abortionist in this city. Miss Cardaso will pose as his sister or companion, whichever is more believable."

"I'd prefer companion," said Sutton.

"Please, allow me to finish. As I said, Miss Cardaso will pose as your sister or companion. You're to attempt to amass as many details...prices, places of business, medical training of the practitioners...as you can. A month or so from now, I want to put 'Evil of the Age,' that's what the story will be entitled, on the front of the *Weekly*. We're going to drive these devils out of business."

"I'm curious, Miss Cardaso, you've done work like this before?" asked St. Clair.

"Yes and more dangerous. Two months ago, I posed as, let us say, a woman of the streets, in exposing a mining scandal."

"Is that so?"

"Yes, Mr. St. Clair, I'm quite capable and a woman of many talents and experiences."

"I have no doubt about that, Miss." He turned to Fox. "And, Tom, what's my role in all of this?"

"Your first priority remains Fowler and the civic corruption. But I want you to work with Sutton and Miss Cardaso as an editor and advisor. I believe your assistance will be invaluable."

Ruth reached for her handbag. "If the meeting has concluded, I would like to freshen up at my hotel. And I do thank you for your hospitality, Mr. Fox. I've stayed in many fine establishments before but the Fifth Avenue Hotel is exquisite."

"I'm glad you approve. Nothing but the best around here, right fellows?" said Fox, patting Sutton on the back. "Molly will see you out, Miss Cardaso. A cab will take you back to the hotel. Why not return in a few hours and you can work with Sutton on completing a plan of attack?"

"You make it sound as if we're going to war, Mr. Fox," said Ruth.

"That's exactly what we're doing."

Ruth stood up and folded her veil back down over her face. She took a few steps and then turned. "Mr. St. Clair, and I trust you'll forgive me for being so forward, but perhaps we can continue our earlier conversation later today or this evening? And," she added with a slight smile, "you can tell me about your adventures."

"Adventures?" he asked turning his head.

She pointed to her eye.

"Foolishly ran into a door," said St. Clair with a shrug, desperately trying to contain his enthusiasm at her offer. Indeed, he found the idea of spending more time with Miss Cardaso extremely appealing.

Chapter Three

INITIAL INVESTIGATIONS

Within fifty minutes, Hudson Depot was swarming with police. Seven patrolmen in their distinctive blue uniforms and caps were first on the scene. They parked their horse-drawn wagons at the front door of the station.

Behind them in another carriage was Detective Seth Murray in plain clothes. He wore an inexpensive and dusty brown suit and black felt bowler hat. Six feet tall and broad shouldered, Murray was large in every way—including his most distinctive feature, his thick black moustache that covered much of his mouth. As he stepped down from his carriage, he could not get one thought out of his head—why had he been asked to investigate this case? There were detectives at precincts closer to the Hudson Depot than he.

Accompanying Murray was Dr. Anton Draper. The doctor had been working with the police as a coroner for as long as anyone could remember.

"As I was saying, Murray, I'm more than a little surprised to see you on this case," said Draper, a short man with a grey beard and wire glasses.

"No more than me, Doc." Murray shrugged his muscular shoulders. "I thought Stokes was going to make sure that I stayed at the Fifteenth chasing pickpockets for the rest of my days. Damn, two weeks ago I was on rat-and-dog patrol breaking up bloody animal fights at Kit Burn's hall. There's nothing more humiliating than that. Then, out of the blue, today O'Brien orders me to meet you here at the depot."

"What exactly happened between you and Stokes?" asked Draper moving closer.

"A difference of opinion, you might say."

Murray had no desire to launch into a lengthy story of his deteriorating relations with Inspector William Stokes. Better to let sleeping dogs lie, he always felt. He doubted the Doc would've understood in any event. After all, what was Stokes guilty of? So what if Murray had discovered that the inspector was accepting payoffs from Madame Philippe and other abortionists? No one on the force cared—except him that is.

His personal feelings in this matter, he now realized, were beside the point. That his younger sister, Caroline, had bled to death from a botched abortion meant nothing to anyone, but him and Caroline's husband, Charles St. Clair. In retrospect, his only real mistake was confronting Stokes about the bribes. Within months after their initial argument, Stokes had him transferred from the Mulberry Street station to the Fifteenth where Stokes's fellow Irishman, Captain James O'Brien, ruled with an iron fist.

"Have it your way." Draper shrugged. "We'd better have a look at the body, don't you think?"

The doctor followed Murray and an entourage of patrolmen into the rail depot. Arriving passengers, wagon drivers, baggage handlers and even the pickpockets and beggars standing in the vicinity moved to the side to allow them to pass.

Some men tipped their hats, while ladies curtsied. Several called out, "Good afternoon, sir," to the detective.

"I bet there's been some trouble. Anything I can do?" asked one of the beggars in a loud voice. He held out a tin cup out for Murray to drop a coin into.

Murray ignored the old soldier, yet he did find this newfound respect from the other men and women curious. There was a time, not too long ago, when he had first started on the job, that New Yorkers would have gone out of their way to spurn the police. Certainly, few citizens would have come to the aid of a patrolman in trouble. Murray had been taught a bit of wisdom the first day of his training. "Depend on your fellow officers, your club, and your pistol," Sergeant Moses Patterson had instructed him.

As Murray well knew from personal experience, attacks on a lone policeman by gangs of ruffians were all too frequent. He, himself, had been jumped and mugged about six years ago while on a routine patrol near the waterfront. He was only slightly roughed up, yet cops like him and others had resisted uniforms for precisely this reason—the less conspicuous they were, the better they could do their jobs.

Some years ago, however, Murray noticed that attitudes began to change.

"It's the fear," he had recently suggested to St. Clair. "Look what happens each evening. The good citizens of this city lose their streets to the pickpockets, thieves, and scoundrels who lurk on every corner and hide in every saloon and theatre."

"I don't disagree with you, Seth. All I'm saying is that the police need to be wary of using excessive force in carrying out their duties. Justice has its limits," St. Clair had suggested, although he hardly sounded convincing.

"That's hogwash and you know it," Murray had argued. "You know as well as I do that the situation in the city has become intolerable. In many neighborhoods, it isn't safe to leave your home once it's dark. I guarantee that anyone in this dangerous predicament welcomes the police and doesn't care how they conduct themselves. If a patrolman occasionally uses too much force with his club or if a robber or thief is shot trying to escape, no one cares much. You know how much I hate to disagree with you, Charlie, but liberty and security are compatible and complementary."

This was one of the few occasions when St. Clair had permitted Murray to have the last word.

Once inside the station, Murray found the baggage master waiting for him.

"It's over here," he said quietly.

"Anyone touch anything?" Murray asked. He covered his nose with his handkerchief as he peered inside at the dead woman. The odor from the trunk was fairly powerful.

The baggage master shook his head. "No, sir. As soon as the trunk was opened and I could see the woman, I sent for you. We didn't lay a finger on the poor girl. But that smell."

"Doc," Murray called out to Draper, "I want you to examine her. See what you can find."

"I know what I have to do, Detective," retorted Draper. "I was doing police work while you were still a whippersnapper."

"Doc, just get on with it," said Murray. There wasn't a detective in New York who had not had to tolerate Doc Draper's quick temper.

"I'll do a preliminary exam here, but we'll have to take the body and trunk back to the morgue."

"Whatever you think, Doc." Murray responded in a more deferential tone. He turned to the patrolmen standing behind him. "What are you standing around for? I want everyone inside and outside the station questioned. That means every wagon driver, deliveryman, carriage and stage driver, every beggar and thief in the area. Three of you outside, the other two speak to the passengers and baggage men inside the station."

"What are we looking for?" asked one of the men.

"How did you ever become a cop, Westwood? You'd make a fine fruit vendor or bookseller," said Murray.

The other policemen chuckled. "Someone delivered this trunk to the station," continued Murray. "It's fairly heavy, so we can assume it came in a wagon. Someone out there saw something. They probably don't even know what they saw, but you are going to encourage them to remember. You understand, Westwood?"

He nodded and the other patrolmen followed him.

Murray motioned for the baggage master to accompany him to a quiet corner of the station.

"Take a seat, sir," he told him.

The baggage master sat down on a wooden bench, filled his pipe with tobacco, and lit it. "In all my years at this job, I've never seen anything like this before. I've caught thieves and pickpockets, of course, but never seen a dead woman before and—"

"And what?" asked Murray.

"She's so young and beautiful. Did you see the look of fear on her face?"

In fact, Murray had noticed immediately, not only how striking the woman was, but how terrified too. Like any seasoned detective, of course, he would never have shared such assessments with any member of the public unless it was in court.

"Who'd do such a damn thing?" the baggage master said shaking his head.

"That's what I'm going to find out, with your help," said Murray.

"Anything I can do to assist you?"

"Tell me about the trunk."

"It came in mid-afternoon. Nothing unusual. Here's the check for it," he said handing Murray the small piece of paper. "The ticket with it was for the eight o'clock to Chicago. Maybe this old lady will show up to claim it like the truckman said."

"I doubt it," said Murray. It was his experience that news like this travelled fast on the street. And who knew for sure about the passenger? Might be an old lady, might not be. "Did you recognize the delivery man?"

"Can't say I do. An Irishman, I'd guess. Medium height. He wore a black cap, brown pants, white shirt with suspenders. I'd know him again if I saw him."

Murray stared for a moment at the claim check. Dumping the body in another city was an ingenious idea. But the murderer wasn't thinking. First, whoever did this should have packed the trunk with charcoal. It would have stopped the smell of putrification. And second, why drop the trunk off hours before the train's departure? It would have made more sense to arrive just before the train left the station. Whoever Murray was looking for had been in a hurry, and it was his experience that people in a hurry make mistakes.

Patrolman Westwood arrived back inside the station with a young man in tow. The boy's clothes were dusty, but not too shabby. He was trying to grow a moustache and beard, but the fuzz on his face was patchy. The hair looked more like dirt than whiskers.

"Who's this?" asked Murray, glaring at the boy.

"Says his name's Azee," replied Westwood.

"Azee? What kind of name is that?" asked Murray. "You look kind of familiar to me. Have we ever met?"

The boy shrugged.

"His name, I believe, is Alexander Lev, but his name on the street is Azee," offered the baggage master. "He's a young Jew pickpocket who fancies himself a cadet for a Hebrew madam on Greene Street. I think the only girl he's ever found for her was his own sister. He's been bothering passengers for about a month now. I chase him away, but he's back every day. Aren't you, boy?"

"Where do you live, kid?" asked Murray.

"Don't have a home. I live on the street. Not ever going home," said Azee staring at the ground.

"Look at me, boy," said Murray more firmly. "You got a mother or father?"

"I don't know who my father is. My mother lives over on Hester Street, near Orchard," he mumbled.

Murray's eyes widened. "Of course, you're Marm Lev's son, aren't you?"

"Marm Lev?" asked Westwood.

"Rebecca Marm Lev, she's a fence. She's probably responsible for half the robberies in New York."

"She pays for police protection. There's nothing you can do to me," said the boy arrogantly.

Murray grabbed Azee by his shirt collar. "You be respectful, Yid. I don't give a shit how many cops your son of a bitch mother's paid off. Now, what do you know about this trunk?"

"He says he saw the trunk being delivered by this Irish truckman," says Westwood.

"Is that right, Azee?" Murray loosened his grip on the boy's shirt.

"Yeah, I saw him."

"So what did he look like?" Murray demanded to know.

"A damn Irishman. A bottlehead with a bracket mug." Azee smirked.

"You mean he was a stupid looking fellow with an ugly face right, kid?" said Murray.

"That's what I said."

"Go on, kid, and wipe that smile off your face."

Azee did as he was told. "He was nothing special," he continued. "Had on pants and this funny-looking hat. I don't know what the fuck you want me to say."

Murray wasn't amused. "I want to know everything. What do you mean the hat was funny looking?"

"That's what I said. It was high."

"A plug hat? He was wearing a plug hat?"

"I guess so," said the boy. "Anyway, I was standing in front of the station. It was about one o'clock in the afternoon. He stops his wagon up front. He gets out and hauls in the trunk with the rope around it."

"What else?" Murray had dealt with enough young thugs like Lev to know that the more he pressed, the more the kid would eventually tell him. It was all inside his head. Murray merely had to unlock it.

"P. Tripp," said Azee, scratching his head.

"What's that?"

"The sign on the truck. That's what was written, 'P. Tripp.'"

"Good. So the truckman's last name was Tripp. That'll help. Anything else, kid?" The tone of Murray's voice softened slightly.

"Yeah, one more thing." Azee now seemed more relaxed. "I watched him come out. He spoke to this beggar for a few minutes. Don't know who he was. Never saw him around the depot before. Didn't hear what they were talking about. This beggar—he was wearing an army uniform, handed him something, maybe money, which struck me as kind of peculiar. The truckman took it and left. So did the beggar. That's it. That's what I saw."

"You can go now, kid. But I may need you again. You're staying with your mother, aren't you?"

Azee nodded. "I hate her, but yeah she'll know where to find me."

Murray returned to baggage area where Dr. Draper was finishing his examination. "Doc, anything yet?"

Draper fixed his tie and jacket. "I can't be certain until I examine her more closely at my office," he said quietly. "However, from the amount of blood on the bottom of the trunk and the cut between her legs—"

"Between her legs? You mean she had an abortion?"

"Exactly. It appears that she was slashed by a knife. She was likely dead when she was put into the trunk."

Murray's face reddened. "When will they stop? Have these animals no sense of decency?" The image of his sister bleeding to death at Bellevue Hospital flashed into his head.

Suddenly Murray felt very hot. He walked out of the station into the sunlight where he could breathe and think more clearly. As a detective he had figured out long ago that success in solving cases depended on having a set strategy in place, much like tackling a chess game against a difficult opponent. Cooling down, he relished the challenge. His first order of business was to find this truckman named Tripp. That was the place to start.

And, as much as he detested it, he was going to have to pay an unannounced visit to Madame Philippe. The woman made him ill, but for a price, she might be able to provide him with key information. He knew that William Stokes, his former boss, had dealt with her—that she was, in fact, still paying him for favors and protection. Speaking with the unpredictable inspector would be necessary.

He knew he would require his brother-in-law's services as well in this investigation. He was certain that St. Clair would be able to help him— he had contacts in every corner of the city—although being an abortion case might be problematic. Charlie was understandably more volatile about the issue than even he was.

Nevertheless, St. Clair was also his ace in the hole. Many detectives on the force had their snitches—bar keeps, madams, and pickpockets— who provided them with much-needed information that often led to a case being cracked. Still, others, and this included Murray, worked with discreet reporters who could plant fake stories and go places where a detective, even in plainclothes, could not. On more than one occasion, Murray had used St. Clair's talents to flush a culprit out of hiding.

It had been St. Clair, for example, who had purposely met the bank clerk, Henry Waters, around the faro table at Darcy's saloon. Then he had cultivated a friendship with him and even interviewed Waters for a magazine article on the New York banking industry. Without that intervention, Murray would never have determined that it was Waters who had been stealing small sums of money from the Greenwich Savings Bank.

While St. Clair enjoyed the adventure police work offered and gained material for new stories, Murray had an indispensable tool at his disposal.

Such outside assistance was generally frowned upon by the department, yet everyone from the chief on down recognized how valuable it was in resolving complex criminal cases. Yes, Murray thought, his brother-in-law would have a role to play in this murder investigation.

As he felt the heat of the August afternoon begin to give way to the cool of the early evening, Murray was struck by a troubling notion—was it more than a coincidence, given his personal view on abortion...a view he had hidden from no one in the police department...that his first homicide case in months involved a woman likely murdered by an abortionist? He wiped his brow and stared into the distance. It was, he contemplated, almost as if this case was intended for him.

Chapter Four

St. Clair Receives an Offer

S t. Clair waited patiently for his informant at a saloon a few blocks from his Park Row office. After sitting for an hour nursing a mug of ale and devouring a plate of fried oysters—served with pepper, mustard and lemon juice, the way he preferred them—he received a hand-delivered message from a young newsy indicating that his companion had been delayed. Their meeting was now to take place later that evening in a saloon down by the waterfront. It was an area of the city St. Clair tried to avoid, especially since there was a chance he might run into Captain Martin's thugs. But business, he figured, was business.

He returned to his office and, along with Sutton, waited another hour or so for Ruth Cardaso to return from her afternoon *toilette*. The trio had eventually established a viable storyline— That Miss Cardaso was Lily Turner from Buffalo and that Sutton was her boyfriend, Samuel. The two were not married and because their families objected to the relationship, Lily, with Samuel's full support, had decided to abort the pregnancy. She was to admit, if asked, that she had experienced quickening. They were to start the following afternoon seeking an appointment with Madame Philippe, the most widely known abortionist in New York.

St. Clair had mixed emotions about the entire escapade, although he tried to keep his feelings to himself. After Sutton excused himself, Ruth Cardaso informed St. Clair that she was not the type of woman to make small talk. She invited him to dine with her at breakfast tomorrow at the Fifth Avenue Hotel. It was an invitation he could hardly refuse—nor did he want to.

~

By the time St. Clair arrived at Victor Fowler's mansion at 511 Fifth Avenue on the southeast corner of Forty-Third Street, it was nearly five o'clock. By reputation, St. Clair knew that the brownstone had forty-five rooms, gas lighting, piped in water from the Croton reservoir, and the most modern water closets money could buy. And in the rear of the property were Fowler's silver-trimmed stables, larger than most homes, for the six black horses he kept in the city.

St. Clair climbed up the wide stoop and rang the bell. Moments later, a Negro male servant answered and let him in. St. Clair noticed that he was dressed in navy pants with a gold cord down the seams, a blue sack coat of navy cut, and a white cloth vest. It was the unmistakable uniform worn by the members of the Liberty Club, the exclusive association Fowler established some years ago near his summer home in Greenwich, Connecticut. The sight of the servant—clearly the butler—made St. Clair smirk. As was well known, the Liberty Club had a closed membership of one hundred—and none of them were Negroes. Fowler always did have a flair for the dramatics, thought St. Clair.

"Right this way, sir," said the butler. "If I can take your hat and coat."

Directly in front of St. Clair was a grand staircase leading to the upper levels. To his right, nearly covering an entire wall, was a mirror with gold trim encircled with green vines. The butler led St. Clair through the main floor parlor over plush burgundy Persian carpets. The room was packed with marble tables, paintings, mahogany chairs, statues, and glass vases and urns filled with every imaginable flower—red and yellow roses, violets, daffodils, and petunias. Mrs. Fowler, he concluded, must have taken up botanizing.

Beyond the parlor was a large oak door. The butler knocked twice and pushed it open. He allowed St. Clair to pass.

"Mr. St. Clair, we meet again. Join us, please. Jackson," he said to the butler, "close the door and keep looking for my gold badge. It's got to be somewhere in this house. Have you any idea the price of those two ruby eyes? I'll take it out of your wages for the next five years if it doesn't turn up."

Jackson showed no emotion and shut the door of the study behind him.

St. Clair turned to face Victor Fowler, who was sitting proudly at the head of a dark mahogany table. His chair, really more of a throne, had a high back and was covered in red velvet. All the Boss was missing, figured St. Clair, was a crown and scepter. He'd have to remember to describe the scene to Peter Stewart for a new sketch. Sitting next to Fowler were the other key members of the Ring—Mayor Thomas Emery, Isaac Harrison, and Bob James. Everyone, except Fowler, was smoking cigars and the haze in the room was thick.

St. Clair surveyed the surroundings. He was in Fowler's private study. There was a wall of books and journals to one side. This was, he thought, peculiar for a man who likely did not read much. Then again, as he well knew, a man's library had aesthetic rather than practical appeal. Beside the shelves of books was a large billiard table with shimmering green felt and smooth leather pockets. It was the finest table St. Clair had seen. The sunlight pouring in from two French windows in front of the table almost made it glisten. The most distinctive item in the room, however, was a mural-size painting of Fowler and his wife, Ellen, dressed in regal attire and looking much like the Hapsburg emperor and empress at a Viennese ball.

"Take a chair, please, Mr. St. Clair," said Fowler. "I think you know the other gentlemen here." His tone was formal, yet friendly. He extended his right hand. St. Clair grasped it tightly and shook hands with Fowler. He had long fingers and a soft, fleshy palm. For such a big man—St. Clair estimated that Fowler must have been more than six feet in height and close to three hundred pounds—he moved with ease.

"I recognize them," said St. Clair. If it was Fowler's intentions to intimidate him, he had succeeded. He sat in the chair and shifted uneasily, astutely aware of the glaring eyes trained on him. They were clearly less friendly than Fowler.

"I'll bet you feel a little like Daniel in the lion's den. Isn't that so, St. Clair?" Fowler remarked with a chortle. He straightened the white cravat that was wrapped around his neck and tucked into his dark suit.

"It remains to be seen if he is to be the lion's lunch, however," added Thomas Emery.

New York's esteemed mayor clearly lived up to the "Prince" moniker that St. Clair had bestowed upon him. He was wearing a tailored grey cloth suit with a matching vest and white shirt and necktie. His ensemble was likely imported from London, St. Clair mused. It must have cost a small fortune.

"Not today I think, Mr. Mayor," said St. Clair. "I don't mean to be rude—"

"That's exactly what you've been," interjected Isaac Harrison, his voice angry and irritated. "Those damn magazine articles and sketches. You've humiliated all of us. I can barely walk down the street any longer without hearing the titters. After what we've done for this city."

Harrison was a short and stocky man with a walrus black moustache and wearing, as he always did, a black suit. St. Clair noticed that a tiny bead of sweat had formed on his brow.

"What you've stolen from this city you mean," asserted St. Clair, his voice cracking.

Harrison flicked the ashes of his cigar in St. Clair's direction. "You're a meddling fool. Since Mr. Fowler's appointment as Tammany's Grand Sachem six years ago and his work before that as an alderman, he's provided sound management and I consider it a privilege to serve him. Why only last week, he donated $5,000 out of his own pocket to a shelter for homeless veterans. They'll erect statues and plaques to honor him one day."

"Spoken like a true loyalist, sir. But you're mistaken. It's certainly true that your Ring will be remembered. But not, I suggest, as you believe. Justice will catch up with all of you. And while donating funds for a shelter is admirable, I'd be most curious to learn where exactly the $5,000 came from."

St. Clair raised his voice slightly and enunciated each word. He always felt that he was at his best when he took the moral high ground. In his view there were principles that could not be compromised and behavior that could not be tolerated. He considered misappropriating the public treasury only slightly less of a transgression than he did abortion—certainly abortion performed by unqualified and incompetent practitioners.

"You're either a brave man or a fool, talking to us in that manner" said Bob James.

"Mr. St. Clair is no fool, I can assure of you of that," said Fowler. "I make no apologies for anything I've done." He stood and the chain of his gold watch grew tight across his belly. "I grew up from nothing, dirt poor in the gutter, and look at me now. In less than twenty years I've gone from the Liberty Engine company as a fire fighter and then brigade commander to improving the life of this city like no one else has before."

"And no one ever will," interjected Harrison.

St. Clair said nothing. He was amused, however, by Fowler's continual efforts to portray himself as the product of a Five Points slum upbringing—an Irish orphan who against all odds made good. In fact, as was well known, Fowler's parents were middle-class English immigrants. He grew up on Cherry Street, not far from City Hall. His father owned a furniture-making shop and his mother pampered him.

"Perhaps you can tell us what you've written for the next issue of Fox's Weekly Hell," said Emery. The other men laughed each time the mayor offered a clever pun. "Why anyone would want to read that *Journal of Devilization* is beyond me."

"Where do you get all of your information?" asked James. "The day I discover who's betraying us—"

St. Clair stood up. "I knew this was a waste of time. If you'll all excuse me."

"Hold on, St. Clair. I invited you here to talk, and talk we shall," said Fowler. "Gentlemen, if you'll be good enough to leave us, Mr. St. Clair and I have a few private matters to discuss."

"After you're finished, maybe we can string him up," murmured Harrison. The other men chuckled.

"Have no fear," said Fowler. "Isaac is not a sporting man. He's all business, all the time."

Once the other men had departed, Fowler stood up and moved closer to St. Clair. "So, what are you going to do about it?" he asked, speaking more softly. His breath reeked of tobacco.

"What am I going to do about it?" St. Clair shifted back. "I'm going to do my job."

"Yes, your job, of course." He reached for an open bottle of champagne that was on a silver tray beside the table. "Can I pour you a glass?"

St. Clair nodded. Fowler poured two glasses and handed one to the journalist. "What shall we toast to? How about the future?"

"The future may not be what you anticipate."

"Perhaps not, St. Clair. But as you well know I rarely surrender without a fight. Speaking of which, I understand," he said pointing to St. Clair's forehead, "that you had a recent altercation with Captain Jack Martin. Isn't that so?"

"Why be coy about it, Mr. Fowler. You clearly know the details."

"Yes, as a matter of fact I do. Gambling can be dangerous to one's health if you're not careful," said Fowler, patting his chest.

"I guess so. My luck will change. It always does."

"Come, Mr. St. Clair, waiting for your luck to change? I thought you were smarter than that."

"What is it you want from me, Mr. Fowler?" St. Clair's tone grew impatient.

"Your luck is about to change, St. Clair, because I have a proposition for you. Interested?" He did not wait for a response. "Here's my offer. I'll ensure that your debts to Captain Martin vanish as if they never existed, plus add in for your personal inconvenience, let us say another $50,000."

St. Clair loosened his necktie and wiped his brow with his handkerchief. "In exchange for what precisely?" He knew that Fowler's outlandish gift must have a price. The question was how high was it?

"For the moment, nothing at all," said Fowler, sipping his champagne.

"Nothing? You want no favors, you don't want me to stop writing my articles, or for Stewart to stop ridiculing you in his sketches?"

"I would never admit this to Isaac. He has no sense of humor. But those sketches are, to be honest, highly amusing. However, you're correct.

I want nothing from you. There may be a day when that will change. Until then..."

What kind of magic was this, wondered St. Clair. The idea that his problems with Martin would be solved and that he would receive such a vast sum were immediately attractive. He could move out of his Bleeker Street flat and find a real home or maybe lodge at the Fifth Avenue Hotel or the Metropolitan for a period of time. The possibilities were endless. So why, then, was his mouth as dry as if he had been lost at sea for many months? Because in his heart he understood that no matter what Fowler offered him, there would be a high price to pay in the days ahead. That at some future time he would be asked, or rather ordered, to act in an unethical manner for the greater glory of Victor Fowler. He did not think he could live with that.

"You'll have to permit me think about this, Mr. Fowler."

"What is there to think about?" His voice became louder. "I've made you the offer of a lifetime. Martin will not wait for you to make up your mind. He'll demand his money and soon."

"Why do you care so much about this?"

"You may be a poor card player, St. Clair, but you're a talented journalist. Ignoring for a moment your recent writings for Fox, which I'm certain I don't have to tell you has indeed caused me considerable grief, I believe that we can complement each other."

"I doubt that."

"This city needs the both of us working together, not in conflict. And I'll tell you this—"

The door to the study suddenly opened and in walked Fowler's wife, Ellen.

"Ellen, my dear, what a pleasure. I thought you had gone out. St. Clair, allow me to introduce my wife." He reached for his wife's hand. "Ellen, this is Charles St. Clair, the journalist I had told you about."

"Mr. St. Clair," she said with a nod. "Your reputation precedes you."

"Madam. So nice to meet you, and you're too kind."

Ellen Fowler, who must have been at least ten years younger than her husband, was not a strikingly beautiful woman, more handsome than anything, in St. Clair's opinion. She wore a dove-colored satin dress trimmed with velvet, one of the hundreds of dresses she was famous for having in her clothes closet. St. Clair had heard that Mrs. Fowler was never seen in the same dress twice and that she was a fixture at the fashion shops along the Ladies' Mile. According to Molly, who diligently kept St. Clair informed on such society matters, this year, when Mrs. Fowler travelled to the family's summer home in Connecticut, six carriages were required to transport her many trunks to the station.

Ellen's dark brown hair hung loosely on her shoulders. St. Clair could see that her skin was smooth and that like most women of her class, she wore cosmetics. He noticed on her dress a broach in the shape of a snake that was filled with diamond chips and that her fragrance was strong but pleasing. Yet, she looked tired and her face was flushed.

"I understand you work for that dastardly Mr. Fox," said Ellen.

"I wouldn't describe him so, but yes, I do work for his journal."

"A pity. All of those dreadful stories about Victor. And those ugly drawings."

"Come now, Ellen. Don't get upset about it again," said Fowler.

"I came to tell you that tea will be served shortly, Victor. Why not invite Mr. St. Clair to dine with us?"

"A splendid thought, my dear. St. Clair, you must join us for tea and pastries from Delmonico's. I believe my nephew, Lewis, is intending to join us. A fine young man. He's been training to be a lawyer and should be admitted into the bar in December," said Fowler.

"Thank you, but I do have to return to work." St. Clair smiled politely at Ellen Fowler.

"I really would like you to sit down with us for tea," she said. Her change of mood was abrupt and her face grew redder.

"Again I must apologize, Madam."

"Help me, Victor," she said holding her hand to her head. "I'm growing dizzy."

Fowler moved quickly to help his wife to a chair. He called for the maid and a Negro woman appeared who escorted Mrs. Fowler out of the study.

"She does have her moments," said Fowler half-apologetically.

"Of course. Now, Mr. Fowler, you'll have to excuse me."

"Think about what I said, St. Clair, what I'm offering you. And don't wait too long to answer. Unless you can find the $1,500 you owe the Captain from another source." He laughed.

"How do you know what my debt is to Martin?"

"St. Clair, there's nothing that goes on in this city from Water Street to Harlem which I don't know about. Every saloonkeeper, every thug and ruffian, every cartman and carriage driver, every harlot and shop owner—my eyes and ears are everywhere. Never forget that."

St. Clair said nothing else. Fowler's butler, Jackson, led him to the door and back outside on to the bustle of Fifth Avenue. The street was, as usual, crowded with late afternoon traffic of stages, carriages, and hansom cabs. St. Clair checked his pocket watch. He had spent more than two hours with Fowler. He would return to the office before meeting his friend at the Hole-in-the Wall.

As he walked, he shook his head in disbelief. The money that Fowler was offering him truly was an astonishing sum. His first instinct was to decline—he had no desire to owe Victor Fowler anything, let alone be in his personal debt. Yet if St. Clair did have a flaw—and in all honesty, he had more than one—it was that he often acted in haste without giving proper consideration to all aspects of a problem. It was what had led to his wife Caroline's death in the first place. Had either of them truly comprehended the potentially dangerous ramifications of their decision to seek an abortion for a baby that they could have had? Why had they not sought other medical advice? His stubborn insistence that Caroline had no other options made no sense to him now. He shook his head at the memory of his foolish intransigence. He realized then and there that this issue of the money required further reflection—especially in light of his gambling debts.

The offer aside, he believed that he had learned another important fact from his visit at the Fowler household. It had been obvious to him the moment he had been introduced to Fowler's wife. Her flushed appearance and her sudden anger and dizziness—Ellen Fowler was using laudanum. St. Clair was certain of it. He had seen the identical symptoms with Caroline.

~

Once St. Clair departed, Emery, James, and Harrison reconvened in the study. Harrison waited until the door was shut before addressing Fowler. "Can his services be bought, Victor?" he asked. "It would make the transition much easier."

Fowler held up his hand. "First things first, Isaac. Find Frank King and have him send out the final plastering contracts to Bruce McWilliams immediately."

"When does he think the courthouse will be completed? It's been nearly two years," said Harrison. "There must be another plasterer in this city who could work faster."

"Patience, my friend," Fowler counseled. "It's our grandest project, yet. They'll be talking of it for generations to come. Hear me, this will be an enduring landmark in this city."

"I assume that at least McWilliams understands the financial arrangements?"

"Of course, Isaac. The percentages have been agreed to, but I'm demanding seventy percent this time in return," said Fowler.

"Seventy percent," said Emery with a whistle. "On all work done?"

"You heard me. For every builder, plasterer, and broom salesman."

"Your audacity never ceases to amaze me, Victor."

"Not audacity, Tom, merely a good business decision for the city and for us. Gentlemen," said Fowler, touching Emery on the shoulder, "our coffers are about to reach new, unimagined heights."

"Isaac's dealt with Ames and Durant then?" asked Emery.

"I have," said Harrison.

"It was like offering a dog a bone," Fowler added. "Was there any doubt they'd accept out terms? The fools should only realize what we have in store for them."

"There's nothing to worry about with them," Harrison responded. "I also had to answer some questions from some of the men today. They weren't happy. They wanted to know why the soldiers and police had fired on them yesterday during the Orange parade, when you and I had assured them there would be no trouble."

"What did you tell them?" asked Fowler.

"Nothing of consequence. That the soldiers had not listened to their superiors or some such excuse."

Fowler waved his hand dismissively. "Pay no attention to this. I'll send out a few cases of whiskey and the matter will be forgotten. What could we do? That damn Orangeman Thompson paid what I demanded."

"And what of St. Clair?" asked Harrison.

Fowler sipped from his glass of champagne. "Mr. St. Clair is an interesting man. He holds his moral principles high and is convinced that this makes him superior. The fact is, he is weak and that weakness will be his undoing. But as I said earlier, it matters not. I won't waste much more time with him. Once I settle my score with Fox, he'll see the light. If he accepts my generous proposal so much the better, and if not—"

"Then, as your friend, Captain Martin, would say, he's a dustman."

A sly smirk crossed Fowler's mouth. "Yes, Isaac, he's a dead man. Now, if you gentlemen will excuse me, I must attend to my wife."

Chapter Five

An Altercation at The Hole-in-the-Wall

Detective Seth Murray paced back and forth in the narrow hallway. He was in the cellar of a red-brick building on Mulberry Street, half a block from police headquarters. And it was hot inside. His shirt, drenched in sweat, was pasted to his body. He was growing increasingly impatient, yet the door to Dr. Anton Draper's medical examination room at the city morgue remained locked. One hour had passed and then another and still he heard no word from Draper. What the hell was he doing to the poor girl, wondered Murray. How much prying, prodding and cutting was required before Draper had some answers?

Murray would not have disputed that his knowledge of medical procedures was limited. In fact, he tried to stay away from physicians altogether. He had found a treatment of bleeding, recommended by his own doctor for each and every ailment, neither restorative nor invigorating, as it was claimed to be. Only last year, when he'd had difficulty passing his urine, he had undergone a painful ordeal—a bleeding from his penis. It took him weeks to recover and it still hurt when he pissed.

He knew, too, that if he should ever suffer from a serious gun or knife wound and survive, the chances were good that he would lose an arm or leg. He had heard of other physicians in the city who claimed they could cure by faith alone—rather dubious, in Murray's opinion—or by using herbal medicines, which seemed to him like an approach he had read the Plains Indians used. When he contemplated this further, he decided that he would be reluctant to place his health in the hands of a healer who followed the ways of the savages.

"Doc, how much longer?" Murray asked loudly.

There was no sound from the other side of the door.

"Shit, this is no goddamn way to run an investigation," mumbled Murray.

Murray had sent his patrolmen into Five Points to search out this truckman, P. Tripp. At least then he might learn how the trunk was delivered to the depot and, if he was lucky, who its real owner was. Did it belong to the old lady the baggage master mentioned? Was she the abortionist who had allegedly killed this young woman? Was Madame Philippe involved in this tragic crime? The more he pondered these various possibilities, the more confusing it all seemed.

He had, however, decided not to run off, half-cocked, to harass or arrest Madame Philippe or any other abortionist. Murray had no desire to return to the dogfight patrol. And, given Philippe's relationship with Stokes, he needed to proceed cautiously. If Draper could confirm his initial opinion that the victim had indeed been killed by a botched abortion, then interrogating Philippe was justified. He'd speak to O'Brien who could intercede on his behalf with the Inspector. He realized, of course, that Madame Philippe's wealth was seemingly unlimited and Stokes, in his judgment, would do almost anything to line his own pockets.

At long last, the door opened. The odor emanating from the room was powerful. Murray felt as if his nostrils were burning. It had been some time since he had visited Draper's office while working on a murder case. He had forgotten how strong the various mixtures and concoctions used by the doctor could be. He peered in and felt a pit in his stomach. Through the early afternoon shadows he could see the female victim, or rather what remained of her, on a slab of wood in the middle of the room. A gaslight hung low from the ceiling, barely illuminating the body. There were pools of blood and guts around the table and on an adjoining bench, a small handsaw, surgeon's knife and other medical tools. A wooden barrel filled with what appeared to be water was nearby. Body parts floated on top. Murray took one step forward when Draper appeared. He wore a white apron on top of his suit. It was soaked in blood.

"Doc, the stench is unbearable. I'd forgotten how bad it can be." Murray covered his nose. "What is that you use?"

"It's the formaldehyde. I use it as a preservative. Keeps the body parts in one piece for further examination. You get used it after a time."

"To be honest, you look kind of pale, Doc, like you saw a spirit. Maybe that formaldehyde bothers you more than you think."

"I doubt it. It's this work. I fear I'm getting too old for it. Seeing young women carved up. It's not natural."

"What can you tell me? What did you find?" Murray continued to hold his nose.

"My earlier assumption was correct. She was with child, maybe seven or eight weeks pregnant."

"You're certain? I thought you said she'd had an abortion."

"That's the strange part, the fetus was not removed. It was as if someone had started the procedure and then once she started bleeding something went wrong, terribly wrong."

"A child, Doc? Are you sure?"

"Would you like to see it for yourself? It's tiny, but have a look inside that barrel."

Murray grimaced. "I believe you, Doc. What else?"

"At some point, she was cut open and stabbed several times between her legs. She bled to death and was then was stuffed in the trunk a few hours later. There wasn't much blood in the trunk. The wounds were fairly deep and abrasive. It's the work of a butcher, not a midwife. Truthfully, Murray, I can't believe Philippe could've done this. But—"

"But, what? What else did you find, Doc?"

"This," he replied. From under his apron he held up two objects, a white lace monogrammed handkerchief with the letter L embroidered on it, and a crumpled-up ball of paper. "The handkerchief was in her left hand. And this," Draper, held up the paper, "I've cleaned it up as much as I could."

"What the hell is that?" Murray stepped closer.

"I discovered this inside of her, fairly deep," Draper replied maintaining an aloof tone.

"Inside? You mean between her legs? Someone pushed up the paper inside of her?" Murray asked, shaking his head slightly.

"That's what I said. Now be careful, it's fragile and still bloody and wet." He handed the paper to Murray as gently as he could.

"This is the damnedest thing I've ever seen."

He walked to Draper's desk, sat down on a chair, and placed the ball of paper in front of him. Carefully he unfolded it, trying not to tear it as he did so. "Looks like a piece of newspaper," Murray muttered under his breath. "Son of a bitch. Look at this, Doc." Most of the words have been smudged, but a few lines were still legible. "It's an advertisement, I think." He began to read aloud:

M . . . Philippe . . . twenty-five . . . experience residence Fifth Avenue . . . she can be consulted with . . . strict . . . confidence . . . on complaints incidental to the female frame. Madame Philippe . . . .

"It's Philippe's advertisement. I've seen it before in the papers," said Murray excitedly. He stood up and walked towards the doorway.

"Where are you going now, Murray?" asked Draper.

"Newsstand at the corner," said Murray as he left.

Ten minutes later, with sweat dripping down his face, he returned clutching an evening copy of the *New York Herald*. He flipped through the pages until he came to the advertisement he was searching for.

"Son of a bitch. I was right. Here it is. Listen to this, Doc." He proceeded to read aloud:

Madame Philippe, Professor of Midwifery, twenty-five years' experience. Residence at Fifth Avenue and Fifty-Second, private entrance second door, where she can be consulted with the strictest of confidence on complaints incidental to the female frame. Madame Philippe's experience and knowledge in the treatment of cases of female irregularity, is such as to require but a few days to effect a perfect cure. Ladies desiring proper medical attendance will be accommodated during such time with private and respectable board. Madame Philippe would apprise ladies that her medicines will be

sent by mail or by the various expresses to any part of the city or country.
All letters must be post-paid. Madame Philippe would also apprise ladies
that she devotes her personal attention upon them in any part of the city
or vicinity.

"The ads are identical. That witch did this or she knows who did. She must be the old lady who was to take the trunk to Chicago," declared Murray.

"It's an odd thing to do." Draper shook his head in disbelief. "Then again, she wasn't intending for the trunk to be discovered at the station."

"Who the hell knows, Doc? She's an immoral woman, proud of her butchery. But maybe, just maybe she's killed her last victim. Even Stokes won't be able to protect her now."

"I suppose not," muttered Draper.

"Was there anything else? Anything identifying who this woman is?"

Draper was silent for a moment.

"Doc, you hear what I said? Did you find anything that can help put a name on the victim?"

The doctor stared directly into Murray's eyes. "No," he said emphatically. "Nothing. I know she was with child, as I said. She was no beggar or domestic servant. Her hands were too fine for that. In fact, I doubt she's done any real labor in years. From her hair and the cosmetics she wore, I'd guess that this was a woman of some means. Other than that, I don't know anything else. Except I suppose," he examined the handkerchief again, "that her first name begins with an 'L.' Leora, Lenore, maybe Laura."

"Thanks, Doc, I get the point. This'll be a big help." Murray stood up.

Murray already knew from his prior investigations that many wealthy women for a multitude of reasons sought out Madame Philippe's services. Some merely had had enough children. Others were young and single with no desire to wed the man who had impregnated them. Still others were married women, bored by their husbands, who had cheated in liaisons with more adventurous, sporting men. Some, like his sister Caroline and St. Clair, had not thought out the full consequences of their actions. They had made an impulsive and terrible decision. Caroline's health was a concern because of his sister's addiction to laudanum. He had tried to help her, but to no avail. What, he wondered, had been the motivation of this woman? What desperation had driven her into Madame Philippe's clutches? In due time, he would ascertain that as well.

He glared at the corpse lying in a heap and his body suddenly seethed with anger. It was the death of his sister all over again.

~

St. Clair walked briskly down Water Street. He gingerly sidestepped the puddles of vomit, bile, and scampering rats and glanced with pity as well as disgust at the numerous drunks lying on the cobblestone road. He also did his utmost best to ignore the half-clad harlots, some of them only girls of fourteen years, who beckoned him for a few moments of unrestrained pleasure—or so they claimed.

In the years since Caroline had died, St. Clair had discreetly visited a brothel on Wooster on more than one occasion—a man had certain needs and urges, after all, like a dry thirst that required quenching. The particular establishment he frequented was run by Madam Helena, a woman he more or less trusted. Its residents were a rare collection of alluring foreign beauties, women from southern Europe, South America, and Japan, who offered their customers a variety of exotic and pleasing services.

On the other hand, St. Clair knew that a man foolish enough to approach a whore in the vicinity of the waterfront was more than likely to be beaten and robbed. In the saloons, they referred to it as the panel game and its players were whores and badgers.

Two months ago, following an extensive investigation, Sutton had written a superb article for the *Weekly* about the dangers of the dockside area. St. Clair had read it with great interest.

A young harlot entices an unassuming victim into a house for what he thinks is a few hours of carnal gratification. The harlot then engages her mark, while her male partner, the 'badger,' a rogue of the worst kind, emerges from behind a secret panel or wall. The victim is then robbed of his pocket book and the badger quietly returns to his hiding place. The harlot quickly finishes her business and her satisfied client departs not noticing his absent pocket book. When he later discovers that his money is missing, the harlot permits him to search the premises knowing full well that he will not discover the secret panel and so nothing of any consequence is found. As a con, it is relatively safe and quite profitable.

St. Clair was certainly not going to be the victim of any panel game on this evening. He looked straight ahead, purposely avoiding eye contact with any stranger who passed him. Even with his pistol in his pocket, he felt uneasy. He knew, as most respectable New Yorkers did, that a man literally took his life into his hands when he ventured down to this area of the city. Its back alleys, saloons, and brothels were frequented by the city's most unscrupulous and dangerous gangs of thieves, pickpockets, and pirates, many of whom would slit your throat for merely glancing in the wrong direction.

It was not only the surroundings that were making St. Clair unusually nervous and anxious. He was still reeling from his meeting with Fowler and his head was swirling with indecisiveness. Accepting the money meant starting fresh, releasing him from his gambling debts. The question he kept asking himself, however, was how in all honesty could he succumb to Victor Fowler's bribe? For that is what it was and there was no getting around it.

St. Clair finally reached the corner of Water and Dover. Pushing his way past several drunken sailors, he descended the stairs into the Hole-in-the-Wall. A thick cloud of smoke greeted him, along with the stench of stale beer and rowdy noise peppered with a dozen different expletives. He looked around.

Groups of unsavory characters huddled around tables in various parts of the saloon. Most of them had not touched a razor in weeks and bathing he guessed was certainly not part of their monthly routine. You only had to come within a few feet of any group to be hit with the pungent odors of human sweat and grime. Most of the men were embroiled in heated conversations, undoubtedly conducting some illegal transactions, thought St. Clair as he further scanned the surroundings.

The Hole-in-the-Wall, as St. Clair and any journalist worth his salt knew, was notorious as the meeting place of thieves and fences, where stolen goods could be traded or sold. The unwritten rule here was that no man took his eyes off of his drink or turned his back. Because if you weren't paying attention, someone was liable to slip knockout drops into your beer and, before you knew what happened you'd find yourself beaten, naked, and robbed in a nearby alley thanking God you were still alive.

Along the far side of the room was the bar. A collection of unpleasant men stood drinking, smoking, and cursing. Beside them were several of the most unappealing harlots St. Clair had ever seen. Their dresses, if that's what you could call the rags they wore, were filthy and their hair was stringy. Two of them were barefoot, while another one had her large right breast out—it nearly touched the top of the bar—easily accessible to men who cared to fondle it for a free drink and a few coins. The conversations among several of the patrons were loud and punctuated with finger pointing and pushing. Many of the men had their knives showing, tucked into their pants. He figured that nearly everyone in the place had a weapon of some sort.

Standing behind the bar in all her glory was the Hole-in-the-Wall's most infamous personality. St. Clair didn't know her real name and didn't care to. Everyone called her Gallus Mag, since she used gallus to hold up her skirt.

She was unlike any woman in the city St. Clair had ever seen. She towered above six feet, had a long nose and large ears. St. Clair always thought she resembled an angry hound dog.

He eyed the crowd, searching for his informant. After a few moments he found the man he was looking for in a corner of the saloon. Frank King was sitting at a table away from the main crowd.

"You trying to get us both killed?" asked St. Clair, taking the chair opposite King. "Needless to say this isn't one of my favorite drinking establishments."

"Just don't stare at anyone. They won't bother you. They're too busy fighting with each other to pay attention to the likes of us. I needed to ensure that absolutely no one of consequence would see us together." He sipped from a mug of beer.

"Why? You think Fowler knows you've been talking to me?" St. Clair wiped the sweat from his palms.

"I'm not certain, but Harrison has been asking me far too many questions lately. That last story you did about the initial courthouse contract and the reference to the amount of money that plasterer McWilliams might have to pay to complete the job made him angrier than I've ever seen him. He was swearing like a sailor. Sooner or later, he and Fowler are going to figure it out. Only so many people are privy to this information. To be honest, I'm surprised that they haven't come after me yet."

Frank King was more stoical than usual. He was a tall thin man, clean-shaven, with a full head of light brown wavy hair. It had long struck St. Clair that he hardly fit the image of a dreary and sober bookkeeper.

"You certain you want to talk in here?" asked St. Clair.

Before King could reply, a knife fight broke out between a young man and a whore on the other side of the room. Immediately, the saloon erupted in screaming and shouting as a circle formed around the combatants.

King motioned for St. Clair to follow him through the back of the saloon just past the bar. Gallus Mag was already on her way to break up the altercation. She held her trusty bludgeon up high, preparing to strike.

"Someone is either going to get their head busted or lose an ear, if she gets really angry," shouted one patron.

Other men hooted and hollered for Mag to add another ear or two to the collection she kept in a pickle jar on a high shelf beside the bar. No one paid attention as King and St. Clair exited through a side door.

It was dark outside and the August air was thick. The alleyway behind the Hole-in-the-Wall reeked of filth and urine. St. Clair nearly stepped on a half-dead rat.

"King, where in the hell are you taking me? Let's finish our business before the rats get us."

King said nothing for a moment.

"Frank, do you hear me?" St. Clair asked, louder.

"Sorry, Charlie, I've got a lot on my mind, that's all." He pulled a small parcel of papers tied together by a string from his coat pocket and handed it to St. Clair. "Here, this should keep you happy for this week's issue."

"What is it?"

"Details about the renovations just finished at Harlem Hall," King explained.

"You mean the old armory that Fowler turned into a church?"

"Right. There's facts and figures here about the purchase and sale of the armory's benches. Fowler pocketed about one hundred thousand in the transaction, money that should've gone into the city's accounts."

"All in a day's work at city hall, I suppose. But I was hoping for something a little bigger."

"Jesus, Charlie, I'm sticking my neck out here, you know. If that bastard Fowler found out what I was doing—"

"Hey, easy, Frank. I only meant that if you and I really want to drive him out of city hall, then we're going to need something that shows what a crook Fowler has become. The sale of a few benches isn't going to impress very many people," St. Clair said more gently.

"There is . . . there's something else," said King moving closer. "I'm not certain of all of the details."

"You mean the courthouse contracts?" St. Clair's voice rose.

"That's worth a lot of money to him, but, no, not that. He's working on some other scheme. I've caught a few conversations between Fowler and Harrison. Let me look into it and I'll get a message to you in a few days."

"But what about . . . ?"

"Charlie, I have to go. We'll talk again soon."

Before St. Clair could reply, King scurried down the dark alley and was gone. That was strange, he thought, but no stranger than any of his dealings with King.

He often wondered about King's motives. After all, from what St. Clair understood, King had known Victor Fowler for many years—they had been neighbors before the Fowlers relocated to their Fifth Avenue mansion—and Fowler had mentored young King. As the Boss rose to power he brought King along with him. He arranged for King to apprentice in a bookkeeping firm on Wall Street and then installed him as the city's chief accounting officer.

Although he had never provided St. Clair with specific details, it was his impression that King had shared in the millions of dollars amassed by the Ring. He was married to a lovely woman named Amanda, who, from what St. Clair understood, was a close friend to Ellen Fowler.

Then, something happened to turn King against Fowler. St. Clair had pried only once, but was rebuffed.

"It's a personal matter," was all King would say about it. King had contacted St. Clair with a request for a meeting and had been revealing confidential information about Fowler and the Ring ever since.

St. Clair put the package of documents inside his pants pocket and was reaching for the door handle that led back into the saloon when suddenly the door swung open.

Standing in front of him was Jack Martin's right-hand man, Johnny 'Fats' Kruger, a 350-pound German hooligan, feared and celebrated in the seedier parts of New York for gouging out the eyes of anyone who dared cross him. Behind him were two other thugs, one of whom St. Clair recognized as a card player from his poker game at Martin's saloon.

"The Captain decided he wants the money you owe him now," said Kruger. He was standing close enough that St. Clair could smell his foul tobacco breath.

"That's not what I was told," replied St. Clair, his voice cracking. Slowly he lowered his right hand towards the inside part of his jacket and reached for his belt where his pistol was tucked.

"Yeah, the Captain makes the rules, you little asshole. And he says he wants the money right now or—"

"Or what?" asked St. Clair, searching in the dark for a possible escape route.

"Or I'm to bring him your eyes in this." Kruger held up an empty whiskey bottle. The two men behind him snickered.

St. Clair could now feel the cool steel of the gun inside his belt. He felt emboldened. "You tell Martin that he'll get everything I owe plus his goddamn interest within two days. And if that's not good enough then...then, he can fuck himself."

St. Clair did not know what came over him. He was seething with anger and was determined that he would not be beaten again by Kruger or anyone else. It was true that he was not a fighter, yet there wasn't a man living in the city, who at one time or another did not have to defend himself—and with a weapon if necessary. In his own case, he had fired his pistol on three occasions in the last year, although he had missed two of his targets—a pair of knife-wielding pickpockets—and only winged the arm of a thief he had caught in his flat.

"You're more of a fool than I thought," said Kruger with a grin. "I think I'm going to enjoy this."

Before St. Clair knew what hit him, Kruger had sent him reeling backwards with a hard punch to his stomach. He could hardly breathe.

"Take him by the arms," Kruger said to his two men. "I was just going to scare you, St. Clair. Just havin' some fun. But now you've gone and made me mad."

The two thugs each grabbed one of St. Clair's arms and yanked him up. Kruger held him by the collar of his jacket. He had just cocked his arm back, when from out of the dark a wooden club struck one of Kruger's men on the head and then the other. They slumped on to the ground.

"What the fuck is going on?" yelled Kruger.

Sufficiently recovered, St. Clair reached for his pistol. Before Kruger could react, he had it pointed at his head. From behind the fat hooligan walked Frank King, holding a wooden club.

"Who the fuck are you?" Kruger roared. "You cocksucker, I'll kill you for this?"

King said nothing. He held the club at his side.

"Another word, you fucking Dutchie, and I'll plug your head with a bullet," said St. Clair, surprised at his own ability to sound threatening given the circumstances.

"You're not that much of a bottlehead," sniggered Kruger.

"You want find out who the real bottlehead is, go ahead," St. Clair snapped back. Beneath his clothes, he was drenched in sweat.

Kruger relaxed his arms.

"You tell Martin that he'll have his money like we agreed. Two days from now. It'll be sent to the saloon."

"That's what you want me tell him?"

"Tell him what I said. Now take your two friends and get the hell out of my sight."

As Kruger pulled his two dazed men to their feet, St. Clair kept his pistol trained on Kruger's head. "Back through the door, go on you."

When the door to the saloon slammed shut, he turned to King. He had begun to shake. "Frank, I'm in your debt. If you hadn't come back—"

"Easy, Charlie. Put that pistol away, I don't think they'll be back. I reached the end of the alley and then heard the noise. When I saw them grab you, I figured I had to do something. So I found this piece of wood. Who is he and why's he after you?"

"It's a long and, I'm afraid, tedious tale. I owe his boss, the nefarious Captain Jack Martin, some money, and I haven't quite determined how I'm going to solve my debt problems."

"You say he works for Jack Martin?" King had a puzzled look on his face.

"Why? You know of him. He runs a saloon in Hell's Kitchen. I should never have stepped into the place." St. Clair sighed.

"Fowler introduced me to him four days ago. He's a real likeable fellow."

"Martin has had dealings with Fowler?" St. Clair shook his head in disbelief.

"Of course," said King. "You know as well as I do that Fowler has an army of thugs and shoulder-hitters working for him ensuring elections are rigged, and contracts and payments are made. The money's got to keep flowing. Hell, you should see Harrison's office on payday. There's a line down the staircase and out the front door. Laborers, hooligans, thieves and other Paddys all come for their cash. But, to be honest, from the little I heard of their conversation my impression was that Martin and Fowler had some other business. Come on, we'd better leave before that German comes back with more of his friends."

St. Clair brushed himself off and returned his pistol to his belt. So Martin and Fowler were partners in some crooked scheme, he mused. Was it merely a coincidence that a few days after King had seen them together, he had lost money in a poker hand that he should've won? Maybe, just maybe, Fowler had conveniently arranged his poker losses. Then Fowler pays off his debts, as he had offered, and St. Clair would be beholden to him. The question was why? Why would Fowler go to so much trouble? What was he planning?

St. Clair followed King back to Water Street, where the revelry had quieted down.

"Frank, I want to thank you one more time," said St. Clair. "If you had not shown up—"

King shook his head. "You'd have done the same for me. Tell me, how are you going to find the money you owe Martin?"

"Honestly, I have no idea," said St. Clair with a hint of resignation.

"Charlie, I think I can be of some assistance. But first, there's something else I need to explain to you."

Chapter Six

PADDY AND CORKIE

S eth Murray glanced at Paddy Tritt out of the corner of his eye, trying to decide how tough an approach to take with the truckman. For a few moments he said nothing, allowing Paddy to sweat it out. He perused Patrolman Westwood's report again, looking for something he may have missed.

Late yesterday, and following several hours of investigation, Westwood had finally determined, after speaking with dozens of truck and cartmen, that the driver he was searching for was called Paddy Tritt, not Tripp, as the witness at the Hudson Depot had told him.

Paddy, he had been told, usually parked his truck and horse at a stand on TwentyNninth Street and Third Avenue. But when Westwood and several other patrolmen arrived at the corner in a police wagon, Paddy was nowhere to be found. Further discussions with other truckmen eventually led the police early this morning to a Five Points boarding house.

Accompanied by two other patrolmen, Westwood had found Paddy's truck and horse in a stable on Baxter Street not too far from the old Brewery in Five Points, where Murray knew that a man's throat could be slit and no one would notice for months. Paddy was asleep inside the adjacent boarding house when Westwood and the other patrolmen barged into his small and sparsely furnished room. According to Westwood, Paddy reached for his knife, but one of the patrolmen knocked it out of his hands. He later claimed that he believed the police were thieves.

As per Murray's instructions, Westwood had brought Paddy to the Fifteenth Precinct for questioning and confiscated his cigarette packet and few coins he had in his pockets.

"Paddy, you're not charged with any crime," Murray finally assured him, "we only want to ask you some questions. But if you've done something wrong you'd better fess up."

"I done nothing to nobody," repeated Paddy. His voice was strained.

Murray poked Paddy in side of his head with his truncheon. "Save your soul and confess," he whispered in Paddy's ear.

He knew he sounded like a preacher, yet it was an approach that often produced results. Never underestimate the power of guilt, Murray enjoyed pointing out to any fellow detective or patrolman who'd listen—even when it came to the most dangerous of criminals.

"Think of the girl's family. Why did you put the body in the trunk? Why did you kill the poor woman?" asked Murray, louder. Beads of sweat dripped down the detective's forehead as he launched into another tirade.

"I didn't kill no one," said Paddy Tritt, his voice cracking. "Don't hurt me. I didn't do it. As Jesus is my witness." Sitting on a wooden stool in a small hot room, he was sweating more profusely than Murray. "Damn it. What do you want to know? Gimme a cigarette and I'll tell you something."

Murray tucked the truncheon under his arm and reached into his coat pocket. He pulled out a small square metal packet and opened it, removing a hand-rolled cigarette. "You mean one of these?" he asked, dropping the packet and cigarettes on the floor. He grasped the truncheon and circled Paddy. Without warning, he brought the truncheon down hard on the truckman's left arm.

Paddy winced. "What in Sam Hill. What'd you do that for? Those are my cigarettes."

Murray picked up a cigarette and held it close to Paddy's nose. "Tell me what I want to hear," he said. He lifted the truncheon above his head again.

"Bloody hell, you make me sick. If I tell you the truth, will you let me skedaddle outta here?" Paddy pleaded.

"Go on," said Murray. His truncheon fell to the side of his leg.

"I delivered the trunk like you said," said Paddy, dropping his head.

Murray kicked the cigarette case towards him.

Once Paddy started talking he could not stop. The detective listened intently as Paddy recounted that he had met a young street urchin named Corkie after the Orange Parade riot, that Corkie had directed him to the alleyway on Broome Street, that he had delivered the trunk to Hudson Depot, and how he had met a former Union soldier by the name of Flint, a nasty son of a bitch who had paid him for the delivery and then put a knife to his throat.

"He was crazy as a loon, if you ask me," muttered Paddy.

"And what about the woman?"

"I swear to you, Detective, I know nothing else, nothing about her. I didn't know she was in the trunk. And," he whimpered, "as the Lord is my witness, I didn't know she was inside as cold as a wagon tire."

Murray's experience taught him that most suspects in a similar circumstance would likely lie. Yet, in this case, Murray was inclined to believe what the truckman was telling him. It was Paddy's sheepish demeanor that convinced him. Listening to his pleas of innocence, Murray was sure that Paddy was no killer and that he likely had no hand in the abortion and murder of the woman in the trunk.

He was much more interested in this street Arab Paddy called Corkie as well as the beggar named Flint.

As Murray left the room, he figured that Paddy had told him everything he knew about the trunk. But as was his prerogative, he decided to keep the truckman locked in a cell for much of the day in case new evidence materialized—or, if need be, was manufactured.

"Detective, I hear you've cracked the case," said a voice from down the hallway.

Murray turned to face the Fifteenth's captain, James O'Brien, accompanied by Inspector William Stokes. Both men were broad-shouldered, tall, and left no doubt, that if required, they could handle themselves in an altercation. Both, too, like most members of the police force, sported thick black moustaches. Stokes also waxed his whiskers giving him—fittingly—a more sinister appearance.

"Not quite yet, but I have some strong leads," said Murray. "I don't think this truckman is involved. He merely delivered the trunk to the depot as he was paid to do. He's identified two possible suspects— A young kid and a thug named Flint. I already sent out Westwood and a few patrolmen to search for them and another team to investigate the Broome Street alleyway." He mustered as much officiousness as he could.

O'Brien nodded.

"I've also dispatched information about the victim on the telegraph wires so that it can be checked against missing-person reports for the last twenty-four hours," continued Murray. "And I'll speak with the boys from the papers. They've been waiting patiently to find out what's happened. The trunk murder is about to get a lot of attention. Someone is bound to come forward with knowledge about the woman." He removed his bowler hat and wiped his brow with a handkerchief. "And I'm planning to question Madame Philippe later this afternoon." He braced himself for Stokes' angry reaction.

"Then you have everything under control," Stokes responded matter-of-factly.

"That all you've got to say about this?" asked Murray somewhat dumbfounded.

"That's it, Detective. I don't think anything more needs to be said do you?"

"I suppose not."

"The fact is, the body of a young woman was discovered in a trunk in a railway depot. My God, there's nothing, absolutely nothing, that can justify that. We have to protect defenseless women. You do what you have to . . . solve this horrific crime."

"I will," replied Murray.

"Bring Madame Philippe in for questioning, but before you charge her with murder or kidnapping or any other damn thing, make sure there's enough evidence," added O'Brien. "I don't want her walking out of court because you didn't do your job."

Murray mumbled to himself as he walked away. That was far too simple, he thought, still taken aback by the inspector's accommodating attitude. His past dealings with Stokes had been tense and confrontational, particularly on the subject of Madame Philippe. What was Stokes up to, he wondered. Maybe he had already tipped off the abortionist? Maybe had had instructed her to dispose of any incriminating evidence?

As usual, he thought, Stokes was taking the moral high ground—he coveted his image as a defender of the downtrodden and innocent. Still, he wondered about the Inspector's true motives.

A shout from the other end of the hall got Murray's attention.

"Seth, you the one looking for a young beggar goes by the name of Corkie?" asked Sergeant Wilson Hughes.

He was overweight and slightly unbearable, but when Murray had problems with Stokes, Hughes was one of the few cops who had offered him any type of support. Since then, Murray had been more willing to tolerate Hughes's loud and intrusive style. Besides, no one could accuse of him not manning the station house desk properly. The Fifteenth was one of the few precincts in the city that ran like clockwork.

"What did you hear,Sarge? I just sent Westwood out to find the kid."

"It was just over the wire. A patrolman over at the Fourteenth has him. He was in a shed behind Spring Street."

"Will they bring him over here or should I walk over and pick him up? I think the kid will be able to answer some questions for me."

"That might be a problem, Seth," Hughes said.

"Why's that?"

"Because when they found him, his throat was slashed from ear to ear. He's not going to be answering any of your questions today or any day after that."

Chapter Seven

———◆◆◆———

BREAKFAST AT THE FIFTH AVENUE HOTEL

Naked with her hair loose and flowing, Ruth Cardaso admired herself in the long mirror. For a woman of twenty-eight-years, her body was lean and firm. She gently pinched her twenty-inch waist and smiled. Nothing, not even her breasts, moved when she swayed. Her skin was smooth, owing, she maintained, to her conscientious use of Parisian cosmetics. She puckered her lips and repeated the words, "potatoes, prunes, and prisms." She did this each morning again and again so that her mouth would maintain exactly the right shape.

Next, she sprinkled droplets of perfume on her neck and wrists and sipped a cup of coffee she had had delivered to her room. Only the wealthiest visitors at the Fifth Avenue Hotel received such royal treatment, but Tom Fox had spared no expense and she was more than happy to experience everything the Fifth Avenue had to offer. There was a time in her life when she had been far less fortunate.

Her toes squished in the thick plush carpet in her sixth-floor suite. It came with its own parlor, water closet, and Turkish style bath, complete with a generous supply of perfumed soaps and Mexican grass. She bent down to smell the bouquet of fresh flowers that the maid had brought up and marveled at the coolness of her surroundings. Outside, the thermometer was already rising above eighty degrees of mercury, but inside her hotel room it was surprisingly comfortable. Every two hours, a young Negro maid arrived at her door to fill two large silver urns with ice. It was just enough to keep the room from heating up.

What to wear, she wondered? She wanted to look her best for Charles St. Clair. From the short conversation she had had with him, he seemed to be an interesting man, not entirely different from many she had known, but definitely worth a special effort. She was impressed by his intelligence and his handsome appearance. He would make the lucrative assignment she had been given all the more rewarding. Her only dilemma for the moment was to decide how far she would play this part. Her life was complicated enough and she hardly needed another man infatuated with her. Yet the thought of St. Clair in her bedchamber excited her. As always, she understood that the decision would be hers alone to make—for experience had convinced her that no man could resist her charm and beauty for long.

She glanced at the clock and hurried to dress. First came two layers of petticoats and then an apricot silk summer dress gathered together in back over a bustle. It was tight in the front and by design pushed her breasts together and up. She fixed her hair under a small matching colored bonnet and dabbed a little more perfume on her neck. The pleasant and plump woman at the hotel shop who had sold this small expensive bottle had assured her that it was a zesty French fragrance no man could resist. She stopped once more in front of the mirror to scrutinize the finished product and could not help but be pleased. So, too, she knew, would Charles St. Clair.

$\sim$

As St. Clair reached the main entrance to the Fifth Avenue Hotel, he stopped one more time to wipe the droplets of sweat from his forehead. Why, he asked himself, had he opted to wear his best black suit on such a hot and humid morning? Had he been anywhere else, he might have removed his jacket, but not at the Fifth Avenue where gentlemen were expected to be formally dressed at all times of the day or night.

That was, he knew, only part of the answer. He had been up since five o'clock. His room on Bleeker was stifling and the heat made it difficult to sleep. On his mind were several pressing matters, not the least of which was last evening's conversation with Frank King. It remained to be seen whether King could indeed help him solve his problems with Jack Martin. The idea that Martin and Victor Fowler were mixed up in some sordid plot weighed heavily on him. Exposing it, he understood, may be dangerous, but essential to solving his debt problems with Martin. If he indeed had been cheated, then he was not going to give Martin one red-cent of what he owed him. He had paid a few dollars extra for a cab this morning to avoid bumping into Martin's men on the street or omnibus.

His brother-in-law, Seth Murray, had already sent him a message that he wanted to meet later that day. It was urgent, he had written, although St. Clair knew that Murray always considered his police business to be singularly important. Still, he was curious as to what case Murray was working on and how he could assist him.

There was, finally, his weekly assignment for the magazine due tomorrow. He would have to write the story about Fowler's profits from the sale of the armory's benches. It was not quite the revelation of corruption he had promised Tom Fox, but it would have to suffice for the moment.

As important as these various concerns were, they were not the real reason for his lack of sleep. He knew that he was being ridiculous and acting like a love-struck schoolboy with a crush, but as he lay in bed last night tossing and turning he could not stop thinking about Ruth Cardaso—about the way she looked, how she smelled, and what it would be like to touch her. It had been a long time since a woman had gotten under his skin.

The hotel's spacious reception area, with white marble tiles and frescos hanging on the walls, was as busy as usual. As he surveyed the small crowd, St. Clair guessed that these must be the usual visitors who had recently arrived on the early morning trains from San Francisco, Atlanta,

Baltimore and elsewhere. In other corners of the room, he saw business-men chatting, smoking, and reading newspapers, while groups of ladies and gentlemen made their way toward the grand staircase that led to the hotel's magnificent dining hall.

Finally, his eyes found Ruth Cardaso. She was standing beside what appeared to be a large marble statue of Aphrodite and speaking with a tall stocky man in a brown suit. St. Clair took a deep breath and approached her.

"If you do hear anything, please let me know, Miss," St. Clair over-heard the man say.

"Of course, I will." Ruth nodded.

The man bowed slightly and walked away as St. Clair arrived.

"A friend of yours, Miss Cardaso?" he asked.

"Mr. St. Clair, right on time. No, I'm afraid one of the hotel's guests has gone missing. A woman named Lucy Maloney. She was a resident here. In fact, I was introduced to her at breakfast a few days ago. Have you heard of her?"

"I'm not familiar with the name."

"No one has seen her in several days. That man was the hotel's private detective." Her voice trembled ever so slightly.

"Perhaps she took a trip without telling someone. You sound certain that something terrible has befallen her."

"Just a feeling I have, nothing more. I'm afraid I can be quite pessi-mistic at times."

"I'll remember that. Now, before I lose the courage to tell you this," St. Clair continued clearing his throat, "you are a vision to behold." His face reddened.

She turned, smiled, and made a slight curtsey. "You're so kind, sir. I have to say, as well, that you yourself are looking splendid this morning."

St. Clair tipped his hat. "Shall we have breakfast, then?" He held out his right arm for her as they walked up the staircase. His nostrils were filled with the spicy and intoxicating scent of her fragrance.

The dining room, St. Clair noted was impressive—large enough for at least 500 guests. A row of white marble Doric columns framed the hall's interior—each was covered in fine white linen. To the left of the doorway was a long line of neatly attired waiters in white gloves standing ready to begin the meal service. They looked, thought St. Clair, like soldiers waiting anxiously for the order to attack the enemy.

St. Clair glanced around at the other diners. He recognized several prominent merchants and businessmen he had spoken to in the course of his investigations of the Fowler Ring, but, for the most part, the patrons that morning seemed to be families and single men. Some of them, he figured, must live at the hotel year round.

St. Clair and Ruth were seated at a table for two off to the far side of the hall, which provided them with a small degree of privacy. St. Clair ordered eggs with a steak chop, while Ruth selected eggs and toast. There was an awkward silence between them for several moments until the waiter brought fruit and coffee.

"You enjoy your work at the magazine, Mr. St. Clair?" Ruth sipped her coffee.

"For the most part, I do. Certainly it's more enjoyable than the drudgery of daily reporting. I did that for several years here and in Baltimore. But I spent my time writing about traffic accidents and high society. At least, at Fox's, I can make a difference."

"Exposing Victor Fowler and the Ring, you mean?"

"You're well-read, Miss, although I'm hardly surprised. Yes, I believe that Fowler is nearing his end."

"You're happy to ruin him?" Her eyes widened.

"He's ruined himself," St. Clair responded, raising his voice. "The man has stolen millions from the citizens of this city. He deserves to go to jail. His greed has been his undoing. Society has rules and he's violated them. There's right and wrong, it's as simple as that."

Ruth smiled. "I've always believed that the world is more like a hazy and cloudy day. Not, sunny or dark, but a dim grey." She paused. "Has Mr. Fowler done nothing worthwhile, left no lasting legacy?"

"Miss Cardaso, you sound as if you're in sympathy with that scoundrel?" He reached for his coffee.

"Perhaps a little." She dabbed her mouth with a white linen napkin, then gently swept away a long piece of hair that had fallen on to her forehead.

St. Clair relaxed. He found her beauty enormously pleasurable. "And what of you?" He spoke more softly. "You're an actress from San Francisco come to help us catch an abortionist?"

"It's a role, like any other I've played."

"Yet with more meaning than a part in a drama production, correct?" St. Clair broke a piece of a sugar stick and stirred it into his coffee.

"I'm doing it for the money that Mr. Fox is paying me. Does that shock you, Mr. St. Clair?" She raised her eyebrows.

He found her straightforwardness delightful. It was not a quality exhibited by most women he was acquainted with. "Not at all. Trust me, I quite understand. That doesn't detract from the noble cause of what you're doing, however."

"A noble cause? I'm afraid I must disagree. From what I understand," she dropped her voice to a whisper, "Madame Philippe provides a service to many women, some who might well not survive childbirth."

"You're mistaken," said St. Clair. He had no desire to be angry with her. Yet the mere suggestion that Madame Philippe and her ilk deserved the benefit of the doubt or worse, sympathy, made his insides churn.

"And I would suggest again that the world is not so black and white." Ruth leaned toward him.

"Forgive me, Miss, but you don't know of what you speak. There are more than two hundred abortionists in this city. Most are impostors. Yes, some of them have been nurses, but few have genuine medical diplomas. They don't even use their real names like the great Madame Philippe, for instance. Do you think for a moment that this wicked woman is French royalty as she pretends? She's a German Jew, by Jesus, like many of the others. She came to this country with the intention of becoming wealthy and, oh, has she done so. Killing is her true profession. They've murdered thousands of innocents. There's nothing black and white about that."

Ruth could not be appeased. "Does a woman not have any rights in the matter of bearing a child?"

St. Clair stared at her. "What rights do you speak of? In my opinion, no woman with a quick child has such a right. It's nature's way and we shouldn't argue with that."

"What of your wife?" She immediately blushed and covered her mouth.

"How do you know about that? Caroline's circumstances were different. We believed her health was at risk."

"Exactly my point," said Ruth more gently. "You supported your wife's decision and—"

"And nothing. She bled to death and I was powerless to stop it. I will speak no more of this."

"I don't mean to anger you, sir." She reached across the table—her hand brushed lightly against his. "Perhaps, if physicians took more of an active role in this matter instead of attacking midwifery, then women such as your late wife wouldn't have had to seek out the assistance of someone who does not possess the proper medical knowledge. Besides, what of the women who risk death in giving birth? Or, what if it was your daughter who has been raped by a Negro or Indian? Would you still prevent her from visiting Madame Philippe?"

St. Clair stood up. He could barely believe his ears. No woman had ever spoken to him about such matters. His face was flushed. Their heated conversation had now attracted the attention of other hotel diners. "Miss Cardaso, I must leave before this discussion goes any further."

"Please stay and have pastries, Mr. St. Clair." She regarded him with a slight pout. "Can we not have a friendly disagreement?"

"On this issue, I'm afraid not. The truth is that most women seek out Madame Philippe to evade their responsibilities as mothers. The world *is* that black and white."

~

Before Ruth could say another word, St. Clair had rushed from the dining room.

A waiter quickly appeared. "Is there anything else I may get for you, Miss?" he asked. "Perhaps you'd like to take your breakfast in your room?"

Ruth was not listening, nor was she concerned with the stares and whispers of those around her. Damn, she thought, what a fool I've been. How could I have so offended him? There were times to keep her opinions to herself and to heed her words. Even if she thought differently about the rights of women, there were, she knew, bounds of proper etiquette that she had not adhered to. And it was not the first time—or likely the last. Still, she was an actress and she had violated the first rule of the stage— She had alienated her audience and seriously jeopardized her assignment.

Chapter Eight

AN INQUIRY IS MADE

Not even a hot towel draped over his face and a shave at Freddy's barbershop rid St. Clair of the hostility he felt. He prided himself on his usually calm demeanor. As a journalist it was often necessary to remain focused and detached. That was how he had approached the Fowler Ring story at any rate. Occasionally he had allowed his personal dislike of Fowler to impact his writing, yet what he was feeling at this moment was something far different.

He knew he had behaved like a gentleman with Miss Cardaso and that he had checked his temper as much as he could. But he had also walked out on her at the hotel, leaving her alone in the dining room. That was an unconscionable act. A true gentleman, he understood, would not have acted in this fashion. As he tried to relax at Freddy's, he repeatedly reviewed his conversation with Miss Cardaso still irritated at her for being so aggressive and at himself for allowing her words to get under his skin. She was wrong about Madame Philippe and the other abortionists. This was not about a woman's right to bear a child or not—it was about preventing murder. Why could she not see that?

He stopped himself. Who was he trying to fool? Had he not once thought about abortion exactly as she did? That, in certain circumstances abortion was necessary. Wasn't that why he had urged, no ordered, Caroline to visit the midwife? He was as much to blame for the tragedy as the abortionist, no matter how ill-prepared Caroline was to be a mother. His heart ached when he contemplated his behavior in this matter. For perhaps the first time, he understood that it was impossible for him to be reasonable about abortion.

His mind soon returned to thoughts of the alluring Miss Cardaso. Even if he did disagree with her, he admired her spirit of conviction. There was no getting around the fact—he was smitten with Ruth Cardaso, a woman he knew almost nothing about. It made absolutely no sense to him. Yet, the force of the attraction was as powerful as he had ever felt for any woman, including Caroline.

He made his way back to the magazine office where he found Tom Fox studiously editing a story. He hardly glanced up when St. Clair sat down at the chair by his desk.

"Where's my story, Charlie?" asked Fox without lifting his head. "I have the next installment of Sutton's history of the city, a lengthy and interesting piece on the New York Stock Exchange by that young writer, Simpson, and fiction from Howells. But what of the Ring? What of the Boss's latest exploits and corruptions? That's what our readers and the rest of the city will want. And I don't know what I'll tell them. Do you?"

"I've been a fool," muttered St. Clair.

"I've been telling you that for years." Fox peered up from his papers. "You haven't lost more money gambling, I hope?"

St. Clair shook his head. "Worse, I'm afraid. I behaved like a buffoon in front of Miss Cardaso."

"I see," said Fox stroking his beard. He reached for the chewed up cigar that was sitting in the small metal bowl beside him. Striking a match, he lit the tobacco, blowing a cloud of white smoke in St. Clair's direction. "Women can indeed make the most intelligent of men behave like buffoons. It's one of the reasons I've remained a bachelor all these many years. But don't dismay, I'm certain that whatever you've done, Miss Cardaso will forgive you. My impression is that she's a clever woman, although I suspect you know that already."

"Tell me, Tom, when did women become so opinionated? I know my mother wasn't like that. Christ, she'd never have argued with my father about our cows, never mind politics and abortion."

"Miss Cardaso argued with you about abortion?" Fox spat out what was left of his cigar into a spittoon by his feet. "That may not have been the wisest approach to take."

St. Clair shrugged.

"It may not happen in my lifetime, Charlie," Fox continued, "but there'll be a day when the law and society we live in will change. To be honest, between me and you, the idea that after marriage a woman is bound to her husband like some Negro slave on a cotton plantation in the Carolinas doesn't make a whole lot of sense to me. Never has. And there may also come a time when women get the vote."

"That's nonsense," said St. Clair. "Congress will never permit it."

"You're wrong, Charlie. The truth is women are far more persistent creatures than men and a lot smarter. They'll campaign until they win and they'll wear every politician in Washington down until they vote. Besides, how can we reconcile giving Negroes and foreigners the franchise, but not our own women? Does that make sense to you?"

"Nothing makes sense to me today, I'm afraid. In truth I feel humiliated. I behaved terribly."

"Your trouble is, Charlie, ever since you lost Caroline all you do is gamble away your hard earned money or drink with those whores at Madame Helena's."

"There's nothing wrong with a game of faro or poker now and then to keep a man's senses sharp," declared St. Clair. "And as for the whores on Wooster Street, I'll say this... they sure as hell don't argue with me." He glared at Fox for a moment. "Didn't you accompany me the last time? Didn't I see you go upstairs with a redhead by the name of Suzette? From Paris, I think."

"I can't recall," said Fox with a smirk.

"So what makes an old bachelor like you such an authority about women?"

Fox turned and reached for a stack of papers on a shelf behind him. "Read this," he said handing the bundle to St. Clair.

"What is it?"

"I'm sure I've told you about these. For about a year now, I've been receiving long articles on suffrage and temperance from this school-teacher in upstate New York. They arrive every few months composed in the neatest and smallest handwriting I've seen. Her name's Anthony, Susan Anthony. She's as clever as Miss Cardaso, maybe more so. I don't much agree with her about the drink. I mean a man's entitled to his whiskey. But her case that women have legitimate right to vote, believe it or not, makes some sense to me. I was thinking of running a feature on her and her suffrage association in one of the fall issues. Maybe send you up to Rochester to meet with her? You should read this. I'd like your opinion on the writing."

"Send Sutton. He'd do a better job of it. I'd likely get embroiled in a heated argument with this Miss Anthony."

Fox patted St. Clair on the shoulder. "Self-pity is not an attractive quality. Haven't I told you that, Charlie?"

"I agree. I shall make every effort to reform."

"Not too much, I hope. Trust me, you'll survive, I guarantee it. And you might even learn something. Now, enough about this, what about Fowler?"

St. Clair knew Fox was right. That there was no point harping on about this situation. He would have to apologize to Ruth as soon as possible. "I'll have a piece for you by the end of the day tomorrow," he told Fox. "A story of how Fowler pocketed more than a hundred thousand…money that should've gone to the city. And I promise that within a week, we'll know everything there is to know about the Boss and his Ring."

"I'll admit, Charlie, you're resourceful. Although I'll wait to pass final judgment until I see what you actually deliver."

"You still doubt me? Very well, then, I accept the challenge." Both men were silent for a moment, then St. Clair asked in a serious tone, "Where did you find her, Tom?"

"Miss Cardaso? I wired Nathan Scott at the *Chronicle* in San Francisco and he suggested I contact her."

"And you trust Scott?"

"I do. He's a decent man. Likes his drink, but don't we all."

"And what of her background?" St. Clair pressed his friend further. "Her work as an actress in the theatre? From her appearance and name,

I'd guess she's a Spaniard. And after this morning, I can attest that she's as hot headed as a wounded matador."

"From what I understand after briefly speaking with her, is that she was born in London and came to California with her parents when she was a young girl. You'll have to obtain the rest of the story from her."

"That may be difficult. Our breakfast this morning, as I said, did not go smoothly. I doubt," St. Clair mumbled, "we'll be having any meaning-ful conversations in the near future." He added, "By the way, did you tell her about Caroline?"

Fox shook his head. "Not me. Why?"

"It's nothing. Maybe it was Sutton."

"So the two of you argued about abortion, you said." Fox twisted in his chair.

"What is it, Tom? You're awful jumpy."

"There's something you must do for me today. A favor," whispered Fox.

"As I said, I was planning to work on the Fowler story and then meet my brother-in-law. But what's the favor?"

"It's about Sutton, in fact." Fox's eyes glanced around the office.

"Yeah, where is he? Wasn't he supposed to be off masquerading as Miss Cardaso's boyfriend?"

"Sutton's father was in some sort of accident." Fox's voice returned to a whisper. "The family doctor isn't certain he'll survive. Sutton took the seven o'clock train to Boston this morning. Which means—"

St. Clair stood up, his mouth open. "Tom, you can't be serious. There must be someone else to replace him. Not me, certainly. How can I face her so soon?"

"Courage, my friend." Fox glanced at his pocket watch. "You have about one hour. You're to meet Miss Cardaso in front of St. Patrick's Cathedral."

"By Madame Philippe's mansion on Fifty-Second and Fifth?" St. Clair asked. He rubbed the sweat on his palms.

Fox saw the conflicting emotions on St. Clair's face. "Charlie, there's no one else I trust to do this. It's important. You know that better than anyone. Think about Caroline and other women like her. Do you want to drive these buggers from the city or not?"

"You know I do, but...."

"But nothing. Apologize the moment you see her. That's the bravest, and the only, thing you can do. You'll feel more at ease after that, I promise. Now off with you."

Though he'd come to the same conclusion about apologizing to Ruth, St. Clair still shook his head in disbelief. "You don't pay me enough for this humiliation." He moved slowly toward the outer office and then stopped. "Fifteen hundred. That's what I owe Martin," he said over his shoulder.

Without another word, Fox reached for his pocket book. "I shall write you a bank draft and you can stop on your way."

"It's not necessary. I can take care of it... at least I think I can. But I appreciate the offer. You're a talented man of commerce and a gentleman, Tom, and I didn't want to lie to you about it."

"That's generous of you, Charlie, but you still have to meet with Miss Cardaso." Fox laughed so loud that his belly jiggled.

"I had to try," said St. Clair with a smile. He straightened his jacket, fixed his bowler hat and descended into the street.

∾

Precisely one hour later, St. Clair found himself walking up Fifth Avenue's wide sidewalks gazing at the horse and wagon traffic and construction all around him. Everywhere you looked there were carpenters, bricklayers and laborers toiling in the hot summer sun. St. Clair had read in the *Times* only a week ago that land speculators like Victor Fowler and his cohorts had bought up entire blocks. They had rightly anticipated that property values would rise, and sure enough, contractors could not put up new brownstones fast enough to meet demand.

These homes, as opulent as any St. Clair had seen in the city, appeared to be uninhabited—as they were most of the summer months. Had this been any other street in New York, St. Clair would have expected to see women and children socializing on their stoops, especially when the heat was high. It was a common, as well as an entertaining way to pass the afternoon or evening. On Fifth Avenue, however, St. Clair understood such fraternizing was considered terribly uncouth. All you had to do was read the society pages to learn that at this time of the year, the majority of Fifth Avenue residents were out of the city indulging themselves at their summer homes in Newport or Saratoga.

As he reached Forty-Ninth Street, St. Clair could see Ruth a short distance away, standing alone against the backdrop of the majestic Catholic cathedral. She had changed from the apricot silk dress she had worn at the hotel into something much plainer, a dull, dark grey dress—the uniform of a factory girl. His anger had not entirely subsided. Why was it, then, that the closer he approached, the faster his heart beat and the more the blood rushed to his head?

"Mr. St. Clair, you're right on time," Ruth said with an awkward smile.

As soon as he drew nearer, her inviting fragrance again overwhelmed him. Despite his conflicted feelings he forced himself to appear professional and aloof. Tipping his hat with a slight nod of his head, he said, "You don't seem surprised to see me."

"Mr. Fox dispatched a message to the hotel early this morning with news about Mr. Sutton's family misfortunes and wrote that you would be taking his place."

"I see. I'm glad Mr. Fox was so certain I'd accept his offer."

"My impression is that he rarely loses an argument."

"That's so. Miss Cardaso—" St. Clair cleared his throat. "I wanted to apologize for my abrupt departure at the hotel...it was uncalled for...If I embarrassed you in any way—"

"No, please, Mr. St. Clair," she interrupted. "I'm the one to blame. I too often speak my mind and don't know when to stop. A flaw in my character, I'm afraid. I had no right to comment about or suggest anything untoward about your personal affairs."

"Perhaps we should start over? Let us agree that there are certain subjects we should avoid speaking of."

"Agreed."

"And why not call me Charlie? There would be nothing inappropriate about that, would there?"

She smiled again. "I don't believe that would be inappropriate at all, Charlie. And you may address me as Ruth."

He reached for hand and kissed it gently. "A pleasure, Ruth."

A group of four women passing by them on the sidewalk gawked at this spectacle. Neither St. Clair nor Ruth paid them any attention.

"Now that this matter is settled, shall we proceed across the street?" Ruth gestured toward Madame Philippe's house.

"Into the den of evil, by all means." St. Clair responded half-seriously.

She tilted her head. "You're quite firm in your convictions, Charlie."

"About Madame Philippe and others like her, I am indeed. But I thought we weren't going to discuss such controversial issues."

She reached for his arm, brushing his hand ever so lightly. "Come, Mr. Fox is waiting for his story."

"Let me tell you a tale," said St. Clair as they walked. "It is indeed one of the great ironic tales of the city, an amusing and delicious anecdote repeatedly told, I understand, in dining rooms and clubs as well as in saloons and ill-fame houses."

"You have my attention," said Ruth. She loosely held on to St. Clair's arm.

"Back in 1857 or 1858," continued St. Clair, "as St. Patrick's Cathedral was being constructed, Archbishop John Hughes, as imposing and intimidating a religious leader as there was in New York, had his eye on the property at the northeast corner of Fifth Avenue and Fifty-Second. He intended to build a grand rectory to be used as a chief residence for decades. At the land auction a broker acting for an unnamed client outbid the archbishop, who was stunned and incensed by this turn of events. He was even more astonished when he discovered that this sly broker was representing none other than Madame Philippe and her husband, Franz."

Ruth smiled. "Did Madame Philippe do this thing on purpose?"

"Precisely," said St. Clair. "According to the information that I've heard, she had deliberately sought out the property to prevent the church from acquiring it. It was just another episode in a long war between Hughes and Philippe. On more than one occasion, Hughes has publicly condemned her in church and in comments he's made to the newspapers. It likely contributed to her nearly being lynched in the winter of 1847."

"Lynched. Please tell me more," said Ruth. They had stopped in front of the gates to Madame Philippe's house.

"Very well," said St. Clair, enjoying the moment. "But I must warn you it's not a pleasant story."

"I assure you, Mr. St. Clair, few things shock me anymore."

St. Clair smiled down at her and continued. "There was a young girl of approximately eighteen years of age. Her name was Alice Wilson. She was from Philadelphia, had arrived in New York alone and eight months pregnant. Madame Philippe had provided her room and board, nursed her, and delivered her child, a daughter. Alice didn't want the baby and the father was an older married man who had misrepresented himself and his intentions. If you'll pardon me," St. Clair blushed, "he desired only to bed the young girl."

"Yes, and?" asked Ruth, ignoring St. Clair's discomfort.

"Madame Philippe found a family who wanted to adopt Alice's girl, for a token sum of $200. It was, she later said, a fair and reasonable fee for such service. Then, some weeks later, Alice changed her mind. I don't know why, but she wanted her baby girl returned. That, of course, proved impossible, since the couple who'd paid Philippe had already taken the baby and left the city for their home in New Orleans. When Alice's story made the rounds of saloons and pubs, Hughes eventually heard about it and within days, every Irish preacher was castigating Madame Philippe and extolling the virtues of the seemingly innocent Alice Wilson."

St. Clair paused to take a deep breath. "One evening," he continued, "a mob of more than a hundred loud and mostly drunk Irishmen, many of whom were waving flaming torches, gathered in front of Madame Philippe's home. Not this one. She then resided on Greenwich Street. They demanded that Alice Wilson's child be returned. If not for the arrival of the police and Victor Fowler, who was then a fireman, they might have burned down the house and lynched her and Franz. She was forever in Fowler's debt.

"So when the opportunity arose to humble the archbishop, she therefore took it and enjoyed doing so, I might add. She relished the idea that each time Hughes walked out of the cathedral, her mansion stood in his sight. She cared little that it caused him such tremendous discomfort. And that's why this corner on Fifth is called the *Pope and Devil.*"

"I realize, Charles, that you have personal feelings about this, but I must say, my initial impression is that Madame Philippe is an interesting woman," said Ruth.

"Interesting? That's not quite the word I would use. But let us see for ourselves," said St. Clair. He was much happier to be involved in this charade than he would have believed an hour ago. Whatever Ruth's opinions, he enjoyed being in her company.

Before they opened the tall iron gates in front of Madame Philippe's residence, he reviewed with Ruth the parts they were about to play, as actors in a stage drama would prior to the rising of the curtain. With Sutton's absence, they decided that their story required a few modifications. While newspaper advertisements advised callers to knock at the private entrance at the side of the house, they decided to ring the bell at the main door to see for themselves the grandeur of the home's entrance way.

It took only a moment before Hector, Madame Philippe's Negro servant, greeted them. He ushered them into a lavish entranceway decorated with mahogany and white marble. A few steps away was a twisting staircase, also of mahogany, that led to the second floor. The house was cool and the hot sun did not penetrate the thick cloth curtains that covered the windows in the entry way and the adjacent parlor.

On a marble table, St. Clair noticed a vase of fresh flowers and two large busts. One was of Benjamin Franklin and the other of George Washington. This was, he thought, no doubt Madame Philippe's personal statement that, despite any claims to the contrary, she was indeed a true American. He made a mental note of this for his magazine article.

"You are here to see the Madame?" Hector politely asked them.

"We are," replied St. Clair.

"This way then, please."

He led them around the corner and down into the basement clinic, although this was unlike any basement St. Clair had seen. Several gas lamps illuminated the vast room, so that it was not as dim and damp as most cellars. The floor was covered with a reddish-brown Persian carpet and a large Biblical tapestry of Adam and Eve hung on one wall. The irony of commemorating the birth of life in the Garden of Eden was not lost on St. Clair. He and Ruth sat down beside each other on a long sofa.

This room, too, was filled with tables and artifacts of white marble and mahogany.

"May I bring you a cup of tea or coffee?" inquired Hector.

"We're fine, thank you," St. Clair responded before Ruth could utter a word.

They sat in silence for a minute or two before Madame Philippe appeared from behind a folding door at the back of the basement. St. Clair regarded her with surprise. He had never met the woman before and was half-expecting that she would be an ogre—Satan in a dress. Instead, in front of him stood a short, stout, and handsome woman. Her grey hair was tied back and her face showed some lines of weariness and old age. She wore a long black gown covered by a white smock.

"I'm Madame Philippe," she said. Her voice, too, surprised him. It was gentle and kind. "What can I do for you?"

Ruth cleared her throat. "Can you relieve a lady of a physical difficulty?"

"That depends on the circumstances. First, please tell me your names."

"Of course," said Ruth. "I'm Lily Turner and this is my brother, Jack."

St. Clair tipped his hat. "Ma'am. We've travelled from Buffalo so that you can help my sister."

"What is it you need?" Madame Phillipe asked them.

"We came to inquire what you can do and how much are your charges," said Ruth.

"For that you'll have to tell me your symptoms," replied Madame Phillipe.

On cue, Ruth blushed and nervously pulled at the locks of her hair. "I don't know where to begin. I was to be married this week." She covered her face with her hands and cried.

It was a wonderful performance, St. Clair thought, as he comforted her.

"Let me relate to you this sad and unfortunate tale of cruelty," he said modulating his tone to convey both sympathy and frustration. "My sister was engaged to this gentleman from St. Paul, or so we thought that's who he was. His name, dare I speak it, is Peter Munroe. He claimed to be from a well-connected family who operated a mid-western grain company. He was in Buffalo for several months on business and he and Lily became...how shall I put this?"

"He and Lily became intimate," suggested Madame Philippe.

"Precisely. Thank you. Some months ago, my sister learned that she was to have his baby." St. Clair gently touched Ruth's shoulders. "Plans for the wedding were arranged. His family was to arrive from St. Paul. All was set for a wonderful occasion. Our own parents did not know about Lily's condition. We thought it best to tell them after the marriage ceremony. A month ago, Peter vanished, disappeared, as if he had never existed. I made inquiries in St. Paul, something I should've done earlier. No one had ever heard of Peter Munroe, or of a prominent family of grain merchants of that name. The whole story, I'm afraid, had been a lie. The cad fled before he was discovered."

"Am I then to understand," Madame Philippe began slowly, "that you're quick with child?"

Ruth nodded sullenly.

"That does present more of a problem. But have no fear, my dear, every problem like this also has a solution."

"And the fee for such a service?" asked St. Clair.

"For something of this sensitive nature the charge would be $500. This would include board and room for several days of recovery."

"That would be steep, although acceptable under the circumstances," said St. Clair. "Pardon the question, Madame, but I must ask you if there is any danger to my sister's health in such a delicate procedure."

Madame Philippe gazed intently at St. Clair, clasping her palms over her chest. This gesture of earnestness unsettled him. "Mr. Turner, Miss Turner, there are no guarantees in medical procedures, as I'm certain you both are aware. I don't think I have to tell you that I have been practicing midwifery for more than twenty-five years and while I cannot say that I've never lost a patient to infection or some other illness, a vast majority of my clients, I'm proud to say, leave here in good health, satisfied and unharmed in any way." She stepped closer to Ruth. "If you'll permit me to examine you, I'll be able to provide you with more information."

"So," St. Clair interjected, his voice quivering slightly, "there's the risk that my sister may leave here seemingly fit and well and within days bleed to death in her own bed."

"Are we speaking of possibilities or something that has indeed transpired? From your tone, I would think the latter. What do you do in Buffalo, Mr. Turner?" Madame Philippe eyed St. Clair suspiciously.

"Forgive my brother," said Ruth. "Some years ago, the wife of a family friend was attended by a midwife. She died within a week of her procedure."

"And what of the law? Do you have no shame in what you do, that you break the law?" St. Clair blurted. He could not stop himself.

Madame Philippe stepped back and pulled a silk cord that hung from the ceiling. "I think it best that you leave, Mr. Turner, or whatever your name is. I don't know what game you play here, sir, but I suspect that the lady, if she is your sister, which I doubt very much, is hardly quick with child."

St. Clair was about to respond when there was loud banging on the front door of the house. A minute later, Hector came running down the stairs.

"Madame, it's the police," he said catching his breath. "They're waiting at the front entrance and, if I might add, they're in a nasty mood."

Chapter Nine

An Arrangement with Mr. Flint

Frank King felt ill, as if he had consumed a piece of rancid meat or a plate of rotten oysters. His head was heavy as a rock and he was soaked in sweat. For a moment he thought he was going to pass out. Considering that he was sitting in the gentlemen's room at the Fifth Avenue Hotel that turn of events would have been humiliating indeed. He steadied himself, determined to gain control of the situation and decide what his next logical step should be.

In his right hand, drooping by his side so that his fingers almost touched the plush Turkish carpet, King clutched a crinkled page of the *New York Times*. Slowly and methodically, he pulled the paper up to his face again, wiped his wet forehead with his handkerchief, and read the column again. It was as if he hoped the words had changed, but, of course, he knew they had not.

The brief story that had grasped his attention was tucked in the top right-hand corner of page eight under the bold-faced heading, "THE TRUNK MYSTERY."

The nude body of a young woman was discovered yesterday morning crammed into a trunk at the Hudson River Railroad Depot. As of today, the

*police have revealed few details of their investigation. The depot's baggage
master found the poor and unfortunate victim in a trunk but has refused to
answer reporters' questions about this gruesome discovery.*

*Detective Seth Murray will only say that the deceased was a young
woman of approximately 24 to 27 years of age with long blonde hair and
that a white lace monogrammed handkerchief with the letter 'L' was in her
possession.*

*Anyone with information is requested to contact Detective Murray through
Police Headquarters on Mulberry Street.*

"Blonde hair...white lace handkerchief with the letter L...." King
cringed and the paper slipped through his fingers to the floor. Almost
immediately a well-dressed waiter, a young man in a black suit and white
gloves, appeared. "You dropped this, sir," he said handing him the newspaper. "Anything else I can bring for you?"

King waved him away. It was Lucy the police had found in the trunk.
It had to be. The description of the hair matched. But it was the monogrammed handkerchief that was the convincing piece of evidence. He
had given it to her as a gift two months ago.

For the past twenty-four hours, he had been searching for Lucy at the
hotel and on the streets. He had not been home in a day and had lied
to his wife yet one more time, concocting a story about crucial contracts
that had to be scrutinized. She smiled as she always did, ever the faithful and devoted wife. On occasion, he had suffered from bouts of guilt.
Then, one glimpse of Lucy in her black lace corset, her hair dangling on
her shoulders, and her body so tender and inviting and he forgot who he
was and where his loyalties and obligations lay.

All he could ascertain from the hotel's doorman was that Lucy had left
the Fifth Avenue early on Tuesday morning and had not returned. Samuel Buckland, the Fifth Avenue's manager, a pompous and polished man
with long lady-like fingers, confirmed that no one had been in Lucy's
suite since Monday morning. Nor had she had left information about
her whereabouts at the front desk. Next, he had spoken to Lucy's friend,
Mildred Potter, the daughter of the wealthy financial baron Rupert Potter
and a gossipmonger whom he could barely tolerate at the best of times.
She, too, surprisingly had not seen or heard from Lucy since Sunday and
was now equally concerned.

At first, he had figured that Lucy might have gone to visit her family in St. Louis. He knew that she had not seen or spoken to her parents in many years—they had become estranged when Lucy had decided to move to New York and she rarely, if ever, mentioned them—yet it was his impression that she had become slightly homesick in the last few months. Perhaps she had wanted to reconcile with them.

As he glanced at the handful of impeccably tailored and trimmed gentlemen who were reading, smoking and chatting about business, baseball or women, one thought kept racing through his head— What if Fowler and Harrison had discovered that he had betrayed them and had sent one of their thugs to harm Lucy as a way to punish him? He suspected that Harrison knew of his relationship with Lucy—that he might have seen them together on the street some weeks ago. What if he had paid someone to kidnap her and was intending to extort or blackmail him?

The more he contemplated these nefarious possibilities, the more he realized they made no sense. Why involve dear Lucy in his dealings with Fowler? When he considered all of the facts, he concluded that neither Fowler nor Harrison would have wanted to harm Lucy, unless she was a direct threat to them or the Ring. In fact, his last meeting with them had run smoothly. That was on Monday morning and they had not acted overly suspicious.

As much as he did not want to admit it, he had no idea who might have wanted to kill Lucy—if indeed she was the woman discovered in the trunk—or why. However, should she prove to be the dead woman, and in his gut he knew that his suspicions were correct, he would be in a difficult predicament. His plan to end his role in the Ring was moving forward and under no circumstances could his name be linked with a murder or adultery.

He couldn't believe he had allowed himself to be torn between two women. He loved his wife, Amanda, dearly, but the lust he felt for Miss Lucy Maloney excited his passions—often beyond all reason. And in this regard, he was likely no different than half the married men—or in some cases women—in New York. On more than one occasion he and Lucy had utilized a house of assignation on Greene Street. No one there asked any questions.

Other than Buckland, whose discretion he had bought for a high price, he did not think that an investigation into Lucy's life would link him in any way. Not even the hotel's doormen knew his name. His comings and goings at the Fifth Avenue, as well as his financial obligations—the money was routed through two banks—had been conducted with the utmost prudence.

Yet, the idea of Lucy lying on a slab of wood at the morgue, as if she were a piece of meat, weighed heavily on him. At that moment, he made up his mind to reveal her identity to the police, but anonymously and carefully. He would send an unsigned message to St. Clair, who would without question relay the information to his detective brother-in-law. At least in that way, Lucy would be properly laid to rest. His broken heart he feared would take much longer to heal.

~

Victor Fowler always enjoyed making as grand an entrance as possible into Harry Hill's concert saloon, a legendary establishment on Houston Street. On cue, the three musicians on stage stopped playing and the voluptuous trio of female burlesque singers halted their dance routine. Fowler moved smoothly across the wide dance floor. He shook the hands of the men and kissed the outstretched hands of giggling and trembling women.

Dressed in his trademark dark suit and white cravat, Fowler resembled a domineering male lion among his loyal and admiring pride.

He had spent the day paying his respects at a funeral in Kleindeuschland, spoke to Hebrew businessmen at the Temple Emanu-El at Fifth Avenue and Forty-Third Street, and chatted with a group of Italian organ grinders on the Bowery. Still, several issues weighed heavily on him, even as he waved to the crowd at Harry's.

Fowler was concerned not only about the continuing assault on his character in *Fox's Weekly* and the newspapers, but also about his wife, Ellen. She was consuming far more laudanum than her physician had prescribed. Her mood was unpredictable and her behavior erratic. One moment she was laughing with glee, and the next she was despondent and in a depressed state for which there seemed no solution. He needed her healthy, fit, and by his side at public gatherings. Much counted on this.

Trailing behind Fowler, as always, was Isaac Harrison, his eyes purposefully scanning the crowd for potential threats and enemies. And close to Harrison and Fowler were two hefty, muscular, and thoroughly unpleasant looking toughs. Thin smoldering cigars protruded from their mouths. The duo—known only as Nick and Johnny—scrutinized and intimidated anyone who got within two feet of the Boss.

"Mr. Fowler, it's always a pleasure when you pay us a visit," said Harry Hill, the saloon's short, thick-set proprietor. He was standing behind a long counter covered with glasses and half-empty whiskey bottles.

"I see you're full as usual, Harry. You'll have to stay up half the night counting your cash," said Fowler with a laugh. "I know I can depend on you in the coming battle."

Hill nodded.

"You want to know what they say about you on the street, Harry?"

"Not interested," muttered the saloon owner.

"I'll tell you anyways. That you're worth close to one hundred thousand. What do you have to say about that?"

"What do I have to say? I'd say that you're still a richer man than me," Harry replied.

Fowler laughed again. "You want me and my men to pay the twenty-five cents admission tonight?"

"Never. Just have a glass of whiskey or a beer. That'll be fine. And remember my rules." Harry pointed to a large sign above the bar.

No loud talking
No profanity
No obscene or indecent expressions will be allowed
No man can sit and allow a woman to stand.

Fowler laughed harder.

"By the way, Mr. Fowler, I don't believe anything I read in those rag sheets," said Hill pouring Fowler a shot of his finest whiskey. "You can count on me as sure as the Lord will make the sun rise tomorrow. I know all of the good deeds you've done for this city. Not to mention that you've single-handedly started a building boom for which there doesn't seem to be an end. Who else in the city can match that? Come election time, you have my vote."

"I appreciate that Harry," said Fowler, swigging down the whiskey in one gulp. "Tell me, is Amelia working this evening?" he asked more quietly.

"She is, yes. Do you want me to fetch her? I think she's upstairs."

"Not quite yet, a little later," said Fowler with an air of contentment, "I've some important business to attend to first."

"We're with you, Mr. Fowler," shouted a patron sitting on one of the many benches and chairs scattered about the saloon. He was a bulky man, with dark greasy hair and a diagonal gash across his left cheek. His two front teeth were missing. Surrounding him was a small group of similarly rowdy drinkers, who Fowler knew were former Union soldiers. They were wearing wide dark cloth pants and stained white shirts whose odor—a repulsive mixture of sweat, alcohol and tobacco—was a sure sign that none of them had bathed in weeks.

"Nothing'll change that. We're ready to do whatever you'd like," said the man with the gash.

Fowler sauntered towards them, patting several of them on their shoulders and shaking their hands. His two guards moved closer, their hands never far from the wooden clubs tucked in their belts.

"That's not necessary," Fowler instructed the two men. "We're among friends. These boys are my shoulder-hitters," he said introducing his guards. "They're Tammany's most loyal supporters and they make sure that everyone votes the right way. In fact, I think some of them have even voted for me more than once. Isn't that so?" Fowler chuckled.

"We do what we're told," said Nick.

"You're Little Philly, aren't you?" asked Fowler, directing his question to one of the assembled, a husky man with dark hair. He prided himself on always remembering the names of his shoulder-hitters.

"That's me," said Philly, puffing his chest. He shoved another piece of chaw into his mouth. "This here's Freddie the Barber, Snake Manfred, Punk Tyler, and Big Frank Connolly."

"Glad to see all of you again. Your support, as I said, is appreciated." He shouted in the direction of the bar. "Harry, a bottle of whiskey for these gentlemen."

A moment later, a pretty waiter girl in red boots and low-cut dress brought over a bottle of whiskey and some clean glasses.

"That's mighty kind of you, Mr. Fowler," said Philly. "Why don't you join us for a spell? Snake was about to tell us a real screamer."

Snake Manfred, as thin and slimy as his nickname suggested, grinned. "I heard this happened at the courthouse the other day," he began. "Murphy's brought before the judge. 'Murphy, you're drunk again?' asks the judge. Murphy replies, 'Yes, Your Honor.' The judge says, 'Did you solemnly promise me, when I let you off the last time, that you'd never get drunk again?' Murphy looks down at his boots and says, 'Yeah, Your Honor, but I wush drunk at the time. Your Honor, I wushn't sponsible for what I shaid.'" Manfred slapped the top of his right thigh. The men howled with laughter.

"Shit, Snake," said Philly, "you're going to make me piss in my pants." He looked up at Fowler. "You sure you don't want to help us finish this fine bottle of whiskey. After all, you're paying for it."

"Philly, nothing would give me more pleasure. However, I see the person I've come to speak to has arrived."

"Mr. Fowler, sir, I have one more question for you before you leave." asked Big Frank Connolly.

Fowler turned around, a look of annoyance on his face. "What's your name?"

"That's Big Frank," said Little Philly.

"Right. Big Frank, what would you like to know?" asked Fowler.

"The other day at the Orange parade. I was there. I got hit by a soldier right on the arm," he said, rubbing his elbow. "Didn't you say we'd have nothing to worry about? That the soldiers wouldn't hurt anyone. Jesus, they were shooting at women and children."

Little Philly gave Big Frank a scowling look. "What are you bothering Mr. Fowler for?" He punched Big Frank on his sore arm.

Fowler's face reddened slightly. "That's fine, Philly. To be honest, I was as shocked as anyone by what happened. I tell you, Frank, there are some things that even I can't control. But I aim to speak to the police chief about it real soon. Now, boys, I have some business to attend to."

Standing at the end of the bar was a tall man in a fine-looking dark suit with a black silk tie and bowler hat. His peppery beard was trimmed and it looked as if he had visited the barber in the past day or two. He was smoking a fat cigar and had his left hand firmly planted on the derrière of one of Hill's waitresses, a petite and adorable woman, who stood beside him holding a tall glass filled to the rim.

"Flint, you're a hard man to track down," said Fowler approaching him.

Flint shrugged. "I've been busy. I know I work for you, Fowler, but don't ever think you own me the way you do those other fools over there."

"Fools they might be, but they do what I tell them to do," said Fowler evenly.

"You mean what Jack Martin tells them to do."

Fowler ignored the comment. By now Isaac Harrison and Fowler's two bodyguards had joined them. "I need to speak with you about a private matter," he said. "It's rather urgent."

Flint pinched the waitress on her arse and shooed her away as a man might his pesky dog. "And what about those two?" he asked, gesturing towards the thugs beside Harrison. "I thought you said you wanted to talk privately. You're not afraid of me, are you, Fowler?"

"I wouldn't want to be lost at sea with you, if that's what you mean," Fowler responded. "But I'm hardly fearful of you, Flint. It's merely that I've become a cautious man of late and these two," he pointed at his men, "provide me with a certain degree of comfort."

"Get rid of them or I'm leaving," said Flint matter-of-factly. He gulped down a shot of whiskey and poured himself another glass.

"No one orders Mr. Fowler around," said Harrison, his voice betraying a lack of calm.

"Bite your tongue, Harrison. I wasn't speaking to you." Flint moved closer to Harrison, a short man. He barely reached Flint's chin.

"Your breath is most foul, sir," said Harrison, lightly pushing Flint away.

Instantly, Flint grabbed Harrison, spun him around, and put a knife to his throat.

"Let'm go," barked one of Fowler's thugs. Both men were now holding their batons out, ready to strike.

"If those two fuckers so much as twitch, I'll slice his throat wide open." Flint's voice was restrained, but threatening all the same.

By now a small crowd had gathered around to see if any blood would be spilled.

"Go on, cut him open," someone yelled from the back.

"Yeah, slice that bottlehead," another man said. "Don't worry, Harry, we'll mop up the blood." A roar of laughter echoed through the saloon.

"There'll be no fighting in here, mister." It was Hill and he had a pistol aimed at Flint's head. "I don't tolerate this sort of thing in my place. Now put away your knife and have another glass of whiskey."

"There's no need for any trouble, Flint," Fowler responded calmly. "I'm sure Harrison is mighty sorry he pushed you like that. Aren't you, Isaac?"

Harrison winced. "I apologize if I gave any offence."

"That's all I wanted to hear," said Flint, stepping back. He tucked his knife back in his belt.

"Drinks are on me, fellows," shouted Fowler to great cheers. "Harry, whatever they want." He turned to Harrison, whose face was flushed. "Take Nick and Johnny and wait for me outside."

"Do you think that's—?" Harrison began.

"Just do what I say, Isaac" Fowler barked. He lightly wiped his brow with the white handkerchief he kept in his breast pocket.

Harrison mumbled a few words under his breath and walked toward the door. "Let's go," he growled to Fowler's two guards who followed behind.

"You should control that nasty temper of yours, Flint." Fowler reached for a glass of whiskey, then removed two Havana cigars from a metal case. He offered one to Flint, who grabbed it. Fowler struck a match, lit Flint's cigar, and then his own.

"My temper's kept me alive," said Flint, puffing hard.

"I'm sure it has, but one day someone's going to fight back."

"I don't worry too much about that." Flint smirked. "Most of my enemies don't live long."

Fowler stared at him for a moment. He had no idea how many men Flint had maimed or killed, but he was certain that the number was high. From what Fowler knew, until recently, Homer Flint—though no one dared called him by his first name—had lived in Chicago and before that somewhere out west. Fowler was not certain and Flint rarely spoke of the past. All he knew was that Flint had worked with a notorious Chicago hoodlum named Frankie the Sheeney, an infamous Russian Jewish thief and fence. Together they robbed upper-and middle-class homes, beating or murdering anyone who stood in their way.

A year ago, according to what Fowler had been told by his associates in Chicago, Frankie was discovered behind an alley near Maxwell Street in Chicago's West Side. His throat had been sliced so badly that his head was almost severed from his body. Rumor had it that Flint had found Frankie with his woman, a blonde prostitute named Celeste. No one had seen her since Frankie's death and she was presumed to be dead as well.

Naturally enough, the Chicago police did not spend much time investigating the murder of someone of Frankie's reputation, nor did they concern themselves with a missing whore. They questioned Flint, even roughed him up some, but he told them nothing.

Fowler had recruited Flint with the promise that he would never have to worry about the police bothering him again. Thereafter, he used Flint for special assignments that required his unique talents—arson, debt collections, and beatings. He paid him a substantial retainer of more than fifty thousand dollars a year to ensure his loyalty. Flint also agreed to stay out of trouble when his services weren't required.

"Your private matters are just that... private. I'd rather not know the details," said Fowler.

"What is it you want?" Flint asked, then added with a leer, "I've got an appointment upstairs and I don't like to keep her waiting."

"I've got a job for you, but I must ask you to show some restraint." Fowler reached into the inside pocket on his suit jacket and took out a small piece of paper. He slid it across the bar towards Flint.

"So what's this?"

"The names of two people who need a reminder that they have crossed a line," said Fowler. "But, Flint, I don't want them to be found behind an alley with their throats' cut. I'm merely trying to convey a message. Do you understand?"

Flint said nothing. He unfolded the piece of paper and glanced at the two names—Tom Fox and Charles St. Clair.

"You know who they are?" asked Fowler.

"I do. Never did like St. Clair much. He asks too many questions for my liking. I've seen him over at a whorehouse on Wooster Street once or twice. Fox, I've never met, but I know where I can find him."

"Good then, it's all settled. You can look after this soon?"

Flint threw his cigar on to the floor and stamped it out with his boot. "Yeah, I can look after it tomorrow if you like. But it'll cost you an extra five thousand."

"Why should I have to pay you extra?"

"It's a lot easier to slice their throats. So if you want me to show some restraint, well, I need some extra incentive for that."

Fowler shook his head. "Very well, Flint, another five thousand. But only after I see some results."

"You'll see some results, I can guarantee that. How do you feel about broken arms and legs?" Flint chuckled.

"I'll leave the details to you. Do as you like. Keep in mind that I'll need to speak with Fox in the near future. I have an offer for him that I don't think he'll refuse. As for St. Clair, he owes Jack Martin a few thousand and you may be able to use that to your advantage."

"How do you know he's in debt to Martin?"

"Flint, I'm surprised at you. Who do you think arranged it? I find that confusion is always a good way to keep someone of St. Clair's intelligence off balance. Now, if our business is done, I also have an appointment with a young lady."

Fowler shook a few more hands as he crossed the dance floor again and headed up the stairs. He suddenly felt more at ease. He had no ethical concerns about either ordering Flint to deal with Fox and St. Clair—two thorns in his side—or about seeing Amelia. He and Ellen had not had sexual relations in months. She was either sleeping off the laudanum or too depressed to act as a wife ought to.

Amelia was waiting for him at the top of the stairs. She was young—only twenty-two years old—with ruby lips, a thin nose, and glossy long dark hair. She was wearing nothing but a red corset with matching red boots, which left little to the imagination. Her body was voluptuous and for a moment Fowler was almost mesmerized by her beauty. He quickly threw a few coins on her dresser. "That'll cover Harry's rent of the room," he murmured.

Amelia smiled at him, pushed the coins into the dresser drawer, but said nothing.

Content that his immediate problems would soon be solved, Fowler allowed his head and heart to fill with lust. Amelia's hand slipped into his, then his mouth went dry as he anticipated what came next.

Chapter Ten

—✦—

DETECTIVE MURRAY MAKES AN ARREST

"Charlie, is that you?" Seth Murray's eyes squinted in the dim light of Madame Philippe's basement. Patrolman Westwood and four other constables crowded around him. "What the hell are you doing here?"

"Seth, what's going on?" St. Clair asked. "I'm working on an assignment, or at least I was." He avoided looking at Madame Philippe.

"An assignment about the good Madame?"

"In part, yes. It's a story about abortion in New York. About how easy it is to obtain one and how dangerous it's become." Now St. Clair gazed into Madame Philippe's eyes.

If this fazed Madame Philippe, she did not show it. "Mr. St. Clair, it's a pleasure to meet you finally. I've read and admired your work. I should've realized Mr. Fox would attempt such a stunt. I'm afraid your anger and moral superiority betrayed you, sir."

"Maybe so. But my conscience is clear. Can you say the same?"

"I can, but I fear we may have to have this conversation another time."

"And who's this, Charlie?" asked Murray, looking in Ruth's direction.

Ruth introduced herself. Her voice betrayed her nervousness.

"Miss Cardaso has come all the way from San Francisco to assist us," St. Clair explained

"A pleasure to meet you, Miss," Murray addressed Ruth, conscious that there was something vaguely familiar about her.

"This was our first appointment and it may be our last," she responded with a pleasant smile. "Once news of our visit here is spread, I doubt any midwife or abortionist will want to talk to us."

"This intrusion couldn't be helped, I'm afraid. But be patient, there may be a much bigger story to cover than you imagine." He turned to St. Clair. "This is quite a coincidence, Charlie. I wanted to discuss with you later the very case that's brought me here."

"And that's what exactly, Detective?" Madame Philippe interjected hotly. "Why have you and your men descended on my home like a pack of wolves?"

Murray's body stiffened in response. "What do you know about the woman found dead in the trunk at Hudson Depot the other day?" He glared at her. "She has blonde hair and had a handkerchief in her hand with the letter L sewn on it."

"Why should I know anything about something so horrific?" Madame Philippe's hand fluttered to her breast. Her tone softened. "Who was she?"

"That's what we're still trying to determine. We have good reason to believe that she was one your clients."

"Do you think I murdered this poor woman and stuffed her in a trunk? Is that what you believe, Detective?" She began to shake. Hector, who had led the police to the basement, moved closer to her and steered her to a chair.

"I read something about that in the *Times* this morning," St. Clair interjected. "Seth, why do you think Madame Philippe knows anything about this?"

Murray reached into his inside coat pocket and pulled out a small package wrapped in brown paper. He laid it down on a nearby table and carefully unfolded the covering. He held up a tattered piece of newsprint.

"Looks like newspaper?" St. Clair commented.

"That's exactly what it is," said Murray. "This is a *Herald* advertisement for Madame Philippe's services. It was found on the victim."

"Found on the victim?" St. Clair repeated. "I understood that she was discovered in the trunk without any clothes on."

"It was on her person, that's all I can say about it."

"What does that prove? That she read the newspaper." Madame Philippe shook her head in disbelief. "Tell me, Detective, does Inspector Stokes know you're here troubling me?"

"He ordered me to do so," said Murray, with an uncharacteristic grin.

"And Mr. Fowler?" asked Madame Philippe.

"That I can't answer, Madame, one way or the other. But I'd expect if Inspector Stokes approved this search, then as sure as eggs Boss Fowler approved it, too."

"I see." Madame Philippe grimaced. "Trust is a rare gift. Betrayal, on the other hand, comes easy for most people. Would you agree, Mr. St. Clair?"

"I'd say that you've been putting your trust in the wrong people," St. Clair responded.

"Perhaps I have. Often we've no choices in these matters. So what is it you plan to do with me, Detective?"

Murray pulled out a folded document from his jacket pocket. "This is a warrant signed by Judge Smith giving me the right to search your premises as I see fit." He handed it to Madame Philippe and turned to his men. "Westwood, I want this house searched from top to bottom. Report anything of a suspicious nature to me. Do you understand?"

Westwood nodded. "Yes, sir."

"Well, get on with it then."

For nearly two hours, the patrolmen opened every drawer, pried in every closet and cupboard, and searched every nook and cranny in Madame Philippe's mansion. They found a treasure trove of potentially incriminating material—a bundle of blank state marriage licenses, death certificates, and adoption documents . . . several letters written to Madame Philippe in German . . . a dozen drug recipes scrawled in pencil on a series of white cards . . . various bottles of medicines including iodine, calomel, opium, belladonna, laurel water, sulfuric acid, and French pills, Madame

Philippe's special blend for ladies…and an assortment of scalpels and other strange-looking surgical utensils—spoon handles bent in different directions, long forceps, and a large glass tube closed at one end with wax and covered with cerate.

Meanwhile, Madame Philippe made tea, which she offered to St. Clair and Ruth, as well as the patrolmen. Only Ruth, who resisted St. Clair's entreaties to return to the magazine's offices, accepted a cup.

"As I told you, Detective, there's nothing unusual to be found here," Madame Philippe said.

"Nothing unusual? What do you call these?" Murray brandished the metal forceps. "They're right out of the Spanish Inquisition. And these phony documents are enough for me to arrest you."

"Come now, Detective, my solicitor will have me out of your custody in less than an hour. The papers can be explained. And these tools are for legitimate medical purposes, as any physician in this city will verify, even the ones who detest me. You must face facts. I had nothing to do with that young woman's death."

"And I don't believe a word you're saying," said Murray. "Doc Draper's examination confirmed that this poor girl was killed by a botched abortion. Whether it was deliberate, I don't know. But at this moment I figure either it was you or someone you know."

"Another witch hunt, Detective, that's all this is," Madame Philippe said, her voice rising. "Why don't you ask yourself as to the reason why so many upstanding women seek the services I provide?"

"This isn't about merely abortion, Madame," snapped St. Clair. "It's about bloody murder."

"What of her office on Broome Street?" Ruth blurted out.

"What's that?" asked St. Clair.

"Yes, go on, Miss," Murray urged.

Ruth placed her cup of tea on a table and opened her handbag. "It's in my notes, I'm certain." She took out a small black leather bound journal and began flipping quickly through the pages. "Yes, here it is. I was reading old clippings on Madame Philippe in the magazine's files when I came across a reference to her working from an office on Broome Street close to the Bowery. You still own the building, isn't that correct, Madame?" asked Ruth.

"I do, yes," said Madame Philippe. She frowned, as if perplexed. "What of it? I once used it as a clinic, but I've not worked there for many years. I rent the lower part of the building to a carriage merchant." Her eyes shifted away.

"Where on Broome Street is this?" Murray asked sharply.

"As Miss Cardaso said, just off the Bowery."

"The address, Madame, please," Murray insisted.

"One hundred and five Broome Street. Why's that so important?" Madame Philippe continued to look perplexed.

"It's a red brick building with an alleyway beside it." Murray raised an eyebrow. "Isn't it?"

"As a matter of fact, it is," replied Madame Philippe.

"Westwood," Murray yelled. The patrolman came running. "Send Joe to fetch that truckman, Paddy Tritt. Tell him to bring Tritt to 105 Broome Street." He turned to Madame Philippe. "If you'll check the fine print, you'll see that the warrant I gave you includes all property you own or reside in. So the Broome Street office can be searched as well."

"What's going on?" St. Clair interrupted.

"I'll tell you, Charlie. I think we're about to solve the trunk mystery. Not only did the victim have a piece of paper linking her to Madame Philippe, but the trunk itself was picked up by this Tritt at an alleyway on Broome Street, right beside 105 Broome Street to be precise."

"That's not possible," muttered Madame Philippe, twisting the search warrant she held in her hand.

"Why's that?" asked St. Clair.

"Charlie, please let me do the talking here." Murray put his hands on his hips. "Madame, what do you know about a man named Flint? He dresses in an army uniform and poses as a beggar. Or a young street Arab named Corkie?"

"I don't know either of them. I've never heard of a Mr. Flint," Madame Philippe pleaded, sinking into the chair. "I have no idea who they are."

"I'd expect you'd say that. No matter, we're leaving for Broome Street shortly." He turned to St. Clair. "You and Miss Cardaso may ride along if you wish."

"I'm ready, you know that," St. Clair responded. He didn't always appreciate Murray's gruff manner or patronizing attitude, but he rarely turned down an opportunity to shadow his brother-in-law. What journalist with a nose for a good story and a keen sense of adventure would? Last year, his series on New York's pickpockets had attracted a great deal of attention and publicity and sold a lot of magazines. And he owed it all to Murray. Few journalists were permitted the direct access to police work in the city that St. Clair was.

"I had nothing to do with that young woman's death," Madame Philippe again pleaded, her voice now strained. "Nothing, at all."

"You may protest all you wish, Madame," said Murray, "but you'll come with us at once. And I won't hesitate to place you in wrist shackles. Your Negro can stay here, but I'll want to question him later."

∾

Madame Philippe was stunned by Murray's orders. She had spent a considerable amount of her money paying off the police and civic officials so she could work without interference. Why Stokes, for one, had abandoned her, she had no idea. Her contributions to his retirement fund had been substantial. Until now, he had interceded in any legal matters confronting her.

And, as for Victor Fowler, she was dumbfounded. She had known him for many years. She had supported both him and Tammany with money and votes. During the last six months alone, she had willingly paid the Ring more than a hundred thousand dollars. Fowler had made a personal and urgent request for the money and he had promised that he would always protect her. What, she wondered, had happened to so abruptly change this situation? The answer, as much as she did not want to admit it, was staring her directly in the face— The dead woman in the trunk at Hudson Depot.

As soon as the detective had described the victim and the handkerchief with the letter L found in the girl's hand, she knew at once of whom he was speaking—Miss Lucy Maloney.

Two days ago, this sweet young woman had visited her at the Broome Street office. Yet, there had been no procedure, no abortion. At the last minute, Miss Maloney had decided not to follow through with the operation and had hastily departed. That was the last she had seen or heard of her until she had read about the trunk murder in the newspaper.

As she followed the police outside to their waiting carriages, she contemplated the difficulty of her predicament. Once they learned of her interaction with Miss Maloney she was certain that they would never believe her version of events.

Despite the fact that it was God's honest truth.

~

"I was to be fitted for a gown later this afternoon," Madame Philippe sighed, staring out the carriage window, seeking to distract her thoughts. "It arrived from Paris only days ago, a lovely dress of silver brocade. For the Fowlers' annual summer ball, no less."

"Madame, with all due respect, your social calendar doesn't interest me," said Murray gruffly. "My only concern is determining the identity of the girl in the trunk and who murdered her. Do you understand?"

Madame Philippe nodded, but she pursed her lips.

She was crunched in the covered carriage between Murray and Patrolman Westwood. St. Clair and Ruth sat opposite them. Two more police carriages followed behind making their way down Fifth Avenue and then Broadway. As the lead horses ambled past Bleeker, the cobblestone road became much bumpier, tossing everyone back and forth.

"This is intolerable," complained Madame Philippe. "We should have used my own carriage. Hector had it out in Central Park only a few days ago—"

"What's intolerable, Madame, is how you paid for that carriage and your grand home," St. Clair retorted, shifting uneasily in his seat. Being so near to Madame Philippe only intensified his anger.

"I've done absolutely nothing wrong, but I fear I may never convince you of that."

"Madame," Ruth interceded, attempting to ease the tension in the carriage, "your accent, I notice, is not French as your name would suggest."

"She's German and a Hebrew. Isn't that correct, Madame?" said St. Clair before Madame Philippe could respond. "Anna Jacoby, I believe is your real name. You were born in Frankfurt and came to New York in the early 1830s when you were about twenty or twenty-one years of age." St. Clair summoned what he had gleaned earlier in his research. "You worked as a servant for a well-to-do German-Jewish family and married their son, Franz. After the family lost some of its money in poor land investments, you and your late husband created your persona as Madame Philippe and you became the most renowned abortionist in New York and beyond. The sales of your French pills and your so-called medical work have made you one of the wealthiest women in the city." St. Clair leaned back in his seat and lit a thin cigar.

"I've never heard my life story related so well," said Madame Philippe, with more than a hint of sarcasm in her voice. "Unfortunately, Mr. St. Clair, your less-than-diligent research into my background has also omitted the most relevant facts. The truth is that you've merely skimmed the surface. To you, I'm Madame Killer. I'm afraid you've allowed your personal feelings to color your brief and inaccurate interpretation of my life. And I was under the impression that you were a talented journalist. This is not the time or the place for me to explain to you my inner passions or hopes or the reasons I've been compelled to do what I do. Perhaps someday you'll understand."

"That won't be today," snapped Murray, scrambling out of the carriage to the dry mid-caked walkway in front of the Broome Street address. "We've arrived."

The carriage abruptly lurched forward and Ruth fell out of her seat onto the dusty floor. St. Clair grabbed her by her right hand and helped her up. It felt good to touch her and for a moment he did not let go. Ruth made no effort to remove her hand from his.

"I think you can let the lady out of the carriage," said Murray gazing at St. Clair with amusement.

"Of course." St. Clair's face had turned a light shade of red. He stepped down first and then assisted Ruth. Her lips held the hint of a smile. She drew close to him and whispered, "Thank you." Her sweet breath tickled his ear.

Patrolman Westwood followed and offered his hand to Madame Philippe. Moments later, the other two police wagons arrived. Behind them was a fourth wagon with two patrolmen and Paddy Tritt.

The truckman's appearance was disheveled. His shirt was hanging over top of his trousers and his hair, minus his stovepipe hat, was messy. He looked as if he had been roused from a deep sleep.

"We finally found him at a whorehouse on Mulberry," said Patrolman Eddie Garnett. "He was right in the middle of his business with one and he had another hooker with large titties waiting naked in a chair beside the bed for her turn."

Several of the other policeman laughed and Paddy stood straighter, his pride in his prowess evident.

"That's enough of that," Murray said. "We've ladies present here."

"My apologies," said Garnett, tipping his cap towards Ruth and Madame Philippe. "I should have been more discreet. Please excuse me."

"Show me where you picked up the trunk," Murray ordered Paddy.

"It was over there." Paddy pointed to the back part of the alley. "Next to the building. That's where I found the trunk and that street Arab. Why don't you ask him? How come you're not bothering that little hustler?"

"I wish I could," said Murray. "But he's dead. His throat was slit open. You know anything about that?"

Paddy stumbled backwards in shock. "That soldier, Flint, did that I'd wager."

"Yeah, you're probably right," Murray gave Paddy an assessing gaze, "but we don't know who Flint is or where we can find him. If I were you, before you go running back to your crib-house, I'd be watching my back," he added, dismissing the truckman.

A small crowd of curious onlookers had gathered in the meantime, including a gang of young boys, half of them barefooted, who had been playing stickball on the street. Behind the boys loitered a couple of men with pushcarts loaded with fruit, and an assortment of beggars, and neighborhood mothers and their children, who came to see what the excitement was about. Above them, bare-shouldered women peered out of windows from nearby brothels. "Up for a visit, mister?" one of them addressed the departing Paddy.

Upon Murray's orders, Madame Philippe led the way into building. The official entourage walked past the entrance to Anthony's Carriage Supplies and moved en masse around the back to a door in the alley—close to the spot where Paddy had said he picked up the trunk. The police waited impatiently while Madame Philippe fumbled with her key, before she finally opened the lock. Murray instructed Westwood to take four men and carefully search the alley—he led the remaining patrolmen, along with St. Clair and Ruth, up the stairs into Madame Philippe's second floor office.

The detective then ordered her to sit on one of the chairs and be silent while the police conducted a search of the premises. Madame Philippe reluctantly did as she was told.

The window shutters were closed and her operating room was dark. One of the policemen knocked on the shutter lock with his club and pushed it open, giving the room some sunlight.

Murray surveyed the room and turned to Madame Philippe. "You don't use this office for medical procedures anymore?"

"That's correct," Madame Philippe mumbled.

"It's curious. There's no cobwebs." He walked to a wall, stroked it with his finger, and held it up. "And no dust. It's almost as if someone had cleaned this place in the last few days."

"Detective," Ruth interrupted, "would you mind terribly if I looked around the office?" Alert to the coquettish tone in Ruth's voice, St. Clair wondered at her ability to be manipulative. The evidence was in his brother-in-law's response.

"I wouldn't normally allow that." Murray pushed back his cap. "But as long as you keep out of the way, go ahead."

"Do you mind if I join you?" St. Clair asked.

As methodically as the police had searched through Madame Philippe's house, they now tore apart her office. Every drawer and cabinet were opened, every wooden box and canister emptied.

St. Clair and Ruth wandered into a back alcove behind the main surgical area. Suddenly a large rat scurried across the floor. Ruth screamed. Four policemen came running.

"Nothing to worry about, it's only a rat," St. Clair said calmly to the policemen who chuckled and returned to their work.

Ruth took hold of St. Clair's arm, and again he was stirred by her touch.

"I promise to protect you from any other rodents we may discover on our journey."

She beamed. "Your chivalry is noted, sir. Though I grew up in the city, I've never been too fond of rats."

"When I was a boy, maybe ten or twelve, we didn't live too far from here. My father was a clerk in a mining business that went bankrupt and we had a few bad years. To help out, me and my friends would—and I hope this won't make you too squeamish—capture as many rats as we could."

"What on earth for?" asked Ruth.

"There used to be a saloon in Five Points run by a scoundrel named Patsy Hearn. The bar was famous for its sporting parlor. Hearn needed as many rats as he could for his rat-and-dog fights. He paid us a penny a rat. And the men, hundreds of them as I remember, would wager how many rats the dogs could kill."

"That sounds dreadful."

"It was. Once I snuck in to watch, but it was so bloody and cruel that I gave up the business. Thankfully, my father got a new job in Baltimore and we were able to move to a much better neighborhood. I never captured any more rats after that."

"Except for Mr. Fowler, that is."

St. Clair laughed. "Your wit is stellar, Miss." He took a few more steps and his left boot jammed into something hard. It was a barrel covered by several large Indian blankets. He grabbed hold of them and yanked them off.

"Perhaps we should call for the police," Ruth suggested.

St. Clair shrugged. "There's no harm in looking, is there?"

He pried open the wooden lid, which was loosely held on by two bent nails. He peeked inside and nearly choked. The odor from the barrel was overpowering. Covering his mouth and nose with his handkerchief, he gingerly stepped forward and again attempted to look inside.

"It's filled with liquid, certainly not water by the smell of it. Maybe acid. And I think there's something floating on top," said St. Clair.

"What is it?"

"It looks like parts of a small body."

"Bless my soul," Ruth declared.

"Seth, you'd better come and see this," shouted St. Clair.

"What is it? What have you found? Charlie, didn't I tell you not to—"

"Will you just look at this." St. Clair pointed to the barrel. "Be warned, it stinks bad."

Murray moved closer. "Damn right," he said before noticing Ruth standing beside St. Clair. "My apologies Miss. I don't usually have ladies present during my investigations."

"Think nothing of it. But that smell's worse than a livery stable on a hot July day," said Ruth.

"Agreed." Murray peered at the strange brew. "And what in tarnation is floating in that muck?" He turned to a policeman who was standing at the entrance to the alcove. "Bring Madame Philippe."

A moment later Madame Philippe stood before the three of them.

"What is this?" Murray demanded.

"I told Hector to clean this up long ago. I'd forgotten it was even here."

"Is that why it was covered by these blankets?" asked St. Clair.

"Hector must've done that. I have no idea why."

"What's inside and why does it stink so badly?" asked Murray, his nose crinkling.

"It's a mixture of lime and acid."

"And if I dare ask," Murray continued, "what's floating in it? Is it what I fear?"

Madame Philippe moved closer, untroubled by the odor.

"It looks like baby parts," said St. Clair, with mounting horror. "Is this where you've been throwing the corpses of the dead children?"

"Of course not, Mr. St. Clair. I believe these are the remains of pigs."

"Pigs?" Murray glanced again at the detritus in the barrel. "Why on earth would you have pigs floating in a barrel of lime and acid?"

"Some months ago, I was conducting experiments on a new combination of ether and chloroform...an anesthetic that could help women in pain. I tried it on several pigs, and some of them died. Hector threw the corpses in the barrel. That's all there is to it."

"I have no reason to doubt you, Madame, but I shall have our doctor examine the contents, nonetheless," said Murray.

"Do what you feel best. But he'll confirm what I've told you."

Patrolman Westwood shuffled into the room, slightly out of breath. "Sir, we've found something outside in the alley. It's an odd thing, because I could have sworn on my mother's grave that I searched that corner just the other day and found nothing."

"Westwood, out with it, what is it?" Murray barked.

Another policeman standing behind him was carrying a small bundle of clothing and handed it to Westwood. "This, sir," he said, holding up several pieces of torn cloth. "Half of a lady's chemise with the sleeves ripped out, and this I believe is a piece of a woman's petticoat. There are bloody streaks on it."

"I see it," said Murray. "Anything else?"

"One more important item." Westwood reached into the bundle and pulled out a small piece of white fabric. "Another handkerchief. This one has two letters on it."

"Let me see that," said Murray, taking the handkerchief from Westwood's hands. He spread it open and there in the middle of the white lace were two letters, L and M.

"So now we're getting somewhere," said Murray. "At some point, the woman was in the alley before Paddy took her away in the trunk."

"Perhaps she was killed somewhere else and then moved here," suggested St. Clair.

"That's my thinking, too." Murray turned to face Madame Philippe. "Whatever happened to this poor woman, you were in the middle of it, weren't you?" He did not wait for her to respond. He reached for a pair of iron wrist shackles. "Madame, you're coming with us to the station until such time as we can determine if you should be charged with the murder of, let's call her now, L.M. . . . the young woman found in the trunk."

"I think that . . ." Madame Philippe began softly.

"You have something to say?" Murray glared at her with disgust.

Madame Philippe's mouth remained open, but no sound came forth. Instead she held out her wrinkled hands so that Murray could fasten the shackles.

Chapter Eleven

A Toast to Crédit Mobilier

Victor Fowler leaned back in his chair. Feeling relaxed from his visit earlier in the evening with Amelia—a lovelier, more luscious and pleasurable woman he could hardly imagine—and stuffed from his late-night, five-course dinner, he discreetly undid the top button of his suit pants. Before him were the members of the Ring—his Ring—seated around a heavy, dark oak, oval table in a private dining room on the third floor at Lorenzo Delmonico's fine restaurant near the corner of Fifth Avenue and Fourteenth Street. The men were waiting patiently for him to deliver his weekly *State of the Union*.

He knew he had grown accustomed to his high status and the wealthy style of his life. Yet there were times when even he could not fathom how far he had come from his parent's modest home on Cherry Street. From there he had joined a fire company, the Liberty Engine Company, Number 7, and within a short time was the company's foreman. He had singlehandedly transformed the Big Seven into the city's premier fire-fighting brigade.

After that, it was not that big a leap into local politics in the Seventh Ward, where he learned the fine art of doling out patronage—saloon licenses, road repair contracts, police appointments, and streetcar franchises. Not to mention the experience he gained dealing with madams, pimps, fences, and abortionists. Within a short time, he was proclaimed the king of Tammany Hall—a position he had no desire to relinquish any time soon.

"Now that, gentlemen, was as superb a meal as you can obtain anywhere in the city," Fowler declared. "How about another dish of baked Alaska, Tommy? Or shall we begin again with a lamb kidneys and oysters?" He took a deep drag on his cigar.

"Another glass of Scotch, it shall be. I fear my pants'll split apart if I eat another morsel," said Mayor Thomas Emery. "You'll have to call for a cartman to take me home."

The other men at the table howled with laughter, as they usually did when Emery made a colorful or witty remark.

"You'll walk out of here on your own two feet, I promise you that," said Fowler. "And you might even be sober. Isn't that so, Isaac?"

Isaac Harrison politely grunted. He continued chewing on the last few pieces of his beef like a dog that did not want to be disturbed by its pesky owner.

"Isaac, you're entirely predictable." Fowler goaded him. "How many items does Delmonico's offer on its menu?"

"Three hundred and eighty-six," declared Emery.

"Exactly. And what does Isaac always order each time we dine here?" Fowler addressed the assembled. "Number 86," he said, answering his own question, "a loin steak lightly salted and basted in butter, I might add, and grilled over an open fire."

Everyone except Harrison laughed.

"Don't forget the best part," added Emery. "What of the potatoes-diced, cooked and creamed, topped with grated cheese and buttered bread crumbs, and baked golden brown."

"Thomas, that's quite enough from you tonight," said Harrison.

"Come now, Isaac," Fowler said, "the Mayor was only sporting with you. Where's your sense of humor?"

～

Ignoring the jibe, Harrison kept on eating. In truth, he looked forward to their frequent gatherings at Delmonico's, where he could enjoy the company of his male companions. The price he had to pay to enjoy this meal, however, was tolerating Fowler's patronizing of Emery, admittedly necessary, although annoying all the same.

Harrison rarely found Emery witty or clever—what kind of Tammany man preferred Scotch to Irish whiskey?—although he was prepared to concede that Emery's higher-class background was an important asset. Unlike most of the men around the table, the mayor had not fought his way out of Five Points. His father was said to be an English aristocrat and he had been educated at New York University as well as Harvard Law School. Harrison understood that when the time came and their Washington plan was launched, having someone of Emery's stature on their ticket would be a bonus.

Harrison also acknowledged that, as mayor, Emery had managed himself superbly. The mayor did what had to be done to build up their coffers. Even Harrison chuckled when he learned that Emery had diverted thousands of dollars from the sale of building permits to the Ring's personal accounts. Harrison had examined the records for himself. Whereas in the past, the permit department brought in approximately $100,000 per year, under Emery's direction this had dwindled to $13,000 in 1870 and only about $9,500 thus far this year—and yet there was a building boom taking place. Harrison appreciated that it was Emery's smooth manner and approach that had made this creative bookkeeping possible.

As well, Emery never refused a request to help a Ring family member. It was only two weeks ago that Harrison had spoken to him about his nephew, Jesse. He loved the boy as if he was his own son, but the lad was a bottlehead through and through.

"It's of no consequence," Emery had assured him. "I've just the position for him. He'll become assistant to the furnisher of hacks and carriages to the City Council and at an annual pay of $20,000."

Harrison, as well as his sister, Francis, the boy's mother, was grateful. That was the way Emery usually did business, so Harrison was prepared to overlook the mayor's irritating behavior.

"Have I ever told you fellows the story of the Kissing Bridge on the line of the old Boston Post Road, near where Third Avenue and

Seventy-Seventh Street intersect?" began Emery, launching into another tale. "It was customary that before passing beyond the bridge, you would salute the lady who's your companion. Except one day, the reverend of a nearby church found himself escorting the wife of his wealthiest parishioner across the bridge. The preacher began to sweat for he did not know what to do. He had no desire to insult the lady and yet if he kissed her she would surely tell her husband. Quite unexpectedly the woman moved closer to him so that he could smell her sweet breath. She puckered her lips and opened her mouth slightly."

The men around the table were as silent as children listening to a bedtime story. Only Harrison rolled his eyes in Fowler's direction, but Fowler ignored him.

"So what did he do?" asked Bob James, the city comptroller, who wore his tall stovepipe hat even while he dined.

Emery smiled. "He did what any God-fearing man would do. He moved as close as he could to her, leaned towards her lips and pecked her on her forehead."

A collective groan emanated from the men at the table.

"That was truly awful, Tommy," said Fowler. He then banged on the table with his fist to get the group's attention. "If the mayor is finished with his tales of old New York for the moment, I'd like to take care of a few important business items. I remind you all that whatever is said here tonight remains in the confines of this room. Twiddle-twaddle of any sort and revealing our personal matters to wives or worse, to reporters, is nothing more than disloyalty and will be dealt with accordingly."

"No need for threats," said James, patting his wallet book, "you know you have our loyalty and gratitude."

The other men laughed.

"I think Bob used to make an annual salary of $3,600 as a clerk in some damn shipping business," said Emery. "What do you figure, Bob? You worth a few more dollars today?"

"Yeah, a wee bit more." James smiled.

"What are we going to do about that damn *Fox's Weekly*?" asked Harrison. "There's an edition coming out tomorrow morning and I've been told by a reliable source that there's a wicked cartoon depicting us like a pack of dogs. It's most despicable and undignified, in my view."

"I agree, Isaac, but let's leave Fox's rag for a moment." Fowler turned to James. "What of the problem with Benjamin Beatty?"

"Ah, the good Court Recorder," said James, touching his protruding belly. "I've dealt with the matter quietly."

"How much did it cost?" asked Harrison.

"I made a deal for five-thousand. That'll keep him satisfied for another six months. No Tammany man will be convicted in police court without consent from Victor."

"Excellent. I assume that includes young Master Johnson?" inquired Fowler, grabbing hold of a wine bottle.

James nodded. "Yes, Beatty assured me that his case would be acquitted in a matter of days."

"For those of you don't know all of the details," explained Fowler, "Nicholas Johnson, the son of Bob's cousin has been accused of raping a fourteen-year-old girl, one of Mabel Williams's whores over on Greenwich Street. He says he paid her and we have no reason to dispute his version."

"He's a decent lad with a good future ahead of him. He's already been helping me out in the office. I'd hate to see something like this ruin his future," added James.

Everyone around the table concurred.

"The next item on our agenda is Crédit Mobilier and our plans for Washington. Arch has the report."

All eyes shifted towards Governor Archibald Krupp, a handsome and tall man. He wore a dapper navy suit—direct from Paris, he had mentioned earlier in the evening—which consisted of a frock-coat, trousers, vest, and a high-collar white shirt complemented by a slim cravat fashioned in a bow. His silver hair was oiled down, as was the custom of the day. "I was in Washington three weeks ago and as you instructed, Victor, I hired an agent I trust named Stephenson Kirkland. He met with the brains behind Crédit Mobilier, Congressman Oakes Ames and Dr. Thomas Durant of the Union Pacific. They are, by the way," added Krupp, "two rascally Republicans, who I'd never turn my back on, I can assure you. Someday soon, we Democrats, will regain control of Washington politics. Who knows what would have happened had Stephen Douglas, the Democrat's great champion, not supported the pro-slavery

Kansas-Nebraska Act in 1854? No Abraham Lincoln in 1860, no civil war, no Republicans in power today—"

"Arch, if I had wanted a history lesson I would've asked you for one. Just tell me about the agreement?" Fowler ordered.

"Yes, of course, my apologies. You know how I can be on this subject. Very well, then, Kirkland posed as the representative of a wealthy New York Republican group willing to invest a considerable amount of money in Crédit Mobilier, but anonymously."

"I assume Ames and Durant don't suspect a thing?" Fowler leaned forward.

"Kirkland said they were almost salivating." Krupp smiled. "They're completely convinced this group is only interested in a sound investment. And let me tell you all that it's nothing to snicker about. Since Crédit Mobilier was set up as a dummy company five years ago, and through its building contracts with Union Pacific, it has recorded profits of more than twenty million."

Emery whistled and James nearly fell over in his chair.

"By my estimation," explained Krupp, "they've charged Union's stockholders more than twice as much as necessary for the construction that they fobbed on to another company. Ames is already negotiating another deal for a railway in Missouri. But here's the important point... Durant, with a bit of urging from our agent, has offered shares in Crédit Mobilier to Schuyler Colfax, the esteemed vice-president of our great nation. And he's agreed to speak to other members of President Grant's cabinet as well."

"I have to say, Victor, it makes me ill to be in league with Republicans like Durant and Ames," said James. "If our Democratic Party Tammany supporters ever discovered—"

"They won't, have no fear." Fowler raised his hand to quell his companion. "That's why I had Arch enter into this agreement to begin with. My friends, we can cause havoc in Grant's corrupt-ridden administration. Playing the part of loyal Republican investors we can lead Crédit Mobilier down any path we choose. First we'll reap the profits... and I've several ideas about that I can soon share with you. And then when the time is right, we'll use our newspaper contacts, as well as our new magazine, which we're about to acquire, and expose this sham for what it is, another Republican attempt to swindle American investors. Don't you see, gentlemen, greed, along with stupidity, will be the undoing of this damnable Presidency. Once Grant is forced to resign along with Colfax, Arch and Emery will be ready for the ticket next year. Washington is in our grasp."

"I'd be the last person to argue with you, Victor," said James. "But General Grant is not a man to be taken lightly."

"He drinks too much," Harrison chimed in.

"That maybe so, but he won the war and is a brilliant military tactician. This has served him well as president. Republican or not, he remains popular with whites, and dare I say, with hundreds of thousands of colored voters. God help us all," added Krupp.

"And you're certain the damn reporters will do as we tell them to?" James puffed his cigar.

Fowler looked at each man at the table. He valued their talents and attributes. Krupp provided capable leadership and would make an obedient president, who would heed his every order. Emery, despite an occasional lapse of common sense, was an important link with the elite members of New York high society and every privilege they and their kind represented. James might be as "cold and crafty with a smooth, oily, insinuating manner," as St. Clair portrayed him, yet that was what made him so effective, and Harrison, his right-hand man whose instincts he generally trusted, was as calculating as he was. There was no higher praise than that. At the same time, Fowler loathed the constant questioning of his plans and the often interminable squabbling over his strategy.

"Enough, gentlemen" Fowler raised his voice, but did not shout. In a firm and unwavering tone he continued, "That's quite enough for this evening. All will fall into place. On this, you must trust me."

He reached for the chain of his gold watch and quickly checked the time. "By now I'd imagine our scheme to acquire *Fox's Weekly* is proceeding on schedule. So I want you all to finish your wine and whiskey and retire to your wives and families with full bellies, content in the fact that tomorrow we will be one step closer to the ultimate prize."

∽

Several of the men quaffed down their last few drops of the Rauenthaler Berg Medoc or Irish whiskey and bid Fowler a good evening. Within a short time, the private dining room had emptied. Only Fowler and Harrison remained seated at the table.

"Tell me, Victor," said Harrison, lighting another cigar, "do you ever feel like one of those high-wire performers at Barnum's show?"

"Occasionally," Fowler responded, then added with a satisfied smile, "but I have yet to stumble or fall."

"You'd agree there are several more problems we'll have to overcome before we claim victory."

"Mere formalities." Fowler waved his hand dismissively.

"You've heard about Madame Philippe being arrested in conjunction with that murder at Hudson Depot? I've already spoken to Stokes. I know how you feel about her but we must distance ourselves from this."

"What did you tell him?" Fowler asked, his tone more serious.

"That he should allow the police to investigate as he sees fit. And that Madame Philippe's on her own in this matter. We cannot be associated with the murder of a young woman and certainly not by an abortionist. Our Tammany men will never forgive us."

"They'll do whatever I tell them to do. This is a damn tragedy. A damn tragedy and shame," muttered Fowler. "But I'm of the same mind on this. We can't be connected to this murder. Not now. You did the right thing, Isaac."

For a few minutes the men sat in uneasy silence. Then Harrison said, "Ellen visited Mary for tea and sandwiches this afternoon."

"And what of it?" Fowler asked sharply.

"Your wife, she was in a depressed spirit and quite sullen, even weepy. I distinctly heard crying from our parlor. And I believe she said some unpleasant words about you. Doesn't this concern you, Victor?"

Fowler shook his head. "Sometimes, Isaac, it's as if I have the hangman's noose around my neck and she pulls it ever so tighter. She was so beautiful and gay when we first wed and then—" He stopped himself. "Why review old wounds? There's nothing to be gained. It's the laudanum. She's drinking more than two gills a day. I fear it's slowly killing her. I've tried taking it away, even hiding it. She merely dispatches her servant for more. The situation is impossible."

"A woman needs to have a child. Keeps her sane, if you ask me."

Fowler stiffened. "You know that's not possible, why speak of it?"

"There's one more thing I should tell you." Harrison tried to look directly into Fowler's eyes.

"What is it?" demanded Fowler.

Harrison hesitated for a moment. "According to Mary, Ellen is quite aware of your frequent visits to Harry Hill's. Perhaps that's what compels her to take the medicine?"

Fowler threw his glass onto the floor, smashing it into a dozen pieces. "She knows about Amelia? So what of it? You're acting like an old codger. My assignations with Amelia keep me sane and content. You only punish yourself by refusing to experience such pleasures."

Harrison could have pointed out that his marriage was based on trust, loyalty, and respect. He knew, however, that Fowler would have had no idea what he was speaking of. Harrison accepted that his union with Mary was an anomaly. If anything was certain of marital relations between men and women, it was that men were intent on safeguarding the virtue of their wives and satisfying their passions and pleasures elsewhere.

There was nothing more for him to say. Ellen Fowler was an unwilling victim of an unhappy marriage and there was little she or anyone else could do about it. Harrison was rising from the table when a messenger boy arrived with a note for Fowler.

"What the hell is this?" he tore open the envelope and read the message. His face turned white.

"What is it, Victor? What's happened?"

"It's a message from Stokes. Frank King was killed in some sort of carriage-racing accident out at Harlem Lane. That damn mutton-head."

"You know what we need to do immediately, Victor."

"Send someone over to his office before the police or his family start snooping around?"

"Precisely."

Chapter Twelve

A TREACHEROUS ATTACK

*T*he first development in the trunk mystery has been taken by the
police. Earlier today, Detective Seth Murray arrested the notorious
abortionist, Madame Philippe, in the death of the young woman
discovered murdered at Hudson Depot. The victim's name has yet to be posi-
tively identified, and so far Madame Philippe has refused to co-operate. It
can be told, however, that the young woman's chemise and handkerchiefs
were found in and near, Madame Philippe's Broome Street office, a torture
chamber of unspeakable evils.

*There is something horrible in the idea that human bodies can be packed
like carrion in trunks or barrels and shipped on railroads, yet the revelations of today's investigation, at which this journalist was present, has shown
that it could be done. While there are many phases of the dark side of life
in New York—more sensational because they are more open to the public
view—there is none more sickening than the work of the abortionists such as
Madame Philippe, who ply their infamous trade to a far greater extent than
is believed by those who have studied the matter...*

As was his style, St. Clair reviewed his writing by editing his prose
with an old quill pen he was fond of. Tom Fox had been trying for
months to convince him to switch to a new metal-tipped pen, but he

preferred a bottle of ink and a goose quill—even if it was terribly out of fashion.

He paused for a moment to light his pipe and then took a sip of luke-warm ale.

"What are you so jolly about, St. Clair? With that foolish grin painted on your face, you look like an upper-class half-wit," bellowed Richard Dukes, the bald and stocky proprietor of The Chartist, a small English-style pub half a mile from the magazine office.

"Can't a man have a smile on his face?" St. Clair responded.

"Only if he's cunt-struck," said Dukes, howling with laughter at his own boorish wit.

"Richard, you can kiss my arse. Now, off with you. Go bother some of your other patrons."

"Whatever you say, mate. Just holler when you need another mug."

The truth was, St. Clair was feeling elated, as if all his troubles were far behind him, including his debt problems to Jack Martin. He had taken great pleasure, as he usually did, in watching Seth Murray work a case. And while Madame Philippe had yet to be charged with the trunk murder, Murray had assured him it was only a matter of hours until he wore her down. He had seen his brother-in-law interrogate a suspect on several occasions and had been impressed with his uncompromising and implacable deportment. Sooner or later, he was certain, Madame Philippe would confess all she knew.

Thus he had gathered his notes, sharpened his quill, and went to work on the first installment of "Evil of the Age." He intended to follow this up with an interview and brief biography of Madame Philippe. There was no doubt in his mind that she would speak with him. Indeed, he suspected all that he would have to do is show her a little compassion, and he would learn everything there was to know about her. Whatever discomfort this might cause him, he reasoned that it was a small price to pay.

He dipped his quill into the small vial of ink beside his ale, and then put it down. Dukes had been right that the perpetual grin on his face was due to a woman, although St. Clair would never have put it as crudely as the barkeep. Nevertheless, the intriguing Ruth Cardaso absorbed his thoughts.

He contemplated again what had transpired. The day had been exhausting. He and Ruth had been permitted to watch Murray's initial questioning of Madame Philippe—a session of more than two hours in a hot and stuffy room at police headquarters on Mulberry Street. Throughout the interrogation, they had shared words and knowing glances. She had laughed at his clever quips, which only encouraged him further. Any feelings of anger that he had earlier felt towards her had vanished. He had invited her to stop for refreshments at an oyster cellar on Mott Street, quieter and tamer than most. But she had told him that she was weary and preferred to return to her hotel. He insisted on flagging down a hansom cab and escorting her back to the Fifth Avenue.

They rode for most of the way in silence, exchanging a few words about Madame Philippe's culpability in the trunk murder and what was likely to happen next. St. Clair had assured her that despite Seth Murray's gruff demeanor, he was a decent and honorable cop. Did St. Clair have any doubts about her guilt, she had asked him? He had told her that he believed Madame Philippe had killed the young woman, perhaps not intentionally, and then had tried to cover it up by sending the body to Chicago—an obviously desperate ploy conceived by a desperate individual.

The cab stopped in front of the hotel. He had descended from the carriage first and had offered her his hand. She stepped on to the walkway and they agreed to meet the next day at the magazine office by ten o'clock in the morning. She bid farewell, smiled at him and he climbed back into the cab, telling the driver to take him to The Chartist. The horses were about to pull away, when Ruth ran back. "Wait, wait," she beseeched the driver, who pulled back on his reins.

And then, without a word, she climbed back into the cab and before St. Clair could react, kissed him passionately for what seemed an eternity. The cab driver, who had turned his head, let out a loud whistle. Ruth abruptly pulled away. St. Clair was too stunned to speak and watched in wonder as Ruth silently leapt from the cab and dashed into the hotel.

Her lips, he now recalled, were soft and moist. The scent of her perfume was enchanting. Even as he wrote his magazine article at Dukes', he could still taste her. He knew then and there that no matter what other events interceded, he would have to kiss her again.

～

It was past eleven o'clock by the time St. Clair left the pub to walk the six blocks to his office. As he crossed the street, someone approached him out the darkness.

"What is it you want?" St. Clair demanded, startled.

"A coin to spare, sir, I've not eaten all day?" A beggar held out a metal cup. His long brown hair was dirty and his beard unkempt. He wore a tattered blue Union Army uniform and a torn slouch cap on his head of the type worn by enlisted men.

St. Clair reached into his pocket and threw a nickel into the beggar's cup. "Here's something for you, now be off."

"I'm grateful, sir. I'm very grateful," the man muttered.

The encounter reminded him to check his pants pocket for his pistol. It wasn't there. Then he remembered he had left it in his flat—a foolish mistake.

"Would you like some company, sir?" came the voice from the other side of the street. "Maybe two of us at once?" another woman asked, laughing.

There beneath a lamp, St. Clair could see three young women dressed in long colorful dresses and bonnets. He ignored them, as he usually did, but picked up his pace.

"You're a real gentlemen, I'd bet. Come on over here so we can get a better look," one of them called loudly after him.

St. Clair continued on his way. In a matter of minutes, he was at Park Row. It was quiet and dark—only the scurrying of a few dogs pierced the silence of a hot and humid night. St. Clair stood for a moment in front of the entrance to *Fox's Weekly*, alert to a disquieting sight. The heavy oak door was open.

"That's odd," he mumbled. It was not like Tom Fox to keep the door unlocked, especially at this time of the night. He pushed his way in and ascended the stairs to the second floor, conscious of his heart racing.

"Tom, you here?" he called out. There was no reply.

The office was dark, except for a flickering gaslight coming from behind Fox's private area. The light shone through a crack in the door. It was slightly opened, illuminating one corner of the room.

"Tom, what are you doing here so late?" St. Clair asked, louder. Again there was no answer. His anxiety increased. Cautiously, he approached the light and nudged the door open.

"Tom, you there?"

He peered in and saw Fox slumped over his desk. Two empty bottles of whiskey were beside his head. St. Clair sagged with relief. "Have you drunk too much grog?" he whispered. "Well, my friend, sleep it off, I have work to do."

He closed the door and lit the gaslight hanging near his own desk. He filled his pipe with tobacco and set his finished article before him for one last edit. Then he saw two sealed messages addressed to him near his blotter. He tore open one.

~

Dear St. Clair,
Your debt has been settled. You are welcome at my faro and poker tables at your convenience.
Your servant, Martin.

St. Clair inhaled on his pipe and smiled. Frank King had done as he had promised that night at the Hole-in-the-Wall—he had paid off St. Clair's debt to Martin. A sense of relief engulfed him. Now, he decided that he must abide by his part of their agreement. He reached for the second note and tore it open with the same resolve. It was a white piece of paper with two words scrawled on it, a name:

Lucy Maloney

He stared at it for only a moment. Then he felt like he had been kicked in the head by a mule. "Of course," he murmured, "of course, what's wrong with me? Lucy Maloney, L.M., the name of the woman in the trunk."

He examined the message carefully to see if he could determine who had sent it to him, but there was nothing, no markings or clue as to the identity of the writer. He would have to speak with Murray early the next morning. Surely he or Murray would be able to ascertain who this Miss Maloney was and why she had sought an abortion with Madame Philippe. Fox, he knew, would be pleased at this development and the next installment of "Evil of the Age" began to take shape in his head.

He studied his article and was pleased with its content and style. St. Clair prided himself on his lean and concise prose, which was in his view, rarely excessive and generally as palatable as a fine bottle of Burgundy. He recalled that his father had wanted him to become a lawyer and he had considered apprenticing with Bidwell and Strong, a prominent New York law office. Yet once he sold his first newspaper article—Horace Greeley had paid him a few dollars for a story about a house fire on the East Side—he knew what he wanted to do. Indeed, what he was compelled to do.

Writing always had been much more than a career for St. Clair—on the contrary, it was a calling. He rarely felt complete if he was unable to put ink to paper each and every day, Sundays included. Caroline was no churchgoer, but it irked her, nevertheless, when he worked on the Lord's Day. He tried to explain that he was addicted to writing as some men were to whiskey, or as she was, unfortunately, to laudanum. That was a sore point and usually led to a nasty argument between them.

Even two years later, these memories stirred his anger and reopened old wounds. Caroline had visited her physician, Dr. Fulton, complaining that she was having difficulty sleeping. He prescribed her a few teaspoons of laudanum mixed in a hot cup of tea. And it had the desired effect. It soothed her nerves and relaxed her—so well that she continually increased the amount she drank. It was not habitual at once, but gradually she became dependent on it. When she tried to stop in the weeks after she felt herself with a quick child, she suffered terribly from excruciatingly painful headaches. What could she do? She again sought relief with small doses of laudanum, enough to halt her anguish. It was then that St. Clair had taken the fateful decision to end her pregnancy. Caroline could barely care for herself, he had told himself, how would she have ever taken care of an infant?

Why of all nights was he reflecting on these events, he wondered? Was it the twinge of guilt he felt for kissing another woman and enjoying it?

He re-lit the smoldering tobacco in his pipe and decided that before he retired, he required a shot of whiskey. He knew that Fox kept a bottle of Bushmills on the top of his bookshelf behind a copy of *The Collected Speeches of Lyman Beecher*. The volume, as St. Clair had been told repeatedly, was Fox's favorite piece of temperance writing.

He began to review his article when he heard the shuffling of feet and then a groan—Fox, he figured, wakening from his drunken slumber.

"Tom, did you have too much to drink for a change?" St. Clair shouted.

There was no reply. He got up and opened the door to the small office. Fox was still slumped over his desk.

"My God, what's going on here?" St. Clair said, noting what he hadn't seen before—blood near Fox's head. He advanced only two steps, when he was suddenly grabbed from behind. Someone strong had hold of both his arms. He twisted, then felt the smack of a fist on his head. It dazed him and his knees buckled.

"That, you bloody bastard, was a gift from Jack Martin. Next time, you'll pay your debts on time." The voice was deep and brusque.

"Who are you? What do you want of me?" St. Clair pleaded. He tried to stand up. But his attacker yanked him up by his neck. He squirmed to get free and managed to turn so that for a second or two he could see his assailant's brown eyes and distinctive side-whiskers.

"Who are you?" St. Clair repeated, groggy and confused.

"I'm here to teach you a lesson." He punched St. Clair again, this time directly in his face. Instantly, blood spurted from his nose. He fell forward on top of Fox's desk. His chin was momentarily propped up and his arms stretched. Out of the corner of his eye, he saw an empty whiskey bottle.

"Come here, you frigging sod, once I get through with you, you'll think twice what you write about." He tried to grab the back of St. Clair's shirt collar.

Squirming as hard as he could, St. Clair grasped the bottle, turned on his back so that he was face to face with his attacker. He smashed the bottle as hard as he could on the man's head. Glass flew across the room. The attacker stumbled backwards and St. Clair, blood now freely flowing from his nose, was able to stand erect. St. Clair never had been much of a pugilist. But some years ago, out of precaution, he had learned the art of boxing at a Bleeker Street sparring gym run by James "Yankee" Sullivan, a former boxing legend. He drew back his fist and before his attacker knew what had happened, St. Clair punched him hard in the face, sending him stumbling almost out the door of Fox's office.

"What the hell's going on here?" A shout came from someone in the outer office. "Stop or I'll shoot!" It was Edward Sutton with a cocked pistol. But before Sutton could pull the trigger, the attacker charged him, pushed him out of the way, then scurried down the stairs and out into the street.

St. Clair staggered out of Fox's office. "Sutton, you have no idea how glad I am to see you. Quick, go to Tom. I think he's hurt worse than me."

~

Tom Fox was alive, but barely. Sutton had found a cartman at a saloon down the street, still sober enough to earn a few dollars and ordered him to race north to Bellevue Hospital and send back an ambulance wagon. Within thirty minutes, two male attendants had arrived with a brandy flask, two tourniquets, small sponges, blankets, and white bandages. They used the bandages to stop the bleeding on the side of Fox's head and provided St. Clair with a sponge for his nose. Then, they loaded Fox, who remained unconscious on to their wagon using a stretcher and drove their horses back to the hospital. St. Clair and Sutton followed in the cartman's wagon.

The doctor on duty stitched St. Clair's wounds, with only a minimum of ether to kill the pain. Then he and Sutton spoke with the surgeon about Fox's injuries. He had lost a lot of blood, the doctor told them—there was nothing wrong with bleeding to rid the body of illness and disease, he added, but it had to be controlled. Fox had suffered from a bad head wound and a concussion. He needed to remain in the hospital for several days. It would be some time before St. Clair could talk to him.

"Have you any idea who did this?" asked Sutton quietly, as they sat by Fox's side in a large sterile room filled with at least a dozen other patients, nearly all of them sleeping.

St. Clair shook his head. His nose was throbbing beneath the large white bandage the doctor had affixed. "I saw his face for a moment. And believe me, I'll never forget it. But I've never seen him before tonight. If you hadn't come along..." He left the rest unsaid, then regarded Sutton with curiosity. "What were you doing at the office at this time of the night?"

"I got back from Boston on the ten o'clock train and couldn't sleep," Sutton replied. "So I thought I'd get started on a new piece for next week's issue."

"Ed, you've no idea how pleased I am that you made such a decision. I really think he would've killed me. He must've been inside Tom's office when I first arrived. I thought Tom had drunk too much."

"He'll be fine. You heard what the doctor said. Why do you think you and Tom were attacked? Was it just a random robbery?"

"It wasn't random. I owed Jack Martin some gambling money, although it's been paid. The attacker knew about the debt."

"So why also hurt Tom?"

"I think I know." St. Clair reached into his pocket and pulled out a white sheet of newsprint. "Before we left the office I found this on Tom's desk." He unfolded it. Written in Fox's own blood was one word,

SELL

"Sell?" Sutton frowned, "Someone wants him to sell the *Weekly*?"

"Not just someone," said St. Clair, carefully touching the bandage on his nose. "Fowler. It has to be him. No one else could pull such a stunt or be mad and stupid enough to come after Fox and me. Besides, Fowler knew all about my losses to Martin. In fact, I have good reason to believe he had Martin swindle me to begin with."

Sutton whistled. "Why not just make Tom an offer if he wants the magazine that badly?"

"Tom would never sell, especially to that crooked son of a bitch. Frankly, I'd like to know why Fowler is in such a hurry. I know the articles we've been publishing have hurt him. He told me so himself. But I didn't really understand how much until now. That he could send a thug after Tom and me."

"Easy, Charlie, you'll be lying in a bed next to Tom, if you're not careful."

"I'll recover and then Fowler will pay for what he's done to Tom. And what he's done to me."

"Don't go off half-cocked, Charlie. You might be wrong about Fowler. Or worse, you'll wind up face down in an alley somewhere or maybe stuffed into a trunk like that young girl I read about."

"Her name's Lucy Maloney."

"What's that?"

"Lucy Maloney, the woman in the trunk. She was murdered by Madame Philippe."

"I didn't know they identified her yet." Sutton's face registered surprise.

"They haven't. I just discovered her name this evening."

"This evening? You're not making any sense, Charlie. You certain you didn't get kicked in the head harder? What the hell does the woman in the trunk have to do with Fowler?"

"Nothing, I suppose," said St. Clair rubbing bandage on his nose, "Nothing at all."

Chapter Thirteen

---※❋※---

WHO IS LUCY MALONEY?

S t. Clair and Murray were sitting across from each other in the interrogation room at police headquarters, where Madame Philippe had been questioned the day before. Murray was smoking a hand-rolled cigarette and sipping on a mug of cold coffee, his second cup of the day and it was only eight o'clock in the morning.

"Charlie, it looks like you ran head first into a brick wall."

"It only hurts when I smile," replied St. Clair, "but I'll take one of those cigarettes." His nose remained bandaged and black and blue circles had formed around both his eyes.

"And how's Tom?" Murray asked, handing over a cigarette. "I read the police report. The doctors at Bellevue aren't certain he'll make it."

"He'll make it, trust me. Tom Fox is about the most obstinate old coot I know. When it's his time to kick the bucket, he isn't going to do it lying on a cot at Bellevue." St. Clair struck a match.

"You don't have any idea who the attacker was?"

"None. Never seen him before." St. Clair lit the cigarette and then blew a puff of smoke toward the ceiling.

He had already decided that he would keep his suspicions about Victor Fowler's possible involvement in the attack to himself for the time being. There was no point riling Murray—or Murray riling Inspector Stokes—if there was no hard evidence against Fowler. He also did not want to do anything to distract Fowler further. This was crucial.

"I stared him right in the eyes," St. Clair continued. "If I see him again I'll recognize him. Let me look through your rogues' gallery and I'll try to find him. One thing I can tell you with confidence is that he's dangerous. He would've killed me and Tom, if Sutton hadn't come along when he did."

"Yeah, I wanted to ask you about that. Don't you find it more than a little coincidental that Sutton happened to arrive at your office like a white knight?"

"You think Ed had something to do with this?" St. Clair frowned at his brother-in-law.

"I don't know. It strikes me as odd that he'd be visiting the office at that late hour. Who knows? Perhaps," Murray shrugged, "perhaps he was there to ensure that your attacker didn't kill you."

"Why on earth would Ed be mixed up in such a plan? That doesn't make any sense. He's a good man, Seth. I think it was just my luck that Sutton arrived when he did." St. Clair inhaled sharply on the cigarette.

"I'm sure you're right." Murray sipped his coffee. "Now, you said you had something else to tell me. What is it?"

St. Clair reached into his pocket. "I received a message last night unsigned with this name on it." He unfolded a piece of paper. "It's the name of the victim from the depot—"

"You mean Miss Lucy Maloney?" Murray interjected, twisting one end of his moustache.

"How do you know that? And I thought I'd proven my worth as a detective," said St. Clair.

"You're a fine journalist, Charlie, but as a detective I'm afraid you'll always be a little green," Murray chided him. "The truth is, Madame Philippe finally talked. The appointment was on August fourteenth. She says that Miss Maloney insisted on meeting her at the Broome Street office. And that she was quick with child, or at least she thinks so."

"She thinks so? What the hell does that mean? Didn't Doc Draper's examination confirm that she was with a child?"

"Yes, but listen, Charlie, here's the queer part. She claims that before she could perform the abortion, Miss Maloney changed her mind and left her office... alive. She didn't even have time to talk her out of it. Just stood up and ran out."

"Hogwash! That woman's a liar."

"That's her version of what happened and her Negro servant told Westwood the same story."

"He would, wouldn't he?"

"I suppose so."

"Don't tell me you believe this rubbish?"

Murray pulled his gold watch from his vest and checked the time. "At this moment, Madame Philippe is having breakfast at the Tombs with all of the other female inmates."

"You've charged her with the murder?"

"Stokes got direct instructions from the district attorney, Richard Cady himself. He told me to go ahead, so that's what I've done." Murray flung his cigarette on to the floor close to the heel of his boot. "To be honest, I thought Cady might charge her with causing death through medical malpractice, as he's done with other abortionists in similar circumstances. Stokes, however, says Cady insisted that it be murder in the first degree and not manslaughter. Philippe's supposed to be brought before Recorder Beatty later today or early tomorrow and it's my impression that they want to deal with this quickly. But there's something else, Charlie."

"I'm all ears."

"She made only one personal request of me. She wants to speak with you as soon as possible." Murray shrugged his shoulders.

"With me? What the hell for?" St. Clair threw up his hands. "Why in God's name would that woman request to see me?"

"I've no idea. Didn't you mention to me that you wanted to interview her about her life for your story? So here's your chance. You should be thanking me."

St. Clair mulled over the idea. Of course, Murray was right. He would be a fool to turn down such an invitation. And he had wanted to speak with her for the next installment of "Evil of the Age." The attack last night had not changed his plans, although Murray's description of Lucy Maloney's murder appalled him. Still, whatever anger he felt towards Madame Philippe for her involvement in Miss Maloney's death, he knew that as a seasoned journalist he would have to put it aside.

"Do me a favor, Seth," said St. Clair, taking a last deep drag on his cigarette. "Let whoever has to know that I'll be visiting the Tombs in the next couple of days." St. Clair threw the cigarette on the floor and crushed it with the heel of his boot. "Now, what about Miss Maloney? What do you know about her?"

"Not much. Only that she lived in the Fifth Avenue Hotel."

"The Fifth Avenue? The woman had style and money."

"Or, she had a rich benefactor."

"You think Miss Maloney was being kept?"

"I've no idea. A hunch that's all. I was planning to go by the hotel this morning."

St. Clair's ears perked up. "Mind if I join you?"

"I was wondering when you'd ask. It's not quite up to regulations. You know that?"

"And since when did you follow all of the rules? Besides, I might be able to find out a few things for you."

"Such as?"

"Who the father of her baby was, for one," St. Clair replied. "And, why he didn't accompany her to Madame Philippe's? The people who work at the hotel will likely talk to me a lot quicker than you."

"I'll grant you that." Murray smirked, then added provocatively, "Isn't Miss Cardaso a guest at the Fifth Avenue?"

St. Clair ignored the question. "Seth, I need some coffee. How about a visit to Tiny Jim's across the street before the day begins in earnest?"

"I got a lot of paper work, Charlie, and don't you have to visit Tom?"

"I can't do much for Tom right now. He's in good hands. Tell you what, I'll pay. I'll bet Jim is cooking his flapjacks."

"How can I refuse the invitation of a man who got walloped last night?" Murray rose from his chair. "I have only one condition."

"What's that?"

"You tell me all about that lovely Miss Cardaso." Murray grinned, as they crossed the room.

St. Clair laughed. "As a matter of fact, you won't believe what happened on the way back to the Fifth Avenue last night, before I ended up looking like I was run over by a horse and wagon."

But Murray's mind seemed to have shifted elsewhere. "Charlie, in all the commotion, I forgot to ask if you'd heard about Frank King?"

"What about him?"

"He'd dead, that's what. Some sort of racing accident up at Harlem Lane. He worked for Fowler, didn't he? His bookkeeper, I think."

"That's right."

"That's all you've got to say about it?"

St. Clair affected a shrug. "Nothing much to say. The man was a fool to be racing and he got killed for it. The Ring's got one less grafter on its payroll. Are the police investigating?"

"I think Stokes sent a few men to find out what happened. I haven't heard anything yet. Why, are you curious?"

"No, not at all. I didn't know King very well."

St. Clair hated lying to Murray, but this was not the time or place to tell him about his relationship with King.

"I guess he took all of his secrets to his grave," said Murray, as they crossed the street.

"Yeah," mumbled St. Clair, "I guess he did."

～

By eleven in the morning, the temperature had reached ninety degrees of mercury and was rising fast. With St. Clair riding beside him in the police carriage, Murray turned his two black horses up Broadway, past Washington Square Park, and then on to Fifth Avenue. He let the horses go at their own pace, not wanting to push them any harder than he had to in the heat. Every once in a while, he stopped to water them at buckets set out by friendly merchants.

"Can you smell the stink, Charlie?" asked Murray, as the horses trotted by Union Square.

"Yeah, even through these bandages. It's going to be a long day." St. Clair cast his eyes over the street. "Someday, Fowler might really want to clean up the garbage and the manure."

"A fact of life, I'm afraid," Murray grimaced. "In this damn heat, I worry more about the young children. I'd wager that by the end of the day there'll be a dead kid somewhere in Five Points or the East Side. Happens every time it gets this hot. Those tenements are like a wood stove."

Murray reached Twenty-Third Street and stopped the carriage at the Fifth Avenue Hotel's main door. Three doormen, all Negroes, came running to greet him and St. Clair.

"It's the word *Police* on the side of the wagon," Murray remarked. "I always receive the best of service."

"Bad for business, I'd guess," said St. Clair climbing down. "This carriage'll scare guests away faster than a gunshot."

"Sir, would you mind it very much if I pulled your rig around to the delivery entrance?" asked George, the hotel's doorman.

"What did I just say?" laughed St. Clair.

Murray waved his hand. "That would be fine."

"Thank you, sir," said George, maintaining his mask of deference.

Murray and St. Clair weren't in the hotel's grand lobby a moment when they were set upon by the manager, Samuel Buckland, in a well-cut, beautifully tailored black suit.

"I'm Detective Seth Murray, this is Charles St. Clair of *Fox's Weekly*. Ignore the bandages . . . the other guy looks worse." He shook Buckland's hand. It was soft and delicate, like a woman's.

~

"Gentlemen, please come this way," Buckland ushered them toward his private office. "Now what can I do for you?"

"I have some questions about one of your guests," said Murray, "Miss Lucy Maloney."

"I am not in the habit of speaking to the police about . . ."

Murray cut him off. "She's dead. Her body was found in a trunk at Hudson Depot."

Buckland's face turned white. "I read about that horrific crime. That was Miss Maloney?" He shuddered.

"It was," said Murray, growing impatient.

"Of course, I will assist you in any way I can, but we must be discreet. There's no need to upset the other guests and residents," he added nervously, wiping his brow. He looked askance at St. Clair. "Is it wise for the press to be investigating this unfortunate incident alongside the police?"

"And why not?" snapped St. Clair.

"Why not indeed, Mr. St. Clair? I've found that my guests require the utmost discretion and consideration... about the last sentiments I would expect from a man of your vocation."

"Discretion, in my view, Mr. Buckland, is highly overrated. But I promise you, whatever I discover here today, I will exercise good judgment."

"I do hope so, Mr. St. Clair. I truly do hope so." He studied St. Clair's face for a moment. "Tell me, did I not see you in the dining room with one of our lady guests the other morning? It was with Miss Cardaso, I believe."

"That was me, yes. Why do you ask?"

"I was told the two of you had a noisy disagreement and you stormed out of the hotel."

"I don't think I stormed out. However, if I did anything to offend the other guests, please forgive me." He bowed his head slightly. "Also, you'll be happy to know that the matter with Miss Cardaso has been settled."

"I'd like to see Miss Maloney's room," Murray interrupted.

"Of course, right this way, gentlemen. We can use the stairs or the elevator. Her suite is on the fourth floor."

"Stairs will be fine," said Murray, before St. Clair could respond. "Never had much faith in these contraptions."

"They're the future, Detective. Only one way to go in this city and that's up." Buckland, pointed skyward with one of his lean, long fingers. "Buildings will be high in the clouds in no time. At least that's my view. The property in this city's too expensive. There's no room for expansion other than up."

"I tend to agree with you," said St. Clair. "Still, any building more than four or five stories is high enough for me."

"It's going higher than that, Mr. St. Clair, I assure you."

The trio reached the fourth floor and narrowly missed bumping into Ruth Cardaso.

"Terribly sorry, Miss," said Buckland.

"Bless my soul, Mr. St. Clair, what's happened to you?" she exclaimed.

"He was hit by a runaway wagon," snorted Murray.

"A runaway wagon?"

"Don't listen to a word he says." St. Clair gave his brother-in-law a dismissive glance. "There was an altercation last evening after I bid you farewell."

Ruth's blushed. "An altercation? Please tell me more."

Buckland excused himself for a moment as St. Clair quickly related the story of the attack on him and Fox, the arrival of Sutton, and his close encounter with death. As much as his nose and other injuries pained him, he took a great deal of satisfaction in recounting the tale, with some embellishments, and enjoyed the look of distress that crossed Ruth's face.

"And Mr. Fox, will he recover?" asked Ruth.

"I'm no physician, but I'm certain he will. I was planning on visiting him at the hospital later this morning or early in the afternoon."

"Please do give him my best regards."

"I shall. And where are you off to at this hour?"

"I was on my way to an appointment and then to the magazine to speak with Mr. Fox. Since Madame Philippe has been arrested, I assume our ruse has been well publicized.

～

Only the most foolish of abortionists will speak to us now. So, I was going to tell Mr. Fox—" She stopped herself and deliberately averted her eyes from St. Clair. "I was going to tell Mr. Fox that I was leaving the city in a day or two."

"Leaving the city?" exclaimed St. Clair. He wanted to say so much to her, although this was not the time or place. After last night, he had assumed that they would draw closer together. His astonishment quickly turned to irritation.

She could not look him in the eyes. "You will excuse me, gentlemen. I'm late for my appointment." With that she scurried down the stairs.

"Do you want to go after her, Charlie?" Murray raised an eyebrow.

In fact, he did. He had convinced himself that Ruth Cardaso was his future. It mattered little that he knew almost nothing about her or that they had spent only a few hours together.

"No, let's continue with the search," he responded, as Buckland returned. He followed Murray and the manager down the wide carpeted hallway. His head swirled with a hundred questions— Why was Ruth leaving? Why now? Did their encounter last evening mean nothing?

"Here it is. Suite Forty-Two. Miss Maloney lived here for about seven months," said Buckland pulling a key from his pocket.

"From what I understand, residing in your hotel for such a length of time would be steep."

"It all depends on your point of view, Detective. Or, rather, on who you are."

"And who was Miss Maloney?"

"Miss Maloney was a respectable guest whose credit was impeccable." Buckland fitted the key into the lock.

"I'd figure a monthly charge here would be about one hundred dollars or so? Is that right?"

"Something of that sort, yes."

"And did Miss Maloney pay for this herself? I know she was not employed—"

"That's a matter of privacy, Detective," Buckland interrupted sharply. "How long could a hotel remain in business, if it revealed its guests most personal affairs? All I can say, again," he added turning the lock, "is that Miss Maloney's bills were always paid in a timely fashion."

"Yes, but by whom?" St. Clair asked. "That's the question, Mr. Buckland. Who was the father of Miss Maloney's child?"

Buckland's face immediately flushed. "That, most of all, is absolutely none of my concern. Or, yours, I would venture to say."

"Just open the door, Mr. Buckland." Murray commanded.

The hotel manager did as he was ordered and Murray pushed past him.

"My Lord, what's happened here?" Buckland stared over Murray's shoulder.

The suite had been turned upside down. Every shelf had been emptied, every pillow cut open, and every piece of furniture thrown about.

"I must call a housekeeper immediately." Buckland turned back into the hallway. "Please excuse me for a moment, gentlemen."

"I'd say that someone had the same idea as we did," said St. Clair, picking up a chair that had been turned on its side. "Whatever was here to be found is surely gone."

"Maybe, maybe not." Murray narrowed his eyes. "In all my years as a cop, you'd be astonished at how careless some thieves and hustlers are. Look around you, Charlie. What do you see?"

"A hotel suite that's been smashed and rummaged through."

"Exactly. And how would you judge the actions and behavior of the perpetrator of this crime?"

St. Clair contemplated Murray's question for a moment. "Desperate, no, not desperate. Frantic, I'd say."

Murray nodded. "Charlie, I'll make a detective out of you yet. Whoever did this likely did not find what they were looking for. Somewhere in this room or in the hotel is an item, a gift or perhaps a letter or a diary, that will reveal Miss Maloney's secrets to us."

"So let's begin."

"We could do that, despite the amount of time it'll take. Or..." Murray paused.

"Or what?"

"I can't force Buckland to let me see his books without an order from the court and who knows whether or not that would tell us anything under any circumstances. If, as we both suspect, someone other than Miss Maloney was paying for this suite, then I'd guess the gentleman in question likely took necessary precautions to protect his good name. There's someone else we could speak with, however. Someone who knows every bit of gossip in this hotel...which husbands are cheating on their wives and vice-versa, which businessmen and merchants are crooked, and who's got money."

"One of the doormen?"

"Yeah, but I was thinking of that doorman who showed us in. I'd wager he knows a lot. He just needs a little encouragement." Murray sneered.

"Don't hurt him, Seth."

"Show a little more pluck, Charlie. I won't hurt him, you know me better than that," said Murray. "I'm not like Stokes, for Christ's sakes. But I might scare him out of his black skin a little. Do you want to know more about Miss Maloney or not?"

St. Clair did not answer. At that moment, he was not sure what he wanted.

~

Across the city at the Hudson Depot, a tall man in a black suit and bowler hat paced back and forth, awaiting the arrival of a cart and carriage. About fifteen minutes later, the cart, hauled by a lone dirty white horse stopped at the side of the platform. There was a pine wood casket on its flat bed. Right behind it was a carriage pulled by two brown geldings. Its only passenger was Amanda King. Despite the heat, she was dressed in an ankle length, long-sleeved black linen dress and wore a bonnet with a lace veil. The veil, however, could not hide her puffy red eyes.

"Papa, I'm so glad you're here," said Amanda to the tall man in the bowler hat. "I don't know what I would've done." Simon Struthers, a general store merchant from Albany, put his arm around his daughter.

"The train is ready to go, we just have to load the casket onto the back car," said Struthers. "You sure you want to bury Frank in Albany?"

"That's where you live and that's where I'll be living now. I want Frank close by."

By this time, four more burly men had arrived on another wagon. "Mrs. King," the driver said, tipping his hat.

"Pete, thank you for coming. Papa, these men worked for Frank. They'll help us."

The men grabbed hold of the casket and with considerable ease heaved it up on to their shoulders. They then climbed up on to the platform and placed the coffin carefully inside the railcar.

"Come, Amanda, we'll find our seats."

She was crying again, as was right and proper in the circumstances. She followed her father, and as she stepped into the passenger car, she turned her head ever so slightly. She caught a glimpse of a man behind a shed on the other side of the platform. He nodded to her and she felt both more at ease, and exhilarated. As she sat down beside her father, she knew that Frank was proud of her.

Chapter Fourteen

An Oversight or a Lie?

Victor Fowler could not sleep. That was unusual. On most days, the myriad of issues that he was dealing with rarely troubled him enough to keep him awake. This was especially true after he had had an assignation with Amelia or any of the other dozen young and striking women he regularly called on. They were whores, one and all, but that hardly troubled him. Indeed, he regarded this harem as the ultimate prize of his status and wealth—something that he could not only enjoy, but also something that he was entitled to.

Last evening, he had arrived home late from his dinner meeting at Delmonico's, only to discover Ellen passed out on the sofa in the parlor. A nearly empty bottle of laudanum was, not surprisingly, close at hand. He had had Jackson carry her to a guest bedroom. When she was in such a semi-conscious state—which, admittedly, was far too often of late—he could barely tolerate to be in the same room as her.

She was a liability, both personally and professionally. He knew that. How could she possibly move with him to Washington? How could she possibly act as his hostess for senators, congressmen, and judges? Months ago, he honestly believed that she would conquer her addiction, but recent events had led him to the opposite conclusion. Each day that he drew closer to the fulfillment of political ambitions, he drew closer to one inescapable solution. It was too terrible to even contemplate. And thus, once he had retired to his bed, he had tossed and turned unable to escape into sleep.

He checked his watch. It was just after four o'clock. He lit a cigar, poured himself a snifter of brandy, and settled down in his study with a book. Since he could remember, there were only two books that interested him and he reread them often. His sense of adventure and his insatiable craving for more wealth were momentarily satisfied by Alexandre Dumas's *The Count of Monte Cristo*, which he had acquired some years ago. Who could not be impressed by the daring cunning of Edmond Dantés, he thought.

Yet on this night, Fowler chose the other literary work that made an impression on him, *The Prince* by Nicolo Machiavelli. Ellen had given it to him as a gift on their fifth anniversary. He opened the book to Chapter Seventeen, as he always did, and skimmed the by-now familiar passage etched into his mind:

"Upon this a question arises: whether it be better to be loved than feared or feared than loved? It may be answered that one should wish to be both, but, because it is difficult to unite them in one person, it is much safer to be feared than loved, when, of the two, either must be dispensed with. Because this is to be asserted in general of men, that they are ungrateful, fickle, false, cowardly, covetous, and as long as you succeed, they are yours entirely; they will offer you their blood, property, life and children, as is said above, when the need is far distant; but when it approaches they turn against you. And that prince who, relying entirely on their promises, has neglected other precautions, is ruined; because friendships that are obtained by payments, and not by greatness or nobility of mind, may indeed be earned, but they are not secured, and in time of need cannot be relied upon; and men have less scruple in offending one who is beloved than one who is feared, for love is preserved by the link of obligation which, owing to the baseness of men, is broken at every opportunity for their advantage; but fear preserves you by a dread of punishment which never fails."

Had truer words ever been written, Fowler asked himself? He understood that any so-called love he felt from the rabble on the waterfront, the lowly and middling patrons of Harry Hill's, and the would-be aristocrats of the Union Club was merely a reflection of the fear he engendered. That, in his opinion, was acceptable—provided, of course, he never mistook the adulation for sincere affection. Look at the Ring itself. He was surrounded by competent and shrewd men—true Machiavellians—yet he trusted none of them, not even Harrison. He had dangled both riches and power in front of them and so their loyalty was guaranteed. But he knew that each one, given the right opportunity and incentive, could in the end betray him.

~

"Sir, there's a message for you." It was Jackson, holding a piece of paper in one hand and a silver tray in the other. Fowler had finally nodded off in his study with *The Prince* opened and resting on top of his chest.

"What time is it?" asked Fowler, still groggy.

"Half past seven, sir. I have coffee for you, bread and cheese, and the morning newspaper."

Fowler sipped the hot cup of coffee, thankful for its almost instantaneous arousing affect. He ripped two pieces of bread, placed a small hunk of white cheese between them, and gobbled it. Then, he placed the newspaper aside and reached for the message. The seal, a small dagger was immediately recognizable. The letter was from Flint.

"Sir, the job has been completed. The Wolf, however is in Bellevue. From what I understand his injuries will not kill him. The Scribe survives as well—my lesson with him was interrupted by an unknown. I do not believe I was seen. I will assume the balance of the money will be sent to me by the end of the day at the usual location. F.

Damn, Fowler mumbled, why could Flint not display more self-discipline? He had not wanted Fox in the hospital with serious injuries. He had wanted him merely frightened. For a man governed by fear is easily persuaded to do that which in calmer moments he would not. It was a truism that Fowler had often employed. Now he would have to pay Fox a visit at Bellevue.

As for St. Clair, he appeared to have escaped the beating that was owed to him. In time, Fowler thought as he lit a cigar and then finished his coffee, all in good time.

～

"Jackson, please bring some coffee." Ellen Fowler was wearing an apricot silk robe with white and pink flounces.

Staring at her, Fowler had to concede that she was a vision of loveliness. This was the young and beautiful woman, who had once stolen his heart. As she moved closer to him, he observed her eyes. They were bloodshot and glassy, revealing her weakness. He turned his head away.

She waited patiently until the servant brought her black coffee, which she sipped rapidly. For several minutes, neither of them said a word to each other.

"I do forgive you, Victor," she finally said softly.

"You forgive me? And what have I done now, except discover you lying on the parlor sofa, unable to move, like a drunken beggar."

"I've made a pledge this morning to stop." Her eyes gazed down at the floor.

"I've heard that before." Fowler turned away.

"No, this time I mean it. I've been speaking for more than a week now, each day with Reverend Ingersoll."

"With Patrick Ingersoll? What possible advice could that charlatan give you?"

"He's no charlatan, Victor. I find his words rather comforting. He's told me that I must accept the past and learn from it. And he's directed me to forgive those who have sinned, including you."

"So how do you explain last evening? Why didn't the great reverend help you then?"

"I don't know," she said tearfully. "I truly don't know."

"You speak to Ingersoll all you want, my dear, for all the good it'll do you. I guarantee sooner or later, this morning, sometime this afternoon, you'll feel the burning craving within you and I promise you'll succumb to its temptation." He glanced down at the newspaper Jackson had brought him.

Tears streamed down Ellen's face. "You're as cruel and ruthless as the papers portray you, Victor. Do you think I like to suffer so? Whatever you think, I will stop my evil habits. But I won't stand here and be humiliated. Go to your whores, go to them." She threw her coffee on the floor and ran from the room.

Fowler crushed his cigar in a metal bowl. He felt terribly sad. It was not merely that Ellen was such a pathetic figure—it was that he felt so little sympathy for her plight. Let her go to Ingersoll, he thought. She'll discover in due course what a hypocrite he was.

In the course of his travels, he had visited the Plymouth Congregationalist Church in Brooklyn and had heard Reverend Patrick Simpson Ingersoll on more than one occasion.

If a man be poor, then, it be his fault or his sin. There is enough and to spare thrice over; and if men have not enough of it, it is owing to the want of provident care, and foresight, and industry and frugality and wise saving. This is the general truth.

Fowler had chuckled to himself at the time. He knew that the good reverend suffered from two vices he habitually railed against—greed and a penchant for young girls. Like most men Fowler dealt with, the reverend had an appetite for money that could never be satisfied—despite earning $20,000 a year from his lectures and books, more than President Grant earned.

As for the young girls, Ingersoll had been seen more than once by Fowler's men at a lowly whorehouse on Water Street, close to one of the various missions he had established for work among the less privileged. Fifteen-year-old girls with their painted faces were his favorite request, according to the reports Fowler had received. Fowler wondered if Mrs. Ingersoll and their children were aware of the reverend's enjoyments. More importantly, what would Ingersoll do to prevent such information from being publicized?

Of immediate concern to Fowler was the arrest of Madame Philippe, a propitious event to be exploited. Fowler wanted her convicted and dealt with. In his view, nothing better diverted the city's masses, rich and poor, than a sensational murder trial. And if he could persuade Reverend Ingersoll to steal a moment away from his mission to rescue Ellen, the preacher might be extremely useful to him in stirring up a desirable distraction.

~

"He's done nothing wrong. He knows nothing about Miss Maloney's death." Buckland, the Fifth Avenue Hotel's manager, addressed Seth Murray with exasperation.

But Murray was not listening.

"In the wagon," he ordered.

George obeyed and climbed in.

St. Clair joined them in the police carriage. He glanced at the doorman, trying to determine his frame of mind. It was impossible. If the Negro was apprehensive or frightened about what lay ahead, he did not show it. He remained stoic and silent during the brief journey.

Upon arriving at the Mulberry Street station, Murray decided to lock up George before questioning him. St. Clair thought it unfair, yet it was not his place to question his brother-in-law's police tactics. So he kept quiet. He also noted that no one else at the station concerned themselves with the treatment allocated to George.

St. Clair spent the next hour looking through the pages of the police department's rogues' gallery, a collection of the most crooked and meanest criminals there were in the country. It was a futile exercise. There was no photograph of the man who had attacked Fox and him.

He was nearly finished when a young messenger arrived with a note for him. It was from Edward Sutton.

Tom is not doing well. Doctor suggests you arrive here immediately.

Less than thirty minutes later, St. Clair was at the hospital, fearing the worst.

~

As soon as he walked through the doors of Bellevue, the overpowering odor of chlorine filled his nostrils, triggering terrible memories.

"Dear, sweet, beautiful Caroline," he mumbled to himself as he trudged up the stairs, weak and unable to talk, dying before him and he helpless to prevent it. He remembered her doctor standing by consoling him, informing him that there were no magical medicines or miracle surgery that could save her.

He broke from this reverie of grief only when he realized his mumbling was loud enough to scare a young girl walking beside her distraught mother. He shook his head to clear his mind. Now was not the time to be feeling sorry for himself.

Fox was in a ward on the second floor. When St. Clair tried to enter the room, a group of four young nurses blocked the entrance.

"I'm sorry, sir, only family members are permitted in here," one with large round eyes and a pretty face said. Like the other three, she was wearing a long white apron, which covered her dress, and a diminutive round white pleated cap.

"I was summoned here." St. Clair responded. "I must see Mr. Tom Fox at once."

"Are you a member of his immediate family?" the nurse inquired sternly.

At the best of times, St. Clair had no patience for those individuals whom he sarcastically referred to as the canon sheep—omnibus drivers, nurses, clerks, bank tellers, and hotel bell men who blindly enforced rules and regulations without common sense or discretion. They were the obedient—ready, and willing to do all that was ordered of them and more.

St. Clair was about to argue with the young woman when he heard that distinctive booming voice. "Nurse, let him through. He's the only family I got."

It was Fox, alive and well and irascible as ever.

"Tom, I thought..." St. Clair stammered, "I received a message...."

"Some amusement at your expense, Charlie. My deepest apologies." Fox laughed. "I had Sutton send that message to you. I've made, as you can see, a marvelous recovery...despite my doctor's best intentions to bleed me dry. You, on the other hand, look about as awful as anyone I've seen around here."

The nurse reluctantly allowed St. Clair to enter the room. There were six beds on one side and six on the other, but only seven of them held patients in them. Most of the men were sleeping. A nurse with wide buttocks and a thick neck was attending to one patient, whose head was wrapped in white bandages. Another patient had a visitor, a petite elderly woman.

The floor was remarkably clean and spotless, a rarity in a city of dust and grime. Beside Fox's bed was a small table with the various tools required for a surgical bleeding—a sharp two-edged lancet, a piece of linen, two square bolsters, a medium-sized metal bowl, a jar of vinegar and water, and a sponge.

"Tom, you're a ruthless bugger, but I'm so glad that you're going to survive. I was truly worried that I'd have to bring out this week's magazine by myself."

Fox laughed louder. "I'd never have permitted that. From what I understand, Dr. Richardson was about to bleed me yet again. Look where that quack cut me on my temple. I opened my eyes, told him to keep away from me, and ordered him to bring me a glass of whiskey. If I could, I'd leave now before they took another pint from me. Take a look at that poor sod." He motioned to the man directly opposite him. "They bled him yesterday and he hasn't moved since. I've told them what I need, but no one listens to me. Give me some Ayer's Pills and I'll be on my way."

"You should be hawking that poison, Tom." St. Clair sat down on a white stool close to the bed. "What do you remember?"

"Not a hell of a lot. I was at my desk looking at the *Times* and reading about Frank King's death. Some carriage accident, I think. Didn't you know him?"

"Yeah, I knew him. It was a real tragedy," St. Clair shifted in the stool.

"I'd poured myself a few drinks and must have nodded off," Fox continued, the smile wiped from his face.

"I'd say. You were snoring by the time I'd arrived and there was at least one empty bottle on your desk."

"It was half-empty when I started drinking. Honestly, Charlie, the next thing I know is that I awoke in the hospital with a doctor standing over me with that." He pointed to the lancet. "Sutton's told me some of the story. Tell me your version."

"I figure that at some point, either before I got there or shortly after, you woke up and someone tried to kill you."

"The same thug who did that to you?" Fox motioned at his bruised face.

"Yes. If not for Sutton, I might not be standing here. I got a good look at the thug, but I've had no luck finding his face in Seth Murray's mug books. This had to be Fowler's doing, don't you think? I mean this wasn't just any crook. He didn't steal anything. He was there to deliver a message." St. Clair lowered his voice, "A message from Fowler, I'd bet."

"That I should sell the *Weekly*," Fox finished the thought. "Sutton mentioned that. I don't remember any of it, Charlie. I don't know if he threatened me or not. But I've been thinking about it and I agree with you. Who else but Fowler would be desperate enough to send someone after us? If he thinks for a minute that I'd sell him my business—"

"The question is," St. Clair interjected, "how can we prove it?"

"Have no fear about Fowler. One thing I've learned about our adversary is that he's an impatient man and sooner or later he'll reveal his true intentions."

"I hope you're right. Did Sutton also tell you about Madame Philippe?"

"No. What's happened?"

"She's been charged with the murder of that young woman found in the trunk at Hudson Depot. Her name is Lucy Maloney, although I don't know a lot about her yet. Miss Cardaso and I were present for all of it...the investigation, interrogation, and arrest. I've written something already for next week's issue and I'll follow that with a story on Madame Philippe herself."

"I thought you detested that woman?"

"I do, but I also know a good story when I'm in the middle of it. What kind of reporter would I be if I quit now?"

"You're a decent man, Charlie."

"I can't take all the credit." St. Clair shifted in the chair. "In fact, it was Ruth, Miss Cardaso, who led them in the right direction. She'd studied the magazine's files on Madame Philippe and recalled reading about the office on Broome Street. That's where this Miss Maloney was supposedly butchered and killed. Madame Philippe, of course, is denying the whole thing with a yarn that Miss Maloney didn't have an abortion. She's claiming that this woman left her place before receiving any medical treatment. And she says she has absolutely no idea how Miss Maloney ended up in the trunk. However, I think the police have enough evidence to convict her."

"I see," Fox mused, twisting the thick grey hairs on his bearded chin.

St. Clair studied his friend's expression. "Out with it, Tom, what's troubling you? I've seen that look of yours before."

Fox stared into St. Clair's eyes. "At least three weeks ago I took home the files on Madame Philippe. They're sitting collecting dust on my bureau in my bedroom. I'd intended to return them because I knew you'd want to see them. So—"

"So Miss Cardaso could never have read them?"

"I don't think so. Perhaps she'd read about the Broome Street office somewhere else."

St. Clair's forehead wrinkled in consternation. "Maybe. Or, maybe she lied about it? She's leaving the city. She says that with our assignment finished, her work has been completed. She didn't give me an opportunity to argue."

"When did this come about?"

"I learned of it only today. I met her quite by accident at the Fifth Avenue Hotel when I was with Murray. This Miss Maloney resided at the hotel as well."

"That's most interesting." Fox stroked his beard harder.

"Why?" asked St. Clair. "What's going on, Tom?"

"I only agreed to pay for Miss Cardaso's accommodations there because she absolutely insisted. I had initially reserved a room for her at the Metropolitan, closer to the office and far less expensive. But she was adamant. I suppose it might be a coincidence and we're allowing our imaginations to get the better of us."

St. Clair nodded. Yet, he hardly knew what to believe any more. Had Ruth only thought she had read about Madame Philippe's office on Broome Street in Fox's files? Or had she deliberately wanted to lead the police there? Ruth had said she was not acquainted with Miss Maloney, but had been firm that she should lodge at the same hotel.

Now a hundred thoughts invaded St. Clair's head. Who exactly was Ruth Cardaso? What was she doing in New York City and why was she now in such a rush to leave? Why was she so determined to ensure that

Madame Philippe was arrested for murder? And, most importantly, what did she know, if anything, about the killing of Lucy Maloney?

St. Clair suddenly felt queasy. The pain in his gut was sharp and piercing. For the first time, he started having doubts.

Doubts that he would ever see Ruth Cardaso again.

Doubts about Madame Philippe's culpability and guilt.

Like many citizens in New York, he wanted Madame Philippe punished for the misery and shame she had inflicted on countless numbers of women. But his sense of justice was equally strong. And he could not stand idly by and watch an innocent person hang or rot in jail for the rest of her life for a crime she had not committed.

Not even an abortionist deserved that fate.

Chapter Fifteen

---※◆※---

MR. FOWLER PAYS A VISIT

The enemy was Satan. Of that, there was no doubt in Reverend Patrick Simpson Ingersoll's mind. Who else, he repeatedly asked himself, was to blame for the incessant sinning in his midst? At the brothels, gin-mills, gambling dens, and concert saloons evil was everywhere. Who else, moreover, was to blame for his own immoral transgressions?

Yet he had surrendered to temptation again—only this morning. He returned to the church and prayed for five hours. It was, he believed, his personal repentance for his numerous failings. With his hands clutched to the cross, he swore that this was the final time—that at long last, this uncontrollable urge was exorcised from his mind and body. He declared that his soul was now cleansed and pure. He thought of his wife, Rose, and their two children. And he gave thanks for everything the Lord had bestowed upon him.

From his pulpit in Plymouth Church, holding a letter tightly in his sweaty fingers, he surveyed his sanctuary. Hundreds of empty pews encircled him. There was room each Sunday for more than a thousand people and still he could not accommodate everyone. How proud he was that the Fulton Street Ferry was now dubbed "Ingersoll's Ferry" since each week it brought hundreds of devoted congregants across the river from Manhattan.

He dropped the letter and picked a sheaf of paper from the pulpit and began rehearsing for his Sunday's sermon. He cleared his throat and let his booming voice echo throughout the church, though there were none to hear it.

"From infancy to maturity the pathway of the child is beset with peculiar temptations to do evil. Youth has to contend against great odds. Inherited tendencies to wrongdoing render the young oftentimes open to ever-present seductions. Inherited appetites and passions are secretly fed by artificial means, until they exert a well-nigh irresistible mastery over their victim. The weeds of sin, thus planted in weak human nature, are forced to rapid growth, choking virtue and truth, and stunting all the higher and holier instincts."

Had he ever voiced truer words, he wondered? And yet, this morning, while he was visiting the church mission on Water Street, the disease had returned with a vengeance. He could not explain it. The irrepressible yearning had taken hold of him and once more he found himself standing at Satan's doorstep.

Miss Beatrice was a lovely and interesting young creature. She was red-haired with a slender figure and graceful form. Her eyes were blue and dreamy and her hands were small, but able to perform feats of magic on him. Her voice was pleasing to his ears. She was also young enough to be his daughter—a fact that strangely excited and stirred him. The first time he saw her, more than six months ago, when by chance she had stopped by the mission, he knew then and there that she would consume his spirit and break his will.

He had been reckless and he realized that it would be only a matter of time before someone discovered his sordid conduct. Still, glancing at the letter, which had awaited him on his arrival, he was astonished that the person attempting to blackmail him was Victor Fowler. Until then, Fowler had been a supportive acquaintance. He had visited the church on numerous occasions and had generously donated money to many of the charities Ingersoll regularly supported. It did not trouble the reverend that Fowler had defended the rights of the abortionists—even so far as paying their legal fees—because he had also used his money to feed the poor and heal the sick. And only a fool, Ingersoll excepted, would refuse such benevolence.

Ingersoll stepped down from the pulpit and moved to a pew near the back of the sanctuary. He stroked his thick mutton chop whiskers and contemplated his options. Regardless of Fowler's motives, which were not clear to him, he had no doubt that the Boss would deliver on his promise to reveal his darkest secrets if he did not do as he was ordered. Apart from his wounded pride, what was to be lost from complying? Each time he pondered this question, he arrived at the same answer— Nothing.

He was curious as to why Fowler had unexpectedly abandoned Madame Philippe. However, he was pleased by this surprising turn of events. Whatever retribution lay ahead for Madame Philippe, she most assuredly had brought on herself by her iniquitous actions. Indeed, if anyone was meant to suffer for her sins, Reverend Ingersoll concluded, it was that wicked woman.

～

Tom Fox had been deep in sleep when his mind sensed a disturbing presence. His eyes opened and he was startled to find Victor Fowler's hulking frame hovering over him.

"Fox, I was giving up all hope we'd speak. I thought you might be dead." Fowler half-smiled through his moustache and beard.

"Not yet, I fear. But I assume you wouldn't know anything about it?" Fox deliberately laced his tone with sarcasm.

"Why would I?" Fowler responded with all innocence. "I'm as anxious as the next man about the crime in this city. You know, as well as anyone, that I've done everything in my power to make New York's streets safe for respectable citizens. But thieves and pickpockets are like rats. As soon as you eradicate one bunch, another takes its place."

"Somewhat like city hall politicians."

"You look a little pale. Would you like me to fetch the nurse?" asked Fowler, as Fox sat up in bed and regarded his visitor with growing disdain.

"You've always been far too much of a blatherskite, Fowler. What the hell do you want from me? What are you doing here? Why do you want to buy my journal?"

"Mr. Fox, you're disturbing our other patients," a nurse barked from across the room.

"My deepest apologies, Nurse."

"By the way, Fox," Fowler continued, "have I ever told you that those dreadful caricatures by Peter Stewart are highly amusing? I'd never tell Harrison, of course, he's much too serious. A good man, but he's not one for amusement. Not like you, I'd wager."

"What happened, Fowler? You're angry at me so you dispatch one of your hooligans to beat me and St. Clair? And now you think I'm so frightened that I'll sell my business to you?" Fox's voice began to rise again.

Fowler ignored the outburst. "How's our friend Charles?"

"He's on the mend, but he'll be fine, no thanks to you, I'm certain. He was nearly killed. If not for—"

"What do I have to do to convince you that I had nothing to do with it?"

"Stand up and leave me alone would be a start."

"Your new issue is out today, is that right? With St. Clair's story about the old armory and some unfounded allegations about money I'm alleged to have absconded with?"

"I hope you enjoy it." Fox smiled.

"In fact, Fox, I admire your magazine and your work. I hope you appreciate the enormous power that you hold in your hands. Or is it St. Clair's pen? However, that publication of yours has caused me no end of aggravation. I wonder if the Founding Fathers truly understood the various ramifications of freedom of the press when they included it in the Constitution."

"I have to say, Fowler, I never considered you much of a historian or a philosopher."

"I'm your servant, sir," said Fowler with a mocking bow.

"You do surprise me and I'm rarely surprised any more. You ever read Macaulay? "

"His works are, of course, on my book shelves. But no, not recently."

"Let me see, how does it go? 'Many politicians of our time are in the habit of laying it down as a self-evident proposition that no people ought to be free till they are fit to use their freedom.'"

"I wholeheartedly agree," Fowler said.

"Yes, I'm sure you do. There's more, however. Macaulay also writes that such a 'maxim is worthy of the fool in the old story, who resolved not to go into the water till he had learnt to swim. If men are to wait for liberty till they become wise and good in slavery, they may indeed wait forever.' In short, Mr. Fowler, we must make the best of the freedoms we've been graciously given. Occasionally that might mean men of letters, such as you and me, may be guilty of hasty and ill-conceived judgment. Not in your case, however, I might add. I believe that you have received the press treatment you so richly deserve. So I ask you again, what the dickens are you doing here?"

"Yes, I suppose I should get to the point of this delightful visit." Fowler pulled a folded piece of paper from his inside coat pocket and placed it on Fox's lap.

"And this is what? An offer to bribe me, the way you tried with St. Clair?"

"Not quite. Please read it," said Fowler, his voice slightly strained as if he was exercising a good deal of self-control.

As Fox did so, any color on his face rapidly vanished. "So you do want to buy me out." He glared at Fowler. "You're out of your head. Let me understand this completely. You want to purchase the magazine and the presses for five hundred thousand dollars?"

"Exactly. And I'm prepared to pay you a personal fee for any inconvenience this will cause you of an additional fifty thousand."

"Undoubtedly belonging to the citizens of New York City."

"Undoubtedly. But that's hardly your concern."

"Tell me, why did you send your thug after us? Why not approach me as a gentleman?"

"I truly had nothing to do with the unfortunate incident."

"I see," said Fox, barely containing his anger. "And what of my loyal employees? Several of the pressmen have been with me for fifteen years."

"They can keep their jobs if they wish."

"And St. Clair and Sutton, and the other writers?"

"I'll speak with Sutton in due course. But I suggest that Mr. St. Clair seek other employment. I don't think he would accommodate my plans."

"Yes, your plans. Please humor me further, Fowler. Before I respond to your more-than-generous proposal, I'm curious about your intentions."

"My intentions are my own private affair for the moment. I'm sure you as a businessman can appreciate the importance of privacy. Suffice it to say that I seek to hold the very power, which you are so familiar with but surprisingly do not yet know how to properly wield."

"Why, Fowler, you're the one who surprises me. Isn't all this because I'm about to crush your infamous Ring?"

"Dear Mr. Fox, nothing could be further from the truth." Fowler put on his hat. "Now I must take my leave of you. Please consider my offer seriously. I'll expect to hear from you within three days."

"And if I choose to ignore you?"

"Who is to say, Fox? The city, as you well know, is a mysterious and dangerous place. You say the scoundrel who attacked you and St. Clair remains at large?" A sly grin swept across Fowler's face.

"As if you didn't know." Fox snorted with derision. "That's what St. Clair has told me, yes."

"It would be a shame if he made a return visit. Who knows what might happen?"

"Is that a threat Fowler? If I wasn't confined to this bed . . ." Fox struggled to remove the covers.

"You misunderstand me, sir. I make no threats, only speculations." Fowler tipped his hat and exited the hospital room leaving Fox with one foot dangling from the bed.

He threw the offer Fowler had given him on to the floor, slumped back on his pillow and gazed at the white ceiling. He tried to calm himself and think. Fowler was as cunning as any man he had dealt with, but he was determined somehow to beat him at his own game.

Fox was fond of Dutch proverbs and one of his favorites was the old adage that "it takes a thief to catch a thief." He instinctively understood that if he wanted to deceive Fowler, he would have to do so by thinking as devilishly as he did. As he lay in bed, a plan gradually formed in his head— He would let Fowler think that he would accept his absurd offer to purchase the magazine. And then, when he let his guard down, he would catch him using guile and deceit.

He smiled to himself, recalling a second Dutch proverb that he also liked— "An old fox doesn't go twice into the trap." Or in this case an old Tom Fox. How fitting, he thought, and swore under his breath that neither he nor St. Clair would again fall into Fowler's trap.

Chapter Sixteen

———⟡———

A Bowl of Oyster Stew

St. Clair was in a foul mood by the time he returned to the police station. His visit at the hospital had been pleasant enough and he was glad that Fox was on the mend. But his mind was now filled with deep suspicions about Ruth Cardaso, leaving him feeling more unsettled and anxious than ever.

He opened the door of the interrogation room and was startled to see Seth Murray raise his right hand and slap George from the Fifth Avenue Hotel across the side of his head. Before the doorman could reply, Murray struck him again. George sank to the floor.

"That's enough, Seth," St. Clair shouted without thinking. "I won't stand by and watch you hit him like a dog."

Seth Murray turned and glared at his brother-in-law. He had permitted him access into the interrogation room as a courtesy and just assumed he understood his methods—that a little physical coercion...a slap to the side of the head, say... went a long way to prying information from a suspect, particularly a colored one. He was particularly furious that St. Clair chose to admonish him in front of two patrolmen.

"I won't tolerate that from you, Charlie," Murray shouted back. "Don't ever tell me how to conduct my business. In here, I'm in charge, not you."

"No one's questioning your authority, Seth." St. Clair stood his ground. "But I'd bet the poor man's told you everything he knows." He regarded his brother-in-law with disappointment. "Hell, I thought you weren't like Stokes and the rest."

"You're standing up for him? A Negro?"

"That's what I'm goddamn doing. As far as I know he's not guilty of any crime, other than being loyal. You want to lock him up for that?"

Murray waved his fist close to St. Clair's bandaged nose, then smiled. "You can be a pest, Charlie, and you've been one since the day Caroline introduced me to you." He turned to one of the patrolman. "Let him go. I know where to find him if I need him."

"I'm free to go?" George eased himself up from the floor.

"You deaf?" asked Murray. "Get out of here, but don't leave the city. I may be bringing you back here for another discussion."

∾

St. Clair accompanied the shocked doorman out of the station house.

"I wonder what happened to Mr. Buckland. Didn't he say he'd be bringing the hotel's lawyer to help you?" asked St. Clair.

"Mr. Buckland's a very busy man." George's voice cracked.

"Yeah, I guess he is." St. Clair was suddenly possessed by an idea. "George, can I buy you a mug of ale? There's a cellar across the street I've been to," he said. "It's a friendly place and they serve a dandy bowl of oyster stew."

"That sounds tasty and I'm hungry. With all due respect, sir, do you think that's a wise decision?"

"We won't know until we try, right, George."

In truth, St. Clair had never before sat down with a Negro in a tavern. He knew that there was no law against such socializing, although if pressed by George he would have admitted that proper etiquette and accepted custom generally inhibited such fraternizing—other than in saloons and brothels in Five Points and down by the waterfront. St. Clair understood, too, that Negroes had their own neighborhoods, churches, and taverns, and white New Yorkers had theirs. It was the way of the land before and after the war and not much had changed in the past six years. Even in New York, where blacks had been free for more than a generation, the end of slavery did not usher in a new age of tolerance.

George, accustomed to following orders, obediently followed St. Clair across Mulberry Street, down the steps and through the red swinging entrance doors to Chauncey's, an oyster cellar frequented by off-duty patrolmen and local toughs. It took a minute or so for St. Clair to adjust to the dark and smoky atmosphere. The only light in the small tavern emanated from a dim flickering candle burning slowly under red and white striped muslin that was stretched over a globe-like wire frame.

In the late afternoon, there were only a half-dozen patrons. As soon as St. Clair walked in with George at his heels, every pair of eyes in the place turned. St. Clair recognized one patrolman, who often worked with Murray, a burly cop named O'Hanlan.

"I heard you were in a bit of a fracas the other day," the cop said.

"I'll survive," replied St. Clair.

"Who's the friend?" O"Hanlan nodded in George's direction. "Don't have a lot of his kind in here."

"We just want some ale and stew. There a law against it?"

O'Hanlan chuckled. "None that I know. You go on, St. Clair, I'll watch your back. I don't think anyone in here much cares who you drink with. It's your goddamn business."

"Appreciate that," said St. Clair with a nod, then motioned to a table to the left of the bar. "Take a seat over there, George."

"Hey, boy, my boots need a shine," hollered one young man sitting drinking nearby. The two men with him bellowed with laughter. When he got no response, he flicked his lit cigar butt at George's head. The doorman knocked it away.

"Ignore them, George," advised St. Clair. "They're nothing but drunken swine."

"I don't take kindly to insults, mister," said the man, pushing back his hat as he stood up. He was broad shouldered and slightly taller than St. Clair.

"Maybe we should leave," George muttered.

"Your Negro's right. You should leave. You wouldn't want the rest of your face looking like your nose, would you?"

St. Clair stared into the man's eyes, uncertain what to do next. Walking out seemed like the best option, but long ago he had made it a point to never permit a big-mouth hooligan to chase him away. And unlike last night, St. Clair was prepared. Deftly, he pulled his pistol from his pocket and grabbed the man by the collar.

"You say another word and there'll be a bullet in that fat head of yours." St. Clair held the gun to the man's cheek. He had no intention of shooting, but talking tough carried a lot of clout on the streets of New York.

"Sit down the both of you." O'Hanlan barked, stepping up to them. "Put it away, St. Clair. I promise you, this asshole won't bother you again." The back of his hand caught the man at the side of his head. "Mulder, sit down, finish your beer, and keep your mouth shut or you'll be sleeping on the floor across the street tonight."

St. Clair shoved his pistol back in his pocket. "Thanks, O'Hanlan. I'll mention this to Murray." He walked to the bar where Chauncy Jones was standing, he appeared to be amused by the entire incident.

"That was more entertaining than an evening at Barnum's," the middle-aged portly barkeep declared. "I don't care who comes in my place, Negro, Hebrew, German, as long as they pay, that is. Now, what'll it be?"

"Two ales and two bowls of your oyster stew."

Chauncy poured the ale from a spout sticking into a barrel and handed the mugs to St. Clair. "I'll bring the stew right out to you."

"Drink up, George," said St. Clair taking a seat opposite the doorman.

"It happened before and it'll happen again. I was nearly killed once," George said shaking his head, "back during the draft riots of '63. I was in the wrong place at the wrong time."

"Tell me about it." St. Clair took a swig of his ale.

George pushed his cap back. "I was visiting a friend, who worked at the Colored Orphan Asylum up on Fifth and Forty-Third. All of sudden, there was a mob outside the door shouting, 'burn the damn nest.' Me and my friend, Joshua, tried to stop them while Duke McCafferty took all of the children to the Twentieth Precinct. But it was sure a close shave."

Chauncey set two steaming bowls of oyster stew on the table accompanied by several hunks of bread, a small portion of butter, and pepper and lemon juice, served in a narrow glass jar.

"Help yourself, George," said St. Clair.

"This is mighty kind of you, sir. If Mr. Buckland could see me now, I'd be fired for sure," he said with a laugh. "And this sure tastes good after that talk with the detective." He gently rubbed the side of his head.

"He's not a bad man, you know," said St. Clair.

"The detective, I'm sure he can be a real gentleman if he wants to."

"He's just doing what he has to do."

"So am I. The guests at the hotel trust me and I wouldn't want to do anything to upset them."

"I completely understand." St. Clair dipped a piece of bread into the stew.

"Poor Miss Lucy. She was always kind to me. I can't quite believe she's dead." George frowned.

"Yeah, it's a shame all right."

"Who'd want to do something like that to her? Stuffing her in a trunk."

"Tell me, where are you from, George? You born around here?"

"In New York, no sir," he laughed. "I came here in '41 when I was a lad of eight. I was born on a plantation in Talbot County, Maryland, not too far from the one where Frederick Douglass himself was raised. Likewise, my granddaddy was born there a slave. So were my daddy and mammy. Miserable slaves one and all. I would've been working in the fields too, if not for Mr. Buckland's father, James. He was a New York shipping merchant, a fine old gentlemen and a dedicated abolitionist, who bought my family's freedom and brought us to the city. My daddy worked as Mister James's servant and my mammy did the laundry for the entire household."

"Buckland offered you employment at the hotel?"

"That's right. Started when it opened in '59. I was the first colored man to be hired and been working there ever since." George took a large gulp of his ale. "Mr. St. Clair, I thank you again for this hospitality, but I really need to be returning to the hotel."

"Of course. You have money for a cab?"

"A cab?" he laughed again. "That'd be a sight, me hailing down a hansom."

St. Clair grimaced. "I guess you're right. I'm not thinking clearly." He pointed to his bandaged nose. "I know you don't want to betray any trusts, George, but I want you to think hard about what Miss Maloney would've wanted. You don't want the person who murdered her to go unpunished, do you?"

"No, sir. Miss Lucy deserves a lot better than that," George beamed at him.

"Did she have many friends?"

"Some lady friends, yes. They used to meet every afternoon for tea."

"Any one in particular?" St. Clair pressed him.

George hesitated. He glanced down at his boots. "I guess there's no harm in telling you. Miss Mildred. Miss Mildred Potter."

St. Clair was surprised, but not wanting to scare George off, he kept his tone matter-of-fact. "Rupert Potter's daughter? Lives in a mansion not too far from the hotel?"

"Yes, that'd be her. Miss Mildred and Miss Lucy were always together. More like sisters than friends if you know what I mean?"

"I do, yes," Clair said thoughtfully.

The connection between Lucy Maloney and Mildred Potter intrigued him. He had only met Rupert Potter once in passing, at a gathering of newspaper proprietors. Potter had struck him as an intelligent member of New York's upper crust and it was not only because he had made millions in railways and mining ventures. Potter was naturally charming and literate—as well as being virulently anti-Tammany. "The Irish rabble, that's all they are. And one's more corrupt than the next," St. Clair had heard him declare publicly on more than one occasion.

St. Clair was hardly surprised when he heard several months ago, that Potter was attempting to organize a citizens' association to investigate Victor Fowler and the Ring. Not much had come of it, since Fowler had too many friends and supporters protecting him. But Potter vowed that his campaign—it was more like a crusade in St. Clair's opinion—to rid the city of the Ring was not finished.

Rupert Potter's daughter Mildred and Lucy Maloney were close friends, thought St. Clair. Was it too much to think that Miss Maloney's death was linked to her friendship with Mildred? Or was this merely a coincidence? As he sat with the doorman, another crazy thought popped into his head— What if Fowler was seeking revenge on Potter and aimed to hurt his daughter, yet went after the wrong woman? That was too farfetched. He realized that he was so desperate to defeat Fowler, that he would have believed almost anything. Still, a meeting with Miss Mildred Potter in the very near future was essential. Who better than a close female companion to know a woman's true secrets?

George stood up to leave. "I really must be on my way."

"And what of Miss Maloney's gentlemen callers?" St. Clair chose to ignore the doorman's growing uneasiness.

"None that I know," he stammered.

"Come now, George, a lovely woman such as Miss Maloney must've had at least one gentleman call on her. What of the gentleman who sees to her monthly rent?"

"You'd have to speak to Mr. Buckland about such matters," George responded, then hesitated. "But, I did see her once," he said finally.

"Go on, George, tell me."

The doorman sat back down. Lowering his voice, he said, "It was about ten days ago. I saw her speaking to this man. He was big, with bushy side-whiskers."

"No hair on his head and a thick neck?" asked St. Clair excitedly.

"That's right. How did you know?" George's eyes widened.

"I think I've met him before." St. Clair touched his bandages. "What did he have to do with Miss Maloney?"

"They were arguing about something. I couldn't hear much of it, but she was upset and told him to leave her be. Then she ran back into the hotel. He didn't follow her. Never saw him again." George looked toward the door anxiously. "I really have to go, Mr. St. Clair. There's nothing more I can tell you."

So, St. Clair thought as he watched George climb the steps back to the street, the thug who attacked him also knew Lucy Maloney. Who was this man? What was he doing in New York? And more importantly, who was paying him? Could he have been the father of Miss Maloney's unborn child? For some reason, St. Clair imagined her with someone more respectable.

He gulped down the rest of his ale and picked at this stew for a few moments, contemplating his conversation with George. Damn, he thought, with each new fact, the puzzle of the trunk mystery became more complicated, not less.

~

"Her name is Mildred Potter. She's the daughter of Rupert Potter. You know him?" asked St. Clair. He was sitting in a chair back in the police station opposite Seth Murray.

"Despite what you think, Charlie, I'm no fool."

"I told you I'd get him to talk." St. Clair puffed his chest.

Murray scowled. "Yeah, well, you still shouldn't have done what you done. It was humiliating."

"Never happen again. You know my intentions are always honest," St. Clair grinned.

"Yeah, I've heard. What else did he say?"

"Nothing," St. Clair quickly replied.

"That's it?" Murray regarded him sourly. "You spend an hour with him over at Chauncey's and you got one name. Hell, a few more whacks in the head and I could've got that and it would've taken half the time."

Thinking about it later, St. Clair couldn't explain to himself why he didn't tell Murray about Lucy Maloney's possible connection to the man who attacked Fox and him.

But for the moment, he knew he wanted to keep it to himself.

Chapter Seventeen

———⊱✦⊰———

AN UNEXPECTED KNOCK AT THE DOOR

fter polishing off two mugs of ale, three chunks of bread and butter, and a bowl of thick oyster stew, St. Clair should have been stuffed. And yet several hours later, by the time he reached Bleeker Street, he was hungry again.

After speaking with Murray, he took as leisurely a stroll as was possible down the Bowery. The colorful and noisy street was illuminated by gas-lit white glass lanterns. He deliberately stayed clear of the ruffians, who nightly congregated nearby in the vicinity of Billy McGlory's Amory Hall on Hester Street, as dangerous a concert saloon as Harry Hill's was entertaining. Bloody gang brawls were a regular event, as was fleecing unsuspecting and usually intoxicated patrons who came to witness the nightly spectacle.

Once he got past McGlory's, he enjoyed the rest of the brief walk, despite the typically rowdy atmosphere of a humid summer weekday evening. There were crowds of young men on the prowl for female companionship. Peddlers pushed their wares and vendors were selling hot corn and oysters. Beside them, too, were young children begging for coins and pickpockets searching for their next victims. Excited men and women rushed past him, presumably he thought, to catch the latest theatrical offerings at the nearby Tivoli and Vauxhall Garden.

St. Clair turned left on to Bleeker and the mood noticeably changed. If there was a street in New York reminiscent of the Latin Quarter in Paris, it was Bleeker. Twenty years ago, the neighborhood was fashionably upper class, the address of the city's burgeoning professionals. Now all that remained of the wealth of that era were aging mansions, which, like the one St. Clair resided in, had been transformed into functional, but crowded, boarding houses. As was well known, several of them rented rooms by the hour or day—discretion was always assured.

The street's most colorful and eccentric inhabitant, from St. Clair's perspective, was Eugene Crask, who fancied himself an artist. Crask was, in fact, a drunkard, who rarely cut his hair or washed himself or his clothes, yet every so often produced bizarre paintings that occasionally caught the eye of a Fifth Avenue patron. Rumor was that Crask frequently had utilized the services of ladies from Wooster Street to pose nude for him— although St. Clair saw no evidence of that in his work.

Another of St. Clair's favorites was Emilé Halloway, a former ballerina from Vienna, with seemingly no source of income, although she lived like a Queen. A bevy of callers, both gentlemen and ladies, could be seen coming and going from her flat at all times of the day and night.

St. Clair had every intention of heading home, when he caught a whiff of the veal stew and roast lamb at one of Bleeker's most celebrated eateries, the Restaurant de Grand Vatel. For thirty cents, it was possible to indulge oneself in a four-course gourmet meal fit for French royalty—and all prepared with perfection by Grand Vatel's star chef, Melville Clement. St. Clair dined here at least twice a week and had wanted to invite Ruth to join him for a splendid meal—until he learned that she was leaving the city. The floor of the restaurant was protected with sand and the wooden tables were decorated with pewter crocks that contained oil and vinegar.

An hour later, he was truly satiated. The veal stew—on the menu it was *veau à la Marengo*—was exquisite as were the salad and potatoes that accompanied it. For dessert, he sipped on a gloria, strong black coffee topped with cognac, while chatting with Chef Clement about the latest political news from Paris. All St. Clair had to do was mention the

Emperor Napoleon III. Clement, a Republican through and through, would berate him for hours about the buffoon who had lost Paris to Bismarck and the Germans and extol the virtues of the Communards who had recently attempted to establish a new revolutionary order. A candle at the front of the restaurant burned in memory of the thousands of Parisians who had been killed in April and May, when the National Guard had attacked and taken back control of the city.

From St. Clair's standpoint, Clement's position was overly sentimental and dangerous. Liberty and democracy were fine, but not at the expense of social order. Look what had happened in New York during the draft riots, St. Clair suggested to Clemont. Mob rule of any kind was perilous and an occurrence to be halted at all costs. The chef, however, refused to change his mind.

~

As usual, it was stifling hot and muggy in St. Clair's sparsely furnished two-room flat. Once, as St. Clair himself had researched for a magazine story, it had been the servants' quarters for the home of English shipbuilder Thomas Lawrence, his wife, and six children, in the early 1820s. There was a modest although slightly worn sofa and two French-style high back chairs—a wedding present from Caroline's family—in the parlor. A medium-sized Indian carpet covered the wood floor. He had purchased it more than a year ago at A.T. Stewart's dry-goods shop on Broadway and Fourth Avenue.

At the back was a smaller alcove—the flat's second room—that contained a bed large enough for two people and an exquisite hand-carved wooden table, which had once belonged to St. Clair's great-grandmother. It was the only possession he had that he truly cherished. The water closet and bathroom were down the hall and shared between the other five men on the second floor of the old mansion. St. Clair either ate his meals downstairs at Mrs. Montgomery's or at nearby restaurants like the Grand Vatel.

He undid his shirt, rinsed his face and hands in a basin of cool water, and made himself as comfortable as possible. Next, he poured himself a glass of whisky and lit his pipe—thankful that his otherwise strident neighbor, a lively ladies' garment salesman by the name of Johnson, who constantly entertained his married female clients, was travelling.

Exhausted, St. Clair welcomed the peace and quiet and a chance to stop thinking about Lucy Maloney, Madame Philippe, Victor Fowler, and even poor Tom Fox. He picked up a new book he had recently acquired at Hogan's Book Emporium on Broadway—*The Coming Race*, which all the critics were raving about, although its author, an Englishman, had opted to remain anonymous. There was some speculation in the press that this romantic saga about an imaginary advanced society in the earth's interior was penned by the likes of Benjamin Disraeli or Edward Bulwer-Lytton. Whoever the author was, St. Clair found the writing clever and entertaining—despite the book's witty mocking of the American national character, with its rejoicing of democratic equality as long as proper social hierarchies were maintained.

A steady knocking at the door startled him. He had dozed off with *The Coming Race* resting on his stomach and his smoldering pipe still in his hand. He checked his timepiece. It was one o'clock in the morning. Who could be visiting him at this late hour? One thought immediately settled in his head— His assailant from the other night had returned. He reached for his pistol and cautiously approached the door. It was bolted shut.

"Who goes there?" he asked in a firm voice.

For about a minute there was no response.

"I say again, who's out there. I should warn you I have a pistol and am not afraid to use it."

"Mr. St. Clair, please I need to speak with you, it's urgent."

He instantly recognized the voice. It was Ruth Cardaso.

He unlatched the bolt and opened the door, his pistol still at his side. She smiled warmly when she saw him. She was wearing a cream satin dress with a low heart-shaped neckline and was a vision of loveliness. The sight of her standing in the dimly lit hallway nearly took his breath away. The pistol he was holding slid off his fingers and fell to the floor.

"What are doing here at this hour?" he asked her, attempting without much success to straighten his shirt.

"Please, may I come in for a moment?"

"Of course," he said, and then remembered their last meeting. "I was under the impression that you were leaving the city." His tone was caustic.

She ignored it. "I am, but I needed—"

"You needed what?" he asked sharply.

"I needed to do this."

She moved towards him and her strong fragrance once more excited him. Then, before he could utter a word of protest, she kissed him passionately. Her lips were as soft and moist as the first time they had embraced. He did not resist. He put his arms around her waist and pulled her closer to him, kissing her again harder and longer.

"There are many questions I must ask you—" he mumbled.

"Later, Charlie, not now," she said putting her finger to his lips. He kissed it gently.

She took a step back and smiled at him again. She reached behind her back and undid the buttons of her dress. The garment fell to the floor and she was standing before him wearing a long white cotton petticoat with floral braids on the side that reached her knees. She slipped that off as well. Underneath a pleated waist-length, sheer petticoat revealed the contours of her body.

He noticed that a tiny bead of sweat had formed on the top of her upper lip. He drew her to him, kissed her again and felt the sweat meld with his own. Her heart beat against his chest—his breathing grew more labored. He stroked her cheek softly and she groped for his hand. He grasped it and she led him to his bed.

~

Ruth stared at St. Clair for few moments and lightly dragged her fingers through his hair—careful not to disturb his sleep. He had been gentle, patient, and passionate with her, as she knew he would be. It was, in her mind, the mark of a man who had once loved deeply. She did not relish the idea of hurting him further. She knew, too, that the more questions he asked of her, the more disenchanted he would become. And eventually, the chasm between them would be impossible to bridge. He would never understand her involvement in this impossible situation. He was far too principled and, admittedly, far too uncompromising. She had noted those two qualities shaped in his character and in his writing. She guessed that the memory of his deceased wife likely nurtured his soul and made him unlike most men she had ever been with. How she wished that matters could be different between them.

But they were not and never would be.

She quietly rose from the bed and gathered up her clothes. Fifteen minutes later, she was out on the street and considering her next difficult decision.

~

It was close to six o'clock in the morning when the first rays from the sun stirred St. Clair. His naked body was dripping with sweat under a thin cotton bed sheet. He felt tired, yet contented, something he had not experienced in some time. He reached for Ruth.

His bed was empty.

"Ruth," he called out, "where are you?"

He sat up, peered into the gloom of his bedroom, and listened for the sound of another person. Then, he fell back into his bed. He was alone. Only hours earlier, he had held her in his arms and in the darkness they talked. About the heat, the dance halls, concert saloons, and the magnificent shops in the vicinity of Broadway and Union Square, the so-called Ladies' Mile.

They spoke about the latest Shakespearean drama at Booth's, the most elegant theatre in the city. They would attend the next performance of *Hamlet* together, she had said, not waiting for him to respond. Did she know, he inquired, that the owner of the theatre, Edwin Booth, was the brother of John Wilkes Booth, the notorious assassin of President Lincoln? She did not. He offered to take her for a sumptuous dinner at Delmonico's and, much to her delight, proceeded to list the menu he would select for both of them—scalloped partridge or lamb's kidneys in champagne sauce to start with, followed by consommé soup, broiled capon or compote of pigeon, salmon with caper sauce, crusts of mushrooms, and finishing with Gruyere cheese or cream cake.

Indeed, they chatted about everything except what he really wanted to ask her— Why had she lied about reading Tom Fox's files? What was her interest in seeing Madame Philippe punished? What did she know about Lucy Maloney, if anything? And most significantly, what did she want of him? He had deliberately not broached these subjects, convincing himself that an interrogation was best left for another time.

As St. Clair lay in his bed, already sticky and sweaty from the early morning heat, trying to muster the strength to rise and begin another full day, he realized that he might never learn the truth about Miss Ruth Cardaso. And, that he felt—contemplating what might have been—was a damn shame.

Chapter Eighteen

The Tombs

*N*o matter how hot and sunny it was outside, St. Clair knew that the moment he bounded up the wide granite steps onto the portico facing Center Street, the temperature would suddenly turn cool and damp. He had learned on other visits that the Halls of Justice, otherwise known as the Tombs, was—fittingly for a prison—the darkest, dankest and most depressing edifice in New York.

Three years earlier, St. Clair had written a lengthy article for the magazine about the history of the Tombs to mark the prison's thirtieth anniversary. He had discovered that its distinct architectural design—its resemblance to a massive tomb fit for the ancient Pharaohs was striking—had been inspired by the sketches shown to the city's Common Council by Colonel John Stevens upon his return from travels to Egypt in the 1830s. Once the structure was completed in 1838, it quickly became known far and wide as The Tombs.

He approached the grand entranceway under the Lotus columns and was immediately confronted by a prison guard.

"What do you want? There's no visiting today, 'cause of the hanging." The guard was tall, husky and in a decidedly foul mood.

"Name is Charles St. Clair. I think if you'll look—"

"I don't give a damn if you're the Emperor Napoleon, I said there's no visiting."

"Franklin, let him in now," ordered a man in a stern voice. He stood out of St. Clair's sight behind the main door.

"Mr. Chapman, I was told—"

"I know what you were told, Franklin, I issued those instructions. Mr. St. Clair has the permission of Detective Murray and Inspector Stokes to visit one of our inmates. So for goodness sakes, let the man in."

St. Clair extended his hand to the Tombs' assistant warden. He noted that Thomas Chapman was as tall as the prison guard but much rounder and bald. "I appreciate the assistance. It's an honor to see you again, sir."

"And you, sir. I have only one question…are you armed?"

"I am," St. Clair replied, pulling his pistol from his coat pocket. "I've not had the best week and I don't intend on being caught unprepared again."

"I assure you that security and safety are my priorities, as well. However, I'd ask you to leave your revolver with the guard. You may retrieve it on the way out. It's a rule I must enforce. I trust you understand."

St. Clair reluctantly handed his weapon to Franklin, as he passed through the mammoth doors that led into the prison's outer building.

"Officer Franklin was just following my orders," said Chapman. "You know, we're hanging Bob Bundy at noon. And we're expecting a crowd might try to come by. The warden didn't want any trouble and the Styles family asked that it be as private as possible. They've had a hard time these last few months with all of this talk that Bundy is innocent. The governor ordered the execution to take place and that's what I aim to see happen. My lone concern is that I only have about eight men on duty right now. A contingent of officers from headquarters was supposed to arrive an hour ago, but I have no idea when they'll get here. I've sent three messages with no proper reply."

As St. Clair and everyone else in the city knew, Bob Bundy was a Negro convicted of raping and murdering Elsie Styles, the twelve-year-old daughter of Frederick Styles, a prominent attorney. According to the newspapers, last November Bundy had broken into the Styles' home on Madison Avenue believing that it was unoccupied. However young Elsie had been at home alone—the family's servant was out on an errand.

Mrs. Styles returned to find, she later claimed, Bundy fleeing from the house. "It was that Negro, I swear it," she had testified in court. The poor woman found her daughter lying naked and dead on the floor of the hallway by the top of the stairs. Her throat had been slashed with a razor, which was, as everyone knew, a favorite weapon of the colored's.

It hardly mattered that another witness claimed that Bundy was with him that day hauling freight in Brooklyn. Because he was also a colored, the all-white jury ignored his testimony. After a half-hour of deliberations, they found Bundy guilty and the judge ordered him to hang. Stories soon appeared in the *New York Herald*, which suggested Bundy might well have been out of the city when the murder was committed. Eventually the case landed on Governor Krupp's desk.

As St. Clair later heard it from Frank King, however, Victor Fowler was allegedly courting Frederick Styles to become Tammany's chief lawyer and did not want anything to upset his negotiations. It was a real coup for Fowler to have someone of Styles's stature as one of several attorneys he could call on. In Bundy's case, St. Clair concluded, innocence or guilt was almost beside the point. There was much more at stake. Mrs. Styles had seen the Negro leaving the family's house and that was all there was to it. The governor ordered that Bundy be hanged.

St. Clair followed Chapman into the prison's huge courtyard where the gallows had been erected. Straight ahead, on the other side of the yard, was the entrance to the men's prison, which could only be reached by a narrow stone bridge.

"The inmates call that the Bridge of Sighs," said Chapman with a glint in his eye, "since it's the last walk some of them take. Sure not like the old days when you could see a hanging out on the streets. It was like a day at the fair... only better. They used to give the poor sod a sermon and then a grand procession from the old prison by City Hall to the gallows on the outskirts of the city. Now, it's here in private with invited guests only. But I can tell you that the excitement hasn't disappeared. Any time there's a hanging, the crowds still gather outside the gates and on the top floors of the factories and shops over there." He motioned with his head to several buildings that were higher than the prison's walls. "You're welcome to stay if you wish. The warden told me to tell you that."

St. Clair had witnessed several executions when he worked with the *Times*, but that was a while ago. It had not been an assignment he had particularly enjoyed or wanted to repeat.

"Thank him for me, please," he said to Chapman. "First I must speak with Madame Philippe."

"Of course, our latest and most famous inmate. Come with me this way. She has the finest room in the house," he added with a chuckle. "Who knows? From what I hear, she might be the next one swinging up there." He glanced back at the gallows.

~

Standing on the makeshift wood platform, Reverend Ingersoll surveyed the crowd of clerks, shopkeepers, peddlers, cartmen, and sailors, along with a good assortment of rogues, thieves, grafters, and harlots. Trust Victor Fowler to assemble this mixed horde, he thought. Fowler was as good as his word—you couldn't fault the man for not fulfilling his promises.

He was in front of Grady's, a saloon squeezed between a funeral parlor and a bookshop, on the corner of Canal Street and Center Street, which Fowler had designated as the gathering place for the march to the Tombs. A decade ago, Fowler had loaned the saloon's owner, Michael Grady, an immigrant from Cork, the money to open his tavern. Ever since then, Grady was a rabid Tammany man and one of Fowler's most vocal supporters. "You be needing anything else, Reverend?" Michael Grady asked, handing Ingersoll a mug of beer. "This in case your throat becomes parched."

"That's mighty kind of you, Mr. Grady," the reverend responded, taking the mug in one hand and dusting off of his black suit with the other. "If you can get this rabble to settle down long enough for me to deliver a few words, I'd be most appreciative."

Grady signaled for a husky man with dark hair to come forward. It was Little Philly, one of Fowler's shoulder-hitters.

"Philly, the reverend needs everyone to shut up. Can you and your men handle that?"

"I can do that, sir, if that's what you need," replied Little Philly.

Within minutes, Philly and his gang, including Snake Manfred and Punk Tyler, were moving about the crowd, with thick clubs in their hands, ordering everyone to stop the talking and hollering. And as if by some sort of magic spell, they obeyed—even the tougher and more despicable-looking thieves and brawlers. Ingersoll was impressed, although he did remember that each member of the mob had been assured of fifty dollars—a generous fee Fowler would pay them once their task for the day was completed.

"Can you hear them?" asked Ingersoll. His voice was clear and crisp. "Can you hear them?" he repeated, louder. His long flowing hair blew in the light wind and grazed the collar of his black frock coat. To anyone in this street congregation there was no doubt that before them stood a man of God.

"I know you can," he declared, not waiting for an answer. "That crying you hear is the sound of two mothers, young and old, who have had their daughters stolen from them by sin and Satan."

Several of the thieves and harlots hooted their approval.

"Elsie Styles and Lucy Maloney. Remember those names," the reverend continued. "For they're the innocent victims of two tragedies, who deserve our admiration and respect. And what of Bob Bundy and Madame Philippe? One's a colored man, who covets young white girls. And the other's a witch who pretends to be a physician, but is in truth a murderess. Have no fear, Bundy will meet his maker at noon today."

A boisterous shout of approval emanated through Canal Street. "Death to the Negro," one tough yelled. "Yeah, hang him high and burn the bastard," screamed another. The crowd roared again.

"Ladies and gentlemen, patience." Ingersoll, now in full stride, held up his arms. "Is there a greater evil in this world than abortion? Yes, worse I'd say even than prostitution to which it is closely allied." He ignored the titters among several men standing close to him. "Each day in this city, countless women like Miss Maloney are victims of vile and cruel quackery. Remember, she was left dead and stuffed into a trunk. Then, there are the children. They're not permitted to be born into this world and are disposed of like garbage. They're cast into the fire pits or buried in a heap of dirt without a Christian prayer being uttered. In a civilized world, we must never tolerate this. That's my message for you today."

Ingersoll stopped for a moment, certain that all eyes were upon him. "So I hear you asking me, what can be done about this injustice?" It was time, he thought, to earn his rewards. "I'd argue here and now that Madame Philippe...Madame Killer...does not deserve the benefits of justice, for she does not accord that to her defenseless victims. The gallows are there for Bob Bundy. Why not force the officials at the Tombs to use them on Madame Philippe as well. To the Tombs. To the Tombs," he cried again and again.

The crowd, which had grown to close to one hundred and fifty people, shouted and hollered. "To the Tombs. To the Tombs. Hang the Negro with the witch. Let them both hang."

That was the signal Little Philly and his men were waiting for. They encircled the mob and, using their clubs, began shepherding them down Center Street. Many of them pulled out guns or picked up stones. Others wielded the clubs they had brought with them.

~

Assistant-Warden Chapman turned the large iron key and the heavy wood door of the cell opened slowly.

"Madame, Mr. St. Clair is here to see you," he announced.

Madame Philippe was resting on the narrow bed and swiftly stood up. "Mr. St. Clair, I'm so delighted you've come. I'd offer you a cup of tea, however, as you can see, it'll have to wait."

The cell, one of half a dozen overlooking Centre Street, appeared to be more comfortable than others St. Clair had seen in the prison, but he knew that such cells were available to inmates like Madame Philippe, who were prepared to pay for it. While it had daunting stonewalls like the rest, a barred window situated high above the floor provided sufficient air and light during the day and the bed appeared to have more straw and fewer bugs than most. There was even a feather pillow on the bed and a bucket for water in the corner.

"Please sit down, Mr. St. Clair." Madame Philippe offered him a spot on the bed.

"I'd prefer to stand, thank you, Madame," he said, making no attempt to hide the sharpness in his voice.

"And your injury? Still painful?"

"I'll survive."

"I'm certain you will." She took a seat on a small wooden stool beside her bed. "Mr. St. Clair, I know this might strike you as an odd request, given our surroundings, but would you do me the honor and please tell me about your late wife."

"There's nothing to tell," he said suddenly overcome with guilt. This morning, his mind had been filled with erotic images of Ruth Cardaso. Evoking memories of Caroline was about the last thing he wanted to do.

"She was a beautiful woman?"

"Yes, she was," said St. Clair. Whether he wanted to admit it or not, he found talking about Caroline comforting. "When she was dressed for a ball or a night at the theatre, there wasn't a woman in New York who could compete with her."

Madame Philippe smiled warmly. "I'm sure you miss her terribly. If this is any consolation, I do know that Madame Anna was dreadfully upset about your wife's death—"

"*She* was upset?" St. Clair interrupted. "She assured me that the procedure would be safe and like a fool, I believed her. You've no idea how many times I've regretted that decision. And the worst of it—" He waved his hand in the air. "Oh, what is the point?"

"No, please continue," she said softly.

"The worst of it was," he said with resignation, "the worst of it was that I was the one who forced her into doing it. She wanted to have the child." St. Clair shook his head in dismay. "It was my fault. I even chose Madame Anna because a friend's wife had recommended her. She is dead because of me. Because I foolishly did not heed the newspaper stories of other such tragedies. I trusted Madame Anna. How could I have been so wrong?" He pounded the wall of the cell with his fist.

"It was a terrible accident, I'm certain of it. Anna is an excellent midwife. Many young ladies of the finest families in the city have utilized her services."

"Please, Madame, make no excuses for her incompetence. My wife bled to death at Bellevue and there was absolutely nothing the doctors could do to prevent it. And with all due respect, she has not been the only one to suffer so. Whether it's been the harlots of Wooster and Green or the misguided daughters of Fifth Avenue families...the list of women, to endure tragedy at the hands of you and your kind, is far too long." He glared at her. "I'm certain you know the sad tale of Mary Ryan?"

"I cannot recall." Madame Philippe looked away.

"Let me refresh your memory," St. Clair began. "Some time ago, she visited an abortionist, whose name escapes me, merely to obtain advice. The poor girl was stupefied with chloroform and an abortion was performed on her without her consent. She was robbed of the few dollars she had in her pockets, and then dumped in the ladies' cabin of the Desbrosses Street ferry. Luckily for her, someone found her and she was taken to the hospital for medical treatment that saved her. What of Miss Emily A. Post? She was not as fortunate."

Madame Philippe remained silent.

"Only four months ago, as you well know, she went to see Madame Van Buskirk. She paid the thirty dollars for the abortion, with the promise that her friends would pay another twenty, so that she could stay longer and recover from this ordeal. What happened next was as abysmal as the fate suffered by Miss Maloney, in my opinion. When these so-called friends did not appear with the needed funds, Madame Van Buskirk and her accomplices took the sick woman in the middle of the night and transported her to Brooklyn so they could search for Miss Post's acquaintances. The trip took several hours and Miss Post's health deteriorated to the point that the abortionist did not know what to do. They left her at the first precinct house in Brooklyn. The police there summoned a physician, but it was too late. She died, yet at least she had identified Madame Van Buskirk as the culprit of this horrendous crime."

"You've made your point, Mr. St. Clair," conceded Madame Philippe. "I know that you could tell me more heart-rending stories. Despite what you might believe, I don't have all of the answers. I do know that I've helped many women, abused by drunken husbands, who care little about them. What of the women with six and seven children who cannot, under any circumstances, care for another infant? What other options do they have, sir? I ask you, what other options? Are there not a sufficient number of unwanted children living in the alleyways like dogs and rats? Do we truly need more?"

St. Clair turned his back to her.

"It's true, I grant you," she continued, "that there are far too many young ladies of respectable class who visit me seeking relief, because they are either not prepared to marry the man who they have been with. Or far worse in your view, I'm certain, they do not, for any number of reasons, want to relinquish their status as single and carefree women. I ask you, however, do they not have that right?"

St. Clair turned around. "To be a mother is the most fulfilling role they can play, is that not so?" he demanded. "Is it not their moral duty? How did Dr. Hale recently explain it in his pamphlet? Something like this I believe, 'an abortion is a crime against physiology because it arrests the normal course of the functions of physical life. It is a crime against morality because it is murder to eradicate the receptacle of the soul. And it is crime against the law.' I didn't understand the true meaning of these words until after Caroline was gone and this is something that will haunt me for the rest of my days."

Madame Philippe walked closer to him. "Are you aware that Edwin Hale has said publicly that even if his own daughter was raped by a Negro or Indian, he would still regard abortion as murder? Surely you wouldn't agree with such primitive thinking, Mr. St. Clair. What of your late wife? You said yourself that her personal circumstances made it impossible. Do you know why I do this work?"

"So you may live in a mansion on Fifth Avenue?" he snidely replied.

"The other day in the carriage, when you related to the police and Miss Cardaso the story of my life, you omitted several important aspects. Permit me to educate you now."

"Very well." St. Clair sat down on the bed and took out his pad of paper and a pencil.

"I was indeed born Anna Jacoby in Frankfurt in the *Judengasse*...Jews' Alley," Madame Philippe said. "My mother was a Jewess, my father a Catholic who opted to live as a Jew because he worshipped my mother. He never spoke of his own family and we never asked him about it. I don't believe he saw them again...he was dead in their eyes. Do you know that it was only a decade ago when my older brother Solomon revealed that our father's real name was von Strauss, Wilhelm von Strauss. He changed his name to Jacoby to make our lives easier.

"The *Judengasse* was small, dirty and muddy-far worse than even Five Points, if you can imagine that," she continued. "Jews were nothing in Frankfurt, lower than Negroes here. I remember as a young girl being instructed that in the streets outside of the *Judengasse*, I was not permitted to walk on footpaths nor play in parks. One day...I was likely no more than six years old at the time...I was with my father, who was always assumed to be a Jew. As we walked past a group of rowdy young men, one of them shouted at him in disdain, '*Mach mores, Jud*'...Jew, do your duty. Without a word, my father, this proud man, a talented carpenter, removed his hat and bowed respectfully. He said nothing to me about it, yet I could see the shame on his face. I don't relate this for your sympathy or pity, only that you should understand the world I'm from."

Madame Philippe cleared her throat and continued her story. "When I was ten, my mother became pregnant. She already had four children...I was her third. When she had given birth to my younger brother, Simon, the doctor had told her that she should never have any more children because to do so would put her life in jeopardy. Nevertheless, she and my father were careless and she became pregnant. There was a woman in a village outside of the city, who she knew could help her. But my father, stubborn and as Catholic as he had been the day he was born, forbid it. When the time came for her to deliver the baby, there was nothing the doctor could do. I watched her die in her own bed after giving birth to my sister, Clara, who has had to live with the knowledge of this tragedy."

Tears welled in her eyes. "Even though I was still young," she said, her voice shaking, "I vowed then and there never to allow anyone else to bear such pain as I did that day." She pulled a handkerchief from her sleeve and dabbed her eyes. "By the time I was eighteen, I had apprenticed with an elderly midwife in Vienna and felt confident in my own abilities. That's why I convinced my late husband, against his better judgment, I should add, to assist me in first establishing my office. Have I become a wealthy woman from this work? I would be a liar if I said no. You must believe me, however, that's not what compels me to continue."

St. Clair scribbled her words as fast as he could. He was not sure what to make of her tale. He had insisted for so long that she was a wicked woman, guilty of committing sin and abomination. Nor had his view on abortion suddenly undergone a major transformation. Admittedly driven by terrible guilt, he had taken a vow on Caroline's deathbed, a vow to halt this immoral practice whenever and wherever he could. Still, it was difficult, if not impossible, for him to be rational on the subject of abortion.

And yet, controlling his emotion and listening to Madame Philippe's arguments, he could hardly deny a reality that he had once shared her views. Not every woman was meant to have a child. The question he could not answer was whether there was a middle position acceptable to both Madame Philippe and her ilk and those who vehemently opposed abortion—as he did now. For the moment, he doubted it.

"Mr. St. Clair, I don't expect to make you into one of my chief supporters. But I do hope you see that I may not be the 'Madame Killer' you've read and, indeed, written about."

St. Clair nodded politely and put down his pencil. "I'll admit, Madame, that there's more to you than meets the eye."

"I'll take that as a compliment, sir. And if I may ask you one more question...do you believe me now that I had nothing to do with the death of Miss Maloney? That I'm not the liar you contended I was?"

St. Clair turned to her and was about to respond, when the first rocks hit the barred window.

Chapter Nineteen

"Hang Her!"

The cell door was flung open. "St. Clair, are you all right?" It was Assistant Warden Chapman. He was panting like a dog.

"What on earth is happening?" St. Clair stared up at the window. "Who's out there throwing rocks?"

"There's a mob gathering on the front steps. Could be as many as two hundred people. And from what I've been told by my men, some of them are armed. I don't know where the hell those patrolmen are."

"Who's leading them?"

"That troublemaker Reverend Ingersoll. He's got them all riled up about Bundy's hanging and—"

"And me, I presume, Mr. Chapman," Madame Philippe interjected.

"That's correct, Madame. But you've nothing to fear. I promise you that we'll protect you. No one's ever broken into the Tombs and I don't aim to allow that to happen on my watch today."

"Have you sent another message for help?" St. Clair inquired.

"They've already toppled the telegraph poles so I can't send anything to Mulberry Street or any other precinct, for that matter. I've dispatched an officer. It may take him a while to bring reinforcements."

"Hang the Negro," came screams from outside on the street. "Hang the fiend of Fifth Avenue along with him."

A flurry of paving stones smashed against the cell window. One managed to slip through the bars and nicked Madame Philippe's arm. She was uninjured, but for the first time, St. Clair could see that she was visibly shaken.

"Let me try talking to the Reverend," St. Clair offered. "I've known him for a number of years. I'm sure I can reason with him."

"With him, maybe," conceded Chapman, "but what about that mob? I don't suggest you do this, sir. However, I won't stop you. Heed my words, I don't want to give the order to fire, but if I have to I will."

St. Clair understood. Officials such as Chapman could take no chances. During one of their heated discussions, Tom Fox often told St. Clair that New York at the best of times was like a powder keg ready to detonate. In Fox's view, it was the misery and degradation endured by the lower classes—the slums, disease, poverty, and, above all, hopelessness—that created a tense and fretful environment. All that was needed was a spark. It had happened during the draft riots of 1863 when hundreds of people, perhaps as many as a thousand, were killed, and the city exploded in a convulsion of violence that lasted four days. St. Clair tended to agree with Chapman's assessment. There was no negotiating with a mob—its leader, however, might be reasoned with.

St. Clair reached the prison's front gates where a trio of armed guards stood in front of the main entrance. Without uttering a word, they stepped aside so he could pass. As he did so, he felt the treacherous heat. In a matter of seconds, he felt as if he had washed in molasses and water. Here was another problem that would turn the mob's mood even angrier, he thought.

The voice of Reverend Ingersoll, which earlier had echoed throughout the Tombs, grew thunderous and more distinct as he walked closer to the mob. His anxiety level was high and listening to Ingersoll he could understand why the crowd was in such frenzy.

"My friends, we live in a world of licentiousness and sin. Corruption is everywhere and unless we alter our course, our civilization will die," Ingersoll bellowed. "Travelers have told us of savages who are like monkeys, yet guided by uncorrupted instincts and nothing else are pure in their domestic lives. We need to be like those savages, rather than the so-called civilized men we pretend to be. The time has fully come when we must do something if we would be saved, and that something must be to restore purity and end the murder of our unborn children.

"The colored man is already condemned to die today. Do we wait until justice runs its slow course with the evil woman? Or, my friends, do we stop her and her kind today? No more killing of children. No more slaughtering the innocent."

The mob shouted its approval. "Death to the Negro. Death to Philippe, the fiend." Some of the men beat copper pots, while others held lit torches or fired rifles and guns in the air.

St. Clair walked up from behind Ingersoll. He grabbed him by the collar and spun him around.

"Reverend, what on earth are you doing?" he shouted. "You must disperse them. The warden's given orders to fire on you if anyone tries to break in. For God's sakes, man, stop this. There's more police on the way."

Ingersoll pulled away from St. Clair. "There's nothing I can do, Mr. St. Clair. That woman is a menace, who's murdered her last mother and child."

"You don't know what you've done, you fool. Innocent people will die today and that blood will be on your hands."

St. Clair lightly pushed Ingersoll back and the reverend stumbled to his knee. The crowd let out a collective gasp of anger and several men, led by Little Philly, began to surge forward from the middle of the mob. A woman to the left of St. Clair picked up a stone and hurled it at him. He ducked. The rock missed his head by inches. He stepped back, intending to retreat into the prison. But then something made him stop in his tracks, something just beyond Philly and his men.

At the far back of the crowd, standing off to the side, was the hulking assailant who had attacked him and Fox the other night. St. Clair would have recognized that silver moustache and thick neck anywhere. The man was holding a placard that read, "DEATH TO THE WITCH," and speaking to a woman whose back was turned. The conversation did not appear to be a pleasant one.

"Sir, you must come back in at once," one of the prison guards shouted.

Little Philly and two of his men, Snake Manfred and Punk Tyler, were nearly at the steps. Reverend Ingersoll raised his arms, trying to pacify the mob. It was too late. He had lost control of them. More gunfire and shouting rang through the streets.

"Hang her now," someone screamed and more people joined in. "Hang her," they began to chant.

St. Clair could not take his eyes off the man with the silver moustache. He waved the placard in the air, stepped away from the woman he was speaking to, and then, without warning, forcefully hit her with the sign. She fell to the ground but as she fell St. Clair could see her face. His mouth opened. "My God," he whispered.

It was Ruth Cardaso.

At that moment, his eyes locked with Flint, who nodded and leered ominously. Even in the heat and commotion, a chill ran down St. Clair's spine. Before he could say or do anything, Ruth scrambled to her feet and ran in the opposite direction.

"You son of a bitch," screeched Little Philly. He reached for St. Clair's arm, but missed. Two police guards appeared at the top of the entrance-way. One yanked St. Clair backwards into the prison and the other pointed his pistol directly at Philly.

"Stop right now, you Mick bastard, or I'll shoot."

~

Philly sneered at him and kept advancing. The guard cocked the gun's hammer and fired. Philly instinctively ducked. The bullet whizzed by his head. He bounded up, and before the stunned guard could react he clubbed the man on the head. The prison official slumped to his knees. With Snake Manfred and Punk Tyler close behind, he pushed his way into the prison past the second guard who abandoned his post.

"She must be in there," he said, pointing to St. Clair who he glimpsed running down a hallway to his left.

"What about the Negro?" asked Manfred.

"He's not going anywhere," Philly replied. "We'll get her first and then string them both up."

~

St. Clair found Madame Philippe alone in her cell. She was shackled to the bed, but the door had been left open.

"Madame, where's Mr. Chapman? Where's the guard?" St. Clair's voice rose.

"He said he was going to bring more of his men from the other side of the prison." Madame Philippe's face was pale. "What's happening, Mr. St. Clair?"

He looked at her sitting on the bed chained like a dog and for the very first time felt a twinge of sympathy. The fiend of Fifth Avenue was nothing more than a weak old woman.

St. Clair could hear Philly and his men in the prison corridor. He reached for his pistol and then recalled that he had surrendered it to Chapman. "Damn it, I need a weapon," he muttered looking around the cell. He grabbed the wooden stool in the corner. He had come to a decision—he wasn't going to let them lynch Madame Philippe. At the very least, she deserved her day in court. He thrust the stool legs forward, as if he was about to tame a wild animal.

Suddenly, the cell door was kicked open all the way.

"Stop right there," shouted St. Clair, uncertain of a stool's effectiveness against bullets.

"I told you that there was nothing to concern yourself with." It was Chapman. "I think you can put that stool down now."

St. Clair threw it to the dirt floor. Behind the assistant warden, were five armed guards. They had their guns pointed at Philly, Manfred, and Tyler. Outside, whistles blew, shouts of confusion, followed by gunfire, filled the air.

"I'd say that help from the precinct has arrived," said Chapman, wiping his brow. The tension in his face had vanished.

~

Within an hour, peace and order had been restored in and around the Tombs. A dozen or so culprits, Philly and his men among them, were arrested and taken to police headquarters for further questioning. So was Reverend Patrick Ingersoll, who was charged with disturbing the peace. St. Clair figured that he would be out by dinner.

Before he departed, St. Clair promised Madame Philippe that he would continue to make inquiries about Lucy Maloney. "Please don't think that I suddenly approve of what you do, Madame," he told her. "But matters here today have led me to reconsider certain facts." He had been deliberately vague and she had not asked for any explanations.

Seeing his assailant gloating at the back of the mob was too much of a coincidence. If, as he and Fox suspected, Fowler was behind the attacks on them that meant that this despicable thug was likely in Fowler's employ. Why then was this man supporting a mob intent on hanging Madame Philippe, who claimed she was innocent in the murder of Lucy Maloney? His presence today could not have been merely a happenstance. Had not George, the doorman from the Fifth Avenue Hotel, told him that he had seen Miss Maloney speaking with a man who fit his description? Did Fowler also know Lucy Maloney? For that matter, St. Clair was as curious as Madame Philippe as to why Fowler had deserted her when she required his support the most?

Much of this was, as Seth Murray might say, merely circumstantial evidence. Yet it was also highly compelling. At the very least, it begged more questions that with any luck would soon find answers.

And, then there was Ruth Cardaso. St. Clair could still hardly believe what he had seen with his own eyes. He wanted so very much to dismiss Ruth's interaction with his foe as a sheer fluke. Yet was it? He thought again about what he had witnessed and he knew it was no fluke. It was the way she had stood while addressing this man—not as a stranger, but as someone she had spoken to on many occasions. And the way this scoundrel shoved Ruth to the ground and then smiled at St. Clair afterwards troubled him deeply. It was not merely a look of contempt—it was one of superiority and domination.

Why had Ruth visited him last night? What were her real motives? Now, more than ever, he needed to learn the truth—even if he knew it was painful.

St. Clair left the Tombs with these many thoughts weighing heavy on his mind and heart. As he passed through the main entrance, he glanced back to see Mr. Chapman and a group of prison guards leading a chained colored man across the Bridge of the Sighs towards the gallows. Fifteen minutes later, Bob Bundy, declaring his innocence to the end, was hanged until he was dead.

Chapter Twenty

---※◆※---

MORE QUESTIONS

Whenever St. Clair was distressed, or in the dumps, as Caroline used to say, he headed to Central Park to wander alone through the Ramble. Even on a hot August day, it was a pleasant stroll on the footpaths among the trees, birds, and streams.

The hordes of weekend visitors, who usually crowded the park to listen to Dodsworth's band play on the Mall or accompany their children to the zoo at the Arsenal, were not there early on a Friday afternoon. They would be out in full force tomorrow, St. Clair was certain, along with the wealthy and affluent of Fifth Avenue, eager to display their prized horses and high-priced carriages. Among the rich, trotting in the park was a popular pastime.

St. Clair walked the wooded paths for more than an hour, before hopping an omnibus to take him back downtown. Against his better judgment, he made one stop at the Fifth Avenue Hotel. He was hardly surprised when Mr. Buckland informed him that Ruth had departed that morning and that she had left no forwarding address. The bill for her ten-day stay already had been sent to *Fox's Weekly*.

By the time the omnibus reached Park Row, he still felt no better than when he had left the Tombs. His heart yearned for Ruth—his head kept telling him that only a fool would love an untrustworthy woman and a liar.

"That you, Charlie?" said a familiar voice.

St. Clair climbed up the stairs and entered the main office. He was stunned to see Tom Fox standing beside Molly Lee, who was at her desk taking dictation. Over in the far corner of the room Sutton was reviewing a sketch with Peter Stewart.

"Tom, what are you doing here?" St. Clair asked. "I thought they needed more of your blood."

"The doctor examined me this morning and told me there was nothing more he could do. He said I should go home and rest."

"So, you decided to come to the office instead?" Seeing Fox healthy and back at the magazine was reason enough to perk up—at least temporarily.

"I heard about what happened at the Tombs. You're having a worse week than me, Charlie. But I see your nose is nearly healed."

"Yeah, but it still aches like the devil. As for the Tombs, we need to speak more of that, but in private."

"Okay." Fox leaned back and lit a cigar. "First tell me what you know about Crédit Mobilier?"

"It's a railway company, isn't it? And a successful one at that, if I'm not mistaken. Although, hasn't it been accused of some commercial indiscretions recently? Didn't I read something about the company being accused of charging Union Pacific exorbitant contract fees? Why do you ask?"

"Here look at this." Fox handed St. Clair an envelope. "I hope you won't be too upset, Charlie. This letter arrived by messenger around ten. Sutton gave it to me and I opened it. I didn't know where you were. Sutton heard about the riot at the Tombs from a cop. We thought it might be urgent. Instead all I found were two words . . . Crédit Mobilier. And it was signed KTB. You know what the hell that means?"

"Maybe." St. Clair stared at the letter. "I don't know for certain."

St. Clair knew exactly who had sent him the letter and what it meant. KTB—Kick the Bucket. He usually found Frank King's sense of humor unsophisticated, yet highly amusing. Now, however, was not the time to reveal his secrets to Fox or anyone else. Timing was crucial and Fowler and the members of the Ring could not suspect that anything was amiss.

Frank King's safety, even his very life, depended on St. Clair's silence and discretion. With the help of his wife, Amanda, and a trusted servant who played the role of a physician, King had meticulously faked his own death at Harlem Lane. He had purposely tipped his carriage and before anyone there knew what was happening, his servant, riding on a horse nearby, had proclaimed him dead and had arranged for the body to be whisked away to a funeral parlor.

Initially, when King had broached this idea, St. Clair was skeptical. King had carried off the charade brilliantly, however. And, from what he had heard, Amanda King's performance at the station the other day, when she solemnly supervised the loading of an empty coffin on board the train, was worthy of the Rialto stage.

King now insisted on revealing Fowler's grand scheme to St. Clair gradually. And St. Clair was in no position to disagree. King was rightly concerned about his wife and wanted to ensure that his ruse had succeeded before he fully exposed Fowler. From his past dealings with the Boss and his cohorts in the Ring, King knew that if any of them got so much as a hint of what he was planning, Amanda would be in danger. No amount of arguing by St. Clair changed his position. Thinking about it later, St. Clair could not blame him for being so cautious. If the situation had been reversed, he would have done the same to protect his wife.

In their last conversation, King had indicated that when he was safely hidden away, he would provide St. Clair with a name of a person or institution that would lead him in the right direction. Now he knew what that was—Crédit Mobilier.

"You're a lousy liar, Charlie," said Fox, "always have been. That's why you lose at poker so much. I'm certain you've got your reasons and that you'll tell me when you're ready. I've got Sutton looking into it. See if there's some connection to Fowler."

"That's an excellent strategy," St. Clair said. "I'll give Sutton all the help he needs. Why not send him to Washington? Let him nose around. See what he can find out. I've heard that Oakes Ames is involved with Crédit Mobilier. Isn't he a friend of yours?"

"Ames? Yeah, we've had a few glasses whiskey together. He's as loyal a Republican as you'll ever meet. Would shine Grant's riding boots everyday if he could. But I think he'd talk to Sutton if I asked him to." Fox looked over at Sutton. "Ed, pack your bags, you're taking the morning train to Washington. Molly'll give you money for the ticket and I want proper receipts for your accommodations." He turned back to St. Clair. "Charlie, let's continue this conversation in private."

St. Clair followed Fox into his office, which Molly had cleaned up nicely since the night of the attack.

"I should've married that woman long ago," mumbled Fox.

"Forget it, she's too young and pretty for you."

Fox shut the door and waited until St. Clair sat at the chair in front of his desk. He slid a single piece of paper across to him.

Mr. Victor Fowler, Esq.
Dear Sir,
With respect to our earlier conversation: The price for Fowler's Weekly, its business and printing presses, is $1,000,000.
I await your reply.
Your servant,
T. Fox

St. Clair stared at Fox, a look of astonishment on his face. "Have you gone mad?"

Fox shook his head. "Not yet. At least, I don't think so, but you'd have to speak to my doctor."

"You're not serious about this? You're offering Fowler the magazine for one million dollars? Why on earth—?"

"I haven't actually gone nuts, Charlie. Listen, please."

Fox proceeded to tell St. Clair about Fowler's visit to the hospital, his half-a-million dollar offer to purchase the magazine, and his not-so-subtle veiled threat that his thug might return if the offer was rejected.

St. Clair whistled. "At least we can now be certain that whoever attacked us was indeed Fowler's messenger. I have to tell you something about him. But first, two questions—"

Fox interrupted him. "They are, I imagine, why does Fowler want to buy the magazine in the first place? And what'll happen if he accepts my new proposal? Am I right?"

"Yeah. But I'd be more concerned if he refuses and gets angry. I hope you know what you're doing, Tom."

"I'd be lying to you if I said I'd figured out every angle. But if we can keep Fowler occupied as well as agitated for a while longer, perhaps this Crédit Mobilier connection will be the final nail in his coffin." Fox butted his cigar in the metal dish on his desk. "Now, what about our favorite hoodlum?"

"Tom, I saw him. He was there."

"He was where?"

"Where do you think? That shit was at the Tombs today."

Fox leaned forward on his elbow. "Why would he be in the middle of a mob that wanted to hang Madame Philippe?"

"A good question..." said St. Clair began.

"Unless," Fox sat up suddenly in his chair, "the noble Reverend Ingersoll is also on Fowler's payroll and he was there to lend him a hand."

"That's what I was thinking as well," said St. Clair. "What I want to know is why Fowler turned his back on Madame Philippe, after supporting her for so many years? How many times has he bailed her out of trouble?"

"Dozens, I don't know for sure. Didn't he once get her released from Blackwell's Island? Back in '47, if I'm not mistaken?"

St. Clair started pacing back and forth. "Tom, there's... there's something else."

"You're like a dog in heat. Out with it, Charlie."

"At the Tombs, Fowler's hired hand was arguing with a woman."

"Yeah, so what of it? I imagine a rogue like that would know a few whores," Fox said snidely.

"It was no harlot or maybe it was." St. Clair stopped in his tracks in front of Fox's desk. "Hell, I don't know. And that's the damn problem. It was Ruth, Tom. Ruth Cardaso was speaking with him." He slumped into a chair. "They had some sort of fight. He pushed her to the ground with a wood placard he was holding. I don't think he hurt her too badly. Then she ran off before I could speak to her. But why in the world would she be talking to him? How in the blazes does she know him? Can you tell me that? You brought her here, for Christ sakes. Where's your whiskey? Did Molly restock your supply yet?" St. Clair began shuffling books on the shelf to find Fox's secret stash of booze. "Here it is." He grabbed hold of a half-full bottle,

Fox was silent. "Ruth talking to the bugger who attacked us. That doesn't make any sense." He stroked his whiskers. "Let's be savvy about this, Charlie. I'll send another wire to Nathan Scott at the *Chronicle* in San Francisco and see what I can learn. I'm sure he has a contact in the police department. Maybe he can find out something more useful about her." He stood and walked around to the front of the desk, putting his right hand on St. Clair's shoulder. "Is it possible that she's working for Fowler? That she's been sent to spy on us?"

"It's definitely possible." St. Clair reached for two empty glasses Fox kept on his desk and poured two shots of whiskey. "And I think that she knew Lucy Maloney, the woman who was found dead in the trunk... the woman who Madame Philippe is alleged to have murdered. I don't know how all the pieces of this puzzle fit, but I will soon. I swear to you, I will."

He carefully handed Fox a glass and both men swilled down the liquor in one gulp. Neither uttered another word for a long time.

Chapter Twenty-One

MISS MILDRED

S t. Clair borrowed a rig and horse—an old grey-and-white nag named Sonny—from Tom Fox, so he did not have to hop back on an overheated omnibus. On the other hand, the journey took a little longer than the forty minutes he had anticipated.

As he neared Union Square, there was yet another accident—as common as flies and rats in New York. He was told by a patrolman that an elderly man who was attempting to cross Fourteenth Street had been struck down and run over by a butcher's cart. The poor man appeared to be dead. The initial accident triggered a collision with at least five other carriages and a lot of yelling and confusion by the time more patrolmen arrived. It took twenty minutes before St. Clair could get through the area and pull up with Sonny in front of the Potter mansion on Twenty-Fifth Street and Fifth Avenue, close to Madison Square.

About the last thing St. Clair wanted to do was go to tea with Miss Mildred Potter, a celebrated society gossipmonger. But with so many questions about Lucy Maloney's life and death unanswered—not the least of which were his nagging doubts about Madame Philippe's guilt in this tragic crime—speaking with Miss Potter made sense. Seth Murray was too busy to accompany him because of the trouble at the Tombs and had grudgingly agreed to St. Clair speaking with Miss Potter on his own. St. Clair reminded his officious brother-in-law that he hardly needed his permission.

"Remember, Charlie," Murray had cautioned him, "this is an open police investigation." St. Clair nodded politely to him and left the station figuring he'd handle Miss Potter in any way he wanted.

He had walked by this palatial house many times. Rupert Potter was known to be somewhat conservative with his money, yet he spared no expense on this magnificent French Normandy-style, four-story, fifty-five-room, stately home. It was said that no member of the city's aristocracy lived in finer quarters—not even Victor Fowler.

St. Clair walked up the stone pathway and rang the front bell. In a matter of moments, he was greeted by an elderly Negro butler dressed in a black suit with tails.

The butler led St. Clair down a wide hallway three stories high with the mid-afternoon sun beaming in through a large skylight. The floors were shining oak and immaculately clean. A trio of maids were busy dusting ornamental ceramic vases, which were displayed like museum artifacts in twin glass cases.

At the end of the hall, St. Clair entered into a rectangular picture gallery with dozens of paintings hanging on the walls. Rupert Potter, who fancied himself a connoisseur of the art world, was renowned for his collection of European and American paintings. On the far wall, St. Clair immediately recognized the work *Washington Crossing the Delaware* by Emanuel Leutze. There were also impressive paintings and sketches by other artists that St. Clair did not know.

"This way, sir," announced the butler.

St. Clair crossed through the gallery into a parlor with plush rose carpeting, cluttered with sofas and an assortment of chairs and tables. Tall, striking plants stood in pots by the windows, which were covered in heavy rose velvet drapery.

He found Mildred Potter waiting for him. She was wearing a flowing pink satin dress with red and pink flounces. However, St. Clair was instantly struck by her youthful and angelic face. He knew that she was a woman of approximately twenty-three years of age, yet she reminded him of a girl who was no more than fourteen years old—in no small way accentuated by the blonde ringlets that hung innocently, yet somehow suggestively, on her shoulders. He also noticed that she was unusually thin and that her bright blue eyes were rimmed with red, as if she had been weeping for a long period of time. Still, he noted that she carried herself well and wouldn't have been surprised to learn that Mildred had attended Madam Puff Ball's Finishing School or a similar institution that instructed a young woman on the fine art of becoming a society hostess.

"Mr. St. Clair, I was worried you'd never arrive." Mildred Potter smiled.

St. Clair responded with a slight bow. "My apologies, Miss. I was delayed at the magazine office."

"You're here now and there's plenty of tea and butter cakes left. Please come sit down and meet my companions." She took his arm and led him to two other young women sitting on a sofa sipping tea.

"This is Wanda Williams, a friend all the way from England, and Alice McKinnon, who lives in the city."

"A pleasure to make your acquaintance, ladies," said St. Clair, again bowing courteously.

"And yours, sir. We're both avid readers of *Fox's Weekly* and always look forward to your articles," said Miss Williams, a tall and lanky woman with wire spectacles.

"We're waiting for your next installment about Mr. Fowler and the Ring. What do you have planned, Mr. St. Clair? Please do tell us," said Miss McKinnon, stouter but just as handsome as her friend.

"Oh, Alice, why do you bother with such things? No proper gentleman would want his wife concerned with such complicated matters as the affairs of city hall," cried Mildred. "You'll have to forgive Alice, Mr. St. Clair, she's been listening to Father far too much."

"On the contrary, my dear Mildred, she has much yet to learn," declared a voice from inside the picture gallery.

Rupert Potter sauntered into the parlor. He was dressed in his riding attire—a low black topper, white long-sleeved shirt, a grey double-breasted waist coat, and matching trousers with two stripes down the side that were tucked into high black polished riding boots. Potter was a tall, muscular and elegant man with a trim black beard speckled with grey and white.

"St. Clair, isn't it?" he asked extending his right hand.

"That's right, I wasn't certain you'd remember," he said, firmly grasping Potter's hand.

"Father has the memory of an elephant, Mr. St. Clair. He never forgets a face or anything else for that matter. Isn't that right, Father?" said Mildred.

"Precisely, my dear. St. Clair, I believe you referred to me in your magazine as a stock-jobber, if I'm not mistaken. I was accused of…how did you put it…'spending money with a profusion never before witnessed in our country, at no time remarkable for its frugality.' Did I recall that correctly?" Rupert Potter asked with a glint in his eye.

St. Clair was impressed. "I meant no insult, sir. As I recollect, it was for a story on…" He searched his memory.

" 'The Fortunes of War', about the riches I'd made from the war against the Confederacy," Potter added, lighting a fat cigar.

"Again, if I insulted you in any way…"

"Poppycock! I've been a fortunate man, I'd never disputed that. And I've made a fortune, just as you've written. I was born dirt poor on a farm in Maryland. My father eked out a living his whole miserable life, but never complained once. I happened to be in the right place at the right time. My investment in railways, especially in Ohio, paid enormous dividends and only a fool would turn his back on such rewards. Besides, my daughter can't spend my money fast enough. Mrs. Potter, God rest her soul, would've been stronger with her. Alas," he added smiling at his daughter, "I'm a weak man when it comes to Mildred."

"Oh, Papa, I think you exaggerate." Mildred gestured to the tea tray, "Please, Mr. St. Clair, have a cup of tea."

"Tea! I think Mr. St. Clair would prefer a glass of whiskey and a Havana."

"Father, please, don't be rude. Mr. St. Clair has come to speak with me about a serious and tragic issue." Tears welled in Mildred's eyes.

"Dear, Mildred, come sit with us for a moment, before we take our leave," urged Miss Williams.

"Don't grieve, my darling. I'm well aware of Mr. St. Clair's intentions." Rupert Potter grasped his daughter's hand. "But, if not the whiskey, then at least let him enjoy a cigar. A new shipment arrived today from the West Indies."

He offered St. Clair his choice from a freshly opened box. "Are you much of a judge of horse flesh? You must visit the stables and have a glance at Sultan, one of the finest thoroughbreds I've owned. Colonel Dukes of Powhatan County, Virginia, bred and raised him. He's said to be of Arabian descent and I believe it. I've never seen a horse faster and more graceful than Sultan. I bought him seven months ago and he's already won four races. I'm planning to race him again in Richmond next month."

"I'd be most interested in seeing the animal."

"Good, and here I thought you were merely a clever Dick, fully occupied on Fowler and that damn Ring."

"Papa, please," Mildred admonished him.

"My apologies, ladies. But that's about the kindest word I can use."

"Please excuse me, Mr. St. Clair, while I see Wanda and Alice to the door," Mildred said, as her friends gathered their belongings.

St. Clair waited until the three women had left the room before he struck a match and lit his cigar. "Apart from this dreadful business with Madame Philippe, which I'm talking to Miss Potter about very shortly, I've been busy with Mr. Fowler's scheming and machinations. However," he studied Potter's face, "I thought you'd approve of such efforts."

"Yes, of course, I do. That crook has spawned the greatest corruption this city has ever known, or, I predict, will ever experience again. Trust me, St. Clair, when the whole truth becomes known, Victor Fowler will be spending the rest of his life in jail."

"And what of your Citizens' Committee?"

"I remain committed to it, but I need some assistance." Potter looked thoughtful. "Fowler, as you well know, has friends, most of who have been bought and paid for. They're in every corner of the city and beyond... in Albany, and even Washington. He is, I'd concede, a formidable opponent. However, with the right degree of conniving, he can be defeated. In my opinion, Fowler's main weakness is not greed, but rather arrogance mixed with a healthy dose of over-confidence. It shall be his undoing."

St. Clair inhaled sharply on his cigar and took stock of the man before him. Potter was as wise as he was wealthy. "Sir, if I might broach another topic. Do you know anything of Crédit Mobilier?"

Potter laughed loudly. "I know enough not to invest one penny in that carpetbagger scheme. Before Ames and Durant are done, they'll rook Union Pacific for every dollar it has," he said, stepping closer to St. Clair. "I can't vouch for the accuracy of this information, but I've heard rumors, nothing more than the type of gossip my daughter fancies, that Vice-President Colfax, perhaps Grant himself, is embroiled in this."

"And what of Fowler's connection?"

"That, I'm afraid, I know nothing about. It wouldn't surprise me if he's somehow involved. A common crook is what Fowler is, of the type you'd find scourging by the waterfront. Nothing more than that."

"But not easily cornered, you'd agree?"

"I'm certain you and that cheeky Mr. Fox will devise an ingenious trap that'll snare Fowler. And I'd be happy to assist you in any way possible." He glanced at his timepiece. "Now, I must attend to Sultan."

"It's been an honor chatting with you again, sir. And don't be surprised if I take you up on that offer in the very near future."

"I look forward to it," said Potter, leaving the parlor.

～

"What can you tell me about Miss Maloney?" asked St. Clair. He was alone with Mildred in the parlor. She sat opposite him, sunk into a green sofa covered in pillows.

"I expect George at the hotel told you to speak with me?"

"As a matter of fact, he did."

"Did you grow up in New York, Mr. St. Clair?"

"I was born in the city, but left when I was a boy of twelve for Baltimore. Why?"

"When I was six and seven years old, my father used to take me to Franconi's Hippodrome. It was located on the same spot as the Fifth Avenue Hotel. I remember it as this mammoth arena, much as I imagine the Coliseum in Rome must be like. It was such a shame when they tore it down to build the hotel, but Father says that Mr. Franconi never made any money. I always found that hard to believe. My word, his show was better than any circus I've ever been to. Barnum's hardly compares. At the Hippodrome there was always this procession of elephants and camels. It must've been a mile long," she laughed. "And make-believe gladiator fights. It was much easier then. Life was a lot simpler at that age, wouldn't you agree?"

"Simpler, yes, but certainly not as interesting," St. Clair paused for a moment gauging Mildred's emotional state. "Miss Potter, what of Miss Maloney?"

"I told her to see a physician," cried Mildred. "I had no idea she'd go see Madame Philippe. My Lord…" Tears welled in her eyes again and spilled on to her cheeks.

"Then you didn't know that she was with child?" St. Clair inquired as delicately as he could.

"I suspected." Mildred patted her eyes with her handkerchief. "But, no, we didn't actually speak of it. I'd planned to raise it with her. And then…you'll have to forgive me, Mr. St. Clair, I consider Lucy my dearest friend. I don't know why she didn't confide in me about this. She'd been unwell for some time and I knew she was courting."

"Yes, please tell me more about that."

"There's nothing to say. She never permitted me to meet him, nor do I know who he is."

"That strikes me as very peculiar, Miss Potter."

"Odd as it is, I'm afraid it's the truth."

St. Clair said nothing. He suspected that she was lying to him, but he sensed that employing Murray's tactics to berate an answer out of her would accomplish nothing.

"George mentioned to me that he'd seen Miss Maloney with a man one day, somewhat rough, with bushy side-whiskers. Not a pleasant fellow, nor someone who'd frequent the Fifth Avenue Hotel, I suspect. Do you know who he meant?"

Mildred shook her head. "No. I know no one like that." She stroked her hair.

St. Clair decided to change his strategy. "How did the two of you meet?"

That query made her smile. "Two years ago at a masked ball given by the *Cercle Français de l'Harmonie*," she replied in an impeccable French accent.

"I attended one myself last season at the Academy of Music. It was quite festive and even rowdy at times. Most are like that, I believe, isn't that so?"

Mildred blushed slightly, but did not respond.

St. Clair was purposely being polite. As far as he knew, the masked or French balls presented by the French societies were notorious for attracting impure and reckless women and their male friends—men who actually dressed in women's clothing. The costumes worn by the women were usually daring and the dancing often vulgar and excessively passionate.

He recalled that some months ago, before Seth Murray had had his problems with Stokes, he had investigated the murder of a young woman who had attended a ball at the French Theatre on Fourteenth Street. Murray's investigation eventually revealed that the woman had been killed by her jealous husband. He had been infuriated by his wife's lewd public behavior. "These affairs are nothing but unruly excuses for debauchery," Murray had then remarked. "Husbands and wives often go, however, they usually go with somebody else's wives and husbands." St. Clair wondered what someone of Miss Potter's stature was doing at one of these orgies along with the mysterious Miss Maloney.

"I'm curious, Miss, did your father have knowledge of your presence at this ball?"

Mildred's face became redder still. "My father's not my keeper, sir. He has encouraged me to be independent. And I am. Lucy tried to be as well, although it was more difficult for her."

"Why's that?"

"Lucy didn't have much contact with her family in St. Louis. She was resourceful, but quite on her own. On numerous occasions, I begged her to leave the hotel and move in with Father and me, but she steadfastly refused. She could be quite stubborn."

"Or, perhaps, merely independent?" St. Clair raised an eyebrow.

Mildred tensed. The smile swiftly vanished from her face. "If you'll excuse me, Mr. St. Clair, I've an appointment before dinner this evening."

"One more question before I depart," said St. Clair, unwilling to be cowed by the young woman's sudden hauteur. "I assume the father of Miss Maloney's child, whoever he might be, was also paying her monthly rent at the hotel?"

Mildred stood, extended her hand. "It was a pleasure meeting you, Mr. St. Clair. One of the servants will see you to the door. Forgive me for being rude, but I must attend to an important matter at once."

Before St. Clair could respond, she had fled from the parlor.

Chapter Twenty-Two

SECRETS

Seth Murray collapsed in his chair. It had been a long and exhausting day. A dozen people, eight men and four women, had been charged with disturbing the peace. Not surprisingly every one of them was a member of what Murray—borrowing freely from the *Times*—usually referred to as the criminal and degraded classes. He reasoned that as long as these unruly and violent people, whose miserable existences were spent in prisons and almshouses, kept having children, the police department would never run out of work.

The only fact that Murray found truly interesting was that each person arrested claimed that they had been promised fifty dollars to take part in the protest at the Tombs. He had asked each to reveal the source of this generous payment, but none would. It didn't matter. He had already determined that the culprit who had organized the demonstration at the prison and the ensuing riot was none other than Victor Fowler.

An hour earlier, he had seen Isaac Harrison march into Stokes's office. Shortly after that, Reverend Ingersoll was released, along with Little Philly and two of his thugs, all of whom had been charged with assaulting a prison guard and attempted murder.

"Not enough evidence," Stokes had announced to him.

To Murray's dismay, he said it as if he meant it. He wanted to strike the inspector where he stood for being so crooked and weak, but he was smart enough not to act on such an impulse. The consequences would have been severe.

As he rolled himself a cigarette, one matter still puzzled him—Fowler's support of Madame Philippe was well known. Why, he wondered, had he deserted her? What did he have to gain by her death? Or, was it merely a distraction from Fowler's own political problems?

He lit his cigarette and his elbow inadvertently pushed three of his rogues' gallery books on to the floor. One of the mug books split open.

"Shit, this is all I needed," he muttered.

He reached down to clean up the mess, picked up several pages, when his eyes caught sight of a photograph of a woman. He stood up and examined it more carefully. According to the caption accompanying the mug shot, this female rogue had short, sandy brown hair. Murray stared at it. The woman's general appearance was audacious like that of a woman of pleasure who worked the customers at Harry Hill's or one of the other spirited concert saloons. Below the photograph, it stated that she was wanted on a suspected murder charge in Chicago. Allegedly, she had stabbed to death a man named Linus "Piker" Andrews, a saloon owner. There were no other details.

The name of the woman in question was Estelle Perera. But Murray knew her by a different name. The more he stared at the photograph, the more he was certain of his discovery.

Estelle Perera was none other than Miss Ruth Cardaso.

~

St. Clair did not fancy himself a spy, yet on more than one occasion he had been put in this uncomfortable role. As Tom Fox liked to tell him, "see not what you see and hear not what you hear." St. Clair always regarded that bit of wisdom as sound advice—except to accomplish such a task usually required a fair amount of patience.

He had moved his carriage a safe distance from the Potters' main gate and waited with his horse, Sonny, for Miss Potter to make an appearance. Sonny dozed, while St. Clair reviewed his conversation with the young lady.

It was not only her evident nervousness that had made an impression on him, or even that she out and out lied to him about not knowing the name of the man keeping Lucy Maloney in such style at the Fifth Avenue Hotel. She was clearly evasive, although he understood that she was protecting her friend's privacy. There was something else that troubled him, although he could not quite put his finger on it. Her tears for Miss Maloney seemed genuine, yet he got the feeling when they chatted that her mind was wandering and that her real concerns lay elsewhere.

St. Clair removed his hat and wiped the sweat from his forehead with a handkerchief. He checked his watch. It had now been two hours since he had left the Potters and still Mildred had not departed. Had she not said she had an important engagement? He supposed that Rupert Potter might have insisted that his daughter remain for supper. She did not seem to him, however, the type of person who would allow even her father to stand in her way.

He was suddenly taken by another notion. What if she had departed from the house using the servants' entrance in the rear by the stables? He might well have missed her an hour ago. He glanced at his watch again. She was not coming, he decided. He gathered up the reins and was about to rouse Sonny from her nap, when he saw her.

She had changed her clothes and was now wearing a plain blue dress and small bonnet, an outfit that a shop girl might have worn. No one would have guessed that she was the daughter of an aristocrat.

St. Clair's curiosity was piqued. He steadied Sonny as he watched Mildred climb into a hansom cab, suddenly excited at the prospect of his clandestine mission. He nudged his horse forward, but kept about half a block back from Mildred's cab so as not to arouse her suspicions.

The traffic was unusually light. The hackney driver proceeded briskly down Fifth Avenue until he reached Washington Square. He then swung his carriage left on to Broadway for several blocks, right on to Spring Street, and pulled up at the corner of Spring and Greene Street. St. Clair rode past Mildred's cab and stopped behind a row of carriages parked in front of one of the neighborhood's many lively brothels.

What was the daughter of Rupert Potter doing down here? St. Clair wondered. She was alone with no chaperone. Thieves and pickpockets were everywhere, not to mention drunken rowdies, who would find her easy prey. It made no sense.

He gazed behind him and watched Mildred pay her driver. Then, to his astonishment, she turned and strode directly towards the front door of what appeared to be a typical parlor house. Except St. Clair, like most men in New York, knew otherwise.

In one of his first Street Scenes columns, St. Clair had tackled the delicate issue of New York brothels.

As is common knowledge among most New York men, there are two types of brothels south of Houston Street—Public bawdy houses for common riff-raff or scoundrels with a few coins in their pockets. These are essentially noisy saloons with uncontrolled drinking, fighting, and whoring.

There are also private residences or parlor houses, run by discreet madams. At these upscale brothels, a gentleman, for five or ten dollars, can enjoy the company of beautiful women, drink whiskey, play cards, or often watch a titillating performance that is certain to excite his passions.

The resourceful madams, who operate these establishments, have a bevy of helpers at their disposal—cabmen who bring them customers, and cadets…ambitious young men, who supply them with whiskey, do house repairs, and recruit wayward women for them. I have it on good authority that the cadets receive twenty dollars for luring women from other brothels or tramping areas and upwards of thirty-five dollars and as much as fifty for delivering untouched women.

Mildred pulled the bell on the outside of the house and a minute later was permitted entry. St. Clair hopped out of his carriage. He found a young lad of about thirteen years and negotiated with him to watch Sonny and the carriage for a fee of two dollars. He made his way up to the front door of the parlor house and rang the bell. A moment later, an iron panel located in the middle of the door slid open. Two dark eyes peered at him.

"I'd like to come in," he said.

"Is Miss Kate, expecting you?" asked the female voice on the other side of the door.

"I don't believe so, but I'd like to visit with you." St. Clair replied using what he knew to be the correct phrase to gain access.

"Well, you appear to be respectable enough."

St. Clair stood patiently while a latch was unlocked and the door opened. A petite colored woman stood before him.

"Come in, sir. Come in and welcome to Miss Kate's House of Southern Belles. Please follow me. Let me take your hat."

St. Clair walked down a short darkened hallway and entered into a magnificent parlor with turquoise velvet carpeting and low gas-lit chandeliers. Directly in front of him, sitting and lying on a row of four plush sofas and divans, were about ten women, some wearing long frilly dresses, others in costumes that he had once seen ballerinas wear. They were drinking, smoking, laughing, and entertaining several male clients, young and old, who reclined on the sofas beside them. The air was hot and smoky.

"Your first time here, sir?" asked a buxom woman wearing a black satin robe. Her red hair was done up and pinned at the back. By the sound of her accent, St. Clair would have guessed she was from Georgia.

"You must be Miss Kate, I presume?"

"I am indeed, sugar. Now, what are you looking for this evening?" She clapped her hands and immediately four young women in various states of dress stood smiling before him. One of the girls moved forward and began gently stroking his hair.

"That's Josie, don't mind her," Miss Kate grinned. "She does that to all of my clients. She's just eager to please, if you know what I mean? Mr....?"

"St. Clair, Charles St. Clair."

"Mr. St. Clair, it's a pleasure to make your acquaintance. Have you ever experienced genuine southern hospitality? Because that's what my girls do best. You look like a discerning gentlemen, perhaps I can interest you in young Flora, she's newly arrived and still a virgin. Only fifteen dollars for you, this evening."

He stared momentarily at the young woman. She was dressed in a white satin gown buttoned right up to her neck. He doubted very much that she was a virgin.

"Or what about Sally? She fancies ropes and braces? Whatever your heart desires, Mr. St. Clair, I can offer you. Also you must stay for our performance. In fact, Sally is on stage in about five minutes. Isn't that so, my dear?" Miss Kate turned to a girl wearing a pale yellow low-cut silk gown.

"That's right, Ma'am," the girl replied in southern drawl. "You've never seen anything like this, sir, I can guarantee that." Sally pushed Josie aside and stroked St. Clair's cheek with her painted fingernail.

"Miss Kate, ladies, I thank you for your kind offer and at any other time, I'd be happy to partake," said St. Clair, taking a step away from the women. "But what I really require is some information." He reached into his jacket and pulled out his billfold. "Here this is for your trouble." He handed Miss Kate ten dollars.

She quickly tucked the money inside her cleavage. Then she clapped her hands and, like obedient and well-trained dogs, Josie and Sally returned to the sofas.

"What type of information are you interested in, Mr. St. Clair?" Miss Kate moved close enough that he could smell her sweet breath.

"A young woman in a blue dress and hat came in the house just before me. I don't see her anywhere. Does she work here?"

Miss Kate pondered St. Clair's query for a moment. "You mean Millie?"

"Yes, exactly, Millie."

"Oh, no, she doesn't work for me." Miss Kate tittered. "Although she could if she wanted to. Millie has other interests. You can find her on the top floor in a special part of the house."

"Why special?"

The madam smiled. "That, you'll have to discover for yourself. Now, why don't—" A loud shout and the sound of a ruckus from the next room stopped her in mid-sentence. "Johnny, what the fuck is going on?" she shouted.

A muscular young man with greased-backed hair appeared at once. To St. Clair he looked like a man who could handle himself in a fight if he had to.

"It's Flint again," Johnny sighed. "Says he doesn't like the show and wants his money back."

"That man is the biggest hell on wheels, I've ever encountered. If he didn't have so much money, I'd never let him in here." Kate frowned.

"You want me to throw him out?" asked Johnny.

"That'll only make him angrier and meaner. Let me speak with him. Please excuse me for a moment, Mr. St. Clair," she said, turning to leave.

"What's in there?" St. Clair asked Johnny when she was gone.

"The stage. You ever seen a show here before? Go have a look-see."

St. Clair figured Millie or Mildred was not going anywhere fast and he was curious about Miss Kate's entertainment. He walked up to the doorway and looked in to see a small theatre with about thirty chairs lined up in front of a stage. A quarter of the size of the one at Harry Hill's saloon, the room was dark, except for the light on the stage. The male audience was loud and boisterous.

What St. Clair saw shocked as well as mesmerized him. He was no novice when it came to brothels or concert saloon shows. The women at Madam Helena's were as adventurous as any he had been with. Recently, he had even witnessed two women doing a strip dance at the newly opened Parisian Café in a show called *The Ladies of Marie-Antoinette's Court*. By the end of the finale both women were, for all purposes, naked. But this scene at Miss Kate's was something completely different.

There were three women on the stage, one of them was Sally. Off stage a large and husky black man played a slow tune on a grand piano. Sally had changed into a short black robe that hung open, exposing her naked body. In her hand, were two sets of rope braces. The other two women, a petite blonde and a brunette, similarly scantily clad, danced beside and around her. In the middle of the stage was a green divan.

The brunette allowed her robe to fall to the floor, which drew howls and hooting from the patrons. She held out her hands in front of Sally. Slowly to the rhythm of the music, Sally wrapped the braces around the naked woman's wrists and led her to the divan. The woman lay down, ensuring that her legs were wide apart. At Sally's urging, the blonde advanced on the brunette, first only pretending to suck her breasts and then doing so. Her fingers wandered all over the woman's body and then her head slowly moved downward. She turned to the audience with her tongue sticking out and, as the men shouted encouragement, she plunged her head between the brunette's legs. Her partner squirmed in ecstasy.

St. Clair took his eyes off the stage and glanced to his right. A few feet away, in the corner of the theatre he could see Miss Kate speaking into the ear of her unruly customer, the man she referred to as Flint. She beckoned him and another man, presumably his companion, to leave with her.

"I've paid my money, you whore, and I'll leave when I'm God damn ready to do so," the man screeched.

St. Clair nearly fell over. It was his attacker. It was the thug he had seen earlier in the day at the Tombs. He was here. And now St. Clair knew his name.

Flint.

St. Clair steadied himself and stepped away so that he could not be detected.

"Will you shut your fucking mouth, you asshole?" said a patron in Flint's direction.

"Yeah, listen to Kate and leave or…" echoed another.

"Or, what exactly?" said Flint, yanking his knife from its sheath and grabbing one of the men by the hair. He pressed the blade to the man's throat.

The women on stage stopped abruptly. Johnny rushed to illuminate more gas lights. St. Clair dived to the floor to keep out of sight. Flint's friend reached for the knife and gently pushed it away from the man's throat. St. Clair gasped. Though the man was wearing a plain dark-colored suit—and his derby hat, a size too large for him, was pulled low over his head, he was certain that Flint's companion was the Reverend Patrick Ingersoll.

Remarkably, Flint heeded Ingersoll's advice and pocketed his knife. He spit a wad of tobacco in Miss Kate's face and followed Ingersoll out of the theatre. Johnny hustled the two men to the main entrance. Miss Kate wiped the beads of brown spit from her cheeks and forehead. Apologizing to her customers, she invited everyone to stay for the next show on her, an offer that drew a loud and sustained applause.

Once he was sure Flint and Ingersoll had left the house, St. Clair approached Miss Kate. "Are you okay?"

"Nothing I can't handle, Mr. St. Clair. All in an evening's work, I'm afraid." She brushed the last drops of tobacco juice from her face. "That man reminds me of a wounded bear. It's hard to believe that he once had a mother."

"What do you know about him?"

"You're a curious fellow, aren't you? What is it you do for a living?"

St. Clair took out his pocket book again and pulled out a few bills.

Now it was Kate's turn to laugh. "No need for that. This one's on the house. I don't know much about him. He's here, whenever he's in New York. I think he's from Chicago or maybe St. Louis, I'm not positive. He fancies one of my girls, Lauralynne. But he's as unpleasant a patron who I've ever allowed in here."

"So why do you let him in?"

Kate laughed even harder. "And here I thought you were a wise and intelligent man. I'm paid handsomely to keep him content. And it's an offer that I'm unable to refuse, if you understand?"

"Victor Fowler," whispered St. Clair.

"So you are man of some intelligence after all. Yes, the Boss does me favors with the police and, in turn, I do some favors for him...for a price. It all works out for the best...at least on most days. This evening was an exception." She smiled. "One does what one has to do to survive. That's the law of this city, is it not?"

"It all depends on your perspective, Madam."

St. Clair knew that she was right. Had he not read last year a book by the English philosopher, Herbert Spencer, who suggested, "survival of the fittest implies multiplication of the fittest?" In short, either women such as Miss Kate made compromises and tough choices, or like thousands of others who did nothing, they would go adrift in the sea of poverty and misery that engulfed New York. The question, as always, was how far did one have to lower one's morals and ethics? From St. Clair's perspective, coming to terms with Fowler was akin to making a deal with the Devil. And that, he was not ready to do.

His sleuthing, on the other hand, had been fruitful and the evening was not yet over. Not to mention that Miss Kate's sexual theatre had been an unexpected and interesting diversion. Perhaps he would allude to it in a future "Street Scenes" column. More importantly, he had learned that the name of his assailant was Flint and thanks to Kate had finally confirmed the man's association to Fowler, who he reasoned must have facilitated Ingersoll's quick release from jail.

"The man accompanying Flint, you know who he is?" Miss Kate coyly asked him

"I think I do, yes. Reverend Patrick Simpson Ingersoll, was it not?"

She nodded with a grin. "Correct. The reverend is a frequent visitor. I believe he enjoys my theatrical productions."

"And you've seen him before in the company of this thug, Flint?"

"Yes, on several occasions. If memory serves me, it was Ingersoll who first brought Flint here. That must've been at least a year ago. Does that help you at all, my sweet?" Miss Kate touched his shoulder.

"It does indeed, Madam. Has Fowler ever accompanied them?"

"Never," she said slyly. "Mr. Fowler's much too clever to be seen with the likes of those two in public. Now why don't you come with me and I'll introduce you to a pretty young thing that'll take your mind off your troubles."

"Another time, Madam," St. Clair responded stepping away. "First I must see about this woman you call Millie. What's she doing up there?" He pointed the direction of the staircase.

"That you must discover for yourself. But take this." She handed him a narrow strip of red cloth. "You'll need it to enter."

"Madam, I thank you again for your assistance. It'll not be forgotten."

He kissed her hand and excused himself.

Chapter Twenty-Three

—❊—

ARABIAN NIGHTS

*T*he noise from the alley below startled Ruth Cardaso from her sleep. She roused herself and peered out the second floor window of her room. Directly below in the muddy street, a small crowd of drunken ruffians and streetwalkers had surrounded two sailors.

"Get your fuckin' hands off that wench. She's mine," said one of them.

"You get your fuckin' hands off her or I'll slit your gut open, you arse-kissin' scab," yelled the second one.

Ruth could see that the object of their desires was a plump woman with stringy dark hair and a torn green dress who stood off to the side smiling and laughing, obviously intoxicated. She was missing a front tooth and on her face were red scratch marks. She was hardly a beauty worth fighting for, mused Ruth. Nevertheless, two sailors were about to come to blows over her.

"Pluck his bloody eyes out," shrieked one of the women in the crowd.

"A little blood is what's needed," called another to a roar of laughter.

Just then, one of the sailors lunged for the other and the battle commenced.

Ruth stepped away from the window. She turned to gaze in dismay at the room she found herself in. It was cramped and filthy. There were dry bloodstains on the ratty piece of rug by her narrow cot and mouse droppings on the wood floor. A dirty bowl of water had been placed on the shelf near the window, but she dared not wash in it, never mind drink it.

Two hours earlier she had rented this room above the Jack-Tar, a shoddy little saloon off of Water Street where forty cents went far. She badly needed a place to hide, rest and think. And the Jack-Tar, as rowdy and seedy a drinking establishment as there likely was in the city, seemed like the only choice. Now, as the cries from the street grew louder and more vicious, she questioned her decision.

Desperation had driven her here. Desperation and fear. She had pleaded with Flint at the Tombs that she wanted to leave the city. He had forbid it and dismissed her with a shove to the ground. Her assignment was not yet finished, he had told her, and his threatening tone and actions could not be taken lightly. She knew all too well that he was capable of the vilest of acts. Greed not only governed his brutal behavior. So, too, did the great pleasure of inflicting pain on others. She understood that he owed no man loyalty.

Why had she allowed herself to become embroiled in his senseless scheming? She pondered this question again and again. She was no saint, she would admit that. Yet could she honestly stand by while innocent people were hurt, even hanged?

And then there was Charles St. Clair.

She reached for the bottle of whiskey she had brought with her and took a swig. The liquid nearly scorched her throat, but its numbing effect was calming. Her thoughts were of the other evening when she lay with him. He had held her tightly and she had wrapped her legs around him. The fit was perfect and she had almost forgotten her dreaded role and task. For a few tender moments, she was indeed Ruth Cardaso, an accomplished actress from San Francisco, and not Estelle Perera, a wanted criminal.

How had she got herself into such a predicament? And more importantly, how could she extricate herself from it? Her first instinct was to run, but she knew that Flint would eventually find her. What kind of life could she have constantly watching out for him and guarding her every move and action?

Initially, the charade had been as easy as shelling peas. She had used her natural ability and flair for dramatics to obtain and keep a job with a stock company at the California Theatre in San Francisco. Her role as Ophelia in Shakespeare's Hamlet had been, quite surprisingly, brilliant. It had garnered her superlative reviews and, most notably, an avid admirer in Mr. Nathan Scott of the *Chronicle*. He was a good and decent man and upon further reflection, she was troubled by the way she had deceived him so easily. He had been her entrance ticket into the city's high society. It had won her further theatre parts and more admirers, rich gentlemen, seeking the company and affections of an actress.

As she took another gulp of whiskey, she decided then and there that she could not permit Flint to blackmail her for one more second. It had to stop, even if that meant a potentially deadly confrontation with him and revealing the truth to St. Clair. She had at least one more part to play and she intended to give the performance of her life.

～

The smell of the smoke, sickly and sweet, was the first thing that St. Clair noted as he reached the top floor of Miss Kate's parlor house. There was a cramped hallway that led to a closed door. He approached it cautiously and knocked. The door opened and a dense cloud of scented smoke overwhelmed him.

A tall and stocky lad of seventeen or eighteen years stood before him. He said nothing but extended his open hand.

"The cloth, of course," muttered St. Clair. He fished the red strip out of his pocket and gave it to the boy, who smiled. It was a strange smile, not that of a man who had drank too much whiskey, but of a dazed person who had been nearly knocked unconscious.

"Come, my friend, come and experience the pleasure," the boy whispered in a French accent. "Please you'll find this much more comfortable. My name is Didier, but you may call me Deedee."

Didier insisted St. Clair give him his hat, suit jacket and shoes, and presented him with a long black silk robe, slippers, and a tasseled smoking cap. He felt foolish, yet dressed as he was instructed.

The curtains in the parlor were closed. Two hanging gaslights covered in a purple fabric colored the room violet. On the floor were large Oriental vases filled with a variety of colored flowers and green shrubs. Two paintings, both of fire-breathing dragons, nearly covered the far wall.

The young man led him through this room and into the next where some fifteen or twenty men and women, similarly arrayed in robes and tasseled caps, were sitting or lying on plush sofas, of the type Miss Kate had on the first floor of the house. The other three walls were almost entirely covered in mirrors, edged in gold. St. Clair noted that most of the men were of a dark complexion and he guessed that they must be Greek or Spanish. Several of them stared at him, but no one said a word. There was also no sign of Mildred, although at least four of the women wore multicolored masks, so he could not be certain.

The air held a haze of the sweet smoke sustained by several of the patrons who were puffing on what looked to be Indian or Persian pipes. These devices had glass decanters, which were filled with a clear liquid, likely water, St. Clair deduced. On the top of each was a silver bowl holding herbs and tobacco. Two long silver tubes protruded from the decanter, allowing the user to smoke from it. It was a scene, thought St. Clair, right out of *Aladdin* or one of the other tales of *Arabian Nights* that he had enjoyed so much as a young boy.

"You have the two dollars?" asked Didier.

St. Clair had no idea what he was talking about, but handed him the money. From behind a round table next to a wood shelf, Didier removed two items—a small bronze urn filled with a dry green herb and a tiny box containing five black lozenges.

Didier noticed the puzzled look on St. Clair's face and chuckled. "This is the *gunjeh* or hashish, the dried leaves of the hemp plant, which you'll soon smoke," he explained pointing to the herb. "And these lozenges are called *El Mogen*, and my favorite."

"What are they made of?"

"The resin of hemp, henbane, crushed datura seeds, butter and honey," Didier recited, as if he had been asked the same question many times.

St. Clair was familiar with the hemp plant and had heard rumors that there were groups of young people in New York who smoked it the way you would opium. The other ingredients in the *El Mogen*, apart from the butter and honey, he had never heard of before.

"Sit with me, here," said Didier, inviting St. Clair to join him on one of the unoccupied sofas. He complied, curious about the strange practice. Didier helped St. Clair off with his slippers, placed a soft pillow behind his back, then clapped his hands once. A colored male servant appeared bearing one of the Oriental pipes in one hand and a silver tray in the other. On the tray was another silver bowl filled with tobacco.

"I enjoy mixing this with the *gunje*." Didier took a spoonful of the tobacco and mixed it with the hemp. He then lit the pipe and offered St. Clair one of the silver tubes.

"Like this," said the young man, inhaling and holding the smoke in his lungs for a moment before blowing a whiff upwards. St. Clair imitated him as best he could and found the taste very smooth and pleasing. He coughed slightly after releasing the smoke, but tried it again without any problem. He lay back and indulged himself. Finding Mildred, he reasoned, suddenly did not seem as critical.

"Didier—I mean Deedee—I must tell you that I haven't felt this tranquil in many months. Even the recent injury to my nose isn't painful anymore." St. Clair laughed. "Do the doctors at Bellevue know about this?"

"*Vous êtes très amusant, monsieur,*" said Didier.

"I have no idea what you're talking about, and I'm certain I don't care." St. Clair said with a wave of his hand. He started to find everything strangely droll.

Didier put one of the black lozenges in St. Clair's hand. "You must now try one of these," he said.

"I definitely cannot. I believe this *gunje* I've smoked is quite enough."

Didier laughed again. "You are reaching Hashishdom. Is it not a tranquil state of relaxation?"

St. Clair had to concede that he had never felt more at peace. For some reason he could not take his eyes off the patterns in the Oriental ceiling. Its border of the red and green serpents and dragons appeared to dance and swirl while the white-faced women waving their fans at the center seemed as real as if they were standing in front of him. His senses never before had been so acute.

"Would you like me to summon one of the ladies from down the stairs for your pleasure?" asked Didier.

St. Clair shook his head, though he had to admit that smoking the herbs aroused him. "I'm looking for a woman named Mildred? Millie? She came in here before me. She's quite beautiful. You'd know her . . . she looks as if she's still a girl. Her hair is blonde—" St. Clair seemed to lose the thread as the ceiling continued to entrance him.

"Millie, *oui*, I know who you mean. You must understand, I cannot disturb her, not in here."

"That's most unfortunate." St. Clair paused. He had lost his train of thought again. He realized the *gunje* was making him dopey. "If you'll excuse me, I must get some fresh air." He staggered up, pushing the tassel on his hat away from his eyes.

"If you leave now, Mr. St. Clair, you'll never learn what you came for, will you now?" said a female voice behind him.

He turned around. Standing before him was a woman in a red silk robe with a matching mask. Even in his dreamy state, he could tell that it was Miss Mildred Potter.

≈

Mildred silently grasped St. Clair's hand and led him to the back of the parlor, where they both reclined on a plush divan. She offered him pears and berries. Food had never tasted so full of flavor. Next, she handed him a cup of hot tea. Its effect, too, was almost magical.

"I think you've enjoyed the happiness and peace brought on by the hashish. Have you not, Mr. St. Clair?" asked Mildred, removing her mask at last. Her eyes were redder than they had been earlier in the day, yet she was far more serene.

"Let's say, it's been an enlightening experience. And please, you may call me Charlie."

"You'd do it again, Charlie?"

"I'm not certain. I don't think I'm able to make such a decision at the moment."

She giggled. He smiled. Whether he cared to admit it or not, he found her delightful and genuine—unlike Ruth.

"Dear Lucy first brought me here. She'd been introduced to *gunjeh* on her travels to Europe. I'd never felt so at peace. It's difficult to resist. Don't you agree? Nothing like whiskey or beer, which to my mind brings only anger and resentment."

"No one knows who you are?"

"I'm not certain. But to be honest, it hardly matters. Whether I'm rich or poor, from Fifth Avenue or Five Points, it's unimportant. That world doesn't exist inside this house. At least not for me."

"You never worry that your father will discover your secret?"

She laughed quietly. "He hasn't so far. You're not planning to tell him, are you?"

"Never."

"You shouldn't have followed me, Charlie." She waggled her finger at him. "However, given that no real harm has been done, I've decided to forgive you." She smiled.

St. Clair responded in kind. "That's very generous of you, Miss."

She gently stroked his face. He said nothing nor did he reciprocate. It was difficult to explain yet he sensed that her intentions were friendship and not sexual in nature.

"King," she whispered in his ear.

"What's that?" St. Clair muttered sleepily.

"The man you're seeking is Frank King, or rather was. He worked for City Hall, as a bookkeeper, I think. He was killed in a dreadful horse racing accident the other day. That's why I didn't say anything to you about it. I didn't see the point."

"I don't understand," St. Clair responded dully.

"I think Frank was the father of Lucy's child," Mildred said, adding, "the two of them dead, it's hard to accept."

St. Clair seemed to hear this from deep inside a tunnel, but it had the effect of snapping him back to reality. His jaw dropped. He was stunned. A dozen questions ran through his head. How could he have not known about King's affair? Why had King not said anything to him after Lucy was found dead? What did this mean for the scheme he and King had hatched to bring down Fowler and the Ring? And what did King know about Lucy's death? Had he killed her to stop her from having their baby? Did his wife discover what was taking place? St. Clair shuddered at these thoughts and the room seemed to spin.

"Charlie, you look green. Are you feeling ill?" Mildred ran a soothing hand over his brow.

"Please, tell me about King and Lucy. I must know more."

"There isn't much to tell," Mildred sighed. "They met at the same masked ball two years ago where I first encountered Lucy. She was coy at first. She wouldn't even give him her name. Then, the next day, he put a personal ad in the newspaper. It was something like, 'Will the young lady in the purple dress with the white ribbon who danced with me at masked ball given by the *Cercle Français de l'Harmonie* send her address to F.K.' and he gave a box number at the main Post Office. Lucy replied and you can guess the rest." Mildred giggled. "Mr. King was quite polite and respectful to her. You must understand, given the right circumstances, Lucy could be free with herself. She was an adventurous soul. You should've seen her dance at the ball in her short purple dress. She didn't have a care in the world. I know that Mr. King was attracted to that. What man wouldn't be?"

"Did he tell her that he was married?"

"Not at first, no, but later, he confessed. By that time, it was too late. He was smitten with her and she with him . . . as well as with the generous arrangements he made for her at the Fifth Avenue Hotel. Lucy had been living at a wretched boarding house somewhere near Canal Street. Who could blame her for taking Mr. King up on his offer? Needless to say, she believed him when he told her that he would soon leave his wife. How foolish."

"And what of that unpleasant man the hotel doorman had seen her with?"

"I truly don't know who he is. She said nothing to me of it. I swear it." Mildred saw the grave look on St. Clair's face. "You don't think that he had anything to do with her death, do you? Or, heaven forbid, Mr. King? Certainly not Mr. King."

St. Clair was silent, still trying to ward off the effects of the hashish and to make sense of everything Mildred was telling him. He had been so certain that Fowler and Flint were directly involved in Lucy Maloney's murder. He thought one of them might even have been the father of her child. Put together with anything he or Sutton could learn about Crédit Mobilier, the end of the Boss and the Ring seemed guaranteed. Fowler would surely go to jail, perhaps face the gallows.

But now, he was more confused than ever. He would need to speak with Frank King—and very soon.

Chapter Twenty-Four

A VERDICT OF GUILTY

Madame Philippe, looking frail and tired, held on to the arm of her lawyer, Cedric Lampson. By all accounts, he was the most able criminal attorney in the state.

"Do you have anything to say, Madame? Anything to add before this court passes sentence?" asked Benjamin Beatty, the eminent grey-bearded Recorder at the Court of General Sessions.

"Only that I'm innocent of the crime of which I am accused," she replied softly.

"A jury of your peers have determined otherwise," thundered Beatty. "They have found you guilty of murder in the first degree with a recommendation to mercy. This case was not merely about the death of Miss Lucy Maloney, as tragic as that is. Rather, it is about the condition of our social life and the morals of our community. You have not only repeatedly committed medical malpractice, affecting the lives of countless innocent young women, but you have, by your malicious acts, tainted our civilization. I find, as the members of the jury did, that your plea of innocence rings hollow. And that the evidence presented by the district attorney, Mr. Cady, ably assisted by the police and Dr. Draper, is compelling."

"The only decision I have before me is whether to accept the jury's recommendation of mercy. Ordinarily, I would heed such a recommendation, but in this case I cannot. In my view, the evil that you have perpetrated on the victim is not deserving of mercy. Therefore, by the power vested in me by this court, I order that at the time deemed appropriate by the New York justice authorities, you be hanged by the neck until you are dead. May God have more mercy on your soul than you showed for Miss Lucy Maloney."

~

Seth Murray had been banging on the door to St. Clair's flat for more than five minutes. But there had been no response, despite the landlady's insistence that St. Clair was inside.

"As sure as the Lord Jesus walked across water, I saw Mr. St. Clair stumble in late Friday evening and haven't heard anything from him since," Mrs. Fitzhenry told him. "Looked like he'd been drinking again. That's what I think, at any rate."

Murray had sent at least four messages to him yesterday and had not received a reply to any of them.

"Charlie, you still alive? Open the door," hollered Murray one more time.

"Who goes there at this hour?" asked St. Clair, his voice groggy.

"At this hour? Charlie, it's already noon. Open the door, you soaker."

"Seth, is that you?" St. Clair fumbled with the door latch.

"What the hell is going on, Charlie?" asked Murray, barging in. "Jesus, you look like a real shit-sack. Your eyes are as red as a beet. Where've you been? What have you been drinking? I sent at least four messages. Christ, Charlie, you missed the entire trial."

St. Clair held up his hand, a plea for his brother-in-law to halt his loud interrogation. "First, coffee. Go ask Mrs. Fitzhenry for a cup of black coffee. Please," he begged holding his head in his hands.

"Shit, Charlie, I'm not your bloody servant," Murray muttered, leaving the flat.

Moments later, the detective returned with a mug of Mrs. Fitzhenry's strong coffee. St. Clair grasped the steaming cup in both hands and sipped it.

"So you want to tell me why you didn't reply to these?" Murray held up the messages that had been shoved under St. Clair's door.

"I apologize. I don't honestly remember what happened yesterday. I arrived home on Friday evening close to midnight. At least, I think it was Friday evening."

"I don't think I've ever seen you like this." Murray regarded him with concern. "What kind of grog were you drinking? By the look of you, I'd say it must've been red-eye."

"Not red-eye," mumbled St. Clair. "I need to sit down." He placed the mug on the table and collapsed on his sofa. "I entered Hashishdom on Friday. And this is unfortunately the result. I can assure you, no whiskey's ever made me feel this rotten before. I tried to get up yesterday. I couldn't do it."

"What in Christ were you doing at a hashish house with Orientals and heathens?"

"It's not like that all." St. Clair closed his eyes and leaned back on a pillow. "In fact, the one thing I do recall is feeling more at peace with than I ever had. For a while, at any rate, nothing at all troubled me. Anyway, I was following Mildred Potter, that's what I was doing there."

"Miss Mildred, the heiress, uses narcotics?" Murray shook his head in disbelief. "I'm sure you're planning a fascinating article."

"It's not like that at all. True, she's rolling in money. But she's not pampered or stupid, as I had thought. And, the information she supplied me is somewhat helpful."

"She smokes hashish, Charlie, how clever can she be?"

"All I can say is . . . try it once before you condemn her."

"Yeah, and I can look like you. Shit, what did this girl do for you? You didn't fuck her did you?"

"Don't be an asshole. I didn't treat her any way but as a gentlemen would, if you must know. Listen to me," he said taking another sip of coffee, deciding that he needed to be judicious about what he told his brother-in-law. "She met Lucy Maloney two years ago and they were close friends ever since. It was Lucy, in fact, who first took Mildred to the parlor house where she tried the *gunjeh*."

"Huh?" Murray stared at him.

"The hashish, I mean."

"Then who's the father of her child? Who was paying for her hotel room?"

St. Clair hesitated before Murray's probing questions. Under no circumstances could he mention to Murray about Frank King. This would only lead to further questions, which he could not answer—at least not yet. "She didn't know," he replied.

"Or she wouldn't tell you. Hell, Charlie, what wonderful information you discovered. You didn't learn anything. So she has a few secrets, who doesn't?"

"Wait a minute," said St. Clair. "I did find out something else. Almost by accident. Besides whores and hashish, this house on Spring Street also offers theatrical performances, if you can call them that. Three women on stage. You ever see anything like that before?"

"I've seen it once or twice, yeah. Westwood took me by a place on Mercer with the same kind of show by the sound of it. Didn't I ever tell you about it? There was this blonde with the largest titties I'd ever seen and this other woman—"

"Okay, you can tell me more later," St. Clair held up his hand. "I've got something else. You'll never guess who I saw there enjoying this show." He didn't wait for Murray to respond. "Reverend Ingersoll, who, by the way, must've spent about five minutes in jail after the Tombs."

"About that. Harrison got him out fairly quick." Murray sighed.

"Ingersoll was with someone else, however."

"Yeah, so tell me."

"The thug who attacked me and Fox. His name's Flint. That's all I know. From what the madam of this house told me, he might be from Chicago or St. Louis. And that's not all. Seth, I was right. He works for Fowler. And—"

"There's more?"

St. Clair nodded. "I believe this Flint was acquainted with Lucy Maloney."

"How did the madam know that? Or did Miss Potter reveal that to you?" Murray removed a cigarette from his case and offered one to St. Clair.

"Neither. As a matter of fact, it was something George mentioned to me." He sat up reached for his matches in his jacket pocket.

"George, the Negro doorman? I thought you told me he didn't know anything about any men she saw."

"Well, I . . . I fibbed. It's as simple as that." St. Clair lit his cigarette and passed the match to Murray.

"You fibbed? Charlie, that's a bunch of shit and you know it. Is there anything else you're not telling me?"

"Nothing, I swear it." He was lying, but it couldn't be helped.

Murray peered at him through the cigarette smoke. He seemed to weigh St. Clair's response in some balance. "I suppose it doesn't matter," he said finally.

"What do you mean, 'it doesn't matter?' There might be a connection between Flint and the murder of Miss Maloney."

"If you hadn't slept through the day yesterday or if you'd read a newspaper, you might've heard. The murderer has been convicted. Madame Philippe's trial is over. She was sentenced to hang."

"That's not possible. Seth, I really believe she's innocent. She didn't kill Lucy Maloney."

"Can you prove it?"

"I need more time. I know that Flint is involved, maybe even Fowler. Perhaps others. I don't know yet."

"Shit, there's plenty you don't know. Forget about it, Charlie. It's over. Madame Philippe's career as the wickedest abortionist in this city has finished. The sentence'll likely be carried out in a few days. Next Wednesday at the latest from what Stokes tells me. I think her lawyer, that stuck-up asshole Lampson, is appealing the verdict. He won't get anywhere. He doesn't stand a chance."

"Why's that?"

"Because Recorder Benjamin Beatty is one of Fowler's loyal and well-paid cronies. And Fowler wants to see Madame Philippe strung up."

"Exactly my point. Why? Why's Fowler in such a damn hurry to hang her? I'll tell you. He must've had something to do with the murder and wants Lucy Maloney's case closed." St. Clair stood up, walked over to a table and ground his cigarette into a metal tray.

Even as he spoke he thought about Frank King and what role he played in this. It had already occurred to him that Fowler might have known about King's adulterous affair and also discovered that King had betrayed him. What if he ordered Flint to murder Lucy as revenge? It seemed possible.

"Charlie, I'd say you're absolutely wrong, except for one other fact that I haven't yet mentioned."

"Which is what?"

"You got any whiskey?"

"In the cupboard, top shelf. You know where it is."

Murray poured himself a shot of whiskey and drank it down. "I found something else you need to know. Maybe it bears on this case, maybe not."

"Seth, my head hurts enough. What the hell are you jabbering about?"

"You remember how I said I felt like I'd met Miss Cardaso at some other time?"

"Vaguely. Why?"

"I was leafing through the rogues' gallery books and made a fascinating discovery. It was a photograph of a woman named Estelle Perera. She's wanted on a murder charge in Chicago. She supposedly stabbed this barkeep, killed him right in the saloon where they both worked. She was a waiter girl and dancer. Disappeared before the police could speak with her. That was about two years ago."

"What does this have to do with Ruth?"

Murray twisted his face and stared at him. "You care for her don't you, Charlie? I thought so when I first saw the two of you together."

"It's a long story, but I suppose in some strange way I do. It doesn't matter...she's probably left the city by now. You still haven't answered my question. What does this have to do with Ruth?"

Then it suddenly dawned on St. Clair what Murray was trying to tell him. "Ruth Cardaso and Estelle Perera are one in the same? And she's wanted for murder? Is that what this is about? Is that what you're saying? My God." St. Clair took a few steps backwards and leaned against the wall.

Murray nodded. "I'll show you the photograph. Except for the hair, it's her. I'm sure of it. I wired the police in Chicago for more information, but haven't received a reply yet."

St. Clair began to pace. "It all makes sense. Listen to me, Seth. Let's go through this one step at a time. Ruth isn't who she says she is. She might be a murderer, who knows? She's posing as an actress in San Francisco. Then, Nathan Scott at the *Chronicle* recommends her to Fox, who brings her to New York. She agrees because she can't refuse the money Tom's offering her. You following me so far?" Murray nodded.

"Somehow Flint, who's working for Fowler, finds her. Maybe he blackmails her or threatens, I don't know. And she's forced to spy on Fox and learn as much as she can. That might explain a lot."

"What do you mean?" asked Murray.

"It's not important. I'll tell you later. Let me continue. Lucy Maloney is then murdered. Perhaps by Flint on Fowler's orders, as I said before. Or by someone else. By the father of her child, whoever he is. One fact is certain... Fowler is no longer prepared to support Madame Philippe. To this end, he orders Ruth to do whatever she can to implicate her. And on Flint or Fowler's instructions Ruth reveals information about the Broome Street office that leads to Madame Philippe's arrest. So where does that leave us?"

Murray laughed and poured himself another whiskey. "It leaves us nowhere, Charlie. You don't have a leg to stand on. All you've got is a lot of nonsensical speculation. But, okay, I'll humor you. Let's assume for a minute that you might be right about this, that Fowler or this Flint did have something to do with the girl's death. How can we prove it? It seems to me that we only have a few options. We could question Fowler, but he'll deny any involvement and really we can't argue with him. No, we must find Ruth Cardaso or whatever the hell her name is. We also must question Flint, although I doubt if he'd tell us much without a lot of kicking and screaming. And, above all, we need to determine the identity of the father of Lucy Maloney's child and who the hell was paying for her room at the Fifth Avenue. I could go rattle Buckland. I'm sure I could convince him to tell me who was giving him money."

"No, let me do that," St. Clair interjected quickly. He did not want Murray poking around at the Fifth Avenue and possibly discovering Frank King's involvement with Lucy. "Why don't you send out some men to find Flint? You can try the brothel at the corner of Spring and Greene. According to the madam, a Miss Kate, he's a frequent visitor.

Let Westwood or another patrolman keep an eye on the place. Sooner or later, he'll show up. The man's an animal. As for Ruth, if she's indeed left the city, it was likely by train."

"I'll visit the Hudson depot myself," said Murray.

"Why there?"

"Just a hunch. It's where the trunk with the body was discovered after all."

"Seth, there's one more favor I need. Can you also arrange for me to see Madame Philippe later today or tomorrow?"

"That may be more difficult. You know as well as I do that once a prisoner is sentenced to hang, visitors other than family members aren't allowed."

"It's important. Please try. It could be a wild goose chase, but maybe, just maybe, she's forgotten some small detail that could help her. I think it's worth the effort."

After Murray left the flat, St. Clair washed and dressed, grateful that his head had finally cleared. He contemplated his next move. He had no intention of returning to the Fifth Avenue Hotel and speaking again with Buckland. That would have been a pointless exercise. He needed to get to his office and examine the note that Frank King had sent him about Crédit Mobilier. Because if he did not find King soon and question him, or if Murray could not locate Ruth or Flint, Madame Philippe would die.

It was curious, thought St. Clair, as he fastened the buttons on his pants and shirt. Not too long ago, he would have been elated to watch the wicked Madame Philippe hang from the gallows. Now, all he was concerned with was saving her life.

Did she deserve to be punished for her acts? The answer he knew in his heart was yes. Still, he was ready to concede that his position on the abortion issue had wavered. Ever since Caroline died he had vehemently condemned abortion—no questions asked. But that firm stand, he now understood, was rooted in the overwhelming guilt he felt about Caroline's death. It was a heavy burden on him that made him unreasonable—sometimes even irrational. The story of Madame Philippe's life had opened his eyes to factors he had not properly considered and he would have to weigh this matter more carefully in the days ahead.

Regardless, he was certain of one thing—he was not prepared to watch an innocent woman hang for a crime she did not commit. Such an injustice might be acceptable in a world ruled by Victor Fowler and other corrupt despots like him.

But it was not for Charles St. Clair.

Chapter Twenty-Five

—⋇◉⋇—

THE ROORBACK

ehind the thick stone walls, Madame Philippe could hear them. Once the court had sentenced her to death, the authorities at the Tombs had insisted that she be moved from her comfortable cell to the female section of the prison located along Leonard Street. Her new quarters had no window, a rusted bucket for a privy, and only a straw mat for a bed. She thought that at least the constant chanting from the streets demanding her immediate execution now would be silenced. She was not that fortunate. The harsh voices still echoed through the narrow passageways.

"Hang the witch," they screamed. "Death to Madame Killer." Again and again, they cried. The warden promised that he would disperse them, although hours later they remained on their morbid vigil. She tried as best as she could to ignore them, yet it was impossible.

Oddly enough, she had faced such hostility throughout her entire career and it had rarely troubled her. She did not even fear death. What upset her most was the injustice of it all. She had not murdered that woman, Miss Maloney. Nor did she have any idea why or how her advertisement had been placed between the poor girl's legs and her handkerchief discovered near her Broome Street office.

She had had Hector send several messages to Victor Fowler—if anyone knew why she was being falsely accused it would be him. He had not responded and she concluded yesterday that he had abandoned her for good. Justice was rarely speedy in New York, yet she was tried and convicted to hang within a day. She was certain that nothing of that consequence occurred in the city without Fowler's tacit approval.

In the cool darkness, she considered the various enemies she had made over the years—preachers such as Ingersoll, civic politicians whose names she could barely recall, dozens of physicians in the city and elsewhere who deeply resented her work as a midwife, as well as the many husbands, fathers, married and unmarried lovers of the women she had aided—the list was seemingly endless. Any of them could have conspired against her.

Or perhaps the murder was a random act of violence. That would hardly be novel for New York. Why had the prosecutor or her own lawyer, for that matter, not bothered to consider that possibility? What if the perpetrator had watched Miss Maloney leave her office, and then, once he killed her, conveniently blamed it on an easy target—the most infamous abortionist in the city?

For some reason her thoughts turned to Charles St. Clair. Other than her faithful servant, Hector, he was, curiously enough, the only person who she trusted. St. Clair was opinionated and mistaken about abortion, but she felt after their last conversation that she had made a positive impression and swayed him slightly to her views. He struck her as a man in need of love, a lost soul who had not yet recovered from his wife's death. But he was dedicated to his craft and, most significantly, to seeking the truth. He would not refuse her plea for assistance even now. Of this, she was confident.

Time was of the essence. There was one final possibility. Hector had already suggested it more than once, but she had rejected the idea. She had told him that she would not betray the trust that so many had placed in her. Not even in the face of death.

As the chanting on the streets grew louder, she began to reconsider her position. If she could only speak with St. Clair again, and if he would promise her that he'd be discreet—that nothing he learned would be published in his magazine or in any newspaper—she would consent and allow Hector to proceed.

Indeed death did not frighten her. Yet it was equally true that she was not ready to die.

Certainly, not at the end of a rope for a crime of which she was innocent.

~

Tom Fox leaned back in his chair, puffing hard on a cigar. He looked at Edward Sutton sitting opposite him. The pages of Sutton's report on his trip to Washington were scattered on the desk.

"I have to admit, it's a brilliant scheme, Tom," Sutton regarded his boss with admiration. "But aren't you the least bit concerned about the President's reaction?"

Fox waved his hand as if he was swatting a fly. "Ulysses Grant was a fine general. He saved the damn Union. But God help us all if he wins a second term. Besides, I'll deny the whole episode as a case of journalistic sloppiness. Do you think our loyal readers will give a hoot? When St. Clair finally exposes the full extent of Fowler's corruption and you confirm that Ames, Durant, and Colfax have bilked Union Pacific of millions of dollars, no one'll remember any of this—except maybe Grant."

"I hope you're right, Tom. Let me remind you that everyone, including Ames, is fairly tight lipped. Not surprisingly Colfax wouldn't even give me an appointment and Ames was happy to have lunch with me in the Congressional dining room—at your expense, I might add," Sutton smiled. "It was a superb meal, but he denied any wrongdoing. All he said was that Crédit Mobilier has provided 'excellent service' to Union Pacific or some such hogwash. When I asked him about Victor Fowler's involvement, he said I was 'out of my head' and that he'd never do business with someone like Fowler."

"You think he's lying?"

"I'm not certain. I also spoke with this business agent, Stephenson Kirkland. He's a slimy shark, if you ask me. He answered every one of my questions with questions of his own. But when I inquired as to the names of these New York Republicans who had invested more than a million dollars in Crédit Mobilier, he was silent."

"And you believe that Fowler is behind this?"

"I do, yes. Which Republicans do you know have that kind of money and don't want to boast about it? Fowler must be involved somehow. The only real question is why? Why invest in a Republican scheme? Then there's Martin Kent."

"Yes, tell me about him again." Fox blew a ring of smoke toward the ceiling.

"It's there in my report on page three. He's the young aide of Congressmen Todd of Massachusetts. I happened to know his older brother, Hugh, a broker on Wall Street. We went to school together. When I spoke with Martin I was certain he had more to say. He's a clever fellow and highly principled."

"If he's highly principled, why in the hell is working in Washington?" Fox snorted.

"As I was saying," continued Sutton, "five days ago, there was a meeting between Ames and Todd about Crédit Mobilier. But that's all Kent will tell me for now. Tom, I need to go back to Washington in a day or two and see him again. I'll take him to dinner, give him a few drinks and then maybe we'll have an even more enlightening discussion."

"Do whatever you have to do, Ed."

At that moment, St. Clair appeared in the doorway. "Don't either of you ever leave this place?"

"We could say the same thing about you," replied Sutton. "Where's that lovely Miss Cardaso? I thought you'd be strolling with her through the Park on a day like this."

St. Clair ignored the question and the taunt. He planned to tell Fox about Ruth's real identity, but had no desire to discuss it with Sutton, who would only ask too many unnecessary questions. "You going back to Washington any time soon?"

"As a matter of fact, I am. Isn't that right, Tom?"

"Charlie, I'm glad you're here. I want you to see this." Fox handed him a yellow newspaper clipping.

"What is it?" He unfolded the frayed paper.

"It's something I saved from the *Ithaca Chronicle*."

"What's so special about it?"

"Look at the date," urged Fox.

"Yeah, I see it. August 21, 1844," said St. Clair. "What of it?"

"I guess you're too young to remember the presidential campaign of that year?"

"Didn't Polk and the Democrats win over Clay and the Whigs? I recollect my father talking about it. He detested Clay. But didn't the Whigs try something underhanded?"

"Exactly. That's in the clipping. Look for yourself. The *Chronicle* was virulently pro-Whig and hated Polk," explained Fox. "So much so that they ran this story given to them, I believe, by a young and extremely foolish Whig by the name of Daniel McKinney. It was purported to be an account from an anonymous Abolitionist and contained an extract from a travel book, *Roorback's Tour through the Western and Southern States in 1836.* According to this so-called abolitionist, Baron Roorback was supposed to have met a gang of slave traders and their slaves near the Duck River in Tennessee. At the time Polk was the Speaker in the House. Go on, Charlie, read it out so Sutton can hear."

"*Forty of these unfortunate beings had been purchased, I was informed, by the Honourable J.K. Polk, the present speaker of the house of representatives—the mark of the branding iron, with the initials of his name on their shoulders distinguishing them from the rest.*"

Fox laughed loudly. "What balderdash. It was all nonsense. Yes, Polk lived in Columbia, Tennessee, near Duck River and he did have a few slaves, but not in Tennessee. They were on his small plantation in Yalobusha County, Mississippi, and he never hot-branded them. For a slave-owner, the man was decent. There was also no Baron Roorback, nor did he ever write a book. This abolitionist had taken the entire story from a memoir by an English writer named Featherstonhaugh, if memory serves me correctly. Polk was never mentioned in the memoir. None of this, of course, made the least difference to the *Chronicle* or the other Whig papers in Ohio, New York, and Pennsylvania. Recklessly, they ran the story giving it more credence and for a time Polk's moral character was the chief issue of the campaign. It took some digging but the Democratic papers eventually exposed the Roorback hoax, setting off a war of indignation with the Whig press."

"That's a fascinating history lesson, Tom, but what does it have to do with anything we're dealing with at the moment? About Fowler or Crédit Mobilier?" St. Clair felt himself growing more impatient by the minute.

"Tom wants to employ a Roorback," declared Sutton.

"You want to spread a false story?" St. Clair scratched his head. "About what precisely?"

Fox slid a sheet of paper across his desk. There were a few lines written on it.

NEWS FROM THE CAPITAL

The trustees of the Crédit Mobilier of America, representing its shareholders, are pleased to announce that late yesterday President Ulysses S. Grant has joined in partnership with Vice-President Shuyler Colfax in acquiring shares in the company. President's Grant's secretary declined to comment. This is the second major announcement from Crédit Mobilier in the past week. A group of prominent New Yorkers also announced a sizable investment in Crédit Mobilier. It is thought that this latter group consists of Republicans except for one lone Democrat, Mr. Victor Fowler, Grand Sachem of Tammany Hall.

Fox's Weekly

St. Clair sighed loudly. "Tom, I got to admit you've always had spunk. I'm not sure who's going to come hunting for you first, the President or Fowler."

"Both I hope." He held up the piece of paper and admired his work.

"You certain about this?"

Fox checked the watch dangling by a gold chain from his vest. "Too late to change my mind now. I've already wired this out to the *Times* and the *Herald* and, in Washington, to the *Evening Star* and *Morning Chronicle*. I expect they'll all run it. Grant'll deny it, of course, but that's not the point. I want everyone in the capital talking about Crédit Mobilier. The Democrats in the House will smell blood. And the more questions they ask, the quicker we'll figure out what's going on."

"And Fowler?"

"I expect Fowler won't be happy," Fox smirked. "He'll deny any involvement as well. But we'll have to see what he does next, if anything."

"Tom, this Roorback's liable to backfire in your face. What if Fowler sends Flint—that's the name of our attacker, by the way—for another visit? I saw him twice the other day and he wasn't looking particularly friendly on either occasion."

"Flint's his name, is it? We'll be ready for him this time." Fox walked to his private office and returned with a loaded Winchester. "Picked this up from Smythe's Gun Shop just yesterday. I figured I might need it. So help me if I so much as see that asshole up here I'll plug him right between the eyes. No one's going to ever attack me in my own place again. I swear it."

～

St. Clair excused himself, sat down at his own desk, and stuffed his pipe with tobacco. He had no doubt that Fox would be true to his word. And he could think of no more deserving reward for Flint than a bullet in his head. What would be the point of the police arresting him? As long as Fowler was in charge of City Hall and the courts, Flint could do as he pleased without fear of capture or justice.

He had decided that the first order of business was to find Frank King. He located the plain brown envelope in his desk drawer where he had left it and examined it carefully. Had King used the postal service, he might have discovered a relevant marking. But there was nothing.

"Here, Charlie, you look like you could use this," said Molly as she handed him a cup of tea. "I know it's hot out there, but tea always makes me relax so I can think more clearly. Anything I can help you with?"

"Is there anything you can help me with?" repeated St. Clair. "There might be. Tell me, Molly, let's say you had to escape from the city. You couldn't stay in a hotel or boarding house for too long and you needed to be somewhere safe—a place where people didn't ask too many questions."

She mulled over his query for a few seconds. "Between you, me, and the gatepost, I'd find an elderly relative, a grandmother or aunt, and stay out of sight as long as I could. Why?"

"Exactly, what I was thinking. Thanks, Molly, that helps."

St. Clair knew that King had no grandparents still alive. His wife, Amanda, did, however. Her grandmother, Mrs. Irene Tillett, was an elderly widow, still working her farm near Newburgh, a village about fifty-five miles north on the shores of the Hudson River. King had mentioned her once before, marveling at her stubborn resolve to stay on her farm until the day she died. It was the perfect hiding spot, figured St. Clair. Country folk cared a lot more about the weather and bugs than they did about Fowler, the Ring, and New York civic politics. King would be relatively safe there.

"Tom, I may be away tomorrow on a short trip," St. Clair leaned his head into Fox's office.

"You want to tell me where you're travelling to on my expense?"

"Can't."

"You can't tell me where I'm sending you?"

"No."

"You want to explain why the hell not?"

"You'll have to trust me, Tom. I'll say this, it has to do with Crédit Mobilier as well as other matters."

"All right, Charlie, we'll do this your way," said Fox leaning back in his chair, "but as God is my witness, you'd better damn well return with a story that'll crush Fowler once and for all."

"I promise you, Tom, if my instincts are correct, which I think they are, you won't be disappointed." He stepped into Fox's office and shut the office door behind him.

"What's this now, more revelations?"

"I'm afraid so. Let me ask you something, did you receive a reply from San Francisco, from your friend Scott at the *Chronicle*?"

"I have, as a matter of fact." Fox searched through the pile of papers on his desk.

"Let me guess," said St. Clair, "Scott insists that Ruth Cardaso is a lovely actress with a wonderful future ahead of her on the stage. And that he personally vouches for her."

"How did you know?"

"Because if Ruth is anything, she is indeed a gifted actress on the stage and off."

"What have you learned, Charlie?" Fox looked up from his search sharply.

"It was Seth who found it." St. Clair sat down. "He was searching his rogues' gallery books when he came upon a photograph of a woman named Estelle Perera—who is almost certainly Ruth. This Estelle may have killed someone in Chicago, a saloon owner she was working for."

"I can't believe Scott knows about this."

"I'm sure he doesn't. To him and the rest of San Francisco's high society, she was the belle of the ball. As I said, she's talented. She fooled Scott. She fooled you. She fooled me."

"I don't know what to say." Tom stared at the ceiling. "What of her connections to Fowler?"

"I'm still not certain, but it seems likely, doesn't it? She certainly knows this Flint and Flint presumably works for Fowler so—"

"So it follows that she's also in cahoots with Fowler."

"And," added St. Clair, "Fowler and Flint may well have had something to do with the trunk murder that Madame Philippe is soon to be hanged for."

Fox detected concern in St. Clair's voice. "I thought you didn't care what happens to Madame Killer?"

"I don't. I just don't want to see an innocent woman hanged."

Fox raised a skeptical eyebrow, but said nothing. After a moment, he asked, "Where's Miss Cardaso now?"

St. Clair shook his head. "That, my friend, is the two-dollar question, isn't it?"

A knock on the door interrupted their conversation. It was Molly.

"Sorry to disturb you, gentlemen, but I thought you'd want to see this, Tom. It was just delivered by special messenger." She handed Fox a telegram.

"Who's it from? The President?" he laughed.

"No, actually from the Vice-President."

Chapter Twenty-Six

Two More Guests for the Summer Ball

Victor Fowler gazed at his wife across the dining room table. Ellen had been in remarkably good humor all day. She claimed that she had taken no laudanum that morning and felt healthier and happier than she had in many weeks. He decided to give her the benefit of the doubt. They had spent several pleasant hours riding together through Central Park, joining the long parade of carriages and horses. Few of his wealthy friends or enemies could match his Parisian black barouche pulled by his two white geldings.

About the only thing that had detracted from his outing was the fact that he was unable to wear his gold tiger badge with the two ruby eyes that he was so proud of because Jackson—despite days of searching—had still not found it. Fowler had concluded that the badge was unfortunately lost, or worse, stolen, and that threatening his butler further was likely not going to change the situation. He tried to put it out of his mind.

"Would you care for more wine, my dear?" he asked his wife. "The taste is extraordinary, wouldn't you agree? I was very pleased when this shipment from the Château Margaux arrived last week. I'd heard wonderful news about this 1870 vintage and it's all Mr. Stockton claimed it to be. Whatever else people say about that man, he has a fine palate for wine. I doubt that there's a more astute wine merchant in New York."

"Oh, Victor, he's a dreadful philanderer. But why should that trouble you?" Ellen smirked at him. "But, please, replenish my cup."

Fowler ignored his wife's remark and filled her glass with the sauvignon. He had no desire to ruin what up to now had been a pleasant and civil dinner. "Have you spoken yet with Mr. Glover to confirm the menu for the summer ball? And has he made the proper arrangements for the orchestra? It's only two days away or have you forgotten?"

"Two days from now, Victor, you might be in jail," Ellen laughed.

"Perhaps you've had enough to drink this evening," Fowler responded, restraining his temper. He forced a smile. "All of the invitations have been sent and the ball will proceed as it always has. Our friends expect it."

"Our friends expect you to cater to their every whim and desire," retorted Ellen.

"And I shall do my best," Fowler said evenly. "Look around you, my dear, have I not given you everything you ever yearned for?"

"Do you think these paintings and this furniture, even this house will ever be sufficient for me?" Ellen snapped. "The only thing I ever truly wanted was a child. Will you ever understand that?"

"Why do you torture yourself over this time and again? You know as well as I do what the doctor said."

"Yes, Victor, yes, I know," Ellen's voice cracked. "But it is of no comfort."

"There's my nephew, Lewis. He has such a fine future ahead of him. I've been thinking of the State Senate for him in a few years. I told my brother that I'd take care of him and I shall do everything in my power to honor that commitment."

"I'm delighted for Lewis and I do cherish him. But you can't understand that I also need my own child." Ellen stared into her wine glass. "Sadly, you never have. And I believe that's why you treat me so disrespectfully. Seeing those whores in public. It makes me sick to my stomach. I'm nothing but one of your possessions, useful to you at civic ceremonies and balls. You covet all that is in this house, including me. I'm no different than one of your bloody horses." Ellen's eyes welled with tears.

"That's most unfair," Fowler thundered. "Do you think I work like a dog for myself? That I do nothing for you? That this house is solely for my own enjoyment?"

"As a matter of fact, I do. And when Charles St. Clair or some other journalist obtains the financial information on your blessed courthouse or on this Crédit Mobilier scheme, I'll be celebrating our summer ball without you."

Fowler was momentarily speechless. "What do you know of such matters? Who told you about Crédit Mobilier? So help me, Ellen——" He waved his fist at her.

"I may be addicted to laudanum, but I do have ears." Ellen patted her eyes with a handkerchief. "You think everything that goes on in that inner sanctum of yours is private. I listen, I read, and I learn. I think I should contact Mr. St. Clair myself."

Fowler stood up, moved around the table to her, and grabbed her by the wrist. "You'll be silent, woman."

"You're hurting me, Victor, let go of my arm."

"Sir, Mr. Harrison is here to see you." Jackson entered the room.

"Show him in," Fowler snapped. He released his grip on Ellen's arm and pushed her away. He glared at her. "This discussion is not over between us."

~

"I apologize for disturbing you both," said Harrison. He glanced at Ellen sympathetically.

"What is it, Isaac?" Fowler said impatiently as he straightened his jacket. "What's so important that you must trouble me at the dinner hour?"

"I assume you haven't seen the evening papers yet?"

"I was about to retire to the parlor with the *Herald* and a cigar, why?"

"Here, see for yourself." Harrison passed him the newspaper.

PRESIDENT GRANT DENIES INVOLVEMENT
He declares he is not a shareholder in Crédit Mobilier of America
Vice-President Colfax claims Fox's Weekly report inaccurate

In reply to the report by Fox's Weekly *as reported in today's special* Morning Chronicle, *the President issued a statement denying any involvement or connection with the Crédit Mobilier of America, a Pennsylvania construction company responsible for completing a portion of the Union Pacific Railway line.*

Vice-President Shuyler Colfax was equally adamant that he is not now, and has never been, a shareholder in Crédit Mobilier. Nor has he any business or political association with Mr. Victor Fowler, also reported to be a major shareholder in this enterprise.

Contacted by the Chronicle, *Representative Oakes Ames, who is also a trustee of Crédit Mobilier has no idea why* Fox's Weekly *would publish such a falsehood.*

"I'm going to wring Fox's neck for this." Fowler threw the newspaper to the floor. "How could he possibly know anything about this?"

"Maybe he doesn't," Harrison said. "All I know is that one of his men, Edward Sutton, was in Washington the other day asking a lot of questions. He was seen dining with Ames and he spoke with Kirkland."

"That fool must've said something."

"I received a telegram from Kirkland before I arrived here," continued Harrison. "He says he told Sutton nothing of any consequence, although your name did arise in the conversation several times. Fox is merely on an ill-conceived goose hunt. We should do or say nothing. I promise you Ames will figure some way to make his problems disappear. He doesn't relish any more publicity or a Congressional investigation. Leave it for a few days. The papers will have something else to write about and no one will ever remember they read anything about Crédit Mobilier until we want them to."

Fowler looked over at Ellen. "What's that smirk on your face?"

"I do enjoy it when you squirm like an eel," she said rising. "Isaac, if you'll excuse me."

Fowler waited until she had left the dining room. "You're most fortunate, Isaac, you have a wife who's obedient and content. Look at what I must contend with each day."

Harrison said nothing. He had no advice about marriage that Fowler would be interested in hearing. The last time he had offered his opinion about such sensitive issues, at Delmonico's, he had brought on Fowler's wrath. If he had to choose between Fowler and Ellen, he wasn't sure what he would do. True, his relationship with Fowler had brought him much money and the life of an aristocrat, but the moral price had been high—too high, he felt, and no more so than in the past week.

Fowler gulped what remained in his wine glass. "I made Fox a generous offer and this is how he scorns me. Twice now. First he asks for double the price and now he publishes lies and falsehoods. I'm sure St. Clair had something to do with this as well. I warned him, Isaac. I did warn him that he should consider my proposal seriously. And now, he has upset our plans."

"Temporarily, perhaps, but I don't think—"

Fowler slammed his hand down on the table. "It's too late for second chances."

"What are you going to do, Victor?"

"What I should've done months ago, when that rag began insulting me."

"There's much at stake, here."

"Don't lecture me, Isaac. Never lecture me. Just do as I tell you. Find Flint for me and be quick about it."

"What should I tell him?"

"You'll tell him to buy a new suit for my summer ball. Jackson!" he shouted. "Where's that damn guest list? I have two names to add."

Jackson appeared holding a long sheet of paper. "Here it is, sir."

Fowler grabbed it from his hands and took a pencil from the inside of his coat pocket. "Isaac, this will be the ball of the season, I guarantee it."

"What are you doing, Victor?"

"Inviting two of our friends so that Flint will know exactly where they are on August twenty-fifth. He may do with them as he sees fit." At the bottom of his lengthy list that included railway tycoons, Wall Street brokers, merchants, and the elite of Fifth Avenue, he scrawled the names Tom Fox and Charles St. Clair.

"Jackson, I want two invitations sent out by messenger to the offices of *Fox's Weekly* immediately."

"How do you know they'll accept?" asked Harrison.

Fowler chortled. "Isaac, my trusted friend, you've learned nothing. As sure as a pig'll roll in its own shit, they'll be there wearing their Sunday best."

He threw his wine glass into the fireplace and left the dining room leaving Harrison staring at the shards glittering in the flames.

Chapter Twenty-Seven

———❦———

DECEPTION

Ruth Cardaso had crossed Canal Street and was continuing her way up Greene. A young man, who was fashionably dressed in a grey suit and flat-top derby hat, walking closely behind her, brushed passed her and then suddenly stopped.

"I beg your pardon, Miss. I was wondering if you might work at one of these fine establishments." He smiled snidely.

"I do not. Now be on your way," Ruth responded, mildly amused.

He bowed to her and started walking in front of her. He took only four or five paces when he turned to her again. "Would you consider accompanying me to that oyster saloon across the street?"

"Thank you for your kind offer, sir, but I have important business."

"Important business? Around here? In these houses? Then you're for hire, as it were?"

Ruth attempted to walk pass him, but he blocked her path. "Sir, I ask you to leave me alone."

"You're a beauty, you are," he said, reaching for her hair.

She pushed his hand away and tried again to get by him. This time he reached for her arm.

"Leave her be," said a voice from behind Ruth. It was another young gentlemen, a little taller although as elegantly dressed. "Off with you, before I call the police."

The first man hesitated, as if to retaliate, then turned on his heels and darted back toward Canal Street.

"This is no neighborhood for a lady like yourself," the second man said, bowing. "Here, please allow me to escort you to your destination." He reached for Ruth's arm, but as he did so, her elbow caught him hard in the face. He fell to the ground with her purse in his hands. She pulled a small pistol from a hidden pocket in her dress and pointed it at his head.

"You think I'm an easy mark for you and your snot of a partner? Drop my purse on the ground or there'll be a bullet right in the middle of that lovely head of yours."

The man cringed. "Please, lady, don't shoot. We didn't mean no harm."

"Hey, don't shoot him," pleaded the first man, who had returned.

"Don't come any closer," Ruth shouted.

By now, several people had stopped to watch the spectacle of a stylish woman teaching two young pickpockets a lesson.

"Get up slowly," she addressed the man on the ground. "Now, take out your wallet."

The man groped in his pocket. "Let it fall to the ground," she ordered as several members of the crowd cheered and laughed.

"It took us all day to make this money—" the first man pleaded.

"Drop it now or so help me I'll shoot."

The wallet slid out of the pickpocket's fingers. "Now get up," she glared at the man still on the ground. "I want you to turn around, grab your partner's hand and the two of you run from here as fast as you can. And if you ever trouble me again, I'll shoot the both of you right between your legs. Then you'll never be able to enjoy anything any more. Go!"

The two men turned and ran swiftly down Greene Street without looking back. The crowd applauded and Ruth bowed as if she was on the stage. She picked up her purse and the man's wallet. There was fifty dollars in it. She kept ten for herself and gave the rest to an old emaciated soldier sitting nearby on the ground. He thanked her profusely.

She continued walking down Greene, when something up the street caught her eye.

Half a block away, two patrolmen, who must have witnessed her altercation with the two men, had both pickpockets by their collars.

~

Ruth stopped in front of the house at the corner of Greene and Spring Streets. She was still laughing to herself. Imagine, she thought as she walked up the pathway, those two scoundrels trying to pull the wool over her eyes. Little did they know that she had learned such tricks long ago, when they were still wearing short pants.

She patted her dress and fixed her hat. It was time now for her to consider more serious and dangerous matters. She needed all of her wits about her, if she was to successfully string Flint along. She had created the scenes and memorized her lines. The curtain was about to rise.

She took a deep breath, pulled the bell, and waited as patiently as she could until Miss Kate's servant allowed her to enter the premises.

"Will you please tell Bridget that Ruth's here?" she asked.

The house was not too crowded so early in the evening. At least two gentlemen called out to her, but she ignored them and took a seat in the parlor beside the piano player.

"Miss Ruth, are you going to sing for us today?" asked Moses, who had worked for Miss Kate as a piano player since she opened the house.

"I'm afraid I can't right at the moment, Moses. I must speak with Bridget."

Ruth owed Bridget a lot for keeping her informed on Flint's comings and goings. They had been an inseparable trio in Chicago, her, Bridget and Celeste. Life had been difficult, yet she and her friends had survived, working the saloons on the West Side, occasionally participating in some petty theft, and singing and dancing at Linus "Piker" Andrews's concert saloon.

Unlike Bridget and Celeste, however, she refused to prostitute herself even when Andrews had ordered her to do so. It was, in fact, a dispute over pleasing a wealthy client that led to the fateful altercation with the son of a bitch. She was not about to be threatened or coerced into one of Andrews's upstairs rooms, even at the point of a knife.

She had repeatedly chided him to leave her alone, but the obstinate fool had not heeded her. Instead, he had slapped her in public and she had retaliated in self-defense. There was an awful scuffle and Andrews's knife had ended up buried deep in his chest. He had too many friends at the police department and she feared that she would never have obtained a fair hearing or trial. What other options did she have other than to flee the city?

It was also at Andrews's saloon where Celeste first met Flint and through him Frankie. She and Bridget had both warned her about Flint. He was not to be trusted for a second, they had told her. He was the kind of a man who would stab a stranger, young or old, it hardly mattered, merely for the sheer pleasure of watching the person die. Celeste, initially at least, refused to listen to them. It was almost as if she obtained a thrill by being close to someone so wicked.

And then Celeste met Frankie. He was a notorious fence and cheat, although he worshipped the ground Celeste walked on. He treated her like a queen. She soon realized that she wanted to leave Flint. But, as it turned out, it was too late for her and Frankie.

"I didn't think you'd go through with this, Estelle," whispered Bridget, breaking Ruth's reverie. She was wearing a long black silk robe that was loosely tied and hung open at the top.

Ruth pulled her friend into a corner of the parlor. "Will you stop calling me that? Your mouth'll get us both caught."

Bridget nodded sheepishly and took Ruth by the arm. "I know. I know. I promise to be more careful."

"Is he here?"

"Upstairs. How much longer must I continue this dodge? He makes me feel seedy. If it wasn't for dear, sweet Celeste, I wouldn't let him touch me with those disgusting hands. And you know the worst part, honey?"

"What is it?"

"His cock is the size of my pinkie."

"It isn't?" Ruth chuckled.

"That murdering arsehole doesn't even know how to fuck. What good is he?"

"You do surprise me." Ruth planted a kiss on Bridget's cheek and embraced her tightly. "Now, which room?"

"Up the stairs, third door on your right. You want me to come with you?"

She shook her head. "No, I'd better do this on my own."

As Ruth reached the top of the stairs, she could hear voices and the sounds of moaning from behind several doors. The whiff of hashish from the top floor of the house also filtered down. She had tried it only once—Bridget had insisted—and found it fairly appealing, although she much preferred strong whiskey.

Strange, she now realized, Lucy Maloney and her friend Millie had been in Miss Kate's *gunjeh* parlor that evening as well. It was soon after her arrival in New York. She had immediately recognized them from the Fifth Avenue Hotel, but had said nothing. And later, when their paths crossed again, she pretended as if she had never met them. Either they did not recognize her, which seemed to Ruth unlikely, or they had no wish to acknowledge their previous encounter.

Ruth found the room she was looking for. She pulled her gun from her pocket and eased the door open.

"It's about time you're back, you sweet cunny. Come here now with that whiskey," ordered Flint. He was naked and covered by a thin dirty white sheet pulled up around his belly.

"Just lay still, Flint, or I'll shoot that little cock of yours off." Ruth affected all the anger at her command.

"Estelle," Flint drawled. "Always a pleasure to see you. I'm glad you decided to stay in the city."

"The name is Ruth, you prick."

"Suit yourself. And what the fuck's this about my cock being small?"

"That's what I hear downstairs."

Flint snarled at her. "I'll kill that whore, like I killed your friend, Celeste."

"You touch one hair on Bridget's head and I swear, Flint, I'll cut your balls off and feed them to the dogs in the alley."

"You always did have a good sense of humor, Estelle." Flint snorted. "What the hell do you want from me? Something new to report about Fox and St. Clair?" He sat up, revealing a jagged scar across his right shoulder.

"I want you to listen to me because I've been busy." Ruth clutched the pistol tightly in her sweaty palm. "I've come from Fox's office. I've told St. Clair about you killing Celeste and Frankie in Chicago. And I've given him the name of someone in the Chicago police department who'll confirm what I'm saying is the God's honest truth. I also told him you're working for Fowler."

Flint laughed. "You think that's supposed to scare me, you cunt. How about if I tell him your sad story? Would you like that?"

"I already have. He knows all about what happened. Everything. My fight with Andrews and how he was accidentally killed. And why I ran. He says he'll talk to Fox about hiring me a decent lawyer. So you can't blackmail me any more, you bastard."

Flint edged a leg over the side of the bed.

"Move another muscle, Flint, and I'll shoot. I swear it." Ruth strained to keep her hand from shaking.

"What else you got to say?" He remained where he was.

"Yeah, this is the best part of my little tale. I had a chat with Mr. Fowler, earlier today."

"How the hell did you get in to see him?"

"It's not important. I saw him. Now, shut up and listen. I told him how you've been threatening me and I made him a deal. In exchange for getting Fox and St. Clair to stop writing anything more about him, he's agreed that tomorrow night at his summer ball, he'll announce to his guests that you're the real murderer of Lucy Maloney, the girl found in the trunk at Hudson Depot. And that Madame Philippe is innocent."

"That's bullshit. Why would he do such a dumb thing as that? He'd be putting a noose around his own neck."

"What's that supposed to mean?"

"Nothing. It don't matter. You're a lying whore and I don't believe a word you're saying."

"Believe it, Flint. Fowler's going to hand you over to the police on Tuesday night. Why shouldn't he do it? He'll be a hero. Saving an innocent woman from the gallows." Ruth waved her gun at him.

"Yeah, I don't think many of his damn Paddies will think so. They're more than happy that bitch'll hang." He sneered at Ruth. "I'll talk to Fowler myself."

"He'll deny the whole thing, and why wouldn't he? You're going to have to wait until the ball, aren't you? Or you could leave the city and disappear, never to be seen or heard from again." Ruth slowly backed to the door. "If I were you, I'd watch myself. And by the way, I'd leave through the rear door. There are at least two patrolmen watching the front."

Before Flint could respond, she was through the door and down the stairs. She needed to find Bridget and make sure she stayed away from Flint until he calmed down.

Suddenly, she realized she was shaking and that under her dress, she was soaked in sweat. Still, she was sure she had delivered her lines to good effect. At the very least, Flint was more confused and suspicious than ever. She had no doubt that he would be at the Fowlers' ball.

So would she.

And on that night, she would have her revenge.

Chapter Twenty-Eight

CONFESSIONS

As soon as St. Clair boarded the half-empty train car at Hudson Depot, he could smell a strange repellent odor. This was not how he wanted to start the day. He would be in Newburgh by nine-thirty in the morning and with any luck back in the city by four o'clock that afternoon. Travelling by train was much preferable than several hours wasted on the steamer.

He looked at the passengers around him. To his right, on the other side of the car, was a pretty young woman in a brown suit with matching hat and gloves, next to a debonair young man, likely her husband, who obediently fetched her water and repeatedly pulled the car blinds up and down to ensure that the hot morning sun did not trouble her. Undoubtedly, he surmised, happy newlyweds on their way to Albany for a holiday.

In the seats directly in front of St. Clair was a family of five—a mother, father, and three young children, one an infant. The father was puffing a pipe of clearly inexpensive tobacco and had his nose buried in the *Herald*'s sports section. Glancing at his cheap suit, St. Clair guessed that the man was a clerk or cashier, one among thousands who serviced the ever-changing needs of the city's burgeoning professional middleclass.

No matter what he was paid, he must have been overjoyed to have traded his factory dungarees and check shirt for a shabby suit and a relatively clean white shirt.

The mother's main occupation was her children. She wore a light long-sleeved white flowered dress and bonnet, which likely cost no more than a few dollars each at some low-priced shop on Sixth Avenue. In her right hand, she had a can and a small flat piece of wood. The objectionable smell emanated from it. Carefully, she brushed each child with a blackish thick liquid.

"Madam, if you'll pardon the intrusion, what is it you are putting on the children?" asked St. Clair.

She smiled. "It's no intrusion whatsoever, sir. Here see for yourself." She thrust the can in front of St. Clair's face. "Half sweet oil mixed with the same amount of tar."

"And, why are you doing this?"

"She's mad, that's why," remarked her husband over his newspaper.

"We're on our way to Albany and then a little further north to my parents' farm near the village of Rexford, where I grew up," said the woman. "The mosquitoes and gnats are awfully bad this time of the year. I don't want them bothering the young ones."

"Megan, we won't arrive there for nearly three and half hours. Surely this doesn't have to be done now." Her husband slapped his newspaper down.

Ignoring him, she turned to St. Clair. "It's curious most people don't find this offensive."

"My apologies, Madam, but I beg to differ."

"So do I," her husband chime in.

"Oh, Daniel, hush." She looked at St. Clair, "Sir, the tar is mild and good for the skin."

"I'm certain it is, and I wouldn't want to deprive the children." St. Clair smiled. As the train rolled out of Manhattan north along the Hudson River into the rolling plains and high hills of Orange County, he returned to his thoughts. Newburgh was an hour away—just enough time for him to figure how he would deal with Frank King.

He needed to be clever about this. Obtaining any and all relevant information on Fowler's involvement in Crédit Mobilier and any other incriminating documents on the Ring's activities was paramount. But he also wanted King to explain his relations with Lucy Maloney. He had come to regard King as a friend, especially since King had rescued him from Captain Jack Martin's thugs. Yet if he somehow had been responsible for Miss Maloney's death, St. Clair was not about to let him escape or permit Madame Philippe to hang for his crimes.

As the train rumbled past Irvington, he pushed his hat over eyes for a few moments of rest. For the next half-hour he drifted in and out of sleep, trying to concentrate on the task ahead—instead he dreamed of his night of passion with Ruth.

≈

As St. Clair made his way on to the platform, a young man in dusty leather chaps, buckskin gloves, and a Union Army officer's hat approached him.

"You Mr. St. Clair?" he asked.

"That's right."

"Name is James Case. I work for the town's blacksmith, Mr. Merritt sent me to take you to see the Widow Tillett. Is that right?"

"Good, I'm glad you're here," said St. Clair. "Where's your rig?"

"I'm just out front of the station. You want to see the village first? It's market day, might be something interesting for a city gentleman like yourself—"

"No, just take me to Mrs. Tillett's farm," St. Clair snapped.

As young Master Case and his two horses made their way through the winding stony roads and up around the hills, St. Clair filled his lungs with country air, delighted in the difference from the foul smells of daily life in New York. Several of the farms on the edge of Newburgh appeared fairly large and well maintained. Every white picket fence he came across was in superb condition and much of the land was planted and properly worked, evidence that the area around Newburgh had rich soil, good for growing.

"See that road over there." Case pointed to a small pathway beside one farmhouse. "That's where Mr. Clark was killed last week. It was a real tragedy. He was walking beside his wagon, which had a full load, when his foot caught the reins. That startled his horses and he was pulled underneath the buggy. Ran over his head and arms. The doc couldn't do a thing to save him."

While St. Clair sympathized, he had no time for small talk. He looked at his watch anxiously.

Case finally turned his horses into a muddy trail that led to a small farmhouse. It appeared to be a little more dilapidated than the others he had seen.

"You can stop here," St. Clair ordered.

"You sure, sir? Mrs. Tillett has a few cows in the back. I'd be careful if I was you. Those are awfully fancy-looking boots you're wearing."

"No, it'll be fine right here. I'll meet you back here in two hours."

"Two hours. I'll be here. You want me to call the old widow? She's kind of hard of hearing."

St. Clair pulled out a dollar and handed it to the young man. "How about you take this on one condition—you're not allowed to ask me any more questions."

"It's a deal, Mister. That's mighty generous of you."

St. Clair proceeded up the path, trying to avoid the mud and cow dung—a feat that proved impossible. He reached the wobbly fence gate, wiped off his boots, and walked carefully to the front door of the house. He could hear a dog barking in the back. He knocked on the door, but there was no reply.

"Anyone home?" he cried out. He pushed lightly on the door. "Hello, Mrs. Tillett, are you there?"

"Not another step, stranger, or I'll blow your head off. Get your hands up, nice and slow," ordered the voice from behind him. "Now turn around."

St. Clair did as he was told.

"Charlie, is that you?" Frank King walked out from behind a cluster of trees holding a rifle.

"Can I put my hands down, Frank? Don't do anything foolish."

King let the rifle fall to his side. "Sorry, I've had the shakes the past few days. Nothing to do out here but sit and wait. Amanda's granny can barely hear, so there's no talking to her. She's at the town market right now," added King. "By the way, how in the hell did you know where to find me? I'm certain I didn't say anything to you."

"You didn't. It was a lucky guess. Journalistic instincts."

"I said I'd send you more documents on Fowler as soon as I had them ready. You impatient?"

"Somewhat. There's been some new developments."

"Like what? I've been trying to follow along in the newspapers, but most of the ones from New York are a day late out here."

"Can we go inside?" asked St. Clair, shaking the last bits of manure off of his boots.

"Follow me. I want to show you something. You'll find this hard to believe. I'd love to see Fowler's face when you publish this."

The farmhouse had three rooms, a kitchen with a wooden table and two chairs, a small parlor with a dusty old sofa, and one bedroom. The privy was out in the back. There was no gas lighting. Water had to be hauled in by horse and buggy from a well a mile away.

"I sure can't wait for this to end," King said, offering St. Clair coffee. "I miss Amanda something awful."

"Yeah, I'm sure you do. Before I forget, I want to thank you for settling up my debts with Martin."

"We had an agreement and I always honor an agreement. Shit, it was Fowler's money." King laughed.

St. Clair smiled. "I suppose that's fitting, considering it was Fowler who ordered Martin to cheat me out of the money in the first place." St. Clair sipped the coffee. "Tell me, if Fowler's been paying you so well, why betray him? Why did you start sending me information in the first place? And please, don't tell me it was personal."

"I don't honestly know the answer to that." King lit a cigarette and offered one to St. Clair. "Months ago, I watched Fowler fleece some poor builder out of a few hundred dollars. It meant nothing to him, but to the builder it was money to feed his family. Fowler couldn't have cared less. It made me mad. A week later, I contacted you."

"But you kept on using and sharing the booty?" St. Clair stared hard at King as he lit a cigarette.

King shrugged. "Why the hell not? I deserved it."

St. Clair was not about to get into an argument about King's role in cheating the citizens of New York out of their money. "Frank, I got your message about Crédit Mobilier. What else do you know?"

"Not a lot, but I heard Fowler and Harrison talking about it, and more than once. They didn't know I was listening. At least I don't think so. It's a big railroad company worth millions, but run by Republicans. Crédit Mobilier did all the work for Union Pacific. Maybe Fowler wants to award it the lucrative contract for his grand viaduct train scheme, although I don't know if his Tammany men would be anxious to do that. Imagine building an elevated railway on forty-foot stone arches throughout Manhattan? Think of the possibility for graft."

"We believe that Fowler is secretly buying up shares in Crédit Mobilier to possibly control it. Fox sent Ed Sutton back to Washington to investigate." St. Clair took a deep drag of his cigarette.

"That makes sense. According to the plans I've seen, the company controlling the viaduct railway would be exempt from all city taxes and have the right to build all street railways in other sections of the city. Have you any idea how much money such a project could generate, Charlie? That's why this past March, Fowler ordered Governor Krupp to quash Alfred Beach's Pneumatic Railway. Have you seen it?"

"I've heard about it, of course," said St. Clair, "but, no, I've never seen it."

"It's the damnest thing," continued King. "I was down there right in the bowels of the earth. Beach actually built this three hundred foot tunnel. And there's a giant fan that propels the railcar. The inventiveness is astounding, which is why I suppose the Ring opposed it. Fowler's greed cannot be satisfied, nor his weakness for corruption." King drank the last of his coffee. "Come, I want to show you what I've prepared for you. I was planning to send it on the four o'clock train, but you can take it yourself."

King went into the kitchen and returned a moment later with a sheaf of papers. "Here it is," he said excitedly. "Sit down at the table and I'll show you. It's all of my notes and bookkeeping on Fowler's courthouse. You must see this. The original books are still in my office at City Hall, but I took great pains to make this copy. Because I was also working on other projects and plans, I hadn't realized the extent of the scandal. I have to admit, Bob James did a brilliant job of manipulating figures and books. It took me hours to sort this out."

St. Clair removed his jacket and hat and pulled his chair close to King.

"Let's look first at the accounts of Frederick Stevens, a carpenter and well-known Tammany man. On paper, at any rate, he may be the richest carpenter in the world. On July 20, 1869, he billed the city for a day's work at the new courthouse for $13,692. On the twenty-eighth he invoiced for work on two rooms for $16,092. October 17, for $38,985, and so on. His year-end total for 1869 was $394,998."

"That's staggering." St. Clair gaped at the figures.

"Only Bruce McWilliams, Fowler's favorite plasterer, did better. I understand now why they call him the Prince of Plasterers. For June and July of 1869, he was paid $945,000. He earned $133,847 for two days work. It goes on and on. Jimmy Robinson, the plumber earned more than a million for installing privies and gas light fixtures. How much do you think an awning might cost? Take a guess." King smiled.

"I don't know, Frank, ten dollars or so?"

"Twelve dollars and fifty cents to be exact. Except the city paid $645.26 cents for an awning and they bought thirty-six of them. Here's a bill for three tables and forty chairs for $179,730. And the brushes must've been made of gold. Thirty floor brushes and brooms cost $41,985. Queen Victoria would be shocked. However, the most creative part is how some of the money ended up back in the Ring's accounts at the Tenth National Bank. There were daily deposits into Special Accounts or Department of Finance Contingency Accounts. Never let it be said also that Harrison or James have lost their senses of humor. Here are three cancelled checks for more than $100,000 in total that came from the Comptroller's Office. The first, for $42,000 and dated February 10, 1869, was made to Fillippo Donaruma. A second for May 5, 1870, for about the same was sent to T.C. Cash and a third for about $15,000 to Philip F. Dummey. Funny, right?"

"Yeah, damn hilarious."

"So, here's my best estimate," continued King. "When Fowler first announced the construction of the courthouse he said the total cost to the city would be $250,000. From what I can see here, by the time it opens in September, the taxpayers of New York will have paid out about twelve million dollars. And you can figure that seventy-five per cent of that wound up back in the Ring's pockets."

St. Clair leaned back in his chair and laughed. "If it wasn't so sad, this would be funnier than any showman or song and dance man I've seen on the Rialto. My God, how could he get away with this for so long?" He suddenly felt energized, imagining the role the magazine could play. "I want to take this with me, Frank. I'll write something, of course, and Stewart can produce another series of sketches. I want to show your work to Rupert Potter as well. It might be enough for him to rally his committee to oust the Ring once and for all. And maybe put most of them behind bars. Whatever grandiose plans Fowler has for Crédit Mobilier will amount to nothing by the time we're done with him."

"And then, I can return to a normal life?" asked King

"Potter will want you to testify. So you must remain dead for the time being. Is there anyone out here who can cause you trouble?"

"I haven't left this house and I know that Granny Tillett would never say a word."

"I hope you're right. Because I assure you if Fowler finds out that you're still alive, he'll send his man Flint to visit you. Do you know who Flint is, Frank?"

"I don't. Why should I?" asked King.

"He's a hired thug and murderer. He attacked me and Fox and nearly killed the both of us." St. Clair paused for a moment. "He also knew Lucy Maloney, the woman found in the trunk at Hudson Depot. He may have had something to do with her death."

"Is that so?" King responded. St. Clair noted a bead of sweat forming on his forehead. He reached for his jacket and pulled out a folded piece of paper. It was the unsigned message he had received with Lucy Maloney's name on it. "You recognize this, Frank?"

"Why? What is it?" King paled visibly.

"It's the message you sent telling me about Lucy." St. Clair kept his eyes on King's every gesture.

"I don't know what you're talking—"

"Enough, Frank. I spoke with Mildred Potter. I followed her to Miss Kate's. I even smoked some hashish with her, if you can believe it. She told me everything. How you met Lucy at the masked ball. You were paying for Lucy's hotel room at the Fifth Avenue, weren't you, Frank?"

King leapt to his feet. "I knew Mildred could never keep her mouth shut, especially if she's smoked hashish. I never understood the fascination with it. But yes, yes, it's true what you say. I paid for her suite at the hotel from money I received from Fowler. And the worst part of it is, I miss her terribly. She was so beautiful and lovely. There was never a dull moment with her."

"And Amanda?"

King looked pained. "You think it's possible to love two women, Charlie?"

St. Clair shrugged. There was no answer to this conundrum. "What about Flint?" he asked instead. "The doorman at the hotel says he saw Lucy with a man that sounds like it was Flint?"

"I have no idea whatsoever about that. She never said anything to me. I swear it."

"Frank, were you the father of her baby?"

He put his hands up to his face. "I must've been. Who else could it have been? She never said a word to me. Never told me—"

"Did Fowler know about this?"

"I don't know, Charlie. He may have. He only met Lucy once or twice. We tried to be discreet, but Fowler has eyes and ears everywhere. We dined occasionally at this small Italian restaurant that Lucy liked on Twenty-third Street behind the Opera House. He saw us there. I introduced her as my cousin from Pittsburgh, but I suspect he knew better. Another evening, Lucy was out with Mildred at Harry Hill's. I urged her not to go there without me, but she refused to listen. She could be stubborn. She told me later that she had spoken to Fowler and Isaac Harrison there."

"Did you kill her, Frank?" St. Clair affected nonchalance hoping to catch King off guard.

"What! You think I could've done something like that? Shit, Charlie. How could you ask me such a thing?"

It was St. Clair's turn to leap to his feet. "How about this? You found out that she was pregnant. You talked her into visiting Madame Philippe. She agreed, except she got scared, and at the last second ran out. You were watching and waiting for her. You had a heated argument and in a moment of passion killed her. Frightened yourself, you stuffed her in a trunk and arranged to hide the body out of town. Or maybe you hired Flint to do the deed for you?"

"But—" King protested.

"Except you're a decent man, Frank, and your guilt overwhelmed you," St. Clair continued. "So you let me know who she was. But you're still too scared to admit it. And now you're going to allow Madame Philippe to hang for your crime."

"You're nuts, Charlie," yelled King. "That's the most preposterous story I've ever heard. I swear to you on the grave of my mother that I didn't kill her. And I sure in hell didn't hire this Flint. I don't even know this son of a bitch. I loved Lucy. I could never, ever have harmed a hair on her head. You have to believe me." He put his hands over his face and released a sob.

St. Clair felt helpless. "I believe you, Frank. I believe you. But I had to ask."

St. Clair waited a few moments for Frank to recover his composure. "Frank," he began gently, "do you think it's possible that Fowler discovered that you were providing me with information about the Ring and killed Lucy as retribution?"

King wiped his eyes. "That's what I thought when I first learned of her death. But, Charlie, we've both been careful. No one knows about this. Honestly, I don't believe Fowler knows about you and me. And, it's probably the only secret in the entire city that he's not privy to."

St. Clair walked towards the window. His mind roiled...If King had nothing to do with Lucy's death and Fowler had not ordered the killing to punish King, then maybe Fowler had another motive to kill her. And what about Flint? Why was he talking with her that day that George saw them outside of the Fifth Avenue Hotel?

He needed to learn what they had been talking about. Yes, he decided, as he turned to face King—that was the key to unraveling this troubling enigma.

Chapter Twenty-Nine

———◦❋◦———

A LAPSE OF JUDGMENT

*R*andolph Glover was a tall thin gentleman in his late fifties, fashionably clean-shaven, with long white hair, parted in the middle, which swept over his ears and on to the collar of his suit jacket. Six years ago, Glover came up with an ingenious and profitable idea. He purchased a large and regal mansion on upper Fifth Avenue near Thirtieth Street, tore down a few walls, renovated the interior, and transformed it into the finest private banquet hall in the city.

The main-floor ballroom with its exquisite chandeliers, oak floor-ing, and mahogany tables immediately appealed to the wealthiest of the upper crust, who held their parties, weddings, and festive occasions there. While the price was steep—a social gathering or ball with fifty guests or more cost upwards of $10,000—Glover offered the best of everything—décor, food, and entertainment. He fancied himself as a perfectionist and his services were renowned among the ladies of the well-to-do. The Fowlers had held their annual Summer Ball at Glover's establishment for the past four seasons.

"I must apologize for keeping you waiting, Mr. Glover," Ellen Fowler said, her face pale, her body agitated. "Please forgive me. I lost complete track of the time."

"Think nothing of it, Madam Fowler. You're here now, that's all that is important. Isn't it?" Glover lightly kissed Ellen's outstretched hand. "Pardon the personal nature of the question, but are you feeling well, Madam?"

"As a matter of fact, I do feel a bit faint at the moment, I'm not certain why," she answered. In fact, she was well aware that her decision to abstain from laudanum this morning left her weak and agitated. "But pay no attention to my health, Mr. Glover. I'm determined that this year the ball must be truly special. And money is no object."

"It never is with your husband, Madam."

Ellen feigned a smile. "Yes, that's been the case, but if you've been reading the newspapers, then you'll know that this might be the last ball we host for some time. My dear husband has even managed to raise the ire of President Grant."

"I make it a habit never to read the newspapers, Madam. For the news is always bad. However, it long has been my view that Mr. Fowler is too clever a man to fall into any trap from which he cannot free himself. I look forward to arranging many more of your celebrations in the years ahead."

"Mr. Glover, you're overly optimistic. I've always found that appealing about you."

"Shall we look at the final menu, Madam? Please take a seat."

"You're the Captain of this vessel, sir. Steer the ship as you like." Ellen collapsed into a chair by Glover's large oak desk.

"Very well," began Glover. "We shall start with hors d'oeuvres of scalloped oysters, artichokes *à la poivrade* and pieces of Westphalian ham with mayonnaise of lobster. Served with champagne and rum punch. I recently acquired the recipe for the Tom and Jerry Punch served at the Metropolitan Hotel for many years. I know the ladies will be delighted with this." He cleared his throat. "This will be followed by a choice of *consommé* or green turtle soup. For the main course, Mr. Fowler's favorites—roast lamb and wild duck with a jumble of vegetables, French peas, and crabs with mushroom. I've decided to omit the ragout of pigeon with shallots and mushrooms and stuffed suckling pig that we'd discussed earlier. And finally for dessert, an assortment of cakes and pastry, along with port, Madeira and liqueurs. For the wine, I've selected Chablis, Medoc and Rauenthaler Berg."

"And the orchestra?"

"Ah, the most talented musicians from the Academy of Music accompanied by a trio of Italian singers, visiting from Europe."

"That sounds marvelous. I must say, I can hardly wait. Yes, this should be the grandest Summer Ball we've ever held. A night that Victor will remember for years to come."

"As it should be," said Glover with a smile.

Discussing the plans for the ball made Ellen feel slightly more at ease. The first twenty-four hours after stopping her daily dose of laudanum had nearly driven her out of her head. All day yesterday she lay in bed in a cold sweat. Today, however, was better than yesterday—despite her weak state. For the first time in a long time she could see her life with Victor more clearly and had arrived at one significant decision—either his philandering with whores must stop or she would pack her bags and leave. No matter what Reverend Ingersoll had counseled, the time for forgiveness had past. She knew that Victor did not take kindly to threats—already today the President's statement that Crédit Mobilier was to be investigated by a special committee sent him off screaming at poor Harrison. She only felt a guilty about one thing—enjoying his discomfort so immensely.

Her ultimatum about the future of their marriage, she had decided, would be delivered the night of the ball—at midnight would be most fitting. She could not wait to see the twisted expression on his face. It almost made her giddy with anticipation. Was she wrong to feel this way? The reverend had repeatedly told her that vindictiveness and spitefulness were akin to blasphemy. And that in the end she would be the one to suffer, not Victor. She didn't care. If God chose to punish her later for this and other transgressions, so be it.

~

"Where's Krupp when you need him?" hollered Fowler. "This deal is collapsing before my eyes and I can't find him. He should be in

Washington using every damn contact he has in Congress to stop the committee investigation. Do you hear me, Isaac?"

"You've been ranting for the last two hours, Victor. How could I not hear you?" answered Harrison. "I've already told you, Krupp decided to take the steamer here from Albany. He should arrive before seven. There isn't much we can do until then."

Fowler picked up the stack of telegrams he had been receiving from Washington all day and scattered them about the floor. "Have you read this last one from Grant's office? Political blatherskite is what it is. Rubbish. Listen to me, Isaac. There can be no investigation into Crédit Mobilier or anything else. What is the point of controlling a company that's been brought into disrepute by a presidential special committee? And if I'm associated with it, our plans for the next election will be ruined."

In all the years, Harrison had been associated with Fowler, he had never seen him quite so livid or disturbed.

"What did you tell the Tammany delegation?" asked Fowler.

"That the story was false. That you or any of your chief organizers have no involvement whatsoever in a Republican operated company," Harrison replied as calmly as he could.

"And they believed it?"

"I think so. If this presidential committee does convene, however, and Kirkland is compelled to testify, then we may have serious problems to contend with."

"A few more contracts will take care of that." Fowler narrowed his eyes.

"I'm not as certain about that."

Fowler paused to light a cigar. "You know, I should've told Flint to slit Tom Fox's throat as soon as possible."

"What would that have solved?"

"Nothing, I suppose, but it would've made me feel a lot better," said Fowler with a short laugh. "The fool sent back his reply card for the ball along with St. Clair's an hour after it was delivered."

"As you said he would. It's too tempting an offer. Fox is a clever man. Look how much trouble he's caused already. I think it would be a grave error to underestimate him or St. Clair. I've heard rumors that Fox is planning to publish a special issue about us. Possibly as early as tomorrow and with a story about the courthouse."

"What does he know?" said Fowler waving his cigar. "Nothing. King had all the account books and we retrieved those from his office. Forget about it, Isaac. The courthouse is the least of our problems. No, if we're ever to install Krupp in the White House and ruin Grant, then Crédit Mobilier must succeed." Fowler glanced at his watch. "Now, if you'll excuse me I have an appointment."

"At this hour, with whom?"

"She's about five feet, three inches, twenty-two years old, and howls like a bitch in heat."

Harrison watched Fowler saunter out of his office and was disgusted—yet again. Maybe it was his own recent, intense discussions with Reverend Ingersoll about morals and ethics that were having an effect, he wasn't certain. All he knew was that he was weary of tormenting himself about Fowler's whoring. Look at how much trouble and needless tragedy it had caused already. And for what? So that Victor Fowler could ultimately control the highest office in the land.

"Excuse me, Mr. Harrison." Fowler's servant, Jackson, interrupted his thoughts. "There's a gentlemen here to see you. He says it's urgent."

Harrison sighed. "What now? Please show him in."

A moment later, Jackson led a tall well-built man in an old navy suit and derby into Fowler's office.

"I don't have time for you now, Stokes," Harrison said impatiently. "What are you doing here?"

"Is that anyway to talk to a friend, Harrison? And trust me, from what I've been reading and hearing, you need all the friends you can get." The police inspector glanced around the room. "Any of Mr. Fowler's cigars handy?"

"I have no idea. Stokes, I haven't got time for idle chit-chat. State your business and be on your way."

"Yes, my business. I find myself in a bit of quandary, Harrison. As you know, my meager police department income was being supplemented by Madame Philippe for some time. I now find myself without this since the Madame's regrettable arrest and conviction."

"How much do you want?" Harrison eyed the inspector with growing annoyance.

"Not to be crass."

"No, of course not." Harrison rolled his eyes upward.

"I was thinking of five thousand a month. How does that sit with you?"

"Stokes, you're lucky Mr. Fowler isn't here to listen to this crude attempt to wring more money from us." Harrison walked toward the window, turning his back on Stokes.

"As I said, I didn't want to be crass. But that's my demand. I've done everything you've asked. Didn't I assign the case to that pest, Murray? Didn't I ensure that Madame Philippe was arrested?"

"And if I refuse?" asked Harrison spinning around.

"That would be inadvisable. In truth, I've been experiencing a pang of guilt over what's transpired. The idea that this innocent woman—"

"Come now, she's hardly innocent. How many children does one person have to kill before its murder?"

"Nevertheless, the circumstances in this case are unique, I think you'd agree?"

"I'll have to speak to Mr. Fowler about this."

"Yes, do so, but I expect a reply within a day or—"

"Or what, Stokes?" Harrison's voice was hard.

"Or you may find yourself with even more problems."

"Get the hell out of here, before I do something I would certainly regret."

As soon as Jackson escorted the police inspector out of the house, Harrison helped himself to a glass of Fowler's best whiskey. He detested men such as Stokes, a sanctimonious public official, corrupt from the top of his head to the tip of his boots. New York's citizens deserved far better. But what choice did he have? He had to meet Stokes's demands, as absurd as they were. Nor could he consult Fowler about this. That would merely complicate matters further. He gulped down the whiskey and poured another glass as he reviewed all that had happened.

~

Seth Murray crossed Mulberry Street and headed towards Chauncey's oyster cellar. His search for Flint had been unproductive thus far. He had posted police patrols near Miss Kate's parlor house on Greene Street around the clock, but Flint was nowhere to be seen or heard from. When questioned by Westwood, Miss Kate offered no hint that she even knew the man.

On the other hand, he thought as he climbed down the stair into the bar—two days from now, Madame Philippe would be gone. And whether or not it was Flint or someone else who had actually killed Lucy Maloney would be a moot point. Murray was tired of the whole affair anyway and he doubted St. Clair's theory about Flint or Fowler's involvement. He also seemed to be back in Inspector Stokes's good books and looked forward to other challenging cases in the near future. There would be no more pickpocket patrol for him.

"Murray, I'm glad you stopped by." Chauncy Jones greeted him.

"A pint of ale, Chauncy. And hurry."

The saloon owner motioned with his head toward the corner. There sitting alone talking to himself was Doc Draper. "He's been doing that for about an hour. You can't go near him. He's as ornery as a mad dog and scaring my other customers."

Murray grabbed his ale and swallowed it quickly. "Shit, I can't even rest in here anymore."

"Is that you, Detective?" Draper asked as Murray approached. His eyes were red and glazed over, his hair disheveled.

"Yeah, it's me, Doc. Chauncey says you've been causing trouble. Doesn't sound much like you."

"I need some more whiskey. That's what I need all right," Draper mumbled.

"Tell you what, Doc, I'll fetch you another bottle, if you tell me what's got your dander up?"

"I'm an old fool, that's all. I've done something imprudent. And for what? For a few extra dollars in my pocket from the mangiest beast this city's ever seen." He waved his right hand and it tipped over an empty glass.

"You lost me, Doc. Can I sit down so we can talk about this?"

"Suit yourself. You're a good man, Murray, I've always thought so. You ever take money when no one was looking? Of course you wouldn't. Why would you? Unfortunately, I'm not as strong as that."

"What happened, Doc? What did you do?" Murray righted the tipped glass.

Draper wiped his face and blew his nose into a dirty handkerchief. He stuffed the cloth back into his pants pocket and pulled out a small medical vial. Carefully, he placed it in the middle of the table between him and Murray.

"What is it? Can I look?"

Draper nodded. Murray picked up the vial and held it up close to his face. Inside were two red objects.

"Are those jewels, Doc?"

"Rubies, to be precise," whispered Draper. "Two red rubies."

"Why are they so special?"

Draper looked in every direction to ensure no one was listening and then let his head slump. His chin nestled in his chest. "I found them in the bottom of the trunk."

"What trunk? The trunk from Hudson Depot? You took them out of the trunk that Lucy Maloney was stuffed into? Is that what you're saying, Doc? For Christ sakes, is that it?" Murray's excited voice boomed through the saloon.

"Will you keep your voice down?" Draper pleaded. He picked his head up and looked directly into Murray's eyes. "Yes. Yes. That's it. They were under her head, buried in her hair."

"So why didn't you tell me about this at the time? I mean, you showed me Madame Philippe's advertisement. Why not the rubies as well?"

"You don't understand, do you? You don't recognize those? Those rubies are quite distinct. They're from a gold badge—from a gold badge cut in the shape of a tiger. The rubies are the tiger's eyes."

Murray pushed his hat back. He dropped his voice. "Those are Fowler's rubies? From his tiger badge? Are you certain?"

Draper leaned toward him. "I suspected immediately when I found them. That's why I never said anything to you. Fowler's been good to me. Shit, I earn five times what any other coroner does. And I owe that to Fowler. So I went to his office. I spoke with Isaac Harrison who instructed me to keep it to myself. He said I should send them over to him and he'd get them back to Fowler. But I never did it and it's been gnawing at me."

"How could Fowler's rubies have ended up in that trunk?"

"That's what I've been asking myself for the last week. And I keep coming to the same conclusion. He must've been with her. I'd guess that Fowler knew Miss Maloney intimately. He might well be the father of her child. He," Draper's voice dropped to a whisper, "he might have killed her."

"And the rubies fell into the trunk when he put her in there." Murray absently twisted the end of his moustache. "It's possible, Doc."

Draper face sagged. "What of Madame Philippe?"

"Yeah, what of her? We have a bit of a problem here, don't we? Have you told anyone else about this?"

"No one. I swear it."

"And you're not to until I tell you. Is that understood?"

Draper nodded. "What are you going to do?"

"At the moment, I have no idea. Fowler has got to be questioned, but it has to be done properly. I expect he'll claim his rubies were stolen or he has no idea how or why they were in the trunk. And that would be that. Madame Philippe will still hang on Wednesday." He grabbed Draper's bottle of whiskey and took a swig. "Doc, I know someone who's going to piss in his pants when he hears about this. I'd also wager he'll have a good idea about laying a trap for that bastard once and for all."

Chapter Thirty

A Journal Entry

"Charlie, why so glum?" Fox called from inside his office, as St. Clair entered, back from Newburgh. "Haven't you read this morning's *Times* or *Herald*? There's news of Ames, Crédit Mobilier, and Fowler. Grant's office has denied any involvement. Colfax is screaming that we've libeled him and claims he's going to take the magazine and me to court. So things are looking up. Tell me, do you own a black evening jacket?"

"Why? I still have the one I wore at my wedding."

"Good. That'll be fine."

"Tom, what the hell are you talking about?"

"Sit down and fill your pipe," said Fox holding up two cards with regal printing on them. "These are two invitations to a ball. One was addressed to me, the other to you. Mind you, not just any ball, but Mr. and Mrs. Victor Fowler's Summer Ball tomorrow evening at Glover's. From what Molly tells me, it should be the grandest and most magnificent dance of the year."

"Why would Fowler put us on his guest list? Certainly not to thank you for causing him so much aggravation."

"I have no idea, but I immediately replied that we would be there in full patrician attire. So clean off that suit."

"Tom, have you hit your head again?" St. Clair rolled his eyes. "With everything that's happened, we'd be walking into the wolf's lair. What if Flint's also on the guest list?"

"Then, we'll bring protection." Fox pulled out a revolver from his desk drawer. "And Molly for good luck. It does invite us to both bring ladies."

"That sounds like a fabulous idea, Tom," said Molly, who had been eavesdropping. She bent down to where Fox was sitting and lightly hugged him. "I need to go out for a few hours."

"What's this? We've work to do," exclaimed Fox, as Molly disappeared out the door. "Where are you off to?" he shouted at her.

"The shops on Broadway. I need to buy a gown if I'm going to a ball," came the reply.

St. Clair blew a whiff of smoke upwards. "Put that gun away, Tom. I've a better idea. But first, here's an article I finished about four this morning." He handed him the loose pages. "It's about the construction of the courthouse, in all its glorious detail. The corruption is truly astounding. The Ring may have stolen as much as ten million dollars from the city for this one building. I want to send a copy of it to Rupert Potter as soon as it's ready. It'll provide him with the ammunition he needs to oust Fowler. Stewart should also get to work on a new series of sketches."

As Fox skimmed through the piece, his eyes widened. "$950,000 to McWilliams, $180,000 for chairs, $41,000 for brushes and brooms. Bloody hell, does Fowler really believe he can pull the wool over the eyes of every citizen in New York?"

"Actually, I think he does. You know as well as I do that despite any campaign Potter mounts, Fowler can do as he damn well pleases." St. Clair paused for a moment as Fox continued reading. "What have you heard from Sutton?"

"Nothing yet. This aide he wants to see is away for the day, so we'll have to be patient. Sutton's a good man. He'll dig up something we can use." Fox dropped St. Clair's article on the desk. "Where did you get this information, Charlie? Don't you think it's about time you let me in on your secret source."

St. Clair stood and shut the door of Fox's office. "Tom, there's a man's life at stake here. So what I'm about to tell you cannot leave this room. But with everything that's happened, I had already decided to share this with you. You ready?"

"Charlie, what the hell is this about?" Fox leaned across his desk.

"Frank King's alive," whispered St. Clair.

"Alive! Christ! How?"

St. Clair removed his smoldering pipe from his mouth. "He's been my source for the Ring stories from the beginning. Although Fowler's made him a rich man, he detests him as much as we do. He believed, rightly or wrongly, that Fowler discovered what he had done and was going to kill him. So he faked his own death in order to carry out the rest of his plan—to destroy the Ring. The curious thing is, from what I've heard, Fowler and Harrison really do think that King is dead."

"Where is he now?"

"Hiding out at his wife's grandmother's farm near Newburgh. He doesn't know a hell of a lot about Crédit Mobilier, only that it's linked to some grander scheme Fowler's been plotting for months. He's intending to stay hidden until, or if, there's an inquiry or a trial. And, Tom, there's more." St. Clair sat down. "King was having an affair with Lucy Maloney. It was King who was paying her bill at the Fifth Avenue. He used money that he took from Fowler."

"I need some whiskey." Fox reached for a bottle hidden on his book shelf.

"I asked him directly if he had killed Miss Maloney and he said no," St. Clair watched Fox pour two glasses of whiskey. "He says he loved her, but he couldn't leave his wife and family."

"Yeah, I've heard that before. You don't believe him, do you?" Fox motioned to St. Clair to take one of the glasses.

"Whatever his faults, I don't think King's a liar." St. Clair refused the whiskey. "Yeah, I think he's being truthful. That, of course, doesn't help Madame Philippe. I should also tell you that Miss Maloney was acquainted with Flint. That doorman at the hotel claims he saw the two of them arguing."

"Which means, from what you told me earlier, Miss Maloney might've known Ruth Cardaso, too?"

"I suppose, I hadn't thought of that. I'll say this—and I realize that I have no proof—but before I spoke with King, my view was that Flint, and Fowler for that matter, had something to do with the girl's murder. I haven't changed my mind about it."

"Then we must have a discussion with Mr. Fowler at his ball, Charlie, and see what's what."

"Anyone here?" A voice from the other room startled them.

"Seth, is that you?" St. Clair rose and opened Fox's door.

Detective Murray, his face somber, entered and took an empty chair beside Fox's desk.

"Why so blue, Seth?" St. Clair inquired. "You look as if your best friend just died."

"I need to talk to you."

"Talk. You can say whatever you want in front of Tom."

"Of course. Sorry, Fox."

"No need to apologize, Detective. Would you like a glass of whiskey? St. Clair isn't drinking."

"No, thanks, not right now." Murray pulled a vial out his jacket pocket. "These were found under Lucy Maloney in the trunk under her body."

"What are they?" St. Clair examined the small bottle.

"I'd say two red rubies," said Fox, a sly grin growing across his face. "Two rubies that you might find on a tiger badge."

"Fowler?" asked St. Clair, dumbfounded.

"Exactly," Murray said. "Draper was on Fowler's payroll. That's why he hid this. Except now the poor sap feels guilty that Madame Philippe will hang for something she might not have done."

"That's it, then, Seth. That's the evidence you need to go to the judge with."

"And what do you think he'll do, Charlie? Not a damn thing. I can question Fowler, and I'm certain he'll tell a whopper of a story, but it won't be enough to collar him. Besides, what's his motive? Was Fowler fucking her?"

"You'll have to pardon my brother-in-law, Tom. He's never been in the company of a gentleman before."

"Who me?" Fox chuckled. "Which one of us is a gentleman?"

"My deepest apologies." Murray doffed his hat. "What I meant was, maybe Fowler was the father of her child. Maybe it was Fowler who was paying for her room at the hotel? He discovered she was with child and it became too dangerous to have her around. Now, if we could prove that, then we'd have a case. But until that time comes, there's not much I can do to Boss Fowler."

"Charlie, why don't you ..." began Fox.

St. Clair glared at Fox and discreetly shook his head. Murray appeared oblivious. "What Tom was about to say," he interjected quickly, "was that for some odd reason we've been invited to Fowler's Summer Ball tomorrow evening. And we plan to confront him there about his corrupt business dealings. Mentioning Miss Maloney could catch him off guard."

"You at the Summer Ball, Charlie?" Murray snickered. "And in tails? What a sight." Murray's face suddenly grew somber. "Fowler might've invited you, so the two of you would walk right into his trap. What if this Flint shows up as well?"

"I already thought of that." Fox brandished his pistol.

"Tom, I wouldn't advise that. There'll be a few cops around. Fowler's had Stokes arrange for a detail of ten patrolmen to be on duty protecting the guests."

"That won't stop Flint," added Fox.

"Seth, is there any way you can get that assignment?" asked St. Clair.

"I don't know. It would require a large favor from one of the men. It's possible. What do you have in mind?"

∼

St. Clair was on the street bidding farewell to Murray, promising that they'd meet again tomorrow morning to discuss their plan for the ball, when a silver carriage pulled up alongside him. Hector, Madame Philippe's servant, sat in the driver's seat.

"Mr. St. Clair, sir, please a moment of your time."

"How is she?" asked St. Clair, startled to see the man.

"Terrible. I'm afraid all is lost," Hector replied. "Her appeal was denied this morning and the Governor refuses to consider a pardon. I was told to deliver this letter to you and wait to hear your reply." He leaned down and handed St. Clair a folded piece of paper.

21 August 1871
Dearest Mr. St. Clair,

I had wanted to speak to you in person, but alas the prison authorities have forbidden it. When we last spoke I had asked if you believed I am guilty of the crime for which I have been convicted. Due to the violence on the streets, I never received your answer. But I am hoping, beyond all hope, that you do indeed have faith in my words of innocence. I do not know if you have discovered anything in your investigations and travels that could assist me. As I'm to face the gallows in two days, and without any word from you, I am forced to conclude that no new evidence has been found that might clear my good name.

Trust and loyalty are virtues that I have long regarded as worthy, not to be broken or taken lightly. However, for selfish reasons I now must break that trust.

If you will agree, sir, Hector will show you my client books. In these dusty volumes, accumulated over decades, are the names and details of thousands of women who have come to me in their hour of need.

As you above all people can appreciate, I have made many enemies over the years of my service to the women of New York and elsewhere. Perhaps there is something you may find that will assist my case? I realize that you may regard this as a desperate, even foolish measure, but my options are few and far between.

I only ask one favor of you, that you put aside your instincts as a journalist and think of yourself as the husband you once were. Many of these women were young when they sought me out and are now upstanding members of the community. Many have families and loving husbands. I have absolutely no desire to invade their privacy or breach the bond of trust they once placed in me.

Mr. St. Clair, I beg of you to adhere to my wishes. My life, as it were, is in your hands.

With the deepest respect,
Madame Philippe

St. Clair tucked the letter in his pocket and looked up at Hector. "Where are these volumes she writes of?"

"In the parlor at the house on Fifth Avenue. There's a hidden panel where the records are kept. Please climb in and I'll take you there at once."

It only took a moment for St. Clair to make up his mind. He hoisted himself up beside Hector. "To her house, then, and with all the speed those fine horses can muster."

~

Twenty-five minutes later, St. Clair was standing in the grand entrance-way of Madame Philippe's mansion that he had last visited with Ruth. Except now, the house was dark and deserted.

"They've told her that they intend to take the property as soon as she's gone," said Hector. "Can they do this, Mr. St. Clair? Can they seize her home?"

"I honestly don't know. But with Mr. Fowler in charge of the courts and the city, anything is possible."

"Mr. Fowler's been real good to Madame, at least until now. Real good." Hector shook his head in puzzlement.

"Well, he'll do anything if he's paid enough."

Hector shrugged. "I don't know about such matters. The panel is this way."

He led St. Clair into an immaculate parlor with smooth plush carpeting on the floor and Persian and Indian rugs hanging on the walls. There were elegant sofas, chairs, and mahogany tables. Hector shifted one of the sofas away from the wall. Behind it, close to the floor, was a panel approximately half the size of a door. He slid it open.

"Just watch your head, Mr. St. Clair. Also, I haven't cleaned in there for months, so it might be a little dusty. You'll have to light the lantern. You'll see it hanging on a nail."

Intrigued, St. Clair removed his hat, squatted down, and crawled through on his knees. The room beyond was small and rectangular, no more than eight feet long and six and a half feet wide. He found the coal oil lantern, lit the wick, and peered at the room's contents in the flickering light. Each of the four walls had floor to ceiling shelves on which were stored thin black leather-bound record books, some covered in cobwebs and dust. St. Clair estimated more than a hundred volumes in total.

He pulled out one of the books nearest to him and carefully opened it. Each page contained numerous entries, with names, dates, medical notes, and the amount paid. This particular volume was for the first six months of 1854. For the week of February 10th, St. Clair counted fifteen entries. He glanced down the list at the various notations scrawled in pencil and ink.

Name Address Notes Fee Date

I. Lily Wilkins 79 Howard Street Menstrual Blockage $100—Feb. 6/54 Recommended by Madam Elaina Given savin mixture. Complained of pain after procedure. Stayed two days

II. Jane Sollier 45 Wooster Street 8 mos. $50—Feb. 7/54 Recommended and paid for by Miss Helena Tremont. Patient was well past quickening. Eight months. Healthy baby boy delivered on Feb. 7/54. Adoption fee of $200 paid Feb. 9/54. Boy delivered to Mr. S. Stacks of Boston.

III. Gertrude Taylor Fifth Avenue at 16th Street 3–4 mos. $300—Feb. 9/54
Miss Taylor was accompanied by her mother Mrs. H. Taylor, who insisted that the procedure be done immediately. Recommended that she wait. The girl was suffering from a touch of fever. Required three days rest.

And so it went, page after page. The addresses of many women, like Lilly Wilkins and Jane Sollier, were at well-known brothels. Prostitutes, St. Clair concluded, were avid customers of Madame Philippe. He also counted at least four women who died from "medical complications" during the period from February to April 1854.

But he recognized names such as Gertrude Taylor, the daughter of Henry Taylor, then the head of the Bank of New York, and now Mrs. Gertrude Wilson, prominent wife of Samuel Wilson, the current head of the same bank. She could not have been more than sixteen years old in 1854. There were others, too, wives and daughters of railroad executives, shipping merchants, Wall Street financiers, and political leaders. Married men accompanied their young girlfriends, while pregnant wives pleaded with Madame Philippe to abort babies who had not been conceived with their husbands.

The most shocking case St. Clair found was that of Miss Mavis Lockie, the young niece of John Andrew Lockie, the property magnate, who owned much of Upper Fifth Avenue and the surrounding vicinity. According to the notation, on April 7, 1866, Mr. Lockie, who was then in his late sixties, along with two colored servants, brought in his niece for an appointment. Her age was listed as nineteen years. Mr. Lockie paid Madame Philippe five hundred dollars for her discretion. Had John Lockie impregnated his brother's daughter? St. Clair rifled through the pages. There were no details on the identity of the father or about Miss Lockie's condition after the procedure was completed. St. Clair was fairly certain she no longer lived in the city.

The longer he scanned the names and read the personal, often painful and wrenching stories of hundreds of female patients, the more it became clear to him that during the last two to three decades, abortion had been endemic. Rich, poor, or in between, wealthy matriarch, domestic servant, or whore, it hardly seemed to make a difference to the women of New York. Madame Philippe could not keep up with orders for her Monthly Female Pills—a constant stream of requests came from as far as San Francisco and Montreal—nor work fast enough. St. Clair had clearly underestimated the demand and popularity of her medical services. No wonder the woman was wealthy. Fees in the month of February 1854 alone totalled approximately $3,500.

Four hours passed and St. Clair had found little that could solve his immediate problem. At about seven o'clock, Hector brought him a cup of hot tea with bread and cheese.

"That's much appreciated, Hector. Thank you. But I'm afraid I've made little progress. I've found nothing that will aid the Madame," said St. Clair, sounding frustrated and tired. He placed the cheese on top of the bread and took a bite out of it.

"It's there, I'm certain of it. Somewhere in those books." Hector gazed at the massed volumes.

"You've worked for her for a long time?"

"Oh, yes, many years. May I add a personal comment, sir?"

"By all means," said St. Clair, sipping the cup of tea.

Hector cleared his throat. "I know that you don't think highly of what she does. And that she only does it for the money so that she can live in such a splendid house. I can tell you, though, there's goodness in her soul. You must believe me, she has saved thousands of women from misery and perhaps death." His voice shook.

St. Clair nodded and patted Hector on the shoulder. From what he had already read, he had reluctantly arrived at the same conclusion. As much as he hated to admit it, the abuse inflicted on so many of these women by drunken husbands, dishonest boyfriends, and cruel pimps almost justified the work of Madame Philippe and the other legitimate midwives and abortionists.

At about eleven in the evening, having looked at more than thirty books, St. Clair lay down a sofa in the parlor before continuing. Within minutes he was asleep.

~

He awoke suddenly at about half past one by a flickering light. Hector was standing over him, clutching one of the volumes in one hand and the lantern in the other.

"What is it?" St. Clair asked sitting up. "I must have dozed off."

"I have been reviewing in my mind many of the women Madame Philippe has treated over the years." Hector said quietly. "It occurred to me that there is one case you must read about. Why I did not think of this earlier I have no idea. Madame Philippe has insisted on strict privacy and I have always abided by her wishes. Once a woman sees her, I have put it out of mind. It is much safer that way." He handed St. Clair the volume and the lantern. "I shall make you some tea," he said leaving the parlor.

"Can you see your way in the dark?" St. Clair called out. There was no reply. He brought the lantern closer so that he could see the book. The volume was from July to December of 1862. It appeared to be like dozens of other record books he had already examined. His eyes glanced down the page almost to the bottom, when he saw it. The name was scribbled in small letters, barely legible, but it was there.

"Christ almighty," he blurted.

His hands were trembling and his stomach was churning. He wiped his eyes and carefully read the extensive notation Madame Philippe had made nine years earlier. This patient, some months past quickening, had come to her complaining of terrible pains, caused by the pregnancy. Madame Philippe had prescribed her savin and a strong dose of French Pills, but they did not have the desired effect. An abortion followed the next day. During the procedure, there was excessive bleeding. The patient later claimed it was caused from a faulty instrument, yet Madame Philippe's notes indicated that it was not. She was uncertain what had happened. The patient, nonetheless, had nearly died. After a convalescence of five full days, this patient recovered.

His head was spinning. He tried to make sense of what he had learned. What did it truly mean and how did it fit in with what happened to Lucy Maloney? Assuming Madame Philippe had been honest in her journal, the entry's information wasn't something he could dismiss.

He found his notebook in his jacket pocket and copied the information as it was written in the record.

Moments later, Hector returned with a cup of tea. St. Clair stared at him with a look of astonishment on his face. Hector put down the cup and smiled, apparently content that matters were now well in hand.

Chapter Thirty-One

———◦✦◦———

SUMMER BALL REVELATION

The procession of carriages with drivers and footmen in livery began to arrive in front of Glover's on Fifth Avenue at about nine o'clock in the evening. Half a dozen patrolmen directed the traffic to ensure that it was orderly. As was the custom, Mr. Glover's servants had placed a red carpet from the front door of the house to the curbstone, over which a white awning was assembled.

From the carriages, each one more magnificent than the next, stepped gentlemen in black tails, crisp white shirts, black ties or cravats, and top hats. They were accompanied by ladies, two in some cases, in full satin dresses of royal blue, crimson, and apricot, festooned with flounces and gold lace trimmings, and around their necks and wrists, elegant and expensive necklaces and bracelets of pearls and emeralds. The women were followed closely by their young maids, who fussed over their trains and were attentive to their every whim and desire.

At the entrance to the house was Mr. Glover himself welcoming each guest and taking from the gentlemen their invitations. Once inside, the ladies headed immediately to the dressing room so that they and their maids could fix their hair and gowns one last time before the formal part of the evening commenced.

"Quite a sight, Charlie," said Fox with glee. "Now we know where all of our hard-earned money goes."

St. Clair had arrived with Fox and Molly. She could not stop giggling and looked lovely in a dove-colored satin gown trimmed with velvet with silver ribbon around the low-cut neckline. It was the latest Parisian fashion for which Fox had generously given Molly five hundred dollars.

"Let's stay close together," said St. Clair scanning the crowd inside the house for Flint. He was nowhere to be seen.

"Charlie, enjoy yourself," Fox admonished him. "I say let's drink as much of Fowler's champagne as we can."

St. Clair was not listening. He had barely slept. His unsettling discovery among Madame Philppe's record books had kept him awake, as he pondered various potential scenarios. Each time, he kept returning to the same conclusion, but it seemed so outlandish he couldn't mention it to Fox.

As they edged closer to the main ballroom waiting in line to pay their respects to their host and hostess, Victor and Ellen Fowler, St. Clair recognized many faces. The members of the Ring and their wives were present, of course. Governor Krupp was in a corner sipping a glass of champagne and chatting with a handsome young man, whom St. Clair believed was Fowler's nephew, Lewis. Beside him, holding court, was The Prince, Mayor Thomas Emery, bedecked in a stylish and likely very expensive black suit. He was surrounded by a gaggle of young and beautiful women—no doubt the single daughters of the local aristocracy in attendance.

Bob James, looking bored, sat at a table with his wife. Nearby, Isaac Harrison stood by himself, with his back against the wall. He appeared nervous. His eyes moved back and forth as if he were surveying the crowd for anything unusual. As he looked to his right, he saw St. Clair and nodded. The sly, almost sinister sneer on Harrison's face left St. Clair feeling cold and even more anxious.

Inching closer to the front, St. Clair could hear the soft strains of the orchestra inside the grand parlor. The musicians were playing a lively Viennese waltz. He glanced at Fox, then felt someone tapping on his back. He turned quickly, his hand reaching for his pistol inside his suit pocket, only to see Mildred Potter and her father, Rupert. She was wearing a graceful rose-colored satin dress, trimmed, apron-shape with black Brussels lace and gold and bugle bead trimmings with one flounce going all around the skirt.

He released his grip on his gun and relaxed his guard. "Miss Potter, you look lovely this evening. It's a delight to see you once again, but I must say," he continued, turning to Rupert Potter, "I'm somewhat shocked to see you at Fowler's ball."

"No more than me, St. Clair," agreed Potter. "Blame Mildred, she insisted on me escorting her. To be honest, I was more than a little surprised when the invitation arrived and accompanied by a personal note from Fowler himself. He suggested we speak privately during the evening to settle our differences."

"You're not going to listen to what he has to say, are you?"

"A man can always listen. No harm in that, but, no, I haven't changed my mind about driving him from office. Especially not since I looked over the article on the courthouse you sent me this morning. I've already shown it to several of the gentlemen in this room, in fact, and we're meeting tomorrow afternoon to discuss it. Shocking doesn't quite describe what I read."

"Father, enough business," lectured Mildred. "I was hoping Mr. St. Clair might dance with me."

"Oh, I couldn't," muttered St. Clair.

"Nonsense. After all, you and I think much the same way, do we not?"

"What's she talking about, St. Clair?" Potter spoke sternly. "Have you been courting my daughter without my knowledge?"

"Father, please," Mildred interjected. "I was merely being amusing at Mr. St. Clair's expense. We've only spoken once about dear Lucy and he was the perfect gentleman."

St. Clair bowed. "If your father permits it, I would be honored to escort you onto the dance floor."

"Then it's a date," said Mildred smiling. "And the German it shall be. Do you have your handkerchief ready, Mr. St. Clair?"

"My daughter is an independent spirit, I'm afraid." Potter looked at his daughter fondly.

"No need to apologize, sir. Personally, I find it refreshing, although I haven't danced the German in quite some time."

Potter escorted Mildred into the hall.

"Charlie, eyes front," Fox whispered in St. Clair's ear.

St. Clair turned and found himself face to face with Victor Fowler.

"Mr. St. Clair, Mr. Fox, I'm so delighted you accepted my invitation. As you can see, the evening should be sensational. You remember my wife, Ellen?"

"Of course," St. Clair replied. "If you don't mind me saying so, Madam, you are looking exquisite and much happier since the last time I saw you."

Ellen Fowler smiled warmly at him. She was dressed in white satin gown of exceedingly rich quality with two flounces of deep point with *d'Alençon* sleeves that reached down to her elbows. St. Clair figured that the dress must have cost a few thousand dollars.

"That's very kind of you, sir. And yes, my strength seems to have returned."

"I was wondering if I might have a word with you in private later, Madam?"

"What about?" Ellen's smile vanished.

"It's for a magazine article I'm currently preparing."

"I see," she said smoothing her dress. "Is it another pack of lies about my husband?"

Fowler smiled. "She is quite capable, as you can see."

"Of that I have no doubt," St. Clair returned Fowler's smile, then turned to Ellen. "As a matter of fact, it doesn't concern your husband. I'd prefer to share more about it with you later."

"As long as Victor is present, I would be happy to, but I can't neglect my other guests for too long."

"I promise not to delay you, Madam."

"It's curious you should request this, Mr. St. Clair." Fowler frowned. "I was hoping that the three of us—you, Mr. Fox, and me—could speak in private later, say around midnight?"

"That would be fine," said Fox, "but you might want to glance at this first." He pulled out a sheaf of folded pages from his inside jacket pocket and handed them to Fowler.

"What is it?" Fowler asked sharply, glancing at the papers.

"That, Mr. Fowler, is St. Clair's story on the corruption of the court-house for my next issue. It includes amounts, names, and companies. In short, the entire tale of thievery and kickbacks that you have instituted."

Fowler seemed to vibrate with the effort to restrain himself. "It's fortunate that we are in mixed company, Mr. Fox, for I would surely strike you where you stand."

"Or you could send your thug, Flint, after us? That's his name, isn't it? Flint?" asked Fox coolly.

"I've no idea who you're speaking of," Fowler snapped. "Now, if you'll excuse me, I must attend to my other guests. Remember midnight in the private study up the stairs to the left."

When the Fowlers departed, Fox offered his elbow to Molly. "We must find you a glass of champagne."

"You coming, Charlie?" asked Molly.

"I'll find you two in a moment, I'd like to look around the parlor."

~

As soon as he was away from Fox and St. Clair, Fowler motioned for Harrison.

"Read this," he said, thrusting the papers at Harrison, "and then tell me how bad it is. For the life of me, I can't understand how St. Clair could've got his hands on this information. Besides James and the two of us, the only other person to have had access to those books was Frank King, but he's dead.

"Bloody hell, Isaac." Fowler gazed bout the room with barely disguised fury. Then he remembered something. He whispered to Harrison, "Has he arrived yet?"

"Thirty minutes ago. He's drinking on the third floor with two young women. He's asked to speak with you as soon as possible."

"About what, for heaven's sake?" Fowler boomed, loud enough to make other guests swivel their heads. He wiped the bead of sweat that had formed on his forehead.

"He wouldn't say."

Fowler removed a handkerchief from his pocket. "You tell him to meet me in the men's smoking parlor in an hour and to keep away from Fox and St. Clair until then." He wiped his forehead vigorously. "I swear to you, Isaac, this is damn well going to end tonight."

~

She had no maid to fuss over her *toilette* in the ladies' dressing room, but that hardly mattered to Ruth. She required no special attention, nor did she have to look in a mirror to appreciate her own inimitable style and beauty—especially since she was wearing an eight-hundred-dollar deep royal blue satin dress with Greek sleeves trimmed in velvet and quills of silver ribbon. She had purchased it two days ago at Stewart's and happily did so with Fowler's money.

Still, as she powdered her face and brushed her hair, surrounded by a small crowd of gossipy young debutantes and their doting mothers and maids, she was overly anxious. Her hand dropped to the side of her dress for a hidden pocket that she had sewn in herself late last evening. Her pistol was there, as she knew it was. Flint was close by—she could sense his malevolent presence. But she told herself to be patient. She would wait until the time was right. And then, when she found him alone, she would strike quickly and quietly.

"Ruth, is that you? I had no idea you were invited, but I'm delighted to see you again," gushed Mildred Potter.

"Hello, Millie," Ruth responded, half-smiling. "You look lovely tonight."

"As do you. I'm only sad that Lucy couldn't be here. She so loved a ball."

"Yes, it's still hard to believe." Ruth glanced away.

"However, I also know that Lucy wouldn't have wanted us to despair tonight. A ball is for dancing, is it not? You must meet a friend of mine who has promised to dance the German with me . . . Mr. St. Clair. He's a writer for *Fox's Weekly*. Very distinguished and handsome."

"Charlie, Mr. St. Clair, is here?" Ruth glanced in one of the mirrors. Suddenly her hair seemed in want of attention.

"My dear, you're blushing. Have you met him, then?"

"Yes, we've met. Didn't I mention that it was Mr. Fox who asked me to travel to New York to assist him in a special assignment?" Ruth tried to quell her quivering voice.

"No, I don't think you did. But if you know Mr. St. Clair, surely he'll ask you to dance as well. Come, we must find him."

Before Ruth could utter another word, Mildred had grabbed her arm and led her out of the dressing room. They were met by a crush of guests clamoring to move into the grand parlor.

"What's all the excitement about?" Mildred asked one lady.

"The orchestra just announced that the next dance is to be the German. Trust Mr. Fowler to spring such a splendid surprise."

"Marvelous," cried Mildred. "We must find Mr. St. Clair."

Inside the parlor, Glover's servants had encircled the dance floor with chairs that were tied together with pocket-handkerchiefs. Couples were waiting impatiently for the music to begin and to see who would lead the dance.

Mildred stood on her toes trying to locate St. Clair. "There he is, with that man and young woman by the wine table." She pulled Ruth by the arm again and they were off across the floor.

"Mr. St. Clair, it's our dance," enthused Mildred, stepping beside him.

St. Clair turned. His face went white. "I don't know if I'm ready for this, Mildred."

"Nonsense, all you must do is follow the leader. The German has no rules. That's why I adore it so. Excuse my poor manners, Mr. St. Clair, this is Miss Cardaso, but I believe you've met her?"

St. Clair gazed into Ruth's eyes. "Yes, we're acquainted. It's a pleasure to see you again, Miss," he stammered slightly. "I was under the impression that you'd left the city."

"No," said Ruth gently. "I've some unfinished business that requires my attention."

"Perhaps we can chat about such matters after the dance?" St. Clair inquired coolly, though his heart was racing.

"Perhaps." Ruth smiled faintly.

The orchestra began playing lively waltz music as the Fowlers walked to the middle of the dance floor. In her hands, Ellen Fowler carried two fans of ivory and ostrich plumes and several red, blue, and white handkerchiefs. As was well known by all those in attendance, when doing the German the object was to mimic whatever dance figures the leading couple attempted—no matter how difficult or silly. And once a couple entered the circle of chairs, they were not allowed to leave until the music had stopped.

The Fowlers began with a simple and traditional waltz, which St. Clair and Mildred easily followed as did the other twenty couples participating. Then, without warning and to everyone's great amusement, Ellen pirouetted around her husband, hopped on one foot, and fanned him. Everyone laughed, including Mildred, who twirled around St. Clair and pretended to fan him.

St. Clair tried hard to enjoy himself, but it was impossible. He kept looking over at Ruth. Finally, after what seemed to him an eternity, the orchestra ended the dance and the Fowlers bowed to loud and sustained applause. He looked in Fox's direction, but Ruth was gone. He desperately searched the crowd and spied her making her way to the parlor's doorway. He quickly kissed Mildred's hand, bowed to her, and excused himself. Pushing his way through the crowd, he nearly tripped over an older woman and almost knocked the champagne glass out of the hand of the gentleman who was escorting her.

"Ruth, wait, please."

"I can't talk, Charlie," she pleaded.

He grasped her arm and held it. "No. I must speak with you. Estelle, isn't it? Estelle Perera?"

"I don't know what you're talking about," she said, her voice trembled.

"I think you do. Come with me." He pulled her away from the doorway.

"Charlie, you're hurting me. Let go. I beg you."

Still grasping her arm, he led her to the back of the house and into an empty servants' room. "Sit there and don't move," he ordered pushing her gently into a chair.

"You're hurting me," she said again, rubbing her arm.

"Not as much as you hurt me, believe me."

"Charlie, I don't know what to say," she looked up at him. "How did you find out?"

"It was Seth Murray. He found your photograph in his rogues' gallery. Did you kill him? Did you kill that saloon keeper?"

"Piker Andrews was a beastly man. He got what he deserved."

"So you *did* kill him?"

"He wanted me to work as a whore. I refused and he came after me with a knife. I had no choice but to fight back. He ended up with the knife in his chest. It was self-defense, I swear it."

"Why did you flee and not explain it to the police?"

"There would've been no point. I would've been hanged before I'd said a word. Andrews had too many friends, too many powerful friends."

St. Clair sat down beside her. "I do believe you, Ruth. I can still call you that, can't I?"

She smiled and took his hand. "I'm Ruth. Estelle Perera no longer exists."

St. Clair looked deeply into her eyes. "How do you know Flint? I saw the two of you at the Tombs the other day when I was almost crushed in that mob."

Ruth sighed. "He's another bastard, if you'll pardon my language. How do I know him? This is the God's honest truth, Charlie. Sometime in early August, Mr. Scott asked me if I'd be interested in travelling to New York for a special dramatic assignment. The play I'd been working in was closing and I needed the work. I arrived in the city and Mr. Fox sent me over to the Fifth Avenue Hotel."

"Where you met Mildred and Lucy Maloney?"

"Yes. But please let me finish. I had only been here a day or two. It was before we met at the magazine office. I was walking down Broadway when I literally bumped into Flint. Mr. Homer Flint. There's no more hellish person in the world as far as I'm concerned. He'd slice the throats of little children and puppies if he was paid enough. And—"

"And what?"

"He killed a friend of mine, Celeste. He cut her up and threw her body in Lake Michigan. At least that's what I think. Her body's never been found. But I know he did it. He also murdered the man she was with at the time, a fence named Frankie."

"Where did you first meet him?"

She smiled. "I wasn't always the prim and proper lady you see before you. And I wasn't born rich, like Millie. Flint was one of Andrews's crooked companions. He was always in the saloon, bothering me and the other waitresses. I think Andrews was scared of him, too. He was there the night of my fight with Andrews. He saw what happened. He knows I'm innocent. When I met Flint on the street, he wouldn't leave me alone until I told him what I'd done and where I now lived. About how I'd gone to San Francisco and started my life over. He couldn't have cared less and why should he have? He pestered me until I told him about my assignment at the magazine. Then he said he couldn't believe his good fortune and that he had some work for me to do. At first, I refused. But he found me at the hotel and threatened to expose me to the police if I didn't do what he asked."

"Which was what? To spy on me and Fox?" St. Clair narrowed his eyes.

"Yes. Yes," she responded, lightly touching his cheek. "He's working for Fowler, as I'm sure you've guessed by now. Flint said that Fowler wanted to know everything that was said about him and anything you planned to write."

"He nearly killed Tom and broke my nose," St. Clair intoned.

"I know. I should've warned you, but it was too late. We'd already met and I had lied. I didn't know what to do, so I kept on giving him what he wanted." She covered her face with her hands.

"And coming to my flat that night? This was part of your scheme?" asked St. Clair, his voice rising.

"No! How could you think that? I knew by then I had to leave. I just needed to see you one last time."

"And what about Mildred and Lucy Maloney? Why did you insist that Fox put you up at the Fifth Avenue? What do you know about Lucy's murder?"

"Nothing. As I've already told you, I met Lucy and Mildred at the hotel in the dining room, the day after I arrived. They were friendly and pleasant, but that's all. I wanted to stay at the Fifth Avenue because I'd heard so much about it. There's nothing more to it than that. Then, a day later or so, Lucy was missing and after that she was discovered in the trunk."

"Did Fowler order Flint to kill her?"

"I don't know, Charlie. I swear to you. I don't know anything about it. Why would Fowler want to have her killed?"

St. Clair ignored the question. "But you did search her room when Murray and I saw you at the hotel?"

"No. It wasn't me. I did see her gentlemen friend leave her room. I don't think he saw me in the hallway. I had seen them together in the hotel lobby once or twice. Funny, she never introduced me."

"King. It was King who searched the room," mumbled St. Clair.

"What's that?"

"Nothing. Were you aware that Lucy knew Flint?"

"She did? I had no idea. Truly. Neither of them said anything about it."

"And what of your *brilliant* detective work at Madame Philippe's?"

"That was on orders from Flint. He told me what to say and I said it." She stared at St. Clair. "You think Flint killed Lucy and then put the blame on Madame Philippe?"

"Maybe."

"Well, he wouldn't do anything without Fowler or Harrison saying so and paying him for it."

"When I saw you at the Tombs, Flint pushed you down. Why?"

"I told him I was leaving the city. He didn't take kindly to that. He said I could leave when he was finished with me. I'm not waiting for that."

"What are you planning to do, Ruth? What are you doing here?"

"Harrison insisted I come. I'm supposed to keep an eye on his back."

"Why would Harrison need protection?"

"I don't know, but he paid for this dress. Said it was a gift from Fowler for services rendered."

"You still haven't answered my question."

"Let say this…after tonight, Flint won't be bothering me or anyone else again. He'll pay for killing Celeste and Lucy."

"Don't do anything foolish, Ruth. Leave it to the police to deal with Flint. You have to go back to Chicago to tell your story. I'll help you find a lawyer."

Suddenly, Ruth pushed St. Clair. Caught by surprise, he stumbled backward, crashing to the floor. But before he could scramble to his feet, she had fled out the door. By the time he reached it, she was gone.

St. Clair dashed toward the public rooms, nearly bumping into one of the servants.

"Dinner is now being served. Sir, if you'll proceed to the grand parlor."

St. Clair was not listening. He looked in every direction, but there was no sign of Ruth anywhere.

Chapter Thirty-Two

———❧❦❧———

MIDNIGHT

By half-past eleven, Tom Fox was feeling stuffed and contented. He had gorged himself on scalloped oysters, devoured the roast lamb, tried the French peas and crabs with mushrooms, and washed it all down with several large glasses of white wine. Molly, also slightly inebriated, had been back and forth to the ladies' dressing room innumerable times.

St. Clair, meanwhile, having searched for Ruth for more than an hour, had reluctantly returned to dine with his two friends. No amount of coaxing by Mildred, however, could get him onto the dance floor again. He, too, drank Fowler's wine and champagne, kept a watch out for Flint, and mulled over what Ruth had told him. Now and then, he felt a pair of eyes staring at him and look across the room to find Isaac Harrison scrutinizing his every gesture. More than once, he almost stood up and confronted him, but Fox had convinced him to be patient.

"Where the hell is she?" he muttered to Fox. He had revealed much of Ruth's story to him without passing judgment on her. Tom had a soft heart for a pretty woman and wanted to give her the benefit of the doubt.

"She'll find you when she's good and ready."

"Yeah, except it'll be too late. She'll hang along with Madame Philippe."

"Have faith. Often people have a way of surprising you."

As the orchestra announced that the last dance of the evening would be a second rendition of the German, St. Clair saw that Harrison had left his table.

"Tom, it's time," he said rising from the table. He dropped his hand and brushed against the pistol in his pants pocket.

~

Flint was puffing on a fat Havana in a private study on the third floor of Glover's. The door was open. His hands were all over two young women, probably no more than sixteen years of age, when Fowler found him. The girls had been trying, without success, to free themselves from his clutches. Fowler rescued them and bought their silence with a token gift of fifty dollars. They laughed and giggled all the way down the stairs.

"Fowler, I want to talk to you," Flint growled. "Why in hell would you make a deal with that bitch, Ruth Cardaso? And what are you going to do? Tell the police about me? I hope to Christ you haven't spoken to Fox and St. Clair?"

"You're not making any sense, Flint," said Fowler regarding the man with disgust. "Why would I do such an inane thing?"

"You didn't make any deals with Fox or St. Clair that involved me? You didn't speak about this about Cardaso?" Flint guzzled down another shot of whiskey. He leaned back on the plush sofa, bit off a piece of chaw and with two fingers roughly pushed the tobacco to the back of his mouth between his gum and teeth.

"Trust me, I haven't spoken to either Fox or St. Clair about you. I certainly haven't come to any arrangements with Miss Cardaso. I haven't spoken to her in days. She was your responsibility, not mine. Anyway forget about this. I told you what must happen tonight."

"Yeah, I know. I figured that cunt wasn't telling me the truth. I knew you wouldn't betray me. You wouldn't say I killed that girl or anything like that," Flint mumbled.

"Which girl are you talking about?"

"The one at Hudson Depot."

"You mean, Lucy? Miss Maloney?" Fowler stared at the figure on the couch. "Are you telling me that you killed her and not Philippe? Is that what you're saying Flint? For God sakes, man."

"Victor, stop the shouting. I could hear you on the first floor." Isaac Harrison stepped into the room. "Fox and St. Clair are right behind me."

"I'm not going anywhere until someone tells me what the hell's going on," Fowler roared. Droplets of sweat ran down the side of his face. "Flint, did you kill Lucy Maloney?"

"I'm not saying another word about this." Flint stood up and backed toward the far wall. "Ask Mr. Harrison. I just do as I'm paid to do, like I'm doing right now."

"Isaac, I want an explanation," demanded Fowler.

∾

"Yeah, Harrison, so do I," said St. Clair. He and Fox were standing in the doorway, about two paces away. "It's Mr. Flint, isn't it?"

"That it is, Charlie. You don't mind if I call you Charlie, do you?" Flint sneered.

"You can call me whatever you like. I figure by early next week, it'll be you hanging from the gallows for murdering Lucy Maloney, not Madame Philippe. You did kill her, didn't you?"

"What if I did? What the hell is it to you? Why do you care so much about that old lady? Aren't you the one who's called her Madame Killer? Yeah, what a surprise, I can read. That bitch has murdered hundreds of children."

"Did you kill Miss Maloney, Flint? Did you stuff her in that trunk? Tell us." Fowler lurched toward him.

"I haven't got time for this shit." Before anyone could say another word, Flint had jumped a chair, pushed Fox to the ground, and grabbed St. Clair by his arm. He twisted him around and positioned his razor sharp knife inches from St. Clair's throat.

"I'm not answering any more questions about what I did or didn't do. Fowler, I want the money you promised me for this job and I'm leaving. Do it now."

"You paid him to kill us, Fowler?" Fox stared aghast. "Even for you, this is low."

"Shut up. I admit to nothing."

"Flint, put the knife down," ordered Harrison. "I'll see to it that you'll get the rest of the money. Haven't I taken care of you already?"

"Yeah, but I don't like this shitbag, never have. I should've killed him and this old bugger when I had the chance."

Flint tightened his grip around St. Clair's neck and thrust the knife upward. At that moment, a gun fired and then again from behind them. The first bullet only grazed Flint's left shoulder, but the second caught him in his right leg. He slumped to the ground in agony. St. Clair broke free of his grasp.

"Don't move a muscle, Flint," shouted Seth Murray, pointing his gun on the twitching figure.

"Thanks," St. Clair gasped, turning to see his brother-in-law almost unrecognizable in a patrolman's uniform and without his bushy black moustache. "But you could've shot about five minutes sooner for my liking."

"I'm here, aren't I?"

More patrolmen and a handful of guests, drawn by the gunshots, burst into the room, Ellen Fowler and Mildred Potter among them.

"Victor, what's happened?" Ellen rushed toward her husband. "Is anyone hurt?"

"Everyone quiet," shouted Murray.

And then, suddenly, Ruth Cardaso was at Flint's side, pressing a gun to his right temple. Behind her St. Clair could see an open door and the glistening bottles of liquor in the storeroom.

"Miss, put that gun down now," Murray ordered.

"Ruth, no, don't pull the trigger," pleaded St. Clair. "Don't throw your life away now. What you told me, I believe you. I know that you didn't kill Andrews. If you do this, you'll hang... and for what? He isn't worth it."

"For Celeste. She deserved better than this bastard." Ruth pressed the gun harder against Flint's flesh.

"Ruth," Mildred interjected softly, "whatever this man's done to you or your friend, won't change a thing. You're not a murderer, honey.

Don't become one now. I know that Mr. St. Clair cares for you. I can see it."

For a moment, Ruth appeared trapped in indecision, then a single tear coursed down her cheek. Her face crumpled. She stared pleadingly at St. Clair and at that second Flint saw his opportunity. He lunged for her pistol. Immediately another shot rang from Murray's gun. This time the bullet hit Flint in his arm and he dropped back down.

St. Clair gently took Ruth's weapon from her and handed it to Murray. Then he put his arms around her and held her tightly.

"My darling," he murmured.

She pressed her face into his chest and wept.

~

"I've got some questions for you, Mr. Fowler, Mr. Harrison, if you please," Murray said when Flint had been removed on a stretcher and the room was cleared. "Take a seat over there" He pointed to two chairs.

"Victor, I must see to the guests." Ellen moved to leave.

"Sorry, Ma'am, you too, beside your husband."

"Victor, the guests."

"Over here, Ellen, please." Fowler turned to Murray, "Detective, ask your damn questions and be quick about it. Keep in mind that I speak with Inspector Stokes regularly."

"Inspector Stokes has been arrested by order of a federal judge. For accepting bribes, for dereliction of duty, and for conspiring in the death of Lucy Maloney." Murray's smile blazed with satisfaction.

"What?" Fowler thundered. "Stokes had nothing to do with her death."

"Oh, I think he did," said St. Clair. "Stokes was paid to ensure that Madame Philippe was arrested and convicted of the murder, but she's innocent. Isn't she, Mr. Harrison?"

Isaac Harrison stared at the ground.

"Isaac, what's he talking about?" asked Fowler.

"She's innocent, yes," mumbled Harrison.

"Flint killed Lucy Maloney," said St. Clair. "Here's what I think happened. That day, he watched her go into Madame Philippe's Broome Street office. And then when she changed her mind about having an abortion, he caught her and killed her in the alley. He made it appear that she had suffered from a botched abortion. He then left her clothes and belongings in the alley for the police to find. He defiled her further by placing a newspaper advertisement inside of her, which helped convict Madame Philippe. And for good measure, he threw two rubies from a tiger badge at the bottom of the trunk. If Madame Philippe wasn't blamed for the murder, then you, Mr. Fowler, might've been. These were all things he had been instructed to do."

"My rubies were found at the bottom of the trunk?" Fowler's mouth fell open. "I've been searching for them and the badge for more than a week."

"Allow me to finish," St. Clair continued. "Leaving the body in the Broome Street alley would've been the simplest thing to do, although Flint tried to think as Madame Philippe might have, had she truly been the murderer. So, in an ingenious scheme, he purchased a ticket to Chicago and arranged to have the body shipped to Hudson Depot, as a desperate person trying to get rid of a body might well have. The trunk was discovered and Madame Philippe was blamed, as Flint knew she would be. He sliced the throat of that young street Arab named Corkie for asking too many questions. And finally, he watched and ensured that everything went according to plan."

"That's an excellent yarn, St. Clair, but that's all it is," Fowler snapped. "Why would Flint have killed her? What had she done? And besides, Flint only works for money. Who was paying him? I sure as hell wasn't."

"Why don't you tell us all, Mr. Harrison?" said St. Clair.

"I got nothing more to say," Harrison declared.

"Isaac," Fowler turned to him, "how do you know that Philippe is innocent? You assured me that she was guilty. That's why I didn't intervene on her behalf."

"I think I may be able to shed some light on this, as well," St. Clair interjected. "Yesterday, I spent many hours examining Madame Philippe's record books. They go back decades. They're stored in a hidden panel in her house, which is why the police never found them. Her servant showed me where they were. He also drew my attention to one abortion she had done nearly ten years ago on November 2, 1862."

"What the hell does this have to do with anything?" Fowler crossed his arms over his chest.

St. Clair ignored him. "A young woman came to see her. This person was well past quickening and in great pain. Her husband had convinced her to abort the child, apparently for health reasons and because he had his career to think of. He decided that a child would only complicate matters. I suppose he promised her they would have a child later and Madame Philippe assured her that all would be well. But it wasn't. She tried various medicines to cause a miscarriage, yet nothing worked on this woman. She then aborted the fetus and there were complications. One of her instruments may have injured the patient, I don't know for certain. The Madame maintained that she had done nothing wrong and a physician who examined this woman some weeks later more or less concurred. The worst of it was that this woman was told that she would never be able to conceive another child. And I suspect that it nearly drove her half mad. She blamed Madame Philippe for inflicting this tragedy on her. And she blamed her husband, whom she despised. Nothing made her feel any better. Nothing, except laudanum, which she has taken ever since. Isn't that so, Mrs. Fowler?"

A hush fell over the room. All eyes turned to Ellen Fowler, whose face wore a mask of defiance.

"Ellen, it was you? Why? You paid Flint to kill Miss Maloney? What had she done to you? Tell me, woman."

"Shut up, Victor, please shut up." Ellen regarded her husband with barely disguised contempt. "I can't bear to hear one more word from your mouth." She turned to St. Clair. "Your version of what transpired with Flint is more or less correct. You are to be commended. And you're right about my feelings toward my husband. I do despise him. I despise everything about him, everything he stands for. But I'm married to him. And if I can't have his child, then nobody else can either. I wasn't about to let that little whore have his baby. To have a child that would make a claim on Victor's name and inheritance. And yes, I did want to punish the great Madame for what she did to me and punish Victor as well for making me go through it. I only ever wanted a child. Nothing more."

Her voice quivered. "When I learned Miss Maloney was pregnant, I sent Flint to speak with her. I thought he'd convinced her to have the abortion. He even gave her the money. And she did go meet with Philippe as she agreed to. Then that foolish, stupid girl became frightened and fled. Flint had followed her from the hotel and when he determined that she had not had the abortion, killed her. As I had told him, and paid him, to do."

"My God, woman, what have you done?" Fowler leapt from his chair. "I wasn't the father of her child. I didn't run after her, nor take her to bed."

"Don't lie to me," she screamed. "She was one of your whores, I saw you talking to her at Hill's saloon one evening."

"At Hill's saloon?"

"Yes, I follow you occasionally, Victor. God knows why. I suppose to see which whore you'll fuck. And one night I saw you with her."

Fowler reeled as it he had been slapped. "I was speaking with her, but that's all. She was with Frank King, for Christ's sakes. She was his woman. He was paying for her room at the Fifth Avenue. King must've been the father of her child, not me." He glanced at St. Clair, a look of sudden enlightenment on his face. "King's still alive, isn't he? His death in Harlem Square was a trick. He was your informant all along. All of those magazine stories with personal information about me. He provided you with the account records for the courthouse?"

St. Clair nodded. "That's about the size of it, yes."

"And you, Harrison, what's your role in all of this?" Fowler turned to his colleague.

"Ellen came to me and told me what she'd done."

"And you believed her? You believed that I'd made Lucy Maloney pregnant? That I was the father of her unborn child?"

Harrison crossed his arms defiantly. "Yes, I believed her. Why wouldn't I? I've watched you at the saloons for years parading with a steady stream of whores all fussing around you. You're an astute leader, the finest Grand Sachem Tammany's ever had. But morally you're weak and it's sinful, Victor, that's what it is. Reverend Ingersoll assures me that there's hope with faith, but I'm not certain. You're beyond redemption. At the same time, too much was at stake with Crédit Mobilier.

I couldn't let Ellen's actions stop our plans in Washington. We're too close. If you weren't going to protect yourself I had to do it for you. I spoke with Flint and told him to do whatever was required to ensure Madame Philippe was convicted of the crime. You nicely took care of Ingersoll and the riot at the Tombs was helpful. And I paid off Stokes, District Attorney Richard Cady, and the Recorder at the trial, Benjamin Beatty, and that was that. They all thought the money was coming from you and, really, why would they have thought otherwise?"

Fowler's face had engorged with blood. He turned and slapped Harrison hard across the face, tipping him to the floor. "You wanted to protect our plan? Is that it? Instead you've destroyed everything I've worked for. Everything! And if you must know, Reverend Patrick Simpson Ingersoll is a regular customer at a whorehouse on Water Street where he enjoys the company of fifteen year old girls. And he goes to Miss Kate's parlor house where he watches naked women cavort on stage. You've put your blessed faith in a fornicator, Isaac."

Ellen Fowler dropped to her knees in tears. "Victor, I don't know what to say. I don't know what to say." She wailed with grief.

"You sicken me. I want nothing more to do with you." He turned to Murray. "Detective, do with her as you will."

$$\sim$$

As Murray fished in his pocket for his handcuffs, St. Clair opened the door of the study, seeking fresh air for the claustrophobic room. The strains of the orchestra below filtered up the stairs, followed by the voice of the conductor. "A round of applause for our hosts tonight, Mr. and Mrs. Victor Fowler."

But even the thunder of the cheers could not subdue the metallic snap of shackles closing over Ellen Fowler's dainty wrists.

Epilogue

———❧◆❧———

EVIL OF THE AGE

Madame Philippe was released from the Tombs on August 23, 1871. Her trusted servant, Hector, was waiting for her outside the gates with her carriage. She refused to speak to the reporters who were present. All she wanted to do, she said, was return to her home and take a hot bath. She did, however, send a personal note of thanks to St. Clair inviting him to tea that evening.

Two days later in Washington, before a joint committee of Congress, Martin Kent, aide to Congressman Stanley Todd, testified that Oakes Ames had offered Mr. Todd $100,000 to vote against any further inquiry into the affairs of Crédit Mobilier. When pressed by his colleagues, Todd confirmed Kent's version of his discussions with Ames.

Ordered to appear before the committee, as well, was Stephenson Kirkland, who, under threat of imprisonment for perjury, finally admitted that he worked for Victor Fowler and his New York Ring. His instructions were to buy up as many shares of Crédit Mobilier as possible so that Fowler could eventually gain control of the company from Ames and his cohorts. According to Kirkland's understanding— as had been explained to him by Isaac Harrison—Fowler had intended to secretly award Crédit Mobilier the contract to build his elevated street railway. Then he planned to utilize the substantial proceeds to further discredit President Grant and Vice-President Colfax, in addition to using the profits to install Governor Krupp and Mayor Emery in the White House in the next federal election under the Democratic Party banner.

A full-scale Congressional inquiry was soon launched, exposing Ames's crooked scheme and the enormous corruption involved in Crédit Mobilier's building of the Union Pacific Railway. The company was immediately disbanded, although for the betterment of the Union no criminal charges were laid against Ames, his chief accomplice Thomas Durant, or Vice-President Schuyler Colfax, who was publicly criticized for showing poor judgment in this matter.

In New York, meanwhile, under tremendous pressure to act, Mayor Emery appointed a committee of concerned citizens led by Rupert Potter to conduct a full-scale investigation of Victor Fowler's business operations and, in particular, the construction of the new courthouse. The group's official title was the Executive Committee of Citizens and Taxpayers for Financial Reform of the City, but everyone referred to it as Potter's Committee of Forty. One of Potter's first acts, cheered in some quarters and criticized in others, was to hire his capable daughter, Mildred, as the committee's secretary. When St. Clair bumped into her on Broadway soon after the announcement, she assured him that her days visiting Hashisdom at Miss Kate's were over.

Fowler, despite his preoccupation with the trials of his wife Ellen and Flint for the murder of Lucy Maloney, did not relinquish his power easily. Yet Potter, also an able faro player, outsmarted him. First, he organized a tax boycott—citizens refused to pay their municipal taxes and convinced several banks not to loan Fowler any money. The workmen at the courthouse construction site were not paid and protested daily in front of Fowler's home.

On September 15, Homer Flint, who was so irascible in court that the judge ordered that he be kept in leg irons and wrist shackles for the duration of the proceedings, was convicted of the murders of Lucy Maloney and Corkie Smith. He refused to testify on his own behalf and would not respond to questions about whether or not Fowler had paid him to hurt or kill Fox and St. Clair.

The jury only required twenty minutes. Flint was sentenced to be hanged at the end of September. St. Clair, among others, was there that day to watch him take his final walk across the Bridge of the Sighs at the Tombs. He remained silent as the noose was placed around his neck and the trapdoor was released.

Ellen Fowler had agreed to testify against Flint, in exchange for a sentence of mercy. She was also found guilty of plotting the murder of Lucy Maloney and sentenced to twenty-five years in prison.

Asked if she had any final words, she said, "I am truly sorry for the death of Miss Maloney. Upon reflection, I understand now that it was the actions of a desperate woman caused by an addiction to laudanum. That is no excuse, I know, but it is the truth, so help me God."

Once that ordeal had ended, Potter's committee of lawyers and merchants at long last succeeded in bringing charges of corruption and bribery against Fowler, Isaac Harrison, and Bob James. But it took two trials to convict them. At the first, the jury could not come to a decision, despite the testimony of Frank King, whose seeming rise from the grave became a *cause célèbre*. Potter accused Fowler of bribing at least three jury members—a charge he vehemently denied. Another trial was convened at the end of October and each of the defendants was sentenced to a term of twelve years. As the police took Fowler away to the Tombs in shackles, he vowed that he would never serve two years, let alone twelve. No one in court, including St. Clair, doubted him for a moment.

∾

"Any telegrams from Chicago yet?" asked Tom Fox.

St. Clair looked up from his desk, where he was busy writing. "What's that?"

"I said did you hear anything from Ruth or Lampson?"

"Nothing today, no. The last I heard was that her new trial was set for the middle of November and that Lampson was confident a plea of self-defense would be successful. He's assured Ruth and me that none of Piker Andrews's accomplices in the Chicago police department will be able to testify. And that several, in fact, have been indicted on criminal charges."

"That's wonderful news, Charlie."

"Well, it's thanks to you paying for Lampson. Any other lawyer wouldn't have been able to do it."

"Here, I've got a gift for you." He handed St. Clair a rectangular card wrapped in brown paper and string.

"What the hell is this? It's not Christmas yet." St. Clair untied the string. "A rail ticket to Chicago. Thanks, Tom. It's greatly appreciated."

"It was Molly's idea. You know me . . . I can be as mushy as a woman sometimes."

St. Clair laughed. "Here I've a present for you, too. This damn article is done at last."

"Not a moment too soon, my friend. The issue is going to press in two days. Let me read it through."

"Take your time. I'm going across the street for a lunch of ale and oysters." He turned to his colleagues. "Sutton, Molly, it's on me."

A minute later the offices of Fox's Weekly were nearly deserted, except for Peter Stewart, off in a corner at the back of the room drawing a new humorous sketch for Sutton's story on Victor Fowler's conviction.

Fox retired to his office. He poured himself a full glass of whiskey from his private stock, lit a cigar, and began to read the final installment of 'Evil of the Age' by Charles St. Clair.

Last month Madame Philippe, the well-known abortionist, whose real name is Anna Jacoby, a German Jewess, was nearly hanged for a crime of murder that she did not commit. She had been convicted of killing Miss Lucy Maloney in the case of the so-called "trunk mystery." Miss Maloney's body was stuffed into a trunk and shipped to Hudson Depot, where it was subsequently discovered.

Madame Philippe was innocent. However, the question remains—is she innocent of crimes against civilization? Does she deserve the name, Madame Killer?

Miss Maloney had come to Madame Philippe seeking assistance for a pregnancy and child she did not want. And she was hardly alone. In the past twenty-five years, neither Madame Philippe nor any of the other abortionists operating openly in New York City have lacked patrons. Many of those seeking abortions, in fact, have been married women.

Some readers might argue that these women are merely shirking their duties and responsibilities as mothers. It is true that many do suffer from a lax morality and are consumed with the frivolities of the theatre, dancing, and other social activities. They refuse to surrender their personal amusements and interrupt their giddy pleasures to raise children.

Yet there are women who risk their health in childbirth and have no recourse but to seek the services of Madame Philippe and others of her ilk. Countless others struggle with poverty and heartless husbands, too drunk to comfort or properly support them. These women have decided, and justly so, that they are unwilling and not capable of bringing another human being into the world.

It must be conceded that there are indeed far too many unwanted children roaming the streets of the city, orphans left to fend for themselves. They are the next generation of the criminal element that will continue to wreak havoc on our more respectable citizens.

Miss Maloney, however, was neither a married woman nor unhealthy. Instead, she was a single woman in an immoral relationship with a married man—a much more frequent occurrence than most of us would care to admit. Like Miss Maloney, one day these women find that they are with child and then are placed in a desperate predicament. In most cases they have been fooled by the man into thinking he is about to leave his wife, but, of course, this does not happen. Or in other instances, these single women, by no means innocent, are led astray by nefarious characters who promise marriage. These liars and cheats steal the women's money, possessions, and honor before vanishing.

To date, New York State laws have been limited in curtailing the work of abortionists. Laws implemented more than thirty years ago made abortion after quickening second-degree manslaughter and punishable by up to twelve months in jail. Three years ago, the state legislature also made the death of an unborn child before quickening the same crime. But because the policing of this act has been nearly impossible, few abortionists have been charged or convicted. Advertising abortion services is also now against the law, yet a perusal of any of a dozen newspapers or journals in the city would indicate few adhere to it. If not for this recent incident, Madame Philippe would have continued to do as she pleased.

We have, I would argue, come to an important fork in the road. On religious and moral grounds, abortion is not defensible and all the Madame Philippes should be justly punished. But who is truly to blame for this dire state of affairs? When the moral code that governs society brings shame on a man for seducing a woman, as it shames the woman for succumbing to the man's enticements, then we shall have true change. On that day, some abortionists may be put out of work.

Reverend Patrick Simpson Ingersoll has urged state authorities to ban all abortion and drive Madame Philippe and her friends from the city. During the next session of the legislature, such a bill is being introduced. Is this the answer?

Recently I had the opportunity to speak candidly with Madame Philippe. I have never hidden my personal dislike of her, and yet I now find myself of two minds on this subject. I can say without hesitation or reservation that she is assuredly not Madame Killer. She has her own reasons for doing what she does and they are legitimate and valid. Despite any riches accrued to her through her work, she has literally saved the lives of countless women.

Where, then, does this leave us? Do women deserve such rights? A right that may be repugnant to some, immoral to others, but often one of life or death. That will be the debate for the years ahead. If the "trunk mystery" and the sad fate of Miss Lucy Maloney has taught us anything, it is that any future discussion or campaigns on this controversial issue are sure to be contentious, divisive, and more than likely bloody and violent.

One final thought in light of recent events and the downfall of Mr. Victor Fowler and his notorious Ring. I have arrived, albeit reluctantly, at the conclusion that "Evil of the Age" is in truth not a fitting label for the abortion crisis in this city and others. That to find the real Evil of the Age one must investigate City Hall, Albany and Washington where greed, selfishness and the quest for ever more power has the potential to corrupt even the worthiest of men.

More about that in a future article.

Charles St. Clair

ACKNOWLEDGEMENTS

DURING THE TWO YEARS (or more) that this book was being written, I benefited from the sage advice of many individuals. I must express my warmest gratitude to my two literary agents, Hilary McMahon in Toronto and Peter Riva in Gila, New Mexico, who have consistently looked after my best interests. Peter, in particular, took a keen interest in the project, edited an early draft of the novel, and has shown unwavering faith in my work. For that, I am most appreciative.

For the earlier Canadian edition, I thank the great team at Heartland Associates. And for this U.S. edition, I express my gratitude to everyone at Yucca Publishing.

My wife, Angie, our children, Alexander and Mia (and, yes, our devoted beagle, Maggie, my writing companion) have been supportive and encouraging, always reminding me what is truly important in life. To Angie, for being my sounding board-day and night-and for sticking by me for the past 32 years, generally with a smile, I dedicate this book to you with love.

AL
Winnipeg, Canada
December, 2013

Author's Note

EVIL OF THE AGE is a work of fiction, but it is loosely based on real historical events. William Magear Tweed (1823–1878), Tammany's chief, ran New York City with his "Ring" in the 1860s and early 1870s. "Boss" Tweed and his cohorts, including Mayor Abraham Oakey Hall, Peter Sweeny, the city's treasurer, and Richard Connolly, city comptroller, ran New York as their personal fiefdom and stole tens of millions of dollars from the city's taxpayers.

Tweed himself was president of the Board of Supervisors. He controlled a rich source of patronage as Deputy Street Commissioner and Commissioner of Public Works as well as holding executive positions in banks, railroads, gas, printing, and insurance companies. He was the third-largest owner of real estate in the city. However, he had no involvement in the Crédit Mobilier scandal of the late 1860s and early 1870s—which did lead to the censure of Congressman Oakes Ames and ruined the political career of Vice-President Schuyler Colfax, among others in Washington.

Tweed's downfall came in August of 1871, when the press exposed revelations about the kickbacks and corruption in the construction of his famous courthouse (at 52 Chambers Street in Manhattan). Found guilty of fraud, grand larceny, and 220 misdemeanor charges, he received a twelve-year jail sentence. He died in prison in April 1878, bankrupt and broken.

As well, in August 1871 a woman's body was discovered inside a trunk at the Hudson Railway Depot. A subsequent police investigation soon uncovered that the murdered woman, Alice Bowlsby, had been killed by an abortionist named Rosenzweig. As the murder case proceeded, the *New York Times* ran a series of articles entitled *The Evil of the Age* which condemned the practice of abortion in the city. Several of the newspaper stories focused on the exploits of the notorious Madame Restell—the real life abortionist after whom Madame Philippe is modeled.

In recreating life in New York City during this era, I relied on a number of contemporary sources. Among them, Edward Crapsey, *The Nether Side of New York, or, the Vice, Crime and Poverty of the Great* (New York: Metropolis, 1872); and James D. McCabe, *Lights and Shadows of New York Life* (New York: Farrar, Straus and Giroux, 1970-originally published 1872); George Ellington, *The Women of New York* (New York: New York Book Company, 1870); Gustav Lenning, *The Dark Side of New York Life and Its Criminal Classes* (New York: Frederick Gerhard, 1873); and the *New York Times* for the summer of 1871. A section of Chapter Twenty-Three was based on an article by H.H. Kane, "A Hashish-House in New York: The Curious Adventures Of An Individual Who Indulged In a Few Pipefuls Of The Narcotic Hemp," in *Harper's New Monthly Magazine* (1883) vol. 67, 944–949.

Essential as well was *Gotham: A History of New York City to 1898* (New York: Oxford University Press, 1999), a brilliant historical survey—and winner of the Pulitzer Prize-by Edwin G. Burrows and Mike Wallace. Other key reference sources used included: Alexander B Callow, *The Tweed Ring* (New York: Oxford University Press, 1966) and James C. Mohr, *Abortion in America* (New York: Oxford University Press, 1978).

Elsewhere, the fictional Reverend Patrick Simpson Ingersoll's speech is an adaptation of a passage in Henry Ward Beecher's article "Economy in Small Things," in Plymouth Pulpit, IV March-September, 1875 (New York: Fords, Howard & Hulbert, 1892), 463–64. Ingersoll's sermon is an adaptation of Anthony Comstock's Traps for the Young (Cambridge, Mass.: Harvard University Press, 1967–originally published 1883), 238.

GLOSSARY

—◆—

bottlehead: A nineteenth century slang term for a fool or drunkard.

canon sheep: A play on words to denote blind obedience. 'Canon' denotes religious law, while 'sheep' convey the idea of blindly following a leader.

cerate: A thick ointment consisting of a fat such as oil or lard mixed with wax, resin and other ingredients.

Crédit Mobilier: A construction holding company set up by the Union Pacific Railroad in 1864. It was awarded the contract to build the railway west to California. As part of a scam later revealed in the press and congressional hearings, the company charged Union Pacific millions more than the actual cost of the construction. But that money, about $23 million, was paid to Crédit Mobilier's select key investors, who also owned Union Pacific. In short, the railroad's other numerous investors, who did own shares in Crédit Mobilier—as well as the federal government which had given Union Pacific funds—were bilked out of money by the executives of Union Pacific who were supposed to protect them. Congressman Oakes Ames, who became head of Crédit Mobilier in 1867, made Crédit Mobilier shares available to congressmen at a low rate. These were the same politicians who voted funds to Union Pacific to cover Crédit Mobilier's inflated fees.

Douglas, Stephen Arnold, (1813–61). US legislator, congressman and senator, he drafted the Kansas-Nebraska Act (1854), giving settlers the right to determine whether their territory would be free or slave-holding. Short and thick-set, with remarkable oratorical skills, he was nicknamed "the Little Giant". His senatorial campaign of 1858 featured a famous series of debates with Abraham Lincoln and he ran unsuccessfully for president the year before his death.

Douglass, Frederick (originally Frederick Augustus Washington Bailey, 1817–95). An American abolitionist, he was born a slave in Maryland, escaped from a Baltimore shipyard and changed his name. He settled in Massachusetts and became an agent of the Massachusetts Anti-Slavery Society. He lectured on slavery in Britain, where money was collected to buy his freedom. In 1847, he began his own paper in Rochester, NY, and later was an author of several books. He held various public offices, and served as US minister to Haiti in 1889.

hansom cab: named after its designer, Joseph A. Hansom, this was a covered, two-wheeled carriage with the driver's seat situated above and behind the passenger's compartment.

laudanum: A highly addictive liquid form of opium. In the nineteenth century it was prescribed as a painkiller, often mixed with alcohol and other ingredients, without regard to its dangerous side effects.

roorback: A "roorback" is a political slander, especially an allegation that backfires. During the American presidential campaign of 1844, the Ithaca *Chronicle* in New York State printed some alleged excerpts from an imaginary book called "Roorback's Tour through Western and Southern United States in 1836." It contained malicious and false charges against Democratic candidate James K. Polk, specifically that he was a brutal slave owner. The charges were reprinted in other Whig Party—an American political party of the nineteenth century—newspapers. Polk was nevertheless elected president.

Tammany Hall: New York City's Tammany Society controlled the local Democratic Party and civic government during the late nineteenth century. It was notorious for its corruption and graft. As of 1830, the Society's headquarters was in a building on East 14th Street called "Tammany Hall," which also came to denote the organization.

ALLAN LEVINE

Allan Levine is an award-winning internationally selling author and historian based in Winnipeg, Canada. He has written eleven books, including the Sam Klein Mystery Trilogy. His most recent non-fiction book is *Toronto: Biography of a City.*